the e

PRIDE

VII
UINCENDUM NATUS

J.D. HOLLYFIELD

~~lust~~
~~pride~~
wrath
envy
greed
gluttony
sloth

Pride
Copyright © 2019 J.D. Hollyfield

Cover Design: All By Design
Photo: Adobe Stock
Editor: Word Nerd Editing
Formatting: Champagne Formats

ALL RIGHTS RESERVED. This book contains material protected under International and Federal Copyright Laws and Treaties. Any unauthorized reprint or use of this material is prohibited. No part of this book may be reproduced or transmitted in any form or by any means, electronic or mechanical, including photocopying, recording, or by an information and retrieval system without express written permission from the Author/Publisher.

This is a work of fiction. Names, characters, places, and incidents either are the product of the author's imagination or are used fictitiously, and any resemblance to actual persons, living or dead, business establishments, events, or locales is entirely.

To all the demons inside my head. Thanks for the inspiration.

UINCENDUM NATUS

PREFACE

the elite seven

Since 1942, The Elite Seven Society has created and guided influential leaders, molding the country into something better. This society was birthed by Malcom Benedict II, who wanted more for Americans. More wealth. More influence. More power. Some leaders have the skills, but not the influence, and that simply wasn't fair according to Mr. Benedict. He invested his own money and time to construct a society that bred the best of the best, year after year.

But to be the best, you must be ruthless.

Good leaders make sacrifices. Sometimes the sacrifices are hard, but the rewards are plentiful. Mr. Benedict made sure to indulge these leaders with their utmost desires. A devout Catholic himself, he designed a society that rewarded his leaders with the sins that were frowned upon. If they were giving up love and happiness and joy for the betterment of the country, they deserved something in its stead.

Pride, Envy, Wrath, Sloth, Greed, Gluttony, and Lust.

Choosing leaders for this society takes intense focus. Only seven are to be selected, and the investment and time are showered upon the new seven chosen every four years. The university's acting dean behaves as a liaison for the society, bringing the applicants to the predecessors so the selection may begin. The society members going out will bring forth a candidate the society votes on and approves.

After they are chosen, the initiates are given a token and an invitation to initiation. The initiation tests their character and ability to do what's right for the betterment of the society. Once the initiates pass their test, they are discreetly branded with the mark of the society and groomed through challenges during the course of their elite education to breed them into the influential people they were meant to be.

Once in The Elite Seven, there is no getting out. The money and power are their reward. Should they choose to stray or break the rules, the society strips them of everything. Anything they once had will be removed. Opportunities will never arise. They will no longer have the support of the society. To this day, there have been no known occurrences of anyone from the society having to be banished. Every young man and woman aspire to be a part of the elite group whispered about amongst the privileged. Anyone who is anyone knows of the group and secretly hopes their son or daughter is selected, for good fortune is showered on the family for decades to come.

Pride is more than the first of the seven deadly sins; it is itself the essence of all sin.

—*John Scott*

PRIDE

UINCENDUM NATUS

PROLOGUE

Mason
Seventeen years old…

"That shit's tight. Your girl's gonna flip, bro. I'd make her suck your dick for a whole month if I were you. Swallow too."

I step outside into the sweltering Louisiana heat, my best friend, Micah, on my heels. The grimy door of the tattoo parlor screeches shut behind him, and I pull my shades over my eyes, bloodshot from the joint we just smoked.

"Fuck, she better. I didn't do this for nothin'." I laugh, blowing smoke up his ass. Mine and Dahlia's relationship ain't about that. She's my world, my rock, my safe place—she's who I turned to when life sucked ass and I needed something beautiful to push through the bad shit.

We met when we were still with the Keller family, our

previous foster family, back in Covington. Dahlia and I had both just started our freshman year. She was smart, funny, and kept me clean—made me realize she's the only drug I need. Then the beginning of sophomore year came around and our lives got turned upside down. My little sister and I were told our home for the last seven years was over. Just when we felt we were done being tossed around the broken ass foster system, we were once again spit back out. The Kellers, who had taken us in, were expecting a baby, and they needed the space for their own growing family. That or the government's free money wasn't good enough anymore.

I didn't handle the news well and flew off the handle. I broke a bunch of shit in their house, then went out, got drunk as fuck, and crashed their car into a tree. Our assigned social services counselor said I was lucky they were so caring, because they let us leave without pressing charges, but how was that lucky? We were being thrown out of the fifth home since our parents died, yet again scared and unsure of our future. I didn't give a fuck about getting in trouble, but my sister, Evelyn, did. She cried, worried they'd split us up. That was never going to fucking happen. So, I pulled my shit together and played the part. The next family would see two well-behaved kids and accept us as a package deal.

When we were uprooted, I was also torn from Dahlia. Her everyday smile, for the past year, that gave me a reason to be someone other than a fucking troubled kid in the system, was gone. I swore I'd do anything to keep us together. See her every damn day even if it meant walking the forty-seven miles that separated us.

I press my hand against the bandage covering the fresh ink over my heart—a red dahlia flower on my right pec, the

PRIDE

color etched deep into my skin. No worry of it ever fading. I want her to know, just like the ink, my love runs deep and permanent. I'll love her forever.

We make it to Micah's car, and he tosses me his keys. "You drive. My back stings like a motherfucker."

When we got placed in our newest home and school last year, Micah was the first—shit, the only—dude to befriend me. He came from a rich as fuck family but had a wild side and thirst to piss off his parents any chance he got, hence the large ass skull tatted on his back.

Swapping sides, I slide in, starting up the engine. The Porsche purrs to life, and I throw it into drive and whip through traffic. "You ever figure out what's up with Evie?" Micah asks.

The mention of my little sister has my fingers gripping the Italian leather steering wheel harder. She's been off for months now, and I can't figure out why. Quiet. She's pulled back from me. Something's going on with her. I just don't fucking know what.

"No, she won't talk to me. Something's up, though. After my weekend at Dahlia's, I'm gonna force her to tell me. Don't give a fuck how mad she gets." I've always been patient with Evie. She's been through a lot. Our parents dying. Being thrown into the foster care system when not a single living relative would take us. Family after temporary family letting us down when it came to care for us and our well-being. I've tried my best to shelter her from the hardships of the fucked-up world we live in, but I can't always be around. Especially now, when my weekends need to be with Dahlia.

"Yeah, want nothing to do with that shit. Have fun," Micah says, lighting up a cigarette. Those two can't get along for the fucking life of them, and it's getting old. Sometimes, I feel like I'm the goddamn parent breaking up two kids fighting over a toy.

"Either way, I'm not around to do anything about it 'til Sunday. You still cool with driving me out to Covington, right?"

"Anything for you, bro. But I told you, just take the Porsche anytime. My dad won't even notice it's gone."

No.

"I'll just take the bus if you—"

"Stop acting too proud and fucking take the car. It's me trying to do my best friend a favor. Nothing more, nothing less."

Micah and I are so fucking similar, it gets freaky at times. But there's always one thing that defines our differences: money. Him having endless amounts of it, and me, a fuck-up straight out of the dumps of temporary houses who grew up with nothing. We may both have torn jeans and band t-shirts on, but it doesn't change our backgrounds.

"Take me or don't. I'll figure out how to get home Sunday." Micah shrugs, letting it go. "I need to swing by the house. Gotta grab some things and let Evie know I'm leaving."

He doesn't fight me. He knows when to let things lie. I drive the rest of the way to the house, Dahlia on my mind. I hope she likes the tattoo. Tomorrow's our two-year anniversary and I wanted to show her how much she means to me. I'm sure most pussy boyfriends give their girlfriends flowers and expensive dinners. Spend tons of money on dumb ass shit. Not me. Even at seventeen, I know how to show my love for someone, and not in the form of shit that dies.

I take a quick turn into the Griffins' driveway, and my

PRIDE

stomach drops at the sight of the police cars.

"Shit, what'd you do?"

"Fuck off. Nothing," I joke, but my unease thickens. My first thought is something happened to my sister.

"Damn, then what's the fuzz doing at your crib?"

I don't respond. I park and jump out, jetting toward the front door already being propped open by an officer.

"Excuse me, son—"

"Where's my sister?" I spit out, shoving past him and entering the modest house. I halt when I see my sister sitting on the white leather settee surrounded by another cop and Valery, our social services counselor. "What's going on? You hurt?"

Evie shakes her head, tears cascading down her slender face, though her tortured eyes tell me otherwise. I turn to Lillian, our current guardian. "What happened? What the fuck's wrong with her?"

Lillian takes a menacing step toward me when an officer uses himself as a blockade. "What's *wrong* is your sister is a whore!" she yells, pointing her manicured nail at Evelyn. My sister starts to cry harder. "That's right, cry, because you got caught, you bitch!" She turns to Valery. "I want her out tonight. Him too. They're no longer welcome here."

"What the fuck you talkin' about?" I growl.

"Oh, like you don't know. Your slut of a sister has been trying to seduce my husband! I caught her luring him into her room tonight." My eyes flash wide in shock. "Yeah, that's right. Slut!"

I pull my eyes away from Lillian to stare in confusion at my sister. "Mason, I didn't. It's not…he—"

I throw my hand up, silently telling her not to finish that sentence. My sister is sweet and kind. She would never fucking think about doing anything Lillian is accusing her of. But it also means...

That motherfucker!

Anger erupts up my spine, and my head threatens to explode. "Where is he?"

"Who?"

"That motherfucker! Where the fuck is he? He's dead—"

"Mason, please, no!" my sister cries. She attempts to come for me, but the officer throws his hand out to stop her.

I bring my focus back on Lillian. "She would never do that."

Lillian scoffs and brushes her sleek black hair behind her dainty shoulders. "Well, she did. We just try to give you poor children a home and you take advantage of us. Not to mention the money she stole."

I take a step forward, infringing her space. "She didn't take shit from you," I growl. We both know damn well I was the one who stole from her. She saw me take the money out of her purse. Lillian gazes back at me, her eyes pleading for me to dare challenge her. If we weren't surrounded, I would take her by the hair and bash her head through the glass coffee table.

"Mason, son, I'm sorry, but due to the allegations, we have to remove you both from the home." My chest rises and falls in quick succession. I need to calm down for Evie. I need to pull it together for us both and get us the fuck out of here. Once we're somewhere safe, we'll figure out how to press charges. Get her a rape test. Fuck, will she *need* one?

"Fuck it. This bitch is fucking crazy, and so is her pervert ass husband. Evie, let's go." Evelyn attempts to get up, but Valery steps in.

PRIDE

"Mason, just for tonight, we're going to place you in separate homes."

"What? Fuck no. We're staying together." I reach for my sister, but two officers stand in our way, pulling her from the couch. Evelyn screams, and I go ballistic against the hands restraining me from going after the cops as they drag her out. I swear, and kick, and fight to get to my sister with no luck. My eyes connect with the devil herself, and the sliver of a smile on her lips causes my stomach to drop.

"You bitch!" I yell, jerking to break free.

"Please remove him from my home before my step-daughter returns. I don't want to upset her with this. We will send his things to avoid the worry of whether he might steal anything while packing his minimal belongings."

Like a crazed animal, I throw punches until an officer knocks my legs out with a stick. I howl and lose my balance, falling forward, giving them the opportunity to cuff me. I'm carried outside. Twice, a baton is slammed into my gut. From my peripheral, I see Micah being retained by a cop. He's yelling. I vaguely hear my name and my sister's when I'm shoved into the backseat of a cop car.

My world falters, and the reality of what's happening comes crashing down as I watch the gleam in Lillian's eyes shine alongside her malicious smile. She set us up. Is this because I stole from her? Is what she said about her husband in my sister's room true? Tears sting my eyes, and I squeeze them shut. *This isn't happening. This can't be happening.* It all comes full fruition at the sounds of Evelyn's sobbing voice as she's guided out of the Griffins' home. I throw my shoulders into the secured door, my voice burning as I scream my sister's name, needing to free myself from this car and this nightmare and get to her. The shackles around my wrists shred into my skin as the warmth of my blood drips into my palms and my cries turn into frantic sobs.

But no one comes to my rescue.

My hoarse cries go unheard as they guide her into another car and speed away. The vehicle disappears out of sight, and my wild eyes manage to lock back on Lillian's. Just before she slips back into her house, I watch in disgust as her lips purse and blow me a kiss.

Two weeks later.
New Orleans State Detention Center

Twenty-one, twenty-two, twenty-three...

My muscles burn, threatening to give out on me, but I don't stop. I keep pushing myself until my fingers go numb.

Twenty-four, twenty-five, twenty—

"Blackwell, you've got a visitor."

At the sound of my name, I drop the heavy weights on their latch and lean forward, wiping the sweat off my brow. My biceps are on fire as I stare off at the correctional guard. "You sure it's for me?" I ask. I haven't had a visitor since I arrived at this hellhole two weeks ago. I was given one call after spending the first night in an eight by eight dirty cell with no water or pissing privileges. I spent most of that night yelling to speak to my counselor, a lawyer—anyone who would tell me where the fuck they took my sister. My one call was to Micah. When I finished typing in the last digit, a recorded voice on the other line informed me it was disconnected.

PRIDE

"Wouldn't waste my time walking all the way down here if it wasn't. Let's go," the guard says, jiggling his master keys. He holds the door while I stand up and grab my towel. I wipe the excess sweat from my face and toss it into the dirty laundry bin before following him down the long, dimly lit hallway. The place is like a death warrant. It may be labeled a juvenile center, but it ain't no different than a prison. The limitations, the restrictions, the corruption—it's all the same. We make it to the visiting area, and I look around to see who it could be. My heart begins to race in hopes it's Evelyn, but I don't spot her. "Who'd you say it was?" I ask, as if he would even do me the kind gesture of telling me. He's had the pleasure of taking his fist to my stomach twice already this week just for looking at him in a way he disapproved of.

"Fuck if I know, boy. Your momma?"

"I don't have a fucking mother, asshole," I snap.

He walks up passed the rows of tables filled with other fucked-up kids visiting with relatives who look just as pleased to be here as they do. Once we hit the last row, I see her.

Lillian.

Dressed in a crisp navy-blue dress, her sleek black hair perfectly set and lips, as always, shaded a bold red. My first reaction is to attack. Wrap my fingers around her dainty throat and choke the life out of her. My hands begin to shake as I fight them to stay by my side. I slide into the seat across from her. The sadistic simper playing on her lips causes my stomach to recoil.

"Where the fuck's my sister?"

"Now, now, is that any way to talk to your counselor?"

A low growl rumbles up my throat as I lean forward.

"You ain't my counselor, bitch. Where the fuck is my sister?" My crude wording doesn't faze her. Her vicious smile only widens.

"See, that's where it's your lucky day. I *am* your counselor. Being a high ranked social services counselor in one of New Orleans' top schools, I was able to pull a few strings to get your case. Called in a favor."

She's lying to me. There's no way the system is that cruel. "I'm a legal adult now. You have no hold over me." Which is true. While sitting in this prison, I hit my eighteenth birthday.

Her sardonic grin unnerves me. "That's where you're wrong. It's a good thing I paid attention to your birthday. Just before you turned eighteen, I signed the papers to take legal guardianship of you."

"You can't do that."

"Oh, but I can. And I did. Told them I had a soft spot for the troubled boy who stole from my family and sadly raised his hand to me, but I was forgiving and wanted to help you reform yourself. My name is the only contact in your file. That means your freedom is in my hands."

My fingers clench into white fists. She doesn't and will never own me. "Good luck with that. One call to the foster care center and I'll be out of here."

She laughs, and it turns my stomach. "Oh yeah? And let me ask you, Mason, how many phone calls have you been allowed since you've been in here?"

One.

Only one.

She continues. "Exactly. I have something you want. And you have something I want."

"Fuck you. I don't want shit from you," I spit, slamming

my fists on the table. I prepare to stand when she says the one word that can trap me.

"Evelyn."

My eyes find hers shining with victory. My heart begins to beat faster, my lungs fighting for air. I sit back down.

"Ah, good. I see I have your attention. I want you to know, Mason, all of this…it won't be for nothing."

"Fuck you. Where is she?"

"That mouth of yours. Such passion and determination. If you pan out, you can do such great things for you and I." The smug look she gives me turns my stomach once again. She licks her puckered lips and continues. "I want you, Mason. I want to mold you into something great. But that can only happen if you give yourself to me."

"Are you fucking sick?"

"No, sweetheart. Just driven. Goal oriented, if you will. And to teach the most important lesson of all, I need you."

She's fucking crazy. I don't need her. I'll get out of this place and find my sister. We'll run away. I'll keep us safe until I figure shit out.

"So, what do you say?"

"I ain't helping you with shit. Tell me where my sister is!" My rock-hard fists slam against the table again, catching the attention of a few visitors and inmates.

Lillian's demeanor doesn't change. She brushes fake dust off her hands. "You know, it has to be hard for poor Evelyn. With you being stuck in here. Her being bounced around from tragic foster home to tragic foster home. Especially with the horrible conditions of the one she's in now. I would hate for anything to happen to her."

I jump to my feet and reach over the table. My hand wraps around her cold flesh, and I squeeze. I'm all too quickly ripped off her, fighting to kill her right there, while she holds her neck, catching her breath. "You fucking bitch! I'll kill you if anything happens to her!" My body ripples under the restraint of the two heavy guards.

Lillian gets up and grabs for her purse. "It's a shame we couldn't come to an agreement today, Mason. Maybe a few months in a new facility will have you seeing things differently. Until then, think about my offer." With that, she turns and walks out. I explode, thrashing to free myself and run after her. Stab her eyes out with my fingers until she tells me where Evelyn is. But an electric shock stabs me in the back, suspending every nerve ending in my body, and I fall to the ground.

"Don't fucking hurt her!" I howl, but my voice is missing the fight from just seconds before.

Lillian's heeled shoes disappear through the doors, and a large set of black boots I'm all too familiar with come into view. My favorite guard. "Get his paperwork in order. State pen should teach this pretty boy to mind his manners." And then his boot strikes, sending me into the blackness of oblivion.

Six months later...
Louisiana State Penitentiary

"Walk faster, boy." The guard lunges his shoulder into mine, and I stumble but catch myself before my face meets the cold concrete. Even the dim lighting in the hallway hurts my eyes from being in confinement for the past six months.

PRIDE

As I walk down the dingy corridor, away from solitary, my heart begins to race, hoping I'm finally being released. Maybe it's Evelyn. *Please let it be my sister.* I pick up my speed, the knot in my stomach tightening with each step as we gear toward the visiting area.

After leaving, Lillian marked me as a danger to myself and others. She even went as far as forging paperwork, claiming some sick assault allegations against me. I was transferred out of Juvenile Correctional to the Louisiana State Penitentiary. Basically, one hell to an even bigger hell. They kept me in solitary for six months. My *keeper's* recommendation. It could have been longer, but I lost count of the days after that.

That left me alone with my thoughts.

I spent my days thinking about Evelyn. Was she okay? Does she know I'm trying to come for her? Is she fighting? Will she even be the same little sister I remember from months ago? I was never a praying man, but I found myself begging the man above to keep her safe.

I spent my nights thinking about Dahlia. Her emerald green eyes that shine with laughter and love. The way she threaded her soft hands through my hair and talked about life at our old school. Stories of past friends. Visions of our future. I dreamed about getting the opportunity to show her my tattoo. How she'll tell me she loves it and me. Does she know what happened? Why the fuck hasn't she come to visit? She would wait for me. She loves me. She has to.

As time ticked by, my mind struggled to process. I found myself talking to my sister, but I knew she wasn't there. I saw Dahlia and told her to hold on and wait for me. I fought my mind, confused between what was real and not, but I was so desperate for human contact. I missed the sound of

Evelyn's charismatic laugh. Our talks. The warmth of her embrace when she hugged me for no reason but to show me love. I missed the intimate touch of Dahlia. Being so near to her, the smell of her skin on mine as we fucked. Made love. I was on the verge of losing my mind completely. I pushed myself to stay afloat through the rough sea between real and illusion. But too many times, I would fail, the weakness would drift in, and the tears would fall.

At my lowest point, a sick part of me even begged for Lillian. Just to hear her tell me my sister was okay. Everything was going to be okay.

But none of that happened.

So, I forced myself to fight through it.

I used my body as a coping mechanism. Worked my muscles any way I could to build my strength physically, even if I was losing it mentally. Months of torture and darkness consumed me.

And then, one day, Lillian returned.

"Well, look at you. Keeping busy I see." She smiles, sitting down across from me. She looks the same. Black fitted dress. Hair pulled back into a tight knitted bun. "How are you fairing, Mason? Aside from your workout regimen, which I must say, is a nice improvement."

I lift my hands and thread my fingers together, placing my conjoined hands on the table. "No thanks to you."

"Well, sometimes you have to learn the hard way. Your actions have consequences. I've returned to give you another chance. This is no place for you. You can leave here today with me. It's simple really. You'll give me complete ownership of you, and I'll give you what you want—to know where your sister is."

"I already told you, I'm not yours to own. You some

PRIDE

sick bitch who gets off on kids? Or is that just your husband?" Her Botox-injected forehead may not move a muscle, but I don't miss the twitch of her upper lip. Her eyes squint, making her appear more like the snake she is.

"I'd watch your tone with me. I'm the one who holds the cards here. And I wouldn't refer to yourself as a kid. You're very much a man now. Six months away from nineteen." Her slithery eyes examine me from top to bottom, causing the minimal food in my stomach to churn.

"Why're you doing this? I have nothing you want."

"That's where you're wrong. A lost boy who has nothing to lose. No aspirations in life. Just a troubled kid who is well on his way to spending the rest of his life in a place like this. You see, I want to be your savior. Your God, in a way. Offer you a life you would never have otherwise. What would you say to a scholarship to one of the most elite schools in New Orleans? A future? In return, you belong to me."

"To do what?"

"Well, that's the most enticing part of all, Mason. You don't get to open the box before deciding whether you want the gift or not. Did Eve know the consequences of eating the apple before she took that savory bite?" She resembles every bit the evil serpent, her beady eyes smiling back at me as her tongue slides out and licks her bold red lips.

"You're fucked up. And sick."

"Yes, yes, I may be, but my future isn't the one on the line here. Yours is. Oh, and let's not forget your poor sister. Have I mentioned the struggle we've had trying to find her a safe home? The foster families nowadays. Just in it for the money. They do need to do better background checks on sex offenders and drug addicts."

I erupt from my chair, but before I have the chance to dig my fingers into her neck, two guards rip my arms behind my back and cuff me, restraining me. "You bitch! I swear, you can't keep me in here. I'll find a way to get out of here."

"Good luck with that. But I should advise you, it's your poor, fragile sister who needs it. How long do you think she'll last in those unsafe living conditions? Do you know how high teenage drug overdoses are nowadays? So sad, I must admit."

I pull at my restraints, tearing at my skin. But nothing compares to the pain tearing through my heart at the thought of my sister with a needle in her pure skin. My stomach turns, and bile threatens to expel from my throat. "Why?"

"Because I can. That's the most honest answer, right? You have no authority. No rights at this point. I can keep you in here forever if I truly wanted. That's the perk of being your designated counsel. If I see you unfit, you'll rot in here."

"Why, though? What'd my sister and I ever do to you?"

Her smile falls a smidge, but she masks her hate. "Your sister is just like the rest—willing and able to let married men into their beds. For that, she should be taught a lesson. You, on the other hand...I see potential."

My vision blurs red. My hands shake behind me, and the rumble inside me threatens to burst through my chest. "My sister didn't let your husband into her room. She would never have allowed that unless she was being forced."

Her shoulders raise in a careless shrug. "My focus is not on her. It's on you. It's what I want from you."

"And what the fuck is that!" I bark.

PRIDE

"I want you to run a secret club for me. Be the face behind an elite organization."

"You fucking kidding me?"

"Not at all. I wouldn't spend so much time and effort on a loser such as yourself if I didn't feel you had the potential to be molded into my perfect pet."

I'm gonna fucking kill her. If I have to spend the rest of my life behind bars, so be it. I'll find a way out. I'll seek counsel. Riot until I'm heard. They can't keep me here. The second I'm out, I'll get Evelyn and Dahlia and start a new life.

"Oh, honey, you're certainly not thinking about a plan B, are you? There isn't one."

"Fuck you."

"Ah, that would be fun. You certainly have become a man in here. But...speaking of fucking, I have a present for you." She leans to the side and reaches into her purse to pull out her phone. A few pokes at her screen and she turns it to face me.

A video plays, and I watch in horror and disbelief at the reel: two people fucking behind bleachers. Some dude taking the girl from behind while her pleasurable moans spew through the phone speaker. He pulls out, and the girl turns, and I get a view of Dahlia as she drops to her knees, placing his dick in her mouth. I don't take my eyes away as she bobs up and down on his cock like a fucking slut taking him deep into her throat. Her moans become louder as slobber and semen begin to dribble down her chin.

"So, you see, my little pet. I'm all you have. You're not the white knight at the end of this. I am. Your sister can still be saved. Can't say the same for your whore girlfriend."

My heart turns stone cold. Ice drips from my words

as I lean forward. "Fuck you, bitch." I spit in her face, and satisfaction settles inside me as my saliva drips down her cheek. Her disgusted expression gives me pleasure as she takes a handkerchief from her purse to wipe her face.

"You're going to regret that, Mason." She stands and tosses the silk towel into the trash. "I'm sorry we couldn't come to an agreement. Enjoy rotting in here. Maybe I should do my civic duty and adopt your sister too. She's still under age. She can come back and live with us where she'll be properly looked after. I'm sure my *husband* would enjoy that."

No cuffs or guards are strong enough to hold me back as I leap across the table and catch her by the shoulder. I manage to take her down and bust her nose with my forehead. Her screams enrage me even more, thinking about my sister's cries as she's hurt by strangers, let alone that sick fuck.

"Get this animal off me!" she gurgles, choking on the blood spewing from her nose. I've gone completely mad with hatred and revenge. I bare my teeth, ready to rip the veins out of her neck and watch her bleed to death. But it seems today is her lucky day. A baton strikes against my back, over and over. I hear the snapping of the wood, then two Tasers strike me, paralyzing me. Lillian is freed from under me and carried away, and I'm left on the floor, numb and beaten within an inch of my life.

Six months later....

"You got it?"

PRIDE

"You got that extra bun?" Jinx, aka Jimmy Henson, asks, side-eyeing my hand hidden inside my jumpsuit pocket.

"You know I do, brother," I reply, anxious. I pull out the bread bun from dinner, along with a pack of smokes, and slide it under the lunchroom table. The day Lillian walked out, she took any sort of freedom I had left with her. She fucked me. She made sure I knew exactly who she was to me: the puppeteer pulling at my strings. If she wanted me to go without food, it happened. If she wanted a fight to break out, causing me to go underground for weeks, it happened. Every single privilege a normal inmate received, I was denied.

That was just the start. Phone usage, internet, even visitors—she took it all. I thought there was no way she could have that much control over me, let alone a huge prison facility. That turned out to be so far from the truth. Left and right, guards, wardens—they all turned a blind eye to my allegations, the abuse. I acted out in frustration, but just got more time in lockdown. It'd been six months of hell. No word about my sister, or a peep from Lillian. I couldn't spend another fucking day in a dark, cold cell, so I came up with a plan. A smarter one. When I was brought back up to General Population, I started making allies. Other inmates—lifers, as they call themselves—who didn't give two shits about breaking protocol. It wasn't gonna change their sentence. So, in return for the shit I got my hands on, they did my bidding.

Food, smokes, clean laundry. That was my deal. They get what they want and use their computer to do my research, no questions asked. Secret societies. Underground clubs. I didn't believe Lillian when she went off about running a secret elite group, but I need to finally acknowledge how much power she holds. I changed hands every other day so the warden wouldn't catch on to the fact that I was smuggling info under his nose. There's no doubt he's also deep in Lillian's web of deceit.

I had inmates research everything under the sun about secret, elite clubs. Did they exist? I didn't believe that shit to be real, but per the big bad web, they did. Elite universities, holding secret societies, thriving in conspiracies. All were only rumored to be of existence, because no one could prove any real one existed. But they did. The whispered rumors and lavish stories of what really happened behind closed doors at these ivy league clubs were nothing but sinister. They didn't create these for scholars to rise above the rest educationally. They were created to build a dark path to the forbidden side of evil: hazing, law breaking, bizarre traditions that went back centuries of disorderly conduct and destruction. These clubs weren't for the innocent, the good faith and good hearted—no, they were built and constructed for warriors. If you're searching for an ivy club, turn around, this ain't it.

I did my usual search on Lillian. She was still the headmaster counselor, and an outstanding member of society at the St. Augustine University—an elite school right here in Louisiana. It would make sense, the secret clubs taking place at elite universities. Lillian running the show. Not to mention her scumbag husband was the dean. But why the fuck would she want me? These things were run by rich scholars. Passed down from generation to generation. Definitely not someone like me—which just further confirmed Lillian had plans other than sticking to tradition. And I seemed to be at the center of it.

Jinx grabs the bun and shoves it into his pants.

PRIDE

"All right. Let's have it," I say, looking around for guards.

"Yeah, yeah. Nothing new on Evelyn Blackwell."

My stomach drops, just as it always does when they come back with no new information on my sister.

"Did you try the different spellings on Facebook? Any of those other social pages?"

"Yep. Nada. Plus, them computers are slow as fuck. Only got to print out the—"

"Just fucking give it to me." I snatch the tightly folded piece of paper from his hands, and he gets up and takes off out of the cafeteria. I get up and dump the rest of my untouched food. Heading back to my cell, the small piece of paper burns inside the palm of my closed fist. My muscles strain, driving me to walk faster, but I know I'm being watched. I always am. I turn the corner and get stopped just before I enter my cell.

"In a hurry, Blackwell?" Asshole Berringer, the daytime guard, asks, smacking his baton against my cell bars.

"Yeah, gotta get my daytime jerk off in before my daily prayer session." His baton thrashes against the metal, inches from my face. I don't flinch, which only pisses him off.

"You think you'd learn. Outside." He stands there, waiting for me to obey.

"Yeah. Like I said. Busy. Unless you wanted to help me. You look like a guy who enjoys a good fat cock in your mouth—"

The blow hurts, but the pain isn't unfamiliar. His baton strikes me across my cheek, jerks back, then hits me behind my kneecaps. My legs collapse, and I drop to my knees. The taste of blood fills my mouth, and I raise my hand to my lip. "Sorry, did I read you wrong? I'm not really into ass fucking, but if that's your—"

He lashes out again, hitting my neck, and I stumble forward, losing my balance. My fists hit the concrete, scraping my knuckles. *Fuck*. That one hurt.

"Get up."

"Make me, assh—"

"*Fuck*," I grunt as he kicks me in the side, hitting a still mending rib.

"Boy, you're gonna learn to show some respect. Get up."

I want to fight him more. This ain't my first rodeo with an unwarranted guard beat-down. But my eyes catch my still closed fist, and I remember. He can't see what's in my hand. At least not before I've read what's on it. I do as he says and pull my sore body off the ground. I do it slowly, so he doesn't panic, thinking I'm gonna revolt on his ass, and force my flat hands to the wall, the paper smashed in-between.

"That's right. Fucking pussy boy. Where's that mouth now?" Clutching the note, I turn around and give him my blank face, even though my body's on fire. "Now, why don't you give me what's in that hand of yours."

No.

My fists tighten, my nails digging into my palms.

"Did you just go mute, boy? I said hand me the piece of paper before I make it so that hand don't work." Every muscle in my body tenses, preparing for the fight. He isn't getting this paper. I take a menacing step toward him. With my height and build, I could do quite a bit of harm to him. He may have to fucking shoot me. "You back off, boy!" he hollers.

"Better get ready to shoot me then." I take another slow step, though I'm not sure what the fuck I'm doing. No end to this will be good.

"Boy, I'll shoot ya, and you know they won't tend to ya. You're on the *do not provide medical assistance* list. You'll bleed out right here." I wouldn't be shocked if he was telling the truth. I stop in my advance. "That's right. Hand me the paper like a good little prisoner or I'll shoot your hand off and take it myself." Fuck! The defeat rips at my insides. He retrieves his gun, and I know I lost. "Down on your fucking knees." My knees fall to the concrete, and I put my hands behind my head. The piece of paper falls from my grip, and victory spreads across his face as he bends down and unfolds it.

"Ah…smart little fucker. Having others do your bidding. At least Mrs. Griffin will be pleased at your curiosity." He turns to a guard who's arrived as back up. "Take him back down. Mr. Blackwell just doesn't seem to learn his lesson."

Six months later…

The whistle sounds from the speakers indicating it's time for outdoor recess. It reminds me of when I was a kid, itching in my little school chair, waiting for that bell to ring so I could line up. The anticipation of knowing I was so close to a game of four square or the gigantic playground, or whatever other stupid ass outdoor games I played at that age, flowing through my tiny veins. I can almost still feel the excitement of being that young and carefree.

But it ain't nothing like that here.

It's more like the *Hunger Games*. Inmates stand in corners. Crews segregate themselves from the punks, to the stoners, to the gangsters—you name it. If the movies got one thing right, it's who made friends with who in here and for what benefit. One being to stay alive.

I no longer had anyone doing my bidding. Once I came back up, I had to be even more careful. Some lifers didn't care, but some were hoping for an earlier parole, so they backed off and no longer wanted to be on the warden's naughty list. It seemed that while I was down, word spread. If I was assisted in any way, consequences would come. After being in lockdown for three months, it took me another three to finally get someone to help me out.

I walk down the hallway of the second floor and take the side stairs to get outside quicker. Ricky had a visit with his sister yesterday. In his recent letter to her, he asked her to ask around town about my sister. At this point, I'm only worried about her. I just need to know she's safe. She'll be turning eighteen soon, and I'll be at peace when she does. She'll be free.

I shove through the steel doors and walk out to the open area filled with orange jump suits. I shield my eyes, searching for Ricky, and find him standing in the corner, leaning against the barbwire fence. My boots hit the concrete, making it over to him. "What you got for me?" I ask, wasting no time.

"Today's your lucky day." He fumbles with something up his sleeve, then a small piece of paper appears in the palm of his hand. I go to grab for it, but he yanks it back. "Not so fast. You got something for me?"

I dig in my pocket and slip him the two packs of smokes I jimmied from the laundry room. He stares down at the packs, then hands me the paper. I know I'm not being smart, but I open it right there.

Public files show there's been paperwork filed for the adoption of E. Blackwell submitted by L.P. Griffin.

No.

No.

"No!" I growl, shaking the ground below me.

Ricky takes a step toward me, catching me off guard, and raises his hand. The bright sun gleams off the rusty blade in his grip, and my eyes catch it just as it protrudes into my ribcage. The pain shoots through me, stealing my breath. He draws back, bringing the blade out of my punctured flesh, then stabs me again. My arms shoot up, trying to fight his grip on me, but the pain is too fierce. He lowers his head, his mouth over my ear. "Sorry, bro, but you know how it is. Every man for them self. They gave me a message for you too. Time to make a choice. You know they won't tend to ya. Bleed out or give in." He rips his shank out and drops it next to me. Blood seeps thick and fast from my open wounds. I grab his jumpsuit and pull my arm back to throw a punch, but I'm too weak. My closed fist falls to my side as my knees buckle, dropping myself to the ground. My mind goes to my sister. The regret—shame I couldn't protect her.

My chest tightens, and breathing is more painful than the effort is worth. My body slams against the warm concrete. The strength in my hand weakens, and my palm opens, the small piece of paper falling out of my grip.

I can't leave my sister.

Not in the hands of a monster.

"Tell her she wins," I mumble, struggling to get words out. Using my hands to force myself off the ground, I slip and fall back down. I howl in pain, blurriness creating an overcast in my vision.

"What was that?" I see the steel boot of the warden.

A growl low in my stomach grows, giving me a burst of strength. I reach forward, grabbing the warden's leg and tugging hard. Losing his balance, he howls, slipping and falling to the ground. I pull myself up over his body as he struggles to escape from my grip. "Get the fuck off me!" he yells, fighting and kicking out from under me. I grab the shank he dropped.

"I said tell her she wins, motherfucker," I grit out, then stab him in the ribs.

She finally wins.

That's my last thought before blackness consumes me.

I'm in and out of consciousness.

I remember screaming as they sewed me up. Of course, those motherfuckers didn't use anything to numb me first.

I remember the infirmary. The white room. Beeping sounds of machines.

Then I remember her.

"You made the right decision, Mason. Now, rest. Your recovery puts a damper in our schedule, but we can work around this. I truly do admire the love you have for your sister. The things some do for family. Fast recovery, pet."

I remember the coldness of her lips on my forehead before she left me to spend it in a recovery room—before I can walk out of Louisiana State Penitentiary into a worse hell.

VII
UINCENDUM NATUS

ONE

Two weeks later...

The sun is angry, scorching all of Louisiana with its sweltering temperatures as I step through the prison doors. I shield my eyes, already feeling the heat on my skin, sweat forming into droplets down my back. While being discharged, they handed me a sealed bag containing the shit I came in with. Clothes I've long grown out of. My torn wallet, holding two dollars, a picture of Dahlia, and some receipts. Tossing it in the trash, I walk past the entrance guard. The moment the prison gates are behind me, I breathe a sigh of relief. Two fucking years. I'm finally out.

They don't lie when they say the air smells different when you're free. I inhale the humid air through my nose, and exhale. "Free air is fucking glorious." I laugh, then turn to walk down the mile or so long street where a cab would be waiting to take me wherever I want to go. Fuck if I know where that is, but I have a whole mile to figure it out. A black sedan pulls up next to me as I begin down the gravel sidewalk. When it fully comes to a stop, my steps slow as well, until I'm halted, watching a suited man get out of the car to open the back door.

"Get in."

I don't need to bend down to know that evil voice or the hideous scent of her perfume seeping through the open doorway, choking me along with the humidity and heat. Dread quickly replaces the light feeling of being out of that hell hole, reminding me how fast I had forgotten why—I'd made a deal with the devil.

Lillian slides to the other side of the car and pats the open seat next to her. "Don't make me repeat myself. In. Now."

My eyes light with the fire that holds bright and angry when it comes to Lillian. A rumble deep in my chest sounds, and I throw myself into the back seat.

"That growl... You know, women nowadays have quite a fondness for that rugged, bad boy persona. You should be careful who you use that on. Might give someone the wrong impression." Her hand slides across the seat and lands on my thigh.

I peel her fingers off my skin, throwing her hand off me. "Where's my sister?" I demand, no bullshit in my tone.

She holds up a folder, and I reach for it, but she retracts. "Not so fast, pet. There are some rules we have to discuss first."

"I ain't doin' shit until I see Evelyn," I bark.

PRIDE

"And I think you forgot who makes the rules here. I'm calling the shots. Not you. It's best you quickly realize that."

My hands shake. Keeping them at my sides and not around her neck is almost impossible. I need to see my sister. "Fine. What rules?"

"Good boy." She hands me the file. "As promised, here are all your registration papers. Congratulations, you're officially a student at St. Augustine."

I read over the documents. Acceptance forms, test scores. All bullshit of course. "And how the fuck am I gonna pull this shit off? I didn't even graduate high school, no thanks to you."

She waves her hand. "You have your GED from LSP, and that's for me to handle. Just attend class. I'll take care of the rest. No one will ever bat an eye at my underprivileged pet project."

Fuck her. And fuck this. This is crazy. I continue scanning the papers. "This says I'm eighteen." I look at her.

"And you will be. You should be thankful I devoted so much time to you. But now that you're past your prime, we're gonna have to work around it."

"How's that?"

"Simple. You're eighteen. Newest freshman attendee. Scholarship given by the university for disadvantaged kids."

"I don't understand. You can't just—"

"You don't need to understand anything but what I'm telling you. And what I'm telling you is you need to attend class and sit tight until I come calling." She raises her hand to graze my cheek, but I slap it away.

"Where is my sister?"

"Oh, yes. Well, first, I need you to prove to me your worthiness. I need to trust you won't just take off once I give you what you so desperately want. And even then, I'd be advised not to cross me."

"Where the FUCK—?"

"Oh, hush. All this aggression. You'd be happy to know Evelyn has been given the same specialty treatment as you."

My vision goes blind with rage. *What did they do to her?*

Lillian's laugh has me spiraling. "Down, boy. She's enrolled at St. Augustine as well. Set up with housing and a comfortable class schedule. I hear she wants to be a writer."

A writer. My sister wants to become a writer? Pride fills my chest knowing she has goals. She aspires to be something. She hasn't grown up into a fuck up like me.

"I'm warning you, try anything stupid and all this goes away. That also goes for spilling any of our arrangements to your sister. You *will* obey me. You *will* do everything I ask of you. I promise you, every move you make *will* affect your sister. Do I make myself clear?"

Oh, she's making herself very clear. "All this obeying bullshit, you haven't even told me what you want from me. How the hell do I know what rules I'm breaking?"

Her smile is what nightmares are made of. Hidden behind that sweet lie is hate and destruction. "You will soon enough. For now, here's your housing information, phone, keys, and some cash to get yourself cleaned up. May I recommend some more appropriate attire?"

I take the items she hands me, and the side door reopens. "That's it?" I ask.

PRIDE

"For now."

I sit there, staring back at her.

"This is where you get out, Mason. Hurry along, I have a busy day."

Crunching the items in my grip, I throw my leg out and exit the vehicle. The door shuts, and her henchman climbs back in and speeds off down the gravel road. I stand there confused, shocked, angrier than before. I jingle the set of keys in my hand when I notice the key fob. I press down on the worn off buttons to hear a beeping sound erupt from across the street where a line of cars are parked. I press it again, and the back lights to a vehicle light up.

"How nice. My ride's here."

VII
UINCENDUM NATUS

TWO

St. Augustine College - New Orleans.
Three weeks later...
Mason

"**K**eep going?"

"Don't ask me again. Finish it."

Crow, the tattoo artist, shakes his head, his laugh gruff from the three packs of smokes he inhales a day. "You one bad ass motherfucker. But all right. Prah' got another four hours on this side."

I nod. My skin is on fire, but I welcome the pain. The last two weeks, I've sat in his chair while he covered both arms with ink. Everything on my body has meaning. Symbolization. Starting with the thorns suffocating the flower over my heart. The last two weeks have been hell but sitting in the chair with the buzzing of the

PRIDE

needle permanently bleeding into my skin allows me to feel something other than guilt. Regret. Anxiousness. Lillian has yet to beckon me. She has yet to give me my sister. I'm starting to think she's lying. Only dangling my desperation in front of me so I do what she wants. And right now, it's play nice until she's ready for me.

In the meantime, I've done what she asked. Attended my bullshit classes and laid low. Just as she promised, I was handed a scholarship, all expenses paid. And no one batted an eye at my GED or low-grade point average. Not a single person questioned my jail record or why I'd been locked up the past two years. I don't know how the fuck she thinks I'm going to pull off a full schedule of college classes. She knows this isn't where I belong; it's just another thing she taunts me with. I don't and won't ever have the brains to attend a real university. I told her as much, but it's no concern to her. Her instructions were simple. Just show up to class and she'll take care of my grades.

The housing was a fucking joke. It may have been in one of the nicest areas around campus, but don't be fooled. It was all just a ruse. A ploy to toy with me. Inside the lavish apartment is dingy, used furniture. The couch is covered in rips and tears, and it reeks of vomit. The bed is in the same condition. I have a better chance of escaping bed bugs by sleeping on the floor. She wants me to remember I come from nothing. Same goes for the car. Broken down piece of shit. I'd rather sleep on the streets, but for now, she makes the rules. I stay here or else. I'll hold my chin up, my pride high, because in the end, it's all for her: Evelyn.

The sun peeking through the dingy shutters alerts

me that I've been here all night. I look at the time to see it's going on six in the morning. Crow is just finishing the final touches on the snake around my bicep when my phone buzzes in the back of my worn jeans pocket. Only one person has this number.

Which means I'm being beckoned.

Lillian sure had me at the edge of my seat, anticipating what she had in store for me. But today, now, is when I learn my fate. When I find out what I really signed up for. Agreeing to her terms was no different than signing my death warrant. I knew the day I did, it would be the last time I had control over myself.

Crow patches me up, and I'm out headed to campus. I'm sure my eyes are bloodshot, but they've been that way for weeks now. Sleep is something that hasn't come easily to me in a long time.

I enter through the counselor's office, and see her door, a shiny plaque with her name sprawled across it.

Lillian Griffin, MD
Head Master Counselor

I lean against the wall, thinking how messed up it is that someone as demented as her can have so much power in such a top school—

"Mason?" I bring my focus to the voice calling my name. "Oh my god, Mason, is that you?" Chastity Griffin. Lillian and George Griffin's daughter. It's been years since I've seen her. Two years to be exact. "What the heck happened to you? I came home from cheerleading camp and you and Evelyn were gone. Lillian told me you were placed in a different home."

I'm sure she did. I bet she also left out what a sadistic bitch she is or how her father is a sick fuck who abuses

PRIDE

girls. Looking at her now, I wonder if she even knows—if daddy dearest ever made his way into his own daughter's room.

"Yeah. Fuckin' foster system's a joke," I lie, saving her the truth. She still looks innocent and unaware of the demon living under the same roof. Curiosity begins to build behind those innocent eyes, and I know I need to wrap this up, before she starts asking questions I can't answer—

"Weird though, Lillian never mentioned you went here. What are you, sophomore? Junior now?"

Fuck. Chastity knows how old I really am.

Think...

Think...

"No, actually first year. Took a break for a bit." Actually, your cunt of a step-mother locked me up in a prison until I bowed down to play her little puppet, set out to ruin lives.

"Oh, well cool. Hey! That reminds me! I swore I saw Evie here too!"

My skin prickles at my sister's name. "Where?" I ask, causing her to jump.

"Huh?"

"Where did you see her?" I spit out. Lillian said she was here, but I've yet to find her. I went to the registrars' office asking about her, but those assholes refused to give me any information. Student privacy policy my ass.

"I thought I saw her walking out of the student center. She looked good!" Her eyebrows raise in confusion. "Tell her I said hi and maybe we can do coffee sometime?"

I want to storm off and sit outside the student center in hopes to catch her. Shake Chastity with more questions. What was she wearing? Define good. Did she look like she had endured hell for the last two years? Instead, I rein in my emotions and nod, forcing my lips to curl into a slight smile. "Will do."

That easy-going smile she always carried is back across her face. "Well, cool! I mean, how crazy for all of us to end up at the same school? Are you here to see Lillian?" she asks, unaware of how I truly ended up here.

"Yeah. She's my counselor." And the devil in disguise. The one person I dream about slitting their throat and watching her die slowly. The one who's made it clear she holds all the cards, as well as the strings controlling my life.

"That's great. It's great to see you again. I hope we get to catch up on campus!" She goes in for a hug, which makes me uncomfortable, then disappears in Lillian's office. A short time later, she and another male student exit, leaving the door open as Lillian waits for me to enter.

Fuck.

It's now or never.

"Well, don't you make a handsome college student," she purrs, closing the door and walking in front of me. Her clothes, as always, are form-fitting, her hair pulled back in a tight ponytail. She looks back to inspect me, and it turns my stomach. Deleting the space that separates us, she brings her hands to my shirt and brushes them down my chest with open palms. "Still working out I see. And I'm loving the new additions," she says, inspecting my arms. Not caring if I snap her wrists, I grab for her hands and remove them from my skin. "Always so feisty. You should learn to enjoy this. Us. Because if I want something from you, something as simple as your cock, Mason, I'll get it. Understood?" She doesn't wait for my response.

PRIDE

Pushing away from me, she heads to her desk, sits, and digs in her drawer. "Oh, don't look so grouchy. You're about to get an opportunity of a lifetime. Sit."

Doing as she says, I throw myself into the seat across from her. "I want to see my sister," I bark out.

"And you will. Business first, pleasure later." Shuffling through her desk drawer, she retrieves a manila envelope. "Ah, here we are. Mason, are you familiar with the seven deadly sins?"

I take some time to understand her question. "Like the church shit? Evil versus good?"

"So smart, my pet." She laughs, and my skin pebbles with disgust. "The seven deadly sins. Lust, gluttony, greed, sloth, wrath, envy, and pride. Sins that live inside us all. The excessive desire to want more. The desired evil that's rooted in us all. Every single human being in this world fights the urge to indulge in what God considered a sin. To lie, to steal, to deface. Given the chance, anyone would shame another to rise above. Strip one of their innocence. Harm someone just to boast they have the power to do so."

She's starting to confuse me. "Where the fuck you going with this?"

"Patience. Way before your time, and mine, a secret elite society was formed. The Elite Seven. It was created by guided influential leaders, ones who would go on and flourish in molding our country into something magnificent. Every four years, seven new members are hand chosen for The Elite. But they aren't just hand-picked, they're put to the test—given a task of sin to prove themselves. Once proven, they're initiated for life. They want for nothing. They suffer for nothing. Sins become them, and they become the being of their life."

"And what does this have to do with me?" I ask, uncertain I want to know the answer.

"To be a part of The Elite of course. The leader. The alpha of the seven."

"Yeah, well I want nothing to do with ruining someone's life."

"Oh, but that's not for you to decide anymore, is it? You gave that right to me the second you agreed to my terms. You *will* do as I say, or the liveliness of your sister will suffer."

The power she has over me kills me.

She tosses a sheet of paper at me, and I catch it. I vaguely glimpse at the other names and titles, until I get to mine. "Pride?"

"Of course. Don't you find your sin fitting? You have no regard for others. You'll lead an army. Six, to be exact, and single-handedly assign each sinner a task. You will, with no care for the people they hurt, deface, suffer, make sure each task is completed or they'll be banished from the society. Their lives mean nothing to you."

"But they do. I'm not a fucking monster."

"Aren't you, though? Agreeing to bow down to the devil herself and do her bidding? What does that truly make you, Mason?"

The father of all sins.

My understanding makes her smile. "You get it. The anti-Christ as some would define it. If you agree with me or not, I picked you because you carry the same corrupt sense of values. Just as I, you cannot be fooled by the vices of others. You should see this as a good thing. From someone who has nothing, you'll be seen as someone

PRIDE

who has it all." She shrugs her head. "Arrogant. Probably conceited. Not liked amongst the rest being the alpha, but that's what makes you Pride. You don't care."

This is all too much for me. Run a club? Ruin lives? Taking the sheet of names, I toss it back onto her desk and stand. She doesn't react to my defiance. Simply stands on her heels and walks around her desk, encroaching my personal space. She reaches for the hem of my shirt and her fingers disappear under my shirt. My body stiffens as her fingers latch onto the button of my jeans, then work it undone. "This wouldn't be so bad for you if you'd loosen up a little. You and I...we can have a little fun with this." I want to break each finger that touches me, but I refrain, thinking of Evelyn. "That's a good boy. See? A little playtime between us may turn out to be enjoyable for us both." She pulls my zipper down and reaches into my briefs to cup my soft cock. A sudden knock on the door and the sound of Chastity's voice saves me and she retracts, taking a quick step away.

I pull my zipper back up just as her door opens, and Chastity peeks her head in. "Hey. Sorry. I left my phone on your desk."

Turning, Lillian spots the pink, glittered phone and hands it to her. "Better hurry. Class is about to start," she chirps. I snatch my backpack off the ground and head toward the door. "Hey, Mason?" she calls for me, and I force myself to turn around. "Make sure to read the homework I sent you for our session, okay?"

"Yeah, whatever," I reply before getting the fuck away from her.

What the fuck have I signed up for?

UINCENDUM NATUS

THREE

My biology professor pushes up his bifocals, holding up a stack of papers. "This is just a simple test to see what you remember from high school. Consider it a recap." He walks to the end of each row and disperses small stacks, having the students take one and hand them down the line. I take one and look around, seeing if anyone else is dreading this shit, but people begin scribbling down answers as soon as they get their paper. I take a deep breath and crack my stiff neck. My pencil is tightly gripped between my fingers as I begin to read the first question. Then the second. When I get down to the bottom of the page, I realize I don't know a single answer.

A sound breaks the silence of the room, and a few classmates lift their heads my way. Without realizing it, I've snapped my pencil in half. The number of eyes staring

PRIDE

at me weigh too heavily on my anxiety and I get up. I toss the blank test onto the professor's desk and leave. The anger swirling inside me is a deadly potion of hate and resentment. She did this to me on purpose. Lillian. She created my schedule knowing this shit would be too hard for me. I wasn't a strong student even when I was in high school, and she robbed me of the last two years of a proper education.

I take the stairs down two at a time and burst through to exit the doors of the science building when my phone starts buzzing in my pocket. I reach back and stop at the bottom to read the screen. My breath catches, threatening to knock me flat on my ass at the message.

Cunt Griffin: Bayler Dorm. Room 313. Consider this a gift. Play nice or I'll take your toys away from you.

I'm changing routes before even finishing the text and book it toward the campus dorms. Knocking into people as I storm through the quad, I'm out of breath by the time I make it to the building. I reach for the door, but it's locked. I take my fist and bang for someone to open and get lucky when another student exits. I slide in just as the door closes and head to the staircase. Avoiding the check-in, I take the stairs to the third floor and pound on the door. A girl sees me, and instead of turning me away, her eyes light up as she opens the door.

"Hey there," she purrs in a flirtatious tone. "You know, I could get in a lot of trouble letting you in, but you're cute so—"

"Evelyn Blackwell. I'm here to see her," I spit out, catching my breath.

Her face falls, mistaking my relationship to her.

"Oh…down the hall." I waste no time stepping to the side and racing down, looking at each room number. "I'm in three-oh-one if you get bored of that," she yells as I stop at room three-thirteen. I lift my hand and bang twice. Without waiting for a response, I turn the knob. My heart is racing, and a wave of sickness sweeps through me. I've been waiting for this moment since the night Lillian tore us apart. The door shoots open, and my eyes land on her standing by the window, her back to me.

"Evie?" I've always promised to be strong for her, but seeing her, after all this time apart, it becomes too much. Her name falls from my lips on a coarse whisper. She turns, a tender look on her face. My breath catches at how much older she looks. Her hair, the color of whiskey rests just below her shoulders, her similar gray eyes illuminating the same sadness I see in my own. She's too thin. Her heathered shirt hangs over her slim shoulders, her collarbone protruding. When our eyes meet, it takes a mere flicker of recognition for it to register.

"Mason?" she whispers in disbelief. "Oh god, Mason?" Her face explodes with emotion, tears welling in her eyes as she runs into my arms. I lift her up and hold her tightly to my chest, fighting my own tears.

"It's me, little sister," I murmur, no longer able to stop my own tears from falling. I'm so overcome with emotion, I don't know what to say. I've dreamed about this day—when I got to reunite with her and tell her how fucking sorry I am. How I tried. But right now, nothing seems justifiable. No words can make her understand how crushed I've been since that night. "I'm here now," I whisper in her hair, smelling the sweet scent of flowers and soap. Just like when she was a kid. My heart cracks, and

PRIDE

I lose it. I start to cry, holding her tighter. I'm a fucking bastard brother for not fighting harder. "I'm so fucking sorry," I choke out. Her arms wrap around my neck, and I feel the wetness of her own tears on my skin.

"I love you, Mason."

More words that gut me deeper. How can she still love me? I let her down. I always promised her I'd keep her safe and look what's happened. I don't know what she's endured, but the threats Lillian left me to ponder, I doubt are good. I need to know, but I can't find the right words to ask.

"Where have you been? I've tried…I've looked…" She can't finish her own sentence. Her choked sobs steal the words from her, and we both squeeze tighter to one another. The pain from that night seems fresh all over again. The torment of them ripping her away from me. Her desperate pleas. My failed struggle to save her. Save us.

I don't know what to say to her. I want to tell her the truth. About everything. But Lillian's message is loud and clear. "I got into trouble right after they split us up. I've been in jail since."

She fights out of my hold, her eyes swollen from her tears, but wide with shock. "Jail? Why—what did you do?"

Nothing is what I want to tell her. I chose not to help Lillian sooner. "I got into a bad fight." Which isn't a complete lie. Choking Lillian close to death isn't far from the truth. "I tried to find you, but I was restricted where I was. They didn't allow me to talk to anyone. Well…except one person."

When I see the look of fear in her eyes, I know she knows who I'm talking about.

Fuck.

"Lillian Griffin," is all she says. I want to cry all over again. What did Lillian do to my sister? "She knew where you were, didn't she?" I nod, and bring my hands away from her shoulders, allowing us some distance. She turns away from me, wrapping her arms around her thin waist. "She lied, you know. I never—"

"Don't even finish that sentence," I growl, taking a step closer. "I never thought for a fucking second you did anything wrong." She turns around, hope in her eyes. I continue. "She's a lying bitch. She set you up. She set us both up." Her lower lip starts to quiver, and I eliminate the few steps separating us and engulf her back into my arms. "I don't know where to begin. How to start to explain how sorry I am. I don't know what you've been through, and I don't know how to ask you to tell me. But we're both here now. And things are going to be okay."

Her chest rises and falls, taking a deep breath. "Why us, Mason? What did we ever do to her?"

"I don't know. But I'm gonna figure it out." I pull back and catch her eyes, the same grey color as my own. "I need you to stay away from her though, okay?"

She breaks away, trying to give herself distance, but I grab her arm, stopping her. "I'm serious, Evelyn. She's the fucking devil."

She whips around to face me. "Don't you think I know that?" Guilt stabs me in the heart at her words. "I've tried to run from her. But she finds me every time. And now, I'm here. She's my counselor, Mason. She has all control over my schooling. She'd always tell me I'd be thankful for being such a good little whore because one day…" she fades off, and the look in her eyes gut me. She loses herself in a memory before coming back to me. "And now I

PRIDE

get it. It must have been you she was talking about. I've been good. I've listened. Because I thought…just maybe it would be…" She breaks down. My arms are around her as her knees buckle. I take us both to the ground as her body convulses in deep, gut-wrenching sobs. My heart breaks open in a million pieces, and I pray for time to take us back. If I knew, I could have gotten us out of that house.

"If I could take everything back I would. Fuck, I would. I'm so fucking sorry," I cry into her hair, soaking her soft curls. "I never stopped thinking about you. If I could've done something, I would have. But I was stuck. I had no way…"

She fights out of my hold, bringing her warm hands to cup my cheeks. "Oh, Mason, I know you would have. The whole time, I was dying for you. I didn't know where you were. I didn't know what they had done to you. If Lillian had her claws in you as well…I couldn't imagine what they had done. Was it bad? Were you hurt?"

My body begins to throb all over again.

The horrific pain.

The vivid memory of my ribs snapping from a steel boot, a fist, cracking of a metal rod. Remembering the darkness due to my swollen eyes. The lack of food for days. The solitude for months upon months.

I squeeze my eyes shut, needing the images to go away.

"Hey, it's okay now. We're together."

I open my eyes. She looks back like she's the one saving me. Still, behind the torment, I see innocence. Kindness. "I…I need to ask where you've been."

It's too soon. I fucked up, and she instantly shuts down on me. There's an overcast of sadness in her eyes.

She squirms from my hold and stands, making her way back to the window. "I don't...I can't talk about that."

My heart sinks. My biggest fear was Lillian had been telling the truth. My biggest hope was she hadn't been. I stand. "Evelyn—"

She turns. "Mason, please. In time, but not now. Okay?" Fuck, not now. I need to know. Lillian's life will end tonight. Evelyn can live the rest of hers in peace knowing she's dead, and I'll live mine behind bars knowing my little sister no longer needs to be scared. But I just got her back. Causing her any more stress than I have is the last thing I want. I nod.

"Okay. But I need you to stay away from Lillian."

"Well, I would agree, but that's impossible. She demands I see her twice a week. For counseling sessions."

"Why?"

"Heck if I know. To torture me. Mentally fuck with me. She made it clear, I miss one and I'll regret it. She told me no one likes getting their toys taken away. I'd learn soon enough to play nice."

That fucking cunt.

We're all just toys to her.

My phone buzzes, and I reach for it, knowing who it's going to be.

Cunt Griffin: Hope you're enjoying playtime. But time's up. Check your email.

"Who is that?" Evelyn asks, not missing the low rumble in my chest at the message.

"No one." I shove my phone back in my pocket. "Listen, I know I just got here, but I gotta go do something. I'll come back as soon as I'm done, okay?" Fear radiates across her face. "No, Mason, don't leave me. Just

PRIDE

please stay. I'm sorry. I'll tell you what you want to know, but please!"

She's back in my arms, and I hold her tight. "I don't want to leave, but I have to. Believe me when I say I need to leave to be able to see you."

"Is it her? What does she have on you?" she cries.

I look at her, and there's no way I can deny her the truth. "You." The word is simple and true. "She's kept you from me. And now that I have you back, I'm not gonna do anything to jeopardize that. I can't explain more, but know, in the end, we will be free of her, okay?"

"Mason, please. Don't do anything that'll land you back in jail. I can't do this anymore without you anymore, please."

We stay embraced for some time until her dorm room opens and a girl walks in. I kiss the top of her head and we both pull away. "I'll be back as soon as I can. Take my number. Call if you need anything." She nods, and I type my number into her phone. We say no more as I exit her room.

My mind runs rampant with disturbing scenarios. I should just kill Lillian now. Not waste another second. These years haven't been good for my sister. She doesn't have to confess her nightmarish past for me to know her suffering. I can see it in her eyes. And for this, Lillian needs to die.

I pop out of Evelyn's dorm building, knocking shoulders with some frat asshole on my way out. He turns, giving me a threatening stare but backs down the minute he captures the murderous glare in mine. As I hustle to Lillian's office, I check the email she sent me. The subject line says: *The Elite Seven*. Tonight, I'm to meet at an abandoned nunnery, toward the edge of town. As instructed, I'm to unite and bond with six other members. Six lives I will single handedly help destroy. My conscience doesn't exist here. I will, take part in stripping them of their virtue to earn their rightful place in The Elite.

I despise the person she's about to turn me into. But part of me agrees. Pride won't stop me from doing the tasks doted on me. No one is above my sister. No one. I slow my pace, needing a new plan. I can't risk anything happening to Evelyn. What if it's not just her? What if by deleting Lillian, I'm only deleting a piece of the game? And I doubt she's the only player in this. I need to bide my time wisely until I can figure out a better plan.

One that gives us a life out from under The Elite and Lillian Griffin.

I'm the first one to arrive as I pull my junk Impala up the driveaway of the abandoned nunnery. The wind is fierce tonight, and I fight through the gust of leaves and spitting rain to get inside. It's dark, and the smell of musk and death thick in the air cause me to cough. Walking in farther, I flip a few switches. No power. I spot a bunch of candles displayed along the fire mantel in clusters throughout the main room and take my lighter to them, sparking a dim glow to the beat down room. When I get to the ones on the mantle, I see the scroll, just as her email stated.

There will be a scroll. Read from it. Let them know who they are about to become. Watch as they all stare at you in envy. But no need to fear. Your pride will rise above them all. Enjoy

PRIDE

your new brotherhood. And don't be so grouchy. There's a surprise for you all. Not every sin is bad.

LG

Pulling the parchment off the shelf, I hear someone arrive. I stand silent, as two dudes walk in, one of them staring me down, testing me. Little does he know, whatever superiority he thinks he has over me means shit to me. In this game, I'm the alpha.

"So, do we wait here or...?" Out of nowhere, another guy pops out from the shadows. I didn't hear him enter, and when I make eye contact, it unsettles me.

I hold up the scroll. "I found this on the mantel."

"What does it say?" the entitled douchebag asks, flashing the flashlight on his phone to search around the room.

"We have to wait for all seven of us to be here." It's quiet except the flickering of the candles and wheezing of the heavy wind outside. A few unspoken moments pass before all seven finally arrive. Standing in a circle, I begin. "If you stand in this room, you are witness to the seven chosen candidates. The Elite Seven. Pride, Wrath, Lust, Sloth, Gluttony, Greed, Envy."

"Do we get to choose? Because I can see me being prideful." The douchebag turns to his friend and winks.

My fingers clench around the scroll to keep my calm. I take a labored breath and continue. "The Elite is made up of the best our school has to offer, and you have the honor of proving yourself worthy. Your oath to the society will be given in action. You will perform assignments to show your obedience and dedication to The Elite. In return, you will be welcomed into a society rich, not just in wealth, but in status, influence, opportunity. You've been chosen as the crème de le crème of St. Augustine, and you will be joining the ranks of the most powerful and influential members of society." I take a breather and flex my jaw. "Above all things, we pride ourselves on candidates who will prosper long after school ends. The Elite is for life. It will become a part of you. Keeping the societies' secret is of utmost importance. Any indiscretion will be punishable by the full force of the society.

"Your initiation begins with the bonding of seven. The men in this room are your brothers. The brotherhood of the seven is unbendable. You are no longer one person, you are seven." I lift my eyes away from the words to my audience. Their faces are mostly hidden within the darkness, only a small glare from the candles giving their appearance away. Everyone seems attuned to what I'm telling them. No one looks confused or ready to bail. I inhale a deep breath and continue. "To be chosen for The Elite is of the highest honor, and for this reason, Pride is always chosen as the conduit between the initiating members and The Elite."

"Me," the rich asshole whispers, sticking his chin up, looking high and mighty.

I ignore the urge to take him by the lapels of his expensive shirt and put my fist through his face. I just need to get through this and get the fuck out of here. "Pride leads the seven. Prove yourselves worthy of full initiation and you'll be welcomed into the best society the world has to offer. Your given sin reflects your abilities and personality in life, so shall it be in sin."

"Mason Blackwell, Pride." I peer up at the group and pat my chest. "That's me. Samuel Gunner, Wrath. Rhett Masters, Lust. Rush Demsey, Sloth. Micah—"

I pause on the name, and my eyes raise. I find him

PRIDE

in the darkness of the circle. Micah Dixon, my old best friend. What the fuck? *How...?* I shake it off. Get through this and worry about that later. "Micah Dixon, Greed. Sebastian Westbrook, Envy. Baxter Goddard, Gluttony. Good luck, and may your sins be worthy."

There's a rush of excitement from a few of the guys, Gluttony looks pissed, and a few others have a no care grin on their face. Everyone begins to turn to exit when I speak. "Wait, there's a card." I hold it up. Gluttony walks up, snatches it from my grip, and opens it.

"To bond your brotherhood, you will indulge in the sins of the body, in lust." He wiggles his eyebrows at the group. Annoyed at his cockiness, I rip the card out of his hand, and flip it over to see an address. "There's an address. Let's go."

Everyone takes that as their cue to leave, but Micah and I don't move a muscle. I hear the door creak shut before he makes a move.

"Holy fuck, is it really you?" Micah approaches me, pulling me in for a hug. His arms, also covered in ink, wrap around me, a hand slapping at my back. "Dude! I thought..." He pulls back, the familiar laid-back smile he used to carry still on his face. "I didn't know what happened to you. Shit, I even thought your ass was dead."

More unwanted memories surge to the forefront of my mind. The night I drove Micah and I home, only to watch Evelyn be accused of horrible things and ripped away from the only family she had. The only call I was given in jail.

"I could ask you the same thing." I step back, allowing the anger to filter back in at the betrayal.

"What's that shit supposed to mean?" His expression

hardens. "You fucking disappeared, man."

I go at him and he meets me nose to nose. "I did? How about hours after I got beaten and dragged away, I called you and your phone was disconnected."

His eyes shine with confusion, but they quickly register into understanding. "Fuck. My dad," he begins, shaking his head. "I came home right after all that shit went down. I wanted to ask my dad to look into what happened. But he took my phone. Said I had been hacked or some shit and handed me a new one. I didn't even…"

"Your dad already knew."

"But how?"

Fucking Lillian. The Griffins attended the same church as the Dixons, and on many occasions, those families ended up in the papers together at galas and charity events.

"You think my dad had something to do with—?"

"Lillian Griffin is a cunt liar. My sister never did anything wrong. Her accusations were due to her jealousy that her husband would rather abuse young girls than touch her."

Micah's face turns stone cold. "He fucking do something to Evie?"

"Not sure yet. We've just been reunited as of late and she's not doing much talkin'."

His expression once again morphs into confusion. "Wait. You haven't been with her? Where you been, man? Where's she been? She okay?"

I don't want to admit I've been in hell, separated from my sister with no power or ability to help her. If he even knew what sort of life she was succumbed to live because I couldn't help her, he'd hate me. I hate myself. "I've been

PRIDE

in State Pen. Got myself into some shit."

"Damn. Don't mind me askin', how the hell you end up here, runnin' this crazy ass shit?"

Because I sold my life for another's. "Long fuckin' story." A large gust of wind causes the doors of the church to burst open, startling us both and instantly breaking the moment. "Let's get out of here. Everyone's waiting." I say to distract him from further questions.

He hesitates, but nods. "Yeah, but once we get some drinks in us, you're telling me everything. I feel you have more you're not telling me."

He has no idea.

We all follow The Elite's directions and head to the address. Once everyone arrives, we all jump out of our cars and head up the steps of the lavish two-story mansion, pillars surrounding the property, a grand balcony wrapping around the entire upper floor. "Ready to sell your soul for The Elite?" I ask and slam my fist against the large wooden door. As soon as it opens, the ambiance hits us, sin and pleasure, greeting us at the door. A slow tune fills the room, while women, covered in only seductive masks, and thongs crowd the entire first floor.

Together, we enter the house and once everyone makes it past the threshold of the doorway, a woman, her eyes covered by a peacock mask, walks up to us with a tray full of drinks.

"Welcome gentleman. One for each," she says, offering us a drink and we each grab a goblet from the tray.

"Morality doesn't exist past those doors. Tonight, is about embracing your true sin. Tonight's transgression is to create your very own divine law. Enjoy."

This is The Elite's version of bonding?

The woman walks away without another word, and we all clink our glasses together and take down the sugary liquid. I sneer at the taste. What the fuck was in that?

"You heard her, leave your morals at the door, guys." Sebastian, or *Envy* licks his lips and disappears into the sea of flesh. Everyone else follows suit. Gluttony walks passed and knocks his shoulder into mine. I reach forward to grab him by the fucking neck when Lust stops me.

"Not worth it, man. There's a reason he's Gluttony. Excessiveness in always wanting to be on top." I turn to Lust. Fuck if I care why he earned his sin. Brother or not, he won't make it too far if he thinks he's above me. "Rhett, by the way." He sticks his hand out, and I shake it.

"Mason."

"Pretty badass, this whole Elite thing, right? What'd you have to do to get in?"

Give up everything.

"Whatever got in my way," I reply. Seems like a fitting enough answer, being Pride and all. We both stare off into the crowd, catching Envy who's already locked himself in between two women, getting ready to spring his dick free.

"Well, looks like I need to get myself into some trouble. Good luck tonight, bro." He pats me on the back, then he's off, wrapping his arm around a girl holding a tray of white powder. I'm trying to take the whole scene in, but my vision is starting to blur.

"Fuck," I grunt wiping my hand down my face, realizing those drinks were laced with something. The farther

PRIDE

I walk into the house, the louder the sounds of sex and pleasure get. Rooms filled with women on their knees, and men fucking 'em while they sniff coke off their backs, tits, pussies. I locate everyone in a room sitting in a circle of chairs, women, bobbing, sucking.

"Mason, get the fuck over here. Got her twin sister ready for you." I see Micah, who's getting a lap dance from a blonde. The room spins, and I swear the ground underneath me sways. I grab onto a girl walking past me.

"Hello there, handsome. Can I bring you pleasure?" My eyes land on her, then the mound of coke piled on her tray. The echo of Micah's laugh has my attention back on him. He's laughing at me while pushing a chick's head into his lap.

Fuck.

I don't know what comes over me as I dip low, shoving my nose into the mountain of blow.

VII
UINCENDUM NATUS

FOUR

I stumble into a shithole bar located far from campus and even farther from the place I just left my new *brothers*. I'm drunk and coked out of my mind, not to mention whatever was in that drink. Apparently, being part of The Elite allows easy access to any and everything. A mind-numbing release for starters. A text from Lillian ordered me to stay 'til the party ended, but I needed to get the fuck away. All the sex, the drugs. My new brotherhood. It all took a quick toll and sent me racing to be free of all the chaos happening around me.

I should have gone back to Evelyn, but I can't have her see me in the shape I'm in.

I've been clean for years. Minus the few joints Micah and I used to smoke back in high school. Since I've been out, I've kept it that way. I needed to be on alert and have

PRIDE

my mind clear when it came to Lillian and whatever she had in store for me. But tonight, I gave in and flooded my body with booze and drugs to drown out the reality she's brought down on me.

I throw myself on an open stool at the bar and scan the place around me. The joint is packed with people like me. Trash. Thugs. A group of bikers in the corner, who continue to harass a woman, uncaring of her pleas for them to stop.

"What'll it be?" the rugged bartender asks, throwing his bar towel over his shoulder.

"Five shots of tequila," I say, and slam a hundred-dollar bill on the bar. The last of the tainted money Lillian gave me. The scholarship, the housing, the status—it's all a ruse. Phony image of what she wants me to portray. To the blind, they see prestige, power, an alpha. And in my part of the game, I let them. Because my sinful *pride* won't allow them to see the real person behind the mask Lillian forces me to wear.

The Elite Seven.

A secret society run by a fucking psychopath. But was Lillian the real mastermind? Or was she just another pawn in The Elite? And what do my new band of brothers really know? They all seem pumped to be a part of it. Which confirms they don't know shit behind the masquerade. Being the alpha, I can't let them be fooled. They all need to know and I'm going to be the one to uncover the truth.

I swear to that.

But right now, I need to play nice and do what I need to do to guarantee my sister's safety.

Which is ruin fucking lives.

My head begins to spin and my elbows land on the

surface of the bar as I run my fingers through my hair. And what about Micah? Why the fuck is he wrapped up in this shit? I should tell him to get the fuck out now. He has no idea what's in store for him.

Five shots appear in front of me, and I waste no time going down the line, downing each one with urgency, welcoming the burn as the liquid slides down my throat.

"You good, man?" the bartender asks. I nod and tap my finger on the bar, requesting another round. Seeing Micah again brought up too many unwanted memories. The shit past I wanted to forget. *Dahlia*. My fingers tighten around the shot glass at the memory of the video. Nights when I just wanted to give in to the weakness, I would think of that video. Let the rage consume any urge to surrender. I'd work my muscles 'til they burned. Work my mind with revenge until it almost blinded me. And I would plot. One day, when I was out, if that day ever came, I would get my revenge on Lillian, Dahlia, and anyone who ever dared lay a hand on my sister.

"Hulk smash."

A soft feminine voice to my right tickles at my eardrum. The sweet scent of cherries and vanilla surrounds me, and I turn to sneak a quick glimpse of the chick who's taken the seat next to me. My eyes start at her breasts, full and perked in a skin-tight black halter-top dress. They rise to her bare shoulders, thin neck, and plump red lips. When I make it to her eyes, my cock stirs.

Fuck.

"Say again?" My tone's blank, hiding the jolt of electricity in my pants.

"I said Hulk smash. You look like you're about to crush that shot glass with your fist."

PRIDE

I glance down at my white knuckles and the veins bulging from the top of my hand. The coke is flowing heavily though my blood. Quickly, I release the shot glass, pushing it away. My eyes stay locked forward on the wall of shelved liquor. Not sure why I've piqued her curiosity, but I'm not interested. The last thing I need right now in my fucked-up, complicated situation is to throw a chick into the mix. *If I wanted pussy, I'd have indulged back at the party*, I tell myself, but my sudden alive and throbbing cock disagrees. Unlike the abundance of women back at the house, this one seems to stir life into the guy below.

I turn back to the girl, her hazel eyes glowing behind all the smoky eye makeup. Her plump lips part and spread across her heart shaped face, accentuating her cheekbones. Her smile suddenly warms a dormant part of me that's been cold and shut off. My thoughts quickly turn to the guys, how content they all appeared. Happy. Numb to the world around them. Fuck, maybe some random pussy *is* the perfect way to drown some of my troubles.

But that warmth triggers the reminder of why. Dahlia. That deceiving whore who broke my heart. I rip my eyes away from her, bringing them back to the wall. "Not interested," I grumble and reach for the shot of tequila the bartender sets down in front of me.

Before I grab the glass, a tiny set of fingers snatch it. My furrowed brows follow the glass and I watch in mild shock as the girl slams it. Without a wince from the strong alcohol, she tosses back the shot. *Who the fuck?* My flaring nostrils and darkened sneer would cause most grown men to piss themselves, but this girl ain't the least bit intimidated by my size or death stare.

She only giggles and pats her sexy lips with a bar

napkin. "She-Hulk like tequila." Her laughter fills the air, and it fucks with me. I want her to laugh more. Smile more. Fuck. I need another bump. I scout the crowd, searching out a junkie, hoping to score a bag and snort it all, until I'm completely numb.

"Listen, Betty Ross, said I wasn't interested. Now, run along before Hulk smash *you*." I give her the cold shoulder, waving down the bartender for another shot.

"Ahhh, you know your comics. Betty Ross was Hulk's love interest, though. Later, his wife. I said *She*-Hulk. Technically, I'd be your daughter." Again, she laughs.

The five shots swirling in my stomach are kicking in, and the warmth of the tequila is chipping away at the tension in my shoulders. I swivel my bar stool toward her, and my legs weave in and out of hers. There's a sharp intake of breath at the intrusion of my thick thighs trapping hers in place. She sure as fuck has me intrigued. "You want me to be your daddy?" I ask, my grin growing. "You into that kinky shit, *Lyra*?" I say, using her marvel origin name.

Her facial expression becomes serious as she leans forward, threatening to spill her pretty little tits out of her tight top. Scooting to the end of her chair, she doesn't stop until her mini skirt is hiked so far up her creamy thighs, her barely covered pussy rubs against my knee. "I'm into a lot of things. Just depends on how playful I'm feeling and how adventurous my fellow player is."

She makes another bold move by reaching forward and grabbing my thigh. Her hand may be small, but there's no hiding the power in it. Her thumb tickles the inside of my thigh and she calmly slides her hand up, nearly grazing my cock. The amused countenance shining across her face is no doubt caused by the acknowledgment that

PRIDE

I'm fucking hard.

"I think *someone* wants to play." She giggles, making it harder for me to tame the beast in my pants. "Did you know Lyra's ability, amongst many others, is stamina and durability?" She leans in farther, practically sitting on my lap, and cups my fucking cock to whisper in my ear. "I might be small, but big things come in small packages. My tight cunt would be heaven for this large dick." She squeezes me, and my eyes threaten to shut from the pleasure of her hand. "And trust me, when I take you in my mouth and my cunt, it will be hours until we're done playing."

Jesus.

Who the fuck is this chick?

My raging hard dick doesn't care. It's been years since it's seen any sort of pussy or action other than my fist. The last one being Dahlia. Buried rage resurfaces, and I grab her wrist, squeezing a bit harder than I should. Still, she doesn't seem fazed by my actions. Only more turned on.

"Feisty. Exactly what I need. So, what's it gonna be, handsome?" She licks her lips, and my dick twitches in my jeans. I've never been with someone like her. Her crude mouth. Her lips that would wrap perfectly around my cock as she deep throats me until I explode down her throat. "I see the want in your eyes. Don't deny yourself. It's just a night of harmless fun, filled with excessive sin."

Sin.

Sin.

Sin.

The last of her words are cut short. I squeeze her wrist and tug her out of her chair into my lap. The mention of sin boils my blood. She has no idea the true meaning of it. She wants to take me for a ride and act unfazed by the dangers sin can bring. I dip my mouth low, skimming along her neck. Her scent of cherries overpowers my sanity, and I take a nip at her earlobe. "You're playing with fire," I growl low, and I'm rewarded by the vibration of her trembling body.

She leans back, and our eyes connect. "I'm already burning inside, so we better get out of here."

I slam the door shut of the scummy motel and toss her onto the bed. She laughs, and my dick thickens. If I wasn't so determined to fuck her 'til my dick falls off, I'd beg to just lay here with her and make her laugh until I found peace and sleep took me. Instead, I prowl over to her. She's kicking off her black heeled boots, and in the process, I get a nice view right up her tight mini dress. No fucking underwear.

I didn't realize how starved I was for the touch, taste, and fuck of a real woman until now. I can't wait a second longer to put my tongue to her clit and suck the first of many orgasms out of her. I grab her bare legs and tug her to the bottom of the bed. Her cute little squeal has my smile growing in anticipation of the rest of the sexy little sounds she'll make when I get down to business. I thrust her dress up her thighs, threatening to lose myself just from the feel of her smooth skin. I tell myself to slow down. As hungry as I am, I don't want to fucking blow one before I even get started.

PRIDE

My knees hit the floor, and I position my head between her thighs. She sighs in approval and I spread her legs wider. A flicker of my tongue has her withering under my touch, my own body buzzing at the sweet taste of her. It's been too long. I need more. But I know I need to slow down. Gain control. I extend my tongue back against her lips, and with a slow rhythm, I lick her pussy, steadily sucking her lips into my mouth and tasting absolute heaven.

"Hey, Casanova, no need to play nice down there."

Damn this chick. So much for trying to make this last. I bite her clit and shove my tongue into her opening, sounds of sexual pleasure fill the air. In and out, I tongue-fuck her, feeling drunk. From the tequila or the taste and feel of her, I'm not sure. My cock is rock hard, and my balls are tight as fuck wanting to release years' worth of pent up sexual aggression.

"Oh God, yes. Your tongue is amazing," she moans, riding faster against my face. "But is that all you got? I was hoping for a guy with no manners—*shit!*"

She has no idea who she's messing with. Challenging me. Tempting me. I wasn't curious or adventurous with Dahlia. We were young and still learning one another. But right now, my mind lets loose all the fantasies I've held on to while locked up. The darkness. The dirty thoughts. I pick up the pace with my tongue and shove two fingers inside her. She giggles at my move, which pisses me off. I pull out and thrust into her hard, until my knuckles breach her opening. Her whimpers of pleasure satisfy me, but I need more. I need to take more. I pull one finger out, lubricated by her fluids, and reach behind to her back hole. Smearing juices between her ass cheeks to get her ready, I wait for her to squirm, and deny me, but she shows no sign of refusal. This dirty girl wants me to ravage her there. Pre-cum drips from my cock at the thought of my finger, even my cock, being inside her, fucking her tightness.

She begins to wiggle, encouraging me to get on with it, and I insert my finger into her ass.

"Fuck," she bites down on her lip, and I grunt low with my own arousal. I continue with my tongue as my fingers work her front and back hole. It doesn't take much more until she begins thrashing under my hold and comes all over my tongue.

I don't stop though. It may take an army to pull my tongue away from her swollen cunt. I could lap at the taste of her for a lifetime. Licking her orgasm clean, I want to get her worked up all over again. Lather my tongue with her juices over and over. But the little spitfire doesn't allow it. Sitting up, she untangles her body from under me and jumps off the bed. Her hands are at my belt buckle and my jeans are down and her mouth is around my dick before I know it.

"You're bigger than I thought. My lucky day," she hums, licking at the tip of my dick. Opening wide, she brings it so far back, I swear I hit the back of her throat. *Don't fucking blow,* I coach myself. This is heaven and hell at the same time. And I was right. Her lips do look perfect wrapped around my cock. She sucks me off like a champ, her lips wet and inviting. I grab the back of her head and work her head back and forth, loving the view of her beautiful face as it bobs back and forth. Fuck, this is insane. The coke high is gone, but this new high she has me on is way fucking better. Dark thoughts filter inside

PRIDE

my mind of where I want to take this. She may be little, but that won't stop me. I plan on fucking her all night, hard and ruthless.

Saliva starts dripping from her chin as she cups my balls. I know I've finally lost and pull at her hair, letting her know I'm about to come. She fights my warning and bobs faster, taking me even deeper. "Oh fuck. I'm gonna come." I give her one last warning, but she only hums and works me harder. It's when she starts to hum that I explode, filling her mouth.

She doesn't stop until she's worked me clean. She makes a popping sound as she releases me and stands. "Well...that was fun." She takes her thumb and wipes at her bottom lip. I slowly pull my pants back up and start to tuck myself back in my jeans when she turns and grabs for her purse.

What the...? "That's all you got?" I say, disappointed. Clearly just a tongue fuck was all she wanted. She bends down and digs into her bag, pulling out a bunch of—

"Shit, those sex toys?" I ask, shocked.

"Oh, these things?" She dangles a set of handcuffs and some sort of clamps in her hand. "These are what I like to call ice breakers."

Jesus, I'm not sure if I should run or just fell in love.

She makes her way back to me, her movement slow and seductive. Her fingers still holding the cuffs and with each step, they clink together, heightening my senses. Fuck, the images floating in my head right now are anything but innocent. "Exactly what do you plan on doing with those?" I ask, wanting her to feed my fucked-up fantasy.

"That's up to you. I'm a giving girl. The darkness in

your eyes, I imagine you have some ideas."

Not good ones. I want to take those cuffs and subdue her. Make her beg. Take my heavy palm to her ass. Fuck her until she screams my name over and over.

"I'm yours to play with. What do you want?"

I step forward, snatching her wrist. My fingers dig into her flesh and she almost drops the cuffs. "I think you're a reckless little girl who shouldn't taunt strangers." I yank her into me, our chests colliding, enjoying the way her perfect tits press against me. I shouldn't go along with this, but she wants me to treat her this way. Be her punisher. The way her eyes flare with intense desire tells me, this is exactly how she wants to be treated.

I whip her around and grab her hips, thrusting my stone hard cock in between her ass cheeks. Her moan proves just what a naughty girl she is.

"Are you gonna tie me up and spank me?" she taunts me with her sweet ass, rubbing her plump cheeks into me. I don't reply but take my hand and crack it against her right cheek. She jolts forward, and her hoarse whimper satisfies me. The pleasure that shoots down my spine into my balls is nothing I've ever experienced. Never have I laid a hand on someone, nor has it felt so fucking euphoric. I grind into her again with another hard smack to her ass. This time her whimper is coated with hums of pleasure. She loves this. And so do I.

"Climb on the fucking bed," I order, and she does as she's told. Her mini skirt rides up her milky thighs and I get the perfect view of her glistening cunt. She knows she's giving me a view when she makes it to the top of the bed and bends her head down lifting her ass in the air. I'm fighting not to pull my cock out and stroke myself until I

PRIDE

come all over her ass.

My head is spinning.

This girl has me all out of sorts. She twists her head to speak to me. "I don't need a savior. I need a punisher—tie me up and fuck me hard."

Jesus, my balls just shot into my stomach. My eyes blur. I'm not even sure I can do this. When I don't immediately jump to her offer, she drops the cuffs on the bed. Her hand slides down her belly, and she begins playing with herself. Her fingers rub in a circular motion over her wet lips, and I can't help but grab my cock as I watch one finger slide in. "I want this to be your finger inside me. Fucking me. Your tongue, then hopefully your cock. My nipples ache for those clamps to bite into my skin as you fuck me, hurt me, destroy—"

A growl, unnatural to me, erupts up my chest. I crawl up the bed, grab her hips, and rip her finger from inside her, pulling her arm behind her back. She whimpers in pain, but I'm in a daze. I bend forward, and my mouth wraps around her soaked finger, sucking every last drop of her arousal.

"This what you want? A stranger to fuck you? Hurt you? Can't stop picturing my cock in your mouth again. Your ass. That what you want, *Lyra*?" I almost blow calling her that name.

"Yes," she pants, and I'm done holding back. I reach forward and grab the cuffs and tie her to the bed post. She wants it rough, so I'll give it to her. I work my way back down her body, tearing away at her dress. The thin material rips easily, exposing her smooth pale skin and perfect tits. Just picturing her small nipples in between those clamps has me licking my lips, the taste of her still coating them. In a different life, I'd lie here and savoir her, but it's not tonight. Nor ever. Tonight is about letting go of some deep aggression. Tonight, I plan on crossing a line, and I'm damn sure I'll enjoy it.

"Say another word and I'll gag you with my cock to shut you up," I order, and her head turns. There's no doubt she wants to disobey. Naughty girl. I'm going to destroy her.

I jump off the bed and undress. My heavy cock springs from my jeans, ready and aching, and I grab a condom from the pile lying next to the clamps. I can't help but stroke myself a few times after sliding it down my cock. Snagging the clamps, I work my way back onto the mattress and flip her. Her arms twist, but not enough to cause pain. Her eyes are fogged over as she stares at me in anticipation.

"You have beautiful tits," I compliment as I open the clamp and close it around her left bud. Her chest rises and falls in small pants as I clamp the right one. "Gonna have to fuck you between these sexy things later."

"Hope you do."

Fuck, she's like a dream come true. I grab a handful of her breast and squeeze until the blood flow turns her nipple a dark shade of maroon. "I told you not to talk. I'll not only fuck you in your mouth to shut you up, I'll gag you with my cum."

A normal girl would shudder at the thought. The indecency of the degrading act. Not this girl. Her eyes set on fire. I'd be giving her something she wants. I shake my head in disbelief at the luck that fell into my lap with this girl, a small smile breaching, then flip her back around.

I can't wait any longer to get inside her. My hands

PRIDE

ache to crush her hips between my fingers. Grabbing each side, and without warning, I buck into her, thrusting her a few inches up the bed. "Fuck. You're so tight this way. Are you as naughty as you say you are? Or innocent and want to be bad?" I taunt, pulling out and slamming back inside. I'm rough—ruthless each time I pull her wet cunt off me and crash back inside her. She feels like heaven. Tight around me, warm and slick. The sounds spewing from her lips are music to my ears, a plethora of pleasure I'm igniting inside her. One after another, I pound into her, bending forward so my hand can reach out and squeeze the clamp tighter. She buckles under me, and I ride her faster. Her insides start to crush around me, and since she wants me to be the bad guy, I pull out before she reaches her orgasm.

"Oh god, why are you—"

I smack her ass so hard, she skids up the bed. "No fucking talking," I growl, then take her hips and pull them up so her ass is high in the air. I turn over onto my back and crawl under her, until my mouth is over her nipples. "Can't stop thinking about these." I pluck one clamp off. She cries in pleasure, and I cover her bruised nipple with my mouth, swirling my tongue around her swollen bud.

"More. Fucking more," she pants, and I rip the other one off and suck her into my mouth. I told her ass not to talk, but I don't have it in me to fucking care. My dick is pulsating, needing back inside her. Her legs are giving way as her hips begin to slide down, her slippery cunt rubbing against my stomach. When she starts rubbing herself on me, I lose it.

Grabbing her little body, I place her above my cock, then slam her down on me, over and over, until my eyes begin to squeeze closed. She's purring like a little feline, the sweet sounds of ecstasy fucking me up. My balls tighten, and I work her pussy harder, faster, until a scream, high and orgasmic, breaks through and she death squeezes around me.

I try to catch my breath, but with the booze, coke, and the fucking ride she just gave me, I feel like I'm gonna have a heart attack as her small frame collapses on top of me.

I'm not sure what to say. Or do. Thank her for giving me the best sex of my god damn life? Get up and leave? The problem is, I'm far from done. My appetite for her just got a sample, and now, I'm starved. I flip her, bringing her back to the mattress, trying not to snap her still contained wrists.

She's wearing a carefree smile.

"What's that look for?" I instantly waver on my feet with uncertainty. Was I not good enough? Does she want more?

"Oh, nothing. Pleased you passed round one. I have a full bag of goodies over there. If you're up for it, I say we move on to round two."

It's settled.

I've fallen in love.

VII
UINCENDUM NATUS

FIVE

One week later...

The rain refuses to let up as I make my way back to the biker bar for the second time this week. Lillian just gave me Rhett's, or *Lust's*, task. I showed up at my place after a long day of shit classes and Lillian was in the apartment waiting for me. She handed me the card, wearing her signature smile as she forced me to read it. I didn't want to know what The Elite was asking of him, but Lillian demanded I did anyway. Disgust filled me as I saw her own stepdaughter's name on the card. She wanted me to know what tasks people were willing to do for power. Her words are still ringing in my ears.

"People strive to be invisible, Mason. They want to know they are better than the person next to them. And they may not admit, but everyone is willing to sell a piece of themselves to thrive above."

I told her she was wrong. I'd rather be poor and have nothing than deceive and betray to get ahead. But then she reminded me I was exactly that person. I would hand out each task regardless of whose life would be destroyed in the end. My *pride* would make sure of it. And in some sick way, she was right. These guys—some of them anyway—seemed like they would do anything to join The Elite. Little do they know the destruction it will cause.

I'm about to jump out of my car when my phone dings. Whoever it is can wait as I reach for the door handle. Right now, I need to drink until I forget. The rain suddenly picks up, slashing against my window, and I pause taking the extra moment to catch a glimpse at the screen in case it's Evelyn. She was beside herself with worry when I met up with her the day after our first Elite meeting. I told her I would come back that night and never did. I got too fucked up and literally fucked instead. The pain in my stomach returns. I just got my sister back, and I'm already letting her down. I swore to her it was never going to happen again. Instead of Evie's name, it's a text from Lillian.

Cunt Griffin: Not so fast. You were given a chore my little pet. Be a good boy and do as you're told.

My fists slam into the steering wheel. How the fuck does she know…

My phone dings again.

Cunt Griffin: 14 Manchester Ave. Apartment 45. Get to work.

Fuck.

PRIDE

I'm walking across campus to my first class. The early morning sun is like a fire beam shooting into my eye sockets and I'm tired as fuck. The address Lillian gave me last night ended up being *Gluttony's,* or God, the name he goes by. All the brothers were there, including Rhett. She sent me there for a reason, but I couldn't go through with it yet. Instead, I got fucked up and drank until my mind spun with so much booze, the only thing I cared about was partying with my newly found brothers. The night was a blur, but I had to admit one thing. I was starting to like these guys. Really give a fuck what happens to them. Reconnecting with Micah has been unreal, but he's clearly been through some shit since our time apart. Same went for Sloth, Wrath, and Envy, who all, no doubt were fighting their own demons.

Then, there's Rhett. He came off as a real genuine guy. Not someone who would do what he's going to be tasked to do. The more I got to know him, the deeper I shoved the card into my back pocket. He seemed intense about joining The Elite, but would he risk hurting someone for it? Maybe it was the booze, but last night I pinged him as someone who wouldn't. And when I find the courage to hand his task over, it won't surprise me when he cashes in his coin. A get-out-of-jail coin for each member if they decide they can't stomach their task, or a favor only The Elite can make go away. If they cash it in, they don't get to back out of their second task. They don't follow through, then they're expelled as candidates.

I'm just about to pass the student center when my phone goes off in my pocket. I dig for it and Lillian's name lights up my screen. I'm about to let it go to voicemail, but her evil warning rings in my ear about the consequences if I don't answer when she comes beckoning.

"Yes, queen bitch?" She may have me by the balls, but I refuse to bow down to her.

"Oh, kinky. I like it. Maybe you can call me that at our next meeting. You know I can please you and you'd love it. Or is your *pride* still getting in the way?" She laughs, and chills of hate and disgust run through my veins.

"What do you want, Lillian? I'm busy doing your bidding." I really should meet Rhett and get it over with.

"Yes, yes. And you're about to do more. Time for you to get your own task," she says, no hiding the venom suddenly in her tone. "My office. Now." Then, she hangs up.

I hate her with all my being. I wasn't sure I would have a task. Just assumed all the dirty work she has me doing was my penance. I shove my phone back into my pocket and change directions. My mood darkens along with the weather as the clouds roll in taking the bright sun with it leaving the sky fierce and ominous.

I barge into Lillian's office without knocking. She looks startled when the door whips open, her eyes wild. Rage is it? Shock? Definitely different from the normal sadistic smile she carries. Sometimes I wonder what sin she would be. If I had to guess, I'd say her demise is envy—the one thing I think she drowns in.

"You're late," she snaps, throwing a folder onto her desk.

"Have you seen it outside? It's a monsoon."

"I don't give a shit. Sit down," she orders and walks to the other side of her desk. Sitting, she unlocks the bottom

PRIDE

drawer, pulling out a manila folder—same folder she's pulled out with every other task that's been given.

"You're a little bit bitchier today than normal. Not getting any from the husband?" I say, sitting and crossing my arms over my chest.

"It seems *you* have, though." She tosses the folder at me. It opens as photographs litter her desk, some falling at my feet. I already recognize what they're of before picking them up.

"You fucking following me?" I growl, holding up a photo from last week at the bar. With her. She-Hulk. I woke up in the shithole motel the next day alone. After hours of the best sex of my life, I must have passed out. And in the morning, she was gone. No note or thank you for using me. And that she did, dirty little girl. Her toys…I'd never been so hard. We fucked and played, toys and games. It was nothing I've ever experienced. The best way to describe her was simple. Fucking amazing. She was also in the wind. Which was for the best. I didn't need the added headache. Despite the tightening in my pants any time that night came to mind.

"You think I don't keep my pets on a tight leash? You were supposed to stay at the party. Instead, you leave and go fuck your brains out," she spits out. "You don't get to play around, *pet*." She stands and rounds her desk, coming into my personal space. Using her hands, she spreads my legs and makes her way between my open thighs. "If kink is what you like, I'm more than willing to show you a thing or two. Or was that little whore a good enough teacher?"

My hands clutch the armchair, fighting not to take a closed fist to her face. The random girl may be nobody to me, but having Lillian call her degrading names immediately gets under my skin. Staring down at the photos of her, I'm reminded of how damn beautiful she was. "What is this shit anyway? So, I got my dick sucked. What's it to you?"

"Oh, don't play coy with me. I'm sure you got more than what you bargained for." She doesn't care about the malevolent look I give her or how my skin vibrates with disgust when she positions her body in my lap. "We can make this so easy." She brings her hand between our laps and grabs at me. Unlike the reaction I had with the girl from the bar, my cock doesn't even stir. "Well, that's disappointing," she pouts, dragging her hand away. "I guess you require a ball gag and whip." She leans in and grabs my face, her nails digging into my cheeks. She presses her lips quickly to mine, then pushes off me and stands to make her way back to her seat. "Everyone has a lesson to learn. Even you, Mason. And it seems this one will be perfect for you. It takes a lot of pride to put yourself before others." She picks up a gold card, just like the other tasks. "And I'm gonna have fun teaching you your lesson."

"Aren't you already doing that?" I growl. "Just get to the fucking point, Lillian. I have class."

Her evil laugh chills my blood. "Oh, come on. Are you actually pretending to be a college student?" Her laughter gets louder. "Did you forget you didn't graduate high school? A GED from a prison facility doesn't constitute entrance into a low-grade community college, let alone one of the best colleges in New Orleans. You're only here because I put you here. Don't waste your energy trying to play smart. As I told you, I'll adjust your grades. You just do what you're here to do."

I'm barely hanging on by a thread, fighting from throwing myself out of my chair and cutting off her airways until she's blue and dead. "You're a fucking wretched bitch."

PRIDE

"Thanks for the compliment." She gets up, adjusting her skirt. "Well, this has been fun, but I have other students to see. I assume you can see yourself out." She tosses me the golden card, and I barely catch it before a knock on the door sounds and another student pops her head in. I get up without another glance her way. When I reach the quad, I stand behind the communications building, rip open the seal, and read my task:

PRIDE
Your task is sin of perverse
Megan Benedict
St. Augustine's fresh new Theology professor
Lack of vanity is far from humility
For the sinner who is beneath no one. Expose and ruin at no cost. Teach her secrets are no fun... Secrets will ruin someone.

I finish reading the card, fighting the bile rising in my throat. I need to expose this woman's secret? What *her* secret is, I don't know. Is it that bad I have to destroy her for it? I pull a lighter from my pocket and enflame the corner but stop myself. The rule is cards must be destroyed once the task is read. But there's a nudging feeling I may need this for collateral. I snub out the flame and stuff it in my backpack when my phone dings. Reaching in my back pocket, I see a text from Lillian.

Cunt Griffin: Schedule Change. You're now enrolled in Theology 101. English building. Room 201. Class begins in seven minutes. Better hurry.

VII
UINCENDUM NATUS

SIX

By the time I make it to the English building, I'm soaked to the bone. My backpack hangs heavy on my shoulders, and my shirt is matted to my chest. Unfamiliar with the building, I head down the south hallway and up the stairs. Luckily, I pop out right at the room number, but when I locate the clock on the wall, I'm almost fifteen minutes late. Great. I waste no more time and thrust the door open.

Megan Benedict.

First year college Theology professor.

And now I've been placed in her class to get close to her. I push the guilt of knowing my intentions to the back of my mind. I'm doing this for Evelyn. I'll expose whatever secret she's hiding and be done. I won't have any thought about the consequences or how this will affect

PRIDE

her. Because this isn't about her—a nobody to me. It's only about Evelyn and myself. Her sick but true words burn down my walls of morality, and nothing, especially not my pride, will stop me.

The door to the classroom flies open and slams against the wall as I walk in. The entire lecture hall of eyes whip to the entrance to acknowledge my presence. Professor Benedict, still busy scribbling on the chalkboard, doesn't even bother to turn and address me when she speaks.

"Plato once said, the direction in which education starts a man, will determine his future in life. Translation, lateness is not a good start to success," she says, finishing up some chart on the board.

"Yeah, sorry. Last minute schedule change," I mumble, searching for a seat. Fuck, there's nothing open but one in the front row. I hurry to it, needing the class to stop fucking ogling me. It makes me uncomfortable. All these rich assholes. Some want to be here. Some, like God, are here because Daddy's money put them here. Some, like me, have no business in a place like this.

I drop my bag and sit, tugging at my soaked shirt sticking to my skin. My eyes settle on the back of my professor who's still rapidly scribbling some shit on the board. It's hard not to notice her cute little ass in her tight grey skirt. Makes sense why her class is full. I'd show up every day just for the view. Her legs are on full display, with nude heels to boost her height.

Finishing, she drops the chalk and dusts off her hands. A soft sigh fills the room as she observes her handy work, and my excitement hitches to see the face that comes with such a bangin' body. She turns to address the class—

"You're fuckin' kiddin' me," I growl loudly in disbelief.

My outburst grabs her attention. Her eyes, the most tantalizing color of hazel, go wide as saucers as the recognition almost throws her off her balance. *"Oh hell."* Her high-pitched squeal echoes throughout the huge lecture room as she runs into the corner of her desk. The class erupts into laughter, but I'm far from smiling. Missing are the red lips and black fuck-me outfit, and in their place is a tight grey pencil skirt and white blouse.

Megan.

Her name is Megan. The fierce little spitfire I spent an entire night with, getting to know every nuance of her body, every touch, curve, and dip. Megan Benedict, my professor, who I have to destroy and teach a lesson. This has to be some kind of joke.

What the fuck is Lillian up to?

"Um…um…sorry…" She shakes her head, trying to pull herself together. "So, class…" she begins, struggling to find her bearings. I slowly relax, enjoying just how cute she is fumbling over her words. "Um, sorry…I…uh…" She turns back to the chalkboard, giving the class her back, her shoulders rising and falling as she inhales deep breaths. "Where were we?"

Yeah, she's fucking cute.

The next forty-five minutes are a blur. I can't stop comparing how different she is. Like night and day. Nowhere is the sex kitten with ambiguous eyes and dark tastes, but a sweet college professor with her hair in a perfect ponytail, not a rip in her nylons, and her face clean and almost bare, except for the minimal Chapstick she applies several times probably due to her unease. Damn if just the simple act of her touching her lips doesn't make me harder than hell. She barely gets through her lecture, apologizing a handful

PRIDE

more times as she stutters over her words. Not once does she make eye contact with me again, and I'll admit, I'm disappointed. Knowing how those almond shaped eyes lured me in makes me crave her attention.

It doesn't help that my mind keeps taking me back to the night in the motel. How bendable her small, taut body was. How hungry her cunt was when I fucked her from behind, twice. The scratch marks she left on my back begin to sting all over again at the memory of us both coming so hard, I swore we passed out.

How the hell did she get on The Elite's radar? Is her taste for kink her dirty secret? I sure as hell wasn't complaining.

When the hour hits, ending class, I'm hard as fuck and doubt I can get up without anyone noticing the huge tent in my jeans. Students gather their books and are up, fighting to get out of the classroom. I, on the other hand, don't move a muscle. I wait and watch. Sensing the worry and discomfort in the air. She has yet to look at me, and I know she's all but praying to whatever holy god she worships I get up, leave, and never return.

But I can't do that.

When the last person exits, I make my move. I prowl over to the chalkboard where she's trying to busy herself by wiping the same spot over and over. "Don't they have cleaning staff to do that?" I chuckle as she jumps at the sound of my voice.

She whips around to face me. Since I left her with no room, her warm body brushes against mine. Her cheeks blaze a crimson at our connection, and I have to fight my dick from ripping through my jeans to get to her.

"Um…Mister…Blackwell, is it? Um…how can I—?"

"It's Mason."

"Um, sure. Mason. Please try to be on time for next class..." she trails off, coming to the quick conclusion that playing coy is not worth the effort. A long sigh leaves her lips as her arms fly up in defeat. "*Oh god*. Fuck it. I'm fucked. I didn't...you...I'm going to lose my job! I didn't know...you're a *student*?" she cries. "I was so far off university grounds, no one from this campus would have even been caught dead in a place like that. And oh my god, you're a *freshman*? Please tell me it's because you waited four or ten years to go to school and you're not—"

"Eighteen?" I say.

She covers her face with her hands and groans. "Oh my god."

I want to tell her the truth about my age to ease her stress, but I can't help but laugh. "Don't worry. I'll keep it to myself that you're a cradle robber."

Her hands slide down her face, her eyes wide. "I am *not* a cradle robber! How was I supposed to know you were so young? You were in a bar! And you look...look..."

"Old enough and strong enough to be the Hulk?" Her face explodes with mortified embarrassment. I wonder if she's mentally picturing herself cuffed to the bed while I sucked and devoured her pussy. I can't help it. I bust out laughing.

"Oh my god! What you must think of me! That's not... *I'm* not... *Please*. Please don't report me. I need this job. I've worked really hard to get it. I...I...I was far from campus and didn't think college students even ventured that far. Please..."

I ignore the stabbing feeling in my gut at knowing I plan on doing just that. My task is to expose her, not keep

PRIDE

her secret. "Relax. I ain't gonna say shit," I lie. Her eyes shoot from my chest, where she had yet to blink away from, to connect with mine. This is the first time she's made eye contact with me today, and the moment it happens, my cock starts to stir again. Shit, she's attractive. She's still tiny compared to my large frame, but those sexy nude heels give her just enough height.

"Mason…"

"I told you. Relax. I thought you were way younger yourself. Not into seducing my professors."

"*Younger*?" she gapes. "I'm twenty-three. That's way too old for you." Not when I'm really twenty. But I can't admit that.

I can't help it. I take a step closer, causing her to retract a step, her back hitting the chalkboard. "Didn't think age was a factor last weekend," I taunt, and her cheeks flare red. It reminds me of how flushed and sweaty we both were. My low laughter has her melting farther into the wall. "I'm kidding. Listen, I'm a late start in your class. Maybe in exchange for my *silence*, you help me catch up on what I've missed? I really need this grade."

She studies me, debating whether I'm telling the truth on my vow of silence or fucking with her. I definitely want to be fucking her, but I need to bide myself some time. I ain't doing shit until I get some answers.

A few more seconds pass before her shoulders become less tense, and she replies. "I guess I can do that. But! Last week never happened, okay? It was a mistake. I mean, it wasn't…I had a nice time, but this is my job. We have to stay professional. Okay?"

Professional my ass. Her naked under me sounds more like it. The sexy little tremors of her body when she whimpers at my touch. The taste of her on my tongue. *Not why you're here, asshole.* Reminding myself of that is the bucket of ice water I need thrown in my face to remember this isn't for enjoyment. It's not about having fun with my professor no matter how alive she made me feel. It's about getting my job done and moving on. Completing my task, The Elite, and taking my sister and leaving this fucking town.

"Okay. Sure. I can do that. Sounds like a fair trade. If you stick to it." She raises her brow, hope mixing with worry in her eyes as she stands on pins and needles for my reply.

"Scouts honor," I say, and raise two fingers.

We're both quiet for a moment, until she sighs, the beautiful sound seeping into my skin. "Well, I have some time now. Maybe we can just go over what you missed and start from there."

Bingo.

I'm in.

Those glossed-over eyes confirm, despite our situation, she still wants me. Feeling pleased, I step back, allowing her some breathing room, and toss my backpack to the ground. "Yeah, sure," I reply and take a seat. She scrambles for a sheet of paper in her tote bag and comes to sit next to me.

"Okay, so...um, first, here's the syllabus for class. You'll want to look this over and maybe spend some time catching up on the chapters you've missed."

I'm trying to stay focused on what she's saying, but with the light aroma of cherries and vanilla seeping into my nostrils, it's impossible. I lift my eyes from the sheet and watch as her lips move, aching to trace my finger along her bottom one.

"How familiar are you with theology and religion?"

"Huh?"

"Theology. The class?" She examines me, waiting for an answer.

"Uh, none," I reply honestly. A prison GED doesn't see a need for learning about that shit. Her smile is kind. If she's disappointed in my lacking education thus far, she doesn't show it.

"Oh! Okay. That's not a problem. We can start from the beginning. See if anything rings a bell." She starts highlighting a bunch of shit on the syllabus. "So, the first three weeks we went over the definitions, study of religious scriptures, and how it all aligned with ancient philosophies and worship."

I have no idea what the fuck she's talking about. Shit I couldn't care less about. My eyes follow each line she swipes, but I'm fighting to hide the scowl forming on my face as my thoughts are elsewhere. What is Lillian's angle with Megan? What secret does Megan possibly have that deserves such punishment?

The card.

Sinful enjoyment.

Lillian wants me to punish her for her dark tastes in bed? My fists clench under the desk. I fear I might just turn into the Hulk himself.

"Still with me?"

"What?"

"Sorry, I'm going too fast. Just when I talk, I can sometimes lose myself in…" She scans my face. "God, this is too awkward, isn't it?"

"No, it's fine. Keep going." *Keep talking so the sound of*

your musical voice drowns out all the bad shit in my head.

"Um, maybe I can give you some homework. You can work on it between classes. Some reading maybe?" I study her, searching for the deceit. Ugliness to warrant why I'm really here. But I see nothing behind her sweet beautiful smile. "So, this isn't gonna work, is it?"

It is. It has to. I shake off the doubt and moral battle in my head. "It is. Just last time we were this close, we were doing some pretty heavy shit, not talking lesson plans. Speaking of, wanna explain why you disappeared?"

Crimson creeps into her cheeks. "I thought…I was saving us both the awkward small talk in the morning," she answers, fiddling with her fingers.

"Maybe we could have chatted theology, then I wouldn't be so far behind."

Her mouth parts, and I admire her plump lips.

"Mason, I…I…that night was a—"

"Don't say it. We both know it wasn't a mistake. Let's not degrade what we had. But I get it. You and I, not happenin'. Student and professor. That's all. Cool?"

The last part's a lie. The buzzing around us, the pull that tells me we're far from over. She nods, feeding into my bullshit, or at least shutting down the topic, and I allow her to finish going over the rest of the syllabus. I sit back and listen, her face lit with excitement as she talks. Time seems to get away from us both, and the janitor peeking his head in alerts us to how much we lost track of time.

"Wow, how embarrassing. Why'd you just let me babble for the last hour?"

"You obviously love what you teach."

She shrugs off my compliment. We both stand, and

PRIDE

she gathers her notes and hands them to me. "Or love to bore people to death. Most students use my hour to sleep or catch up on Netflix shows." She grabs her tote bag and slides into her jacket.

"Those people are fucking assholes," I reply, wanting to snap the necks of anyone who disrespects her.

"Ah, well...that's college for ya," she replies. I grab my bag, and together, we walk out of the classroom. Heading outside, I notice the sun's already long gone.

"So, theology, huh?"

"Nerd alert, right?" She laughs at herself but continues. "I practically grew up playing in my dad's office. He had a huge library with tons of books. While most of the kids my age were at parties, building up their reputations and cool factor, I was at home nose deep into history books. Spent two years abroad for college studying religion, Greek theologies, you know, Plato. I almost stayed and taught in Europe, but my mom cried and threw the world's biggest guilt trip, so I came home. Worked super hard and got myself a teaching job here on my own. Despite my family's connections to the university."

"So, you're from New Orleans?"

She smiles and nods. "Yep. Born and raised. My family's here. Everyone, actually. Doesn't seem many of us have gone too far outside of New Orleans. What's your story? Must be pretty smart yourself to land at such a great school." Stiffness ripples up my back, my posture stone still. I falter in my step, catching her attention. "Sorry, I didn't mean to pry. It's really none of my—"

"Scholarship," I say, my tone blank.

"Oh, well that's great. The university is really philanthropic that way."

Satanic, more like it. "Yeah, you can say that." We continue to walk down the building steps. "So, is St. Augustine a family legacy? You have brothers or sisters who also work here? You said family connections."

"Oh no! But family yes! Dean Griffin, he's my uncle actually!" She smiles as I falter in my step. I catch myself before hitting the bottom step. "You okay there?" she asks, unaware of what that information truly means to me.

"Yeah. George Griffin is your uncle?" I ask the words sour on my tongue.

"Yeah! Have you had the pleasure of meeting him yet? Such an intelligent man. And my aunt, Lillian. My dad's sister. She runs the Counseling department. She's so sweet and helpful. If you ever need anything, I could always introduce you. She'd be more than willing to help you out."

I'm dizzy.

Sick.

Enraged.

Her fucking niece?

"Are you sure you're okay? You kinda don't look all right."

I'm far from all right. "Yeah...um, I gotta go. Thanks for the help. I'll see you in class." I turn the opposite direction and storm off without another word.

VII
UINCENDUM NATUS

SEVEN

It's dark on campus, the only lighting coming from the dimly lit street lights. The wind is stronger than normal, casting a spell of leaves to blow across the empty parking lot. Empty but one car. I lurk behind the huge cypress tree, biding my time until I attack. It's later than normal for her to still be at work, but it's perfect for me. Dark, abandoned. No one will hear her scream.

The doors to the admissions building open, and my eyes capture her thin frame as she wrestles with her hair caught up in a gust of wind. She races to her car, searching in her pockets for her keys. I'm in the shadows, right behind her as she makes it to her fancy Mercedes. The key is pressed into the lock when I come up behind her, wrap my large hand around her neck, and slam her into the car. Lillian's cry is loud and laced with fear.

"Take my wallet. I have money in there." Her voice quivers, and it gives me much joy to hear the fear in her tone. She should be scared.

I pull back and whip her around to face me, bringing my hand back to her neck, and smash her up against her car, knocking the wind out of her. "What the fuck have you gotten me in to?" I growl low into her ear. Her hands shoot forward and slaps me in the chest.

"Goddammit, Mason, you scared me. Let me go." She tries to wiggle free, but I only squeeze tighter.

"She's your fucking niece? First your step-daughter, now your *niece*? How fucking sick and demented are you?" I squeeze harder, knowing if I don't stop, I'll choke the life out of her. Her hands squirm, trying to fight me off, but I'm lost in my hate for her. She's gasping and losing strength in her own fight. With the last bit of energy she has left in her, she says the word.

"Evelyn."

I release her, and she almost drops to the ground, grabbing for her neck. "What kind of game you playing here? I ain't ruining her life."

"A game where I make the rules, not you," she rasps, coughing and holding her bruised neck. "You've just made a huge mistake. You think you have any say in what happens here?"

I bend forward, my heated breath striking her pale cheek. "I'm not doing it." I push off her and begin to walk away.

"You will. Because your sister's safety depends on it." My eyelids clamp shut at her words, and I falter in my step.

I turn back to face her. "Then I'm cashing in my fucking coin." I'll accept whatever my new task is, knowing it

PRIDE

doesn't involve Megan.

Lillian raises her chin to the sky and evil laughter spews from her lips. "The coin? You silly boy, *you* don't get a coin. You're the alpha. Pride. I didn't choose you so you can tap out, *pet*. I chose you because you will finish the job, no matter the consequences."

The tornado of rage swirling in my chest scares me. I take a step toward her, threatening to sacrifice everything, just to end her right here, right now. My sister's face comes to mind and I rein in my fury. With a stifled breath I pull back and head in the direction of my car. But not without Lillian leaving me with a warning.

"Mason! Did you know, back in ancient Greece, how they condemned anyone who sinned? The punishment was gruesome. Would you care to know what the punishment for pride was? They'd tie them to a wheel and watch their arms and legs stretch until their bones cracked and limbs ripped."

I don't turn around and feed into her threat. But she still wins. She's filled me full of promise of what's to come if I don't comply. She'll hurt my sister. I pick up the pace until I know I'm out of sight and take my closed fists to the nearest tree, and punch after punch, I destroy the tree until my skin is torn, and my knuckles are bloody. I still haven't caught my breath when my phone dings in my pocket. My adrenaline is already through the roof, but it still manages to step up a notch. *Don't let it be Evelyn.* Thankfully, I find a text from God.

Gluttony: Need you at Lust's place ASAP.
Me: On my way.

I shoot off my text and jump into my car. Tonight's plan was to meet at Rhett's at nine, but it couldn't come at a better time. I need the release like a motherfucker.

I pull up to the address and knock a few times. When no one answers, I invite myself in and glare around annoyed, because I'm expecting some sort of huge ass party. Hitting the foyer, I spot Gluttony, Sloth, and Lust. "What's going on?" I ask, eyeing each one of them.

Something ain't right.

The door opens again, and I nod to the rest of the brothers.

"Oh fuck," Sloth's voice travels from the living room and all eyes gravitate to where he's standing. All the pent-up fury with Lillian instantly dissipates as I stare down at a body on the floor, blood painting the rug around his head. Scanning the photo frames lining the walls, I realize the man on the floor is Rhett's father.

"Okay," God says, nodding his head, glowering between the body and Rhett.

Fuck. This ain't good. I turn my focus on Rhett who's shaking. His chin looks like it took a pretty good hit. "He do that to you?" I ask nodding toward the unmoving body.

"This is bad," Sloth mumbles.

"He hit me, and I just took him down. I didn't…I don't…"

"Breathe," Micah steps in, nodding. "You're not alone in this."

"We'll get rid of the body." Envy shrugs a shoulder, like he's talking about moving a fucking couch. "The swamp. Gators will take care of it."

"It's not an it. It's a fucking person. Christ," Wrath grinds out, sifting a hand through his hair.

Think…

Think…

PRIDE

As the alpha, I need to do something. Rhett doesn't deserve to go to jail because he was protecting himself from a fucking abuser. I don't need to know the reason to know it still ain't right to hit your kid. Too many times in the system have I taken a fist, wishing I could fight back. Do exactly what he did.

"No, Envy is right. We protect our brother. We get rid of the evidence," I say, earning a few raised brows. A round of silence falls upon us until we all snap into action and get down to business.

Dead body.

Bury.

Brotherhood.

Fuck! This is not where I saw my night going.

VII

UINCENDUM NATUS

EIGHT

Megan

E*ighteen...*
 Eighteen...
 Eighteen!

I had sex with my eighteen-year-old student!

No, not just sex. Dirty, kinky, *mind-blowing* sex with my eighteen-year-old student!

"Ahhh!" I cry, throwing myself face first onto my bed, groaning at the soreness of being on my feet all day. How did I not think to ask? And what the hell should I have said? *Oh, hey, by the way, you're of age and not my student before I test out my fantasies on you, right?* I start kicking and banging my fists, having a five-year-old tantrum. I knew I shouldn't have gone through with it. Those damn romance books! I blame all of them. For years I've ached to try something spontaneous. Feed those cravings. I needed to just try. Kink, role playing. Toys. I'd been reading those sweet romance novels ever since I was a kid. But as of late, my tastes have changed. The forbidden books no one talks about. Taboos, BDSM. God, my blood warms just at the mention. It was bringing out a side of me I was unfamiliar with. I had a taste for something dark. I wasn't a virgin by any means, but I just never pushed anything beyond the typical missionary experience. It was nice, sure. But it wasn't hot. It wasn't fulfilling for me. I had a boyfriend once who I tried going just a step further than the typical vanilla sex route. I'd gone online and bought some lotions and went as far as a butt plug. I'd presented it to him on our six-month anniversary, dressed in red see-through lingerie. My gift to him was my body and allowing him free range. I hoped he would pick up what I was throwing down, but the only thing he picked up was his minimal things around my apartment when he dumped me.

I realized maybe I was being silly with my urges and returned the items I bought. I stored those dirty books away and tried to alter my reading back to the lighter, fluffier stuff. But that hunger didn't go away. I would sit in class and imagine myself being spanked. Daydream while at the laundry mat, a stranger tying me up and taking me in all my intimate spots. God, I practically had an orgasm while grocery shopping mentally visualizing being down on my knees and gagging on a large cock. What had been wrong with me! Then, one day I decided to take the plunge. If this was an itch that was never going away, I had to scratch it and move on.

So, I bought a bunch of toys.

I started small, like hand cuffs, a ball gag, and butt

plugs. I shopped at an online kink store for an outfit, and when the weekend came, I searched out the dingiest bar in town. Not only was I a teacher, but the daughter of a prestigious Real Estate Tycoon. My family was heavily involved at the university. Not only was my aunt a high ranked counselor, my uncle was the dean! If I ever got caught, it would not only hurt my reputation, but my family's. And what would it do to my father?

So, I played it smart. But not smart enough. Who would ever imagine, the first time I go out and test my deepest, naughtiest desires, I end up having sex with a student? But how was I really supposed to know he was only eighteen? He perceived to be at least twenty-five. His build and large frame. No doubt anyone would mistake him for a man. "Oh god," I moan, shoving my face harder into my comforter. He's not a man. He's a boy. *A boy with a cock bigger than any dick you've ever had inside you.* Not to mention how well he knew how to use that bad boy. Thank god it was Sunday when I snuck out of that motel room. I had been so sore from the wild ride he gave me, I doubt I would've been able to stand all day and teach.

Even thinking back to that night, there was nothing that would have triggered my acknowledgement that he was so young. He held himself with such fierceness. He was rugged, all muscle, and not to mention the added bonus of his sexy tattoos covering both his arms. If there was anyone that fit my fantasy of a wild night of raunchy sex, it was him. And there was no doubt I picked right. His stamina was exactly what I craved. He worked me, fucked me, devoured me in every way I could have ever asked for.

"Ugh," I moan, curling into the fetal position. My sex begins to pulsate at the memory. My hand strokes between my legs, in hopes to dull the ache, but it only intensifies it. I picture his thick fingers as I pull up my skirt and rub against my clit. His tongue inside me as he licks away my arousal. I push my panties to the side at the mental visual of his cock, his deep voice demanding I watch as the tip of him slides inside me. "Jesus..." I moan again, inserting a finger, my eyes tightly shut. I begin to fuck myself, masturbating to the image of his hard features staring down at me, his cock inside me and the smell of him, tequila and all man, in the air. *"Yes...yes..."* I praise, working myself faster and faster, until my walls close in around my finger, my stomach tightens, and I orgasm, soaking my finger with my release.

Slowly removing my hand, I roll over onto my back. "What in the hell am I doing?" I ask myself, still feeling the high of my fantasy orgasm. I just masturbated to the thought of my sexy student—my *student*, who I shouldn't be thinking of while I masturbate. "God, I'm in trouble," I groan, rolling off the bed to shower. The problem is, the first thing I think about when I undress and start the shower is us back in the motel, him taking me in the bathroom and thoroughly fucking me hard against the bathroom counter before bringing me under the warm spray, using his mouth to lick all intimate parts of me clean.

The second the warm water hits my body, my hands find their way back to my aching folds.

"Dammit. I have no willpower," I moan as I go for another solo mission.

VII

UINCENDUM NATUS

NINE

Mason

Alive.

He was fucking *alive*.

We were seconds away from dumping Rhett's father's body into a marsh to be ripped into shreds by the alligators, thinking he was dead. The anger still flows through me at how careless we all were. But that night, besides all the fucked-up shit that went down, something else happened. We bonded. Truly became brothers. The Elite shit may have brought us together, but watching every single brother step up to protect their own, it gave me a small sense of *pride*, funny as that may be, that I had them all at my back.

I push the rest of that night, and the clear threat I made to Rhett's father out of my head, I refocus on my

PRIDE

current task at hand.

Megan Benedict.

I'm scribbling down notes on my pad of paper, trying to keep up with her as she speed-talks, the passion in her voice hot as fuck. I keep losing my train of thought every time I think about the other night, but the eyeful I get of her taut little ass in that skirt sets me right.

Before class, she grabbed my attention, addressing me by Mr. Blackwell, which turned me on and made her rosy cheeks flush, and invited me to a study session after class if I was available. I had to be insane not to accept. Even though her cute, yet professional invitation was unneeded. I'd been deep inside her. There was no need to be so formal.

Since learning her relationship with Lillian, I've started my research. Googling and trying to find a connection between her and The Elite, but nothing. Everything that had her name attached to it was positive. Perfect grades, perfect background. Perfect family. There was nothing that stated Megan Benedict was anything but what she perceived to be. And that was innocent. I needed to find out the story behind her and Lillian's relationship. Why would she want to do this to her own family? I needed answers—and fast. It was only a matter of time before Lillian beckoned me, demanding a finished task.

Megan turns from the chalkboard, comes to sit next to me, and leans over to see what I've accomplished. "You know, I'm not sure why you think you need my help. You seem to be picking this all up pretty quickly." She uses the back of her hand to brush a loose strand of hair out of her face, and I get a whiff of her floral shampoo.

"You can tell all that from my chicken scratch?" I

examine the last hour of notes I took. My writing is horrible, and half the shit she wrote on the board, I don't understand what it means.

"Sure. It shows you're working hard to understand it. Sometimes taking notes in your own writing helps. When I was in college, I had to rewrite them at least three times before the information sunk in." My brows crease at the thought of having to do this shit over three more times. "Hulk no like taking notes?" she jokes, but her laughter quickly dies off when she realizes what she just called me. "Oh, I'm...shoot, I didn't mean—"

"It's fine. and no, *Hulk* don't like taking notes." I offer her a playful grin, and she eases a bit in her chair. It's hard not to mess with her about the nickname. I haven't stopped thinking about a round two since I walked into her classroom, and I can tell by the glint in her eyes she's having the same issue.

"Anywho..." She breaks away, putting some distance between us, and I instantly miss the closeness of her. "I think you've got this down. Just make sure not to miss any more classes and you should be well on your way to knowing all the ins and outs of ancient Greek theology."

I don't give a shit about Greek anything. Right now, I can't stop staring at her full lips or amber eyes. I can sense my stare is starting to make her uncomfortable, so I pull back my intensity. "Yep, no problem. This is easy shit." I close my notebook, the lie still hanging off my tongue. I would never be able to pass this class on my own. Half the shit she talked about was over my head. Just like Lillian said, with a prison GED, college is no place for a slum like me. But I refuse to let Megan know that.

With the cruel, truthful reality of it, I stand and shove

my notebook in my backpack.

"Oh, you're leaving?" Her smile drops a smidge.

"Thanks for the help. I'll see you tomorrow, *professor*." My lips perk in a frisky smirk. It does its job, because her eyes dilate. We stand there for some time staring at one another, until my phone begins to chirp in my pocket, breaking the moment. Pulling it out, I see a text from Micah.

Micah: 9-1-1 Need you brother. Come alone.

Fuck.

Micah's been acting strange since we've reunited. He's hiding something, I just can't figure out what. Without him telling me, I can tell the last two years haven't been all bells and whistles for him either.

"Gotta get going." I slip my phone back into my pocket, our moment gone. With a simple nod and regret over having to leave, I storm out of the classroom and shoot off a text.

Me: Got you brother. On my way.

VII

UINCENDUM NATUS

TEN

Mason

I'm dead on my feet.

My head aches from no sleep as I trudge through the cold weather to class. My hands rub against my tired eyes when I notice I still have dirt in my fingernails. My stomach turns, but I shove the images to the back of my mind. The smell of death and dirt still lingering on my skin.

Blood.

Blood.

Blood.

I take the steps two at a time and head into the building for biology. The only class I care to attend is Megan's, but it isn't until tomorrow. It's strange to admit it, but I miss her. Her laugh. Her excitement over Greek bullshit.

PRIDE

The way her eyes graze over mine in class, trying to be innocent in her stolen glances. I want to see her. After last night, what I had to do. What we all had to do,

"Micah, what the fuck'd you do?" Every other word escapes me as I regard the scene before me. He doesn't answer me. He's panting like a wild animal, lost in his own rage. Fuck. FUCK!

I'm two steps up the stairs to the building when I stop myself. People race passed me while I stare off at other students disappearing inside. I *need* to see her. I need her to rid all the bad shit in my head. It's then I change course. I fight through the frigid wind in the opposite direction until I'm jogging up the stairs to the communications building. When I open the door to her classroom, I'm greeted by an old guy.

"Coming in?" he asks, handing me a test.

"Uh, no, wrong class," I say, then walk away.

Fuck.

The urge to see her intensifies. Agitation eats at me because I don't know how to find her. It's then I make an irrational move and shoot a text to Lillian.

Me: I'm close but need to know where she is right now.

I wait for a response, regretting the moment I press send, but Lillian is quick to reply.

Cunt Griffin: Library.

I knew she'd come through. I bet she has trackers on all of us. I don't bother putting any more thought into it and race to the library. There's a storm brewing, and I want to get indoors before I get swept up in it. I burst through the doors and a few eyes land on me, their brows crinkling at the unwanted noise. Ignoring the scrutiny, I look around. It's been a while since I've been in a library. I walk up to the help desk, getting the attention of the older woman. She sneers back at me with disgust and confusion, knowing I'm not the normal looking stuck-up rich kid who attends this school.

"Can I help you, sir?" she asks, grabbing for the phone receiver.

I stick my hand in my hoodie for fun and pretend I have a gun just to scare her judgmental ass. "Yeah, I want you to—"

"Mason?" My head whips to my right. Megan stands not three feet away, dressed in a deep plum sweater dress, her hair, as always, up in a cute messy bun. Her reading glasses rest on top of her head as she holds a stack of books in her hand. She stares curiously at the help desk bitch, then back at me.

"Hi, what are you...doing?"

"Oh, I was just asking this nice lady where I can find some Greek literature books." I turn and offer the old hag, who looks about ready to press her panic button, a smile to die for. Her brows scowl at me, and I turn back to Megan. "This nice woman was just about to help me."

She gifts me with her glowing smile, and it instantly wipes all the dread of last night away. She takes a small step toward me and trips, fumbling with her books. I come to her rescue and grab the stack and steady her. "Watch yourself," I whisper, handing her the books, but purposely forget to release her arm.

"Um...well, I can show you where they are...if you want," she says, relieving the prejudice hag. I force myself to release her and nod, instructing her to lead the way. She blushes and her eyes dip to hide how pleased she is I've accepted her offer.

PRIDE

Silently, we walk through the library. A group of douchebags look her way, howling at her, and I clench my fists. A bunch of rich fucks thinking they're entitled to treat an attractive woman like her with disrespect because they have money. Megan smiles politely and continues walking, ignoring it. I wonder if she gets this a lot. I stop as one table starts to whistle, but Megan grabs my arm. "We're almost there," she says, continuing to pull me down a book aisle. If I didn't desperately crave her touch around my arm, I'd turn around and knock every one of those pricks out.

We head down an aisle, taking a few turns until she stops. I purposely bump into her because I'm a selfish prick and need the small contact. Her cheeks blush a soft shade of red, and she reaches for a book out of her grasp. Her arms stretch, hiking her dress up her thighs, exposing her creamy skin.

"Let me help," I say before she falls into the shelf. Reaching forward, I snag the book she's fumbling to reach.

Her eyes light up when I pull it down. She grabs for it, and immediately starts shuffling through the pages. "So, if you want anything Greek literature, this is the book to start with. It's kinda like Greek knowledge for dummies." She glances at me and smiles, but I'm lacking the same. "Oh god, no, I wasn't calling *you* a dummy. It's like a starter book. That's what they call 'em. Oh god, that was rude of—"

I press my finger against her soft lips to stop her from speaking. "I got you," I say, staring her down and loving the warmth of her breath against my finger. She doesn't shove my finger away, which surprises me. We are in public and anyone can see us. I take a step closer, itching to lower my lips to hers. All the bullshit of The Elite is starting to weigh heavy on my shoulders. I can't for the life of me find any dirt on Lillian or Megan, and I know I'm running out of time. And now this shit with Micah. I just want to forget for just a moment what I've gotten myself into and lose myself in her sweet lips. I wonder if she'd let me? Would we get caught? My selfishness only cares about tasting her right in this moment. I bend down, loving the sound of her hitched breath. She's shocked at my bold move, but she doesn't seem to be stopping me. Satisfaction gives me the drive to push her further, so I move my finger and replace it with my lips. Warm, soft cherries. Tasting her again has my mind running rampant with too many inappropriate things. Maybe kissing her was a bad idea, because this is just the beginning of what I need from her. I know I shouldn't be here, and I shouldn't be kissing her, but this is the only thing that's made me feel free of all the fucking shit I've got myself wrapped up in. I press harder into her, using my tongue to part her lips. Her faint moan is the invitation I need to open her wider, tasting her, working my tongue in slow motion around hers.

I know I'm playing with fire, but I can't stop. My arm curls around her waist, and I pull her into me. I'm hard as fuck, my cock pressing against her stomach.

"Mason, we can't..." she moans into my mouth, raising her hand up to my chest. She wants to push me away, but just like myself, she doesn't have it in her. She wants this just as much as I do. Gripping her ass, I lift her up the bookshelf and grind into her while deepening our kiss. My hands shake with the urge to dig under her dress and see how turned on she is. My bet is she's wet as fuck

PRIDE

and craving my finger, even more so my tongue. I grind into her again and swallow her hoarse whimper by kissing her harder. The restraint in me breaks and my hand dips beneath her dress. Her silky skin threatens to break me as I work my hand up her bare thigh. My lips break from hers and trace down to her neck, taking a small bite of her flesh and sucking it in my mouth. The sound of someone dropping a book in the next aisle over breaks the moment, and Megan becomes rigid in my arms. We both stand still until the sound of footsteps disappears down the aisle.

"Shit. That was close," I mumble into her neck. Her fingers are dug deep into my chest as she hangs on to me for dear life. A low chuckle erupts from my chest at how damn cute she is trying to hide herself in my arms.

"Oh my god, why are you laughing? If someone saw us," she panics. Realizing how tightly she's gripping on to me, she wiggles out of my hold.

Forcing myself, I release her. "Well, for starters," I begin, running my hands through my hair, preparing for the brutal pain of blue balls, "Hulk about to smash you through this bookshelf." I stand back, needing to cup my poor balls while she adjusts her dress.

Picking up the book she dropped, she says, "Mason, we can't do this."

"Why the fuck not?"

"Because! It's wrong. That was—"

"Hot?" I finish her sentence.

She sighs loudly. "I was going to say irresponsible."

"You mean hot."

"No. We can't be doing that here."

"But we can do that somewhere else?"

"No!"

"You're confusing me." I fight the laughter that's building.

"You're confusing *me*!" She sighs again. "Mason, I can't...*we* can't. This is my job. You're a student. It's wrong."

Fuck it is.

But she's right. Unlike me. This is her job. She belongs here. I'm just a decoy and a lie.

"Don't look at me like that," she says.

"Like what?" I inquire.

"Like you're disappointed. This, what we're doing... it won't end well. Teacher/student flings...they never do."

She can't be any more correct on that statement, because she has no idea how bad ours will truly end. "You're absolutely right," I say.

She nods in return, but I don't miss the flash of disappointment. A few more seconds of silence pass before the sound of shuffling books and students passing up and down the next row over remind us where we are.

"Well, I should probably get goin'." I hold out my hand for the book she's gripping to her chest.

"Oh, yeah...here." She hands me the book, her cheeks still flushed.

This is where I should turn around and walk away but my legs won't move. "So, is it too unprofessional for a student to walk a professor out to her car? It's probably dark by now and I'd like to make sure you get to your car safely."

She's so damn beautiful when she smiles. A small part of me expects her to turn me down. But when her lips curl into that sexy, sweet grin, I know I won. "A simple, kind gesture from a student? I see nothing wrong with that."

PRIDE

I can't help but match her smile as we begin to walk toward the exit. We pass the group of assholes, but this time, they don't say a peep. Not a single one of them dares to even blink our way. My eyes suddenly catch a shadow in the corner, and I recognize Sloth. What the fuck is he doing here? Casually, he nods, dipping his head as he sucks on a toothpick. I mimic the gesture, confused, but keep walking.

"Excuse me, sir! You can't just take that book! It's stealing!" I snap around to the help desk lady, the receiver in her hand. "I'm calling security!"

"For fucking what?" I bark. Fuck her and her prejudice assumption, the kid from the wrong side of the tracks needs to steal a fucking book. I take a menacing step toward her, wiping the color clear from her haggard face. Megan wraps her small hand almost halfway around my large bicep to pull me back. "Mason, you have to check the book out is all." She turns to the lady. "I'm sorry, Mrs. Willard. That's my fault."

To hell it is. She doesn't have to take the blame for me because this hag lady thinks I'm a fucking thug thief or some shit. The woman's attempt to humiliate me sets me off more. I continue, but Megan digs her nails into my skin, stopping me. "Listen, it's no problem, I'll just check it out for you. Just make sure to get it back in on time, okay?"

"Miss Benedict, you *cannot* do that," she spits, disapproving of her attempt to help me.

"I believe I can. Now, we would like to check out this book. I'd truly hate to discuss my experience here today at a family dinner. I'd hate to admit what a displeasure it was to see one of St. Augustine's veteran staff behave with such animosity toward a fellow student."

Her face blanches, losing any color she has left. With hesitancy, she takes the book and scans the barcode, mumbling about late fees. Megan grabs the book, and with her sweet-as-pie smile, wishes her a good day.

"Thanks. You didn't need to do that," I say, embarrassed I didn't even know how to check out a goddamn library book.

"I know. But you can thank me by reading it and giving me a report on what you learned." God, I want to grab her face, without a care of who sees, and kiss her until her knees buckle, allowing me to carry her back to my place and fuck her—

"Well, well. Look who we have here."

My mood shifts the instant I hear her voice and the blood in my veins turns to ice. My muscles tighten as I face the devil herself.

"Aunt Lillian, what a surprise!" Megan exclaims and steps forward as they embrace in a warm hug. She then steps back, smiling wide. "How've you been? Sorry I haven't been able to make time on campus for lunch. Will we see you at Dad's for dinner on Sunday?"

Someone as sweet as Megan wouldn't notice the simple twitch at the mention of her brother. But I do. There's definitely no love lost for her sibling. She puts that fake smile on and her eyes gleam with fondness, but I know her. The devil wears many hats and the one she wears for her niece is deceit. She hates her brother just as much as she does his daughter. And that sure as fuck sparks my curiosity.

"We'll see, hon. Chastity has a competition which might hold us up." Which is a lie. At one of God's recent

PRIDE

parties, Rhett mentioned he had plans with her. Dear old Lillian is avoiding her family duties. Interesting.

"Oh, well that's too bad. Dad misses you."

There it is again. The simple twitch. No amount of Botox can hide the strain in her eyes.

"Same, sweetheart." In need of a subject change, she veers her hateful stare on me. "And Mr. Blackwell, good to see you again. How is your new class coming along? Accomplishing everything you need to be?" The hidden meaning in that question is clear.

"You know Mr. Blackwell?" Megan jumps in, turning to me with proud eyes. I wish she didn't look at me like that. The moment Lillian notices, her smug grin becomes even more evil.

"Of course. He's one of the many I counsel. Such a promising student, this one." My stomach coils at her words. Even more so at the way her glare feasts on me. Megan doesn't see it. She's blind to the evil that surrounds her.

"I couldn't agree more," Megan says. "By the way, beautiful scarf."

Her eyes flicker to me before she replies. "Yes…well, perfect time of year for them." Bullshit. I know it's because she's hiding the bruises I left on her. She's going to be hiding more too with these games she keeps playing. "I must get going. Meeting with a student to go over his future. Mason, I look forward to hearing about your progress. Do stop by my office in the morning and we can discuss it further." She doesn't stick around for me to reply. She leans in, kisses her niece on the cheek, her eyes creasing in the process, and she's gone.

Megan holds up a conversation as we continue our

trek to her car, but my mind is elsewhere. Murder, new identity, the fucking Elite. How the hell do I juggle all this and stay sane? How do I continue this charade with this perfect girl knowing I'm embedding myself in her life only to ruin her?

"So, this is mine," she says, and I snap out of it. We're standing next to a simple Toyota Corolla. "Thanks again. And I hope you enjoy the book. It's a great one to start with." She's smiling at me, but I find it too hard to return the gesture. Do I tell her now? Come clean that she needs to get out of here? Stay the fuck away from Lillian? How do I warn her that nothing, but destruction is headed her way? I stare down at her, contemplating, when my phone buzzes in my back pocket.

"So…well, I have to get home. I have papers to grade," she says, suddenly looking uncomfortable.

"Yeah, cool. Well I'll see you in class, Miss *Benedict*." My voice is low as I say her last name. Her cheeks flush, and I know I struck a chord with her. As much as she fights to convince herself what we have going on is wrong, she wants it just as much as I do. She digs into her purse for her keys when I grab her phone from her hand and begin to punch in my number.

"Mason, what are you doing?"

"What does it look like? I'm storing my number."

"Mason," she warns. "I don't think that's a good idea."

"Not worried about what you think. Worried about if you ever need it, you'll make sure to use it."

"I'm a big girl, you know," she says.

"Yeah, I know. With even bigger desires. Use it if you need it." With her mouth parted slightly, I leave her and head out. I grab for my phone to check my message, and

PRIDE

my heart drops.

Cunt Griffin: Have you checked on your sister lately?

My hand shakes, threatening to drop my phone. I'm already running through the parking lot to the other side of campus. I barrel through the doors, knocking into a girl carrying a box of pizza. Ignoring her cusses, I take the stairs two at a time. I've been lucky getting on Evelyn's floor since the girls tend to leave the doors perched open for other boyfriends, so I'm thankful when I push through it. Running down the hallway, I hit three-thirteen and throw the door open.

My sister is standing the in middle of her room, her squeal ear piercing as she jumps at the sudden intrusion. There's no hiding she's been crying. "You okay? What's wrong?" I spit out, entering her room and throwing my arms around her checking for wounds, cuts—fuck, I don't know.

"Jesus, what's wrong with *you*? Why wouldn't I be?" she says, wiping at her eyes.

"No, I...I just got a text."

"From who?" My eyes whip to her bed and take in Micah who's seated on the bottom bunk.

I stare at him a few seconds, sizing him up. "The fuck *you* doing here?" I ask, confused. Last time I checked, he and Evie weren't the fondest of one another. I glare back at Evelyn, who refuses to make eye contact, then to Micah. "Anyone gonna fuckin' answer me?"

"She needed someone to talk to. I ran in to her. Just thought we could catch up." My ass. Something's not right here. "Bro, I know that look. It's not what you think. I was just trying to help your sister. You and I are all she has."

"Oh, she *has* you now?" What the fuck? I turn my full body to Micah. "What the fuck is that supposed to mean?"

Micah stands nose to nose with me, but no matter our history, I won't hesitate to take him out if he even thinks of messing with my sister. After last night, I refuse to have her caught up in any of the shit he's involved in. "We're in this together, man. I'd never do anything to hurt your sister. Or you. I thought you knew me better than that."

"I haven't seen your ass in years, how the fuck should I know?" I bark, my defensive wall up high.

"That's right. You *haven't*. You left me just as much as I left you. Neither of us had control over what happened. And now we're both trapped in this shitstorm. But we're in it together. And, together, we're gonna figure out a way to get out."

My eyes dart to Evelyn. "What the fuck did you tell him?" Her guilty eyes tell me too much. "Goddammit, Evelyn."

"He can help. Mason, I'm scared of what you'll do. I'm scared to lose you again." Her eyes swell with tears, and that stabbing in my gut returns at her grief.

I bring my focus back to Micah. "You have no idea what you've gotten yourself into."

"I have an idea."

"Do you, bro? Do you know that soon I'll have to deliver you a task that'll be fucking horrible? It's gonna change you. It's been changing us all."

"I'll just use the coin. It'll be my get-out-of-jail-free card until I figure shit out."

My laugh is deep and cynical. "That coin is worse. Trust me. What you turn down will be child's play compared to what they come back with in return."

PRIDE

"What are you talking about? What coin?" Evelyn steps forward, her voice laced with fear.

"It's nothing. It doesn't concern—"

"Hiding this shit from her won't help her, man."

My anger's back, and I'm in his face. "Yeah and scaring her with details she doesn't need to know about won't help her either." Micah doesn't stand down. The air is thick with tension and fists are about to fly.

"Please, both of you stop," Evelyn cries out, placing herself between us. It doesn't go unnoticed how her hand presses against his chest for longer than needed or the way he instantly calms at her touch. What the fuck is going on between them? "Mason, please. Micah isn't the enemy here. She is."

Micah raises his hand, and I get ready for battle, but he presses his palm to my shoulder. "I'm on your side. I always have been. If I knew…if I had known what the fuck really happened, I would've fought for you. You've always been like a brother to me." My emotions get the best of me. Life has been a whirlwind since I landed on this campus. Between my sister, Lillian, The Elite, reuniting with Micah, and now this thing with Megan…I dip my head in defeat. I'm not as strong as I appear to be. They're both right. I can't do this alone. We need each other to take her down.

"Thank you," I whisper. Evelyn's soft cries are heard as Micah wraps his arm around my neck and hugs me.

"We'll win this one, okay? Lillian, my dad, anyone who gets in our way." I want to believe him. But he doesn't know the whole story. Nor does my sister. Micah knows what Evelyn's told him.

"Mason." My sister calls my name, and I break away

from Micah.

"What is it?" I watch her hand me my phone. It must have fallen out of my jeans when I blasted into her room like a madman. I read the screen.

Cunt Griffin: Bonding time is over. But don't worry, pet. Playtime has just begun. Time to take the life of another brother into your own hands. A philosopher once said, "Needs can always be met, but Greed can never be fulfilled." Enjoy this one.

I raise my eyes to meet Micah's. "You're up."

His face is blank. He nods in acceptance. "Let's do this."

VII
UINCENDUM NATUS

ELEVEN

One week later...

It's been a week since I handed Micah his task. One that rattles me to the core. He showed no emotion by it, which messes me up even more. Since then, the week has been bizarre. Normal even. By some fucking grace of god, it's been quiet and Lillian-free. She shocked me, canceling our one-on-one last minute, with no explanation, nor did she bother to reschedule. I assumed she was probably busy with one of her many pets, which suited me fine. The more she left me alone, the more time I had to spend with Evelyn, catching up and rebuilding the time we'd spent apart.

Surprisingly, I've spent a lot of time with the brothers. Especially Rhett. We may have come from different sides of the track, but our stories were the same. Absent parents. Loss. He opened up about the night shit went down with his dad and what led up to it. He sure as fuck didn't need to explain to me. No one signs up to get hit by their parents. I told him I'd do it over again in a heartbeat. Maybe this time even feed his ass to the gators. He'd talked about the death of his brother. Chastity. His time was running out and I could see the pressure in his eyes to make a choice.

It also left me with more time to pursue Megan.

My sexy little theology professor is fighting hard to lie to herself about what's happening between us, but we both know damn well it ain't over, and I'm not one to give up.

I walk into the lecture hall a few minutes late to make my arrival known and sit in my usual seat up front. I love watching her shoulders tense and her hand slightly shake at my presence. Knowing I make her squirmy makes it all the more fun. But it's not only me playing games. As I sit there playing the perfect student, my sexy little professor stands up front teaching her lesson, avoiding eye contact. I watch the struggle in her eyes, forcing them not to fall on me. Her hands rub together, the nervous sweat building with each passing moment. I know she can't look at me without thinking how good we are together. We're all guilty of our own demises, and I know it's only time before her eyes graze over mine and she sees the heat in my expression. The want. The hunger. And when she does, I go in for the kill.

I take my pen and slide it into my mouth, sucking on the tip, when she gives in. Jesus, there's nothing sexier than the blaze in her eyes as they lock on my mouth while I suck the tip of the pen in and out. The heat in her eyes

PRIDE

threatens to light the entire building on fire. If we were alone, I know she'd let me—no, she'd beg me to give her what we're both desperately craving. My dick is growing in my pants, and I need to rein in my own arousal before shit gets out of hand.

But not yet.

A smile, so dark and devious, spreads across my face. I pop the pen out of my mouth, causing her to snap out of her haze. I can't help but chuckle as I get up, without saying a word, and walk out of her class.

I pull this cat and mouse game with her the next two classes. Each time, waiting 'til she can no longer fight it and her eyes find mine. I toy with her in any which way I know how, watching her lose control. Not in a way that anyone may notice, but in a way I do. In the short time I've known her, I've learned her little signs of arousal. The flush of her cheeks. The way her lips part, or when she glides her tongue along her bottom lip. I work her up until I think she's almost willing to jump me in front of her students, no fucks given, and then I get up and leave. And I'm loving every fucking second of it.

It's Friday, and I'm in my usual seat, enjoying the view of Megan in her tight pencil skirt and pale blue collared shirt. Wondering whether she's wearing panties, I wait 'til she's close enough to the row of desks before I drop my pen. Her body stiffens as the pen rolls to her feet. My smile is predatorial as I lean down and reach for it, no doubt grazing the bottom of her leg in the process. No one catches the intake of breath at my quick move since everyone is taking a test. I retract back into my seat and grab her eyes, loving the way they light up. Fuck, I want her bad. And little miss professor over here can't hide that she does as well.

We're just at the five-minute mark when I bend down to pick up my backpack—

"Okay, class! We're wrapping up early today due to a building inspection. Enjoy your weekend. Mr. Blackwell, can I have a word before you leave?" The class begins packing up and leaving while we stare back at one another. *Smart play, professor.* She taps her heel, waiting for every student to leave until the door finally shuts, leaving only us in the room. "What's your problem? You can't do this in my classroom. What if people suspect—?"

I pop up from my seat, cutting off her words. She stands stone still as I prowl slowly in her direction. My dick begins to swell at her flushing cheeks. She takes a step back before pulling it together. "I'm serious, Mason. This has to stop. You can't be—"

"Looking at you like I want to fuck you over your desk? Turn you around and pound my dick so far into that sweet cunt from behind while your perfect tits brush off your lecture notes of the day? Tell me, Miss Benedict, what can't I be doing?"

I've rendered her speechless. Her pink lips part and close, wanting to tell me I'm wrong—scorn me for the wicked visual now playing in her head.

"Mason, you're my student."

"And a very, very bad one. Who wants to do bad, bad things to you."

Her breath hitches, and my cock jolts. I prowl up to her until there's no space between us, and she has no choice but to press her back against the chalkboard. I say nothing more and reach up, grip her perfect ponytail, and wrap it around my fist. My cock grows with a fierceness

PRIDE

at the way her eyes blaze with excitement, and I bring her head forward until we're nose to nose.

"I'm gonna fuck you right here. In your classroom. And you're gonna let it happen. Because the way you've been eye-fucking me all week has me hard as steel. You're gonna pay for what you've created. Are we clear, Miss Benedict?"

The warmth of my breath heats her cheeks even more. She doesn't fight me. She's completely forgotten we're still in her classroom, where anyone could walk in and see. That or she's aware, and it turns her on even more. She shows no signs of refusal, so I welcome the opportunity and bend forward, pressing my open mouth to her neck. I suck hard, not giving a fuck if I leave a mark. She allows it, her soft whimper egging me on.

"That's my girl," I praise, falling down my own rabbit hole of her scent and the feel of her. "Tell me you don't want me to take you over your desk and spank you 'til your ass is swollen and red. Or should I give you what you want even more and fuck you hard and fast?"

"Mason." she moans my name bringing a triumphant smile to my lips. I nip at her neck and grind into her. I tighten my hold on her hair, but my dirty little girl doesn't plead with me or beg me to release her. She whimpers in pleasure like a wild alley cat in heat. I work my free hand down her ribs and push up her grey skirt until my hand reaches down into her panties. She soaks my fingers the moment I reach her pussy. "Such a naughty fucking girl," I growl, inserting a finger and thrusting as far as I can go.

"Mason…" Again, she moans, and I struggle to keep it together. I push another finger inside her, this time even less gentle. I'm hard as a rock and if I don't pull myself together, I'm gonna pound her cunt straight through the fucking wall. My name falls from her lips again, and the sound is like fucking heaven. I push harder, shoving my fingers so deep, my knuckles restrict me from going any further. "Love the way my name sounds off those lips, babe," I say, working in and out of her.

This is supposed to be a game I'm heading, but I sense myself losing. Her voice, the smell of her arousal, my cock that's fighting not to fuck her hard and dirty. I slam my eyes shut, working faster. She rides my hand, wanting me to punish her. Fuck. I want her. Her walls squeeze me as she orgasms around my hand. I slowly pull my fingers from her soaked cunt and allow her body to slide down the board, her legs barely able to hold herself up. She almost falls forward, and I reach out to steady her. I feast on her glazed-over eyes and crack a smile.

"Perfect," I say, and before she can spew any lies about us being a bad idea, I walk out of her classroom.

One week later...

I'm fucking obsessed.

Everything I do revolves around watching her. Stalking her. Lusting for her.

I can't stop.

The following week played out the same way. Our little game of cat and mouse, until Friday rolled around. This time, I took it a step further and fucked her over her desk. I shoved her cute little silk scarf she wore in her mouth to

PRIDE

muffle her moans and took her from behind. My hands left marks on her smooth pale skin with each spank. God, I've never felt so high being with someone. Even Dahlia didn't take me to this level of euphoria. Megan started the same way, telling me it was wrong, we were wrong, and I would follow through, just like last week, letting her weak plea fall on deaf ears as I plowed my cock so hard into her, the ancient wooden desk even moved.

She was this sweet professor who had this secret craving for being bad. And I wanted to be her enabler. I started attending her classes on the other days just to see more of her. I couldn't get enough of her. She was orbiting into my very own addiction. I wanted more. I needed more.

I may have started this as a game to prove to her we were more than just a fling. A student/teacher disaster waiting to happen. And now, I'm even more so convinced she's mine. And she's going to realize it and stop fighting what's happening between us. Any mention of The Elite has been silenced. No messages or emails to call to. It left me only focused on her and what I wanted her to be for me. And when I wasn't with her or Evelyn, my time was spent trying to find out why Lillian wanted to expose and ruin her. But the problem was, the internet was all dead ends.

I became obsessed with trying to get answers.

Obsessed with her.

I followed Megan home. Watched her in the park when she ran. Sat in my car outside her small little bungalow on the outskirts of town and watched her read in her living room for hours upon hours. I told myself I wasn't a creep or a stalker. It's because I needed to understand. Maybe, just maybe, I would catch her doing something that would make me understand why she deserved what I'm being forced to do. But there's nothing. Absolutely nothing. And I'm close to losing my shit. As I watched her grocery shop, I begged her to steal. Lie when asked the price of a dress while clothes shopping. I even prayed to catch her with another guy. The last thought enraged me, thinking of her with someone else—sharing those moans and orgasms with someone other than me.

But still, nothing.

She was, in every single way, perfect.

And tonight, as I sit outside her house, watching her, and imagining myself inside next to her, being better than the fuck-up I am, I wonder how in the fuck I'm going to get out of my task if I can't find anything on her or Lillian. I'm gonna have to make a move soon. If I don't find what I need, my task will be unavoidable, and I'll have to make choices I don't want to make. But my sister's life depends on it.

My phone buzzes, pulling my eyes away just as she flips her page. Looks like the devil is back up and running. I read the message across my screen. Envy's up.

The music blares to some shitty ass dance music as I finish up my fifth beer. After handing Envy his task, we met up with Rhett and the rest of the brothers at God's lavish apartment for another outrageous party. The more and more I'm around this guy, which isn't much, I see why he's Gluttony. His excess in everything is fucking ridiculous. My eyes scan the room, and I watch as Envy

PRIDE

and Wrath have an argument in the corner. No idea what that shit's about, and I debate on getting involved. As the alpha, I need to keep all my brothers in line. But then I watch as God walks up to them, grinding his teeth and jittery as fuck. He pulls Envy away and drags him into the bedroom, where he popped out of. I'm tempted to follow. Whatever it is they're doing, I could use a jolt of.

"Sup brother."

Rhett walks up and stands next to me sipping on a beer. "Sup," I return, staring off into the crowd of horny college students, drinking and humping each other. "Things work out with your girl?" I ask. Rhett pulled the plug on his task, turning in his coin. I saw relief in his eyes. It's a shame mine didn't mirror the same feeling. I wanted to tell him the coin was evil. But he was blinded by emotion. I understood. I was in the same boat. But the moment Lillian caught wind, I knew she had something more destructive up her sleeve.

"Yeah, things are good," he says, a shit eating grin on his face as he rakes over his girl on the dancefloor as she dances with her friends.

"Just watch your back, brother. You have no idea what they have in store—"

Chastity cuts into my warning and walks up grabbing his attention. He nods his understanding and allows her to pull him onto the dancefloor. I watch them as he holds her tight, staring down at her like he owns every single part of her. Which is just the beginning of how I'm starting to feel about Megan, wishing she was here to drown all the bad shit going on in my head out.

"Don't you look like you can use a little bit of fun." My eyes break away from Rhett and Chastity to the chick now standing in front of me. "You look so angry. Ya know, we can find an empty room and make that frown of yours go away." She tugs at her already too tight shirt, practically exposing her nipples.

I slam the rest of my beer, needing the alcohol to hit me faster. I need to numb my mind and the booze isn't doing the job. Nothing is. My brain refuses to shut down. I haven't talked to Micah since that night he got his task. Wondering if he went through with it. I refused to hear Envy's task. Whatever destruction was in store for him, I couldn't bear the burden of knowing. But there was one thing that's for certain. He was going through with it. That gleam in his eye told me so.

I can't stop thinking about when the next one will be handed down? What horrific things will the next brother have to do?

I just want to leave and find Megan. I'm struggling to find reason in what I'm truly doing with her. I like her. Fuck, it might be more. But I can't imagine doing the horrific things Lillian wants me to do. Why the fuck does she hate her so much? Was she jealous of her? She's her brother's daughter, for Christ's sake. Was she disgusted by her secret fetish for kink? Being a sadist cunt seems worse than having a dark taste for sex. And so fucking what? Megan stands for so much more than her bedroom desires. She's amazing, smart. A hard worker, and a great teacher. She wants to help people. In the last class, she was urging people to sign up for the New Orleans Homeless missionary charity to help support the homeless and less fortunate. How does someone that selfless deserve to be chastised and defaced?

I wasn't going to do it. I couldn't. But every time I told

PRIDE

myself I wouldn't go through with it, my sister's face came into view. No matter how I broke it down, I was fucked. Someone was going to suffer. The more time that goes by, the more questions that arise. How long has this cult society been going on? How long have people been getting away with such disgusting acts? Maybe I was searching for the wrong answers. Maybe if I got down to the root of The Elite, I could expose *them*. Take *them* down. Ruin Lillian herself. Maybe if I did that, I wouldn't have to ruin the only good thing that's come into my life.

"There ain't shit you can do that'll get rid of this look, so move along," I tell her, knowing no one will fire me up the way Megan does. I push off the wall, but she blocks my exit.

"Oh, come on. We can grab some drinks and maybe go in the hot tub. There're tons of private rooms. We can get to know each other a little better." She raises her hand, but before it makes contact with my chest, my fingers wrap around her wrist. She groans at my hard grip. I learn closer with my cruel stare. "What exactly you wanna do? How 'bout you let me tie you up and fuck your ass. Play a little game of who can scream louder? Maybe we can explore what else you like shoved up you while we're at it."

Her facial expression morphs into disgust. She rips her hand from my grip and slaps me hard. "You're a sick fuck," she spits and walks away. Unfazed, I snag a beer from some tool walking passed me and chug it. He dares to turn my way, but the threat in my eyes has him scurrying off like a little pussy. It's late, and I know no one will be on campus. Now is the perfect time to take a little visit to Lillian's office and see what else she has locked up in that desk of hers. I walk by Sloth, who nods at me as if he can read my mind.

I'm out the door and headed to my car. Pulling my keys out of my front pocket, I notice a cloud of smoke in the shadows. I backtrack to see Sloth appear from the darkness. "How the fuck did you—?"

"I wouldn't do it if I were you," he says, taking a huge puff of a joint.

"Do what? How'd you get out here before me?"

He takes a step forward, illuminating himself under the streetlight. "There's persistence in elimination. And in elimination takes strategy."

This guy needs to lay off the fucking weed. "You know, I don't really have time for fucking riddles, so if you could just spit out whatever it is you want to tell me, I got shit to do." He takes another drag and flicks the half-smoked joint in the street. He saunters up to me, lighting up a cigarette. "The best work is done when no one's looking. The problem is, they always are." He turns his head to stare off down the street. I follow his lead but see nothing but an abandoned alley. He returns his gaze back to mine. "I'll see you around, *alpha*. Sooner rather than later." Like a ghost, he disappears back into the shadows of the night.

I jump in my car, weirded out by that encounter. What the hell does he mean? It was a warning, that's for sure, but how does he know so much? I start my car and pull away, unsure where I'm going. My plans to break into Lillian's office are now diverted.

Fuck the whole Elite. Right now, my only thoughts are on seeing Megan and fucking her until all the bad shit floating around in my head disappears. I head toward her house, and my phone dings. I growl at the bad timing and

PRIDE

lift my screen to read my incoming text.

Cunt Griffin: Detour time. Head down Miller to the French Quarter. Enjoy the scenery.

I slam my hands on my steering wheel. I want to message back telling her to go to hell. Ignore her demand, shut my phone down, and spend the entire night with Megan. Besides wanting to take every single part of her until my dick threatens to fall off, I want to get to know her. Her likes and dislikes. What she eats for breakfast, the brand of shampoo she uses. I would even sit and listen to her political views if it meant just hearing her voice.

I run my hands through my hair and tug at the sudden headache making its way through my skull. *Just fucking do it and be done*, I tell myself, taking a detour through town until I find myself in the heart of Bourbon Street. Never a care for what day or time it is, the French Quarter is always alive with music. Street performers block half the streets while people scatter along the sidewalks dancing and laughing, drinking and exposing themselves as if every day were Mardi Gras.

When I come up to the stoplight on Bourbon Street, a group of college kids parade across the street, holding beers and sloshing booze onto the pavement. Just as the light changes to green, a couple ignores the sign and crosses. Annoyance strikes on my nerves, and I raise my fist to slam on my horn when I recognize her. My hand stalls in mid-air as I watch Megan, on the arm of some guy, trotting along the street. The asshole turns to wave at me, thanking me for not running his ass over.

My eyes lock on them as they make it across the street, his hand dipping low on her back to escort her onto the sidewalk. Seeing his hand on her infuriates me.

I want to jump the curb and run him over just to get him off her. A honking car behind me forces me to accelerate and drive just as I catch them popping into a nearby restaurant. I flip the asshole behind me the bird, take a right, and park a few blocks down. Throwing my hoodie over my head, I jump out and head back toward the place they walked in to. I don't know what I'm doing. Why I find myself standing outside the window of the table they were just seated at. I watch in disgust as he pulls out her seat and she smiles at him. The same fucking smile she gives me. They order drinks from the waitress, and every so often, she laughs at something he says. My teeth grind every time he reaches over to pat the top of her hand. The urge to know what they're talking about grates at me. I'm about to storm in there and rough her dorky ass date up. But is that what this is? Is he just another me? Someone she's trying to convince to go home with her and play her dark and twisted games with until she's done getting off? Is this the evidence I've been desperately searching for that proves she's not so innocent?

Fuck! The realization hurts. How fucking stupid of me to think we had something more, deeper. *She was probably just being nice, so you'd keep her secret.* Her dirty little secret. I watch her raise her finger to the waitress. Her lips move, and I read them. *Check please.* That didn't take long to convince him—not as fast as she convinced me.

I pull away from the window, unable to watch any more. My phone dings, and I rip it from my back pocket.

Cunt Griffin: Now that your love-sick puppy dog faze is over, get back to the task at hand. xoxo

The rage inside rumbles deep in my chest. That bitch set me up, wanting me to see this. My anger threatens to detonate. I need to get out of here before I end up inside, ripping that motherfucker's head off. I hang a right, knocking into a college frat boy.

"Hey, watch it, asshole."

He opens his mouth to talk more shit, but doesn't get another word out, because I raise my fist and smash it into his face. Blood splatters as I break his nose. Pulling back, I strike him again, over and over, until the sounds of a girl screaming she's calling the cops compels me back to reality. When the fog finally rises, I pry open my eyes and grimace at the kid, bloody and unconscious at my feet. I glower at the small crowd I've caused. Even people from the restaurant are peeking out the window, curious to the commotion. Jumping up, I take a step back, throw my hoodie back over my head for disguise, and begin jogging down the street. I run past my car to avoid them seeing what I drive. Can't risk them taking down my plates if those pussies really do call the cops. I run for almost a mile until I see neon lights and slip into the hole in the wall bar.

VII

UINCENDUM NATUS

TWELVE

Megan

"Yes, Mother…I know…I am! Tell Dad I love him too. I won't, Mom. I'll see you both on Sunday. Love you too!"

I throw the phone down and snatch my book back up in my hands. I flip to where my favorite worn bookmark holds my place, and curl back into my chair, wrapping my feet under the large cashmere blanket Mom bought me for Christmas last year. My eyes find where I left off when vicious pounding on my door has my arms shooting to the sky, tossing my book. Startled by the intrusion, the book falls to the floor, losing my page.

Bang. Bang. Bang.

"What in god's name…" I get up and peek out my bay window. It's too late for anyone to just stop by. It's not my

PRIDE

parents since I just spoke to Mom. I don't see anyone, and my nerves begin to spike. This is a safe neighborhood, but no matter the location, New Orleans has its danger. More banging sounds, and the hairs on my arms stand on end. My hackles rise as I get up and grab for the bat hidden in the large vase holding my umbrellas. "Who is it?" I call to the door as I tiptoe to the side, using the bat to pull back the curtains. My eyes widen in shock when I see Mason.

"Open up," he yells through the barrier.

I drop the bat and start working on opening the locks. Once I get the last one undone and twist the knob, the door pushes open and Mason falls through the threshold.

"Mason…what are you…are you *drunk*?" He stumbles forward again, almost taking us both to the ground. His foot manages to kick back and shut the door. "You can't just show up at my—"

"Why'd you do it?" He steadies himself with the help of my hallway end table. I get a glimpse of his hands. His knuckles are cut up and bloodied.

"Do what? What happened to your hand?"

He ignores my question. His hair is as wild as the look in his eyes. "The night we met, you got me in that motel room and we fucked like animals." I suck in a breath at his crude choice of words. "Yeah, you know, when I ate your cunt until you screamed. Tore your nails deep into my back until I tied you up." My body heats at the memory. The way he smelled that night at the bar. The ferocity in his eyes that had me wet before even saying a word to him. The way he looked so damaged, I knew giving him a way to forget would be what we both needed. "Why'd you pick me?"

"You seemed like you could use—"

"Don't play games with me. Why? I could've been some fucking serial killer. Rapist."

"You looked lost, not murderous," I say, speaking the truth. If I felt any danger about him, I would have never done what I'd done.

"How many guys have you taken home like that and fucked?"

"That's none of your—"

"How many fucking *guys* have you allowed to put their fingers in your sweet tight ass, their cocks in your cunt—"

My open palm, with a fierce quickness, strikes across his face. The pain shoots through my wrist and up my arm. My breath catches in my throat as he attacks me. His large hands scoop me into his arms, backing us farther into the house.

"Why would you put yourself in danger like that? I could have hurt you. I *can* hurt you."

I raise my arms around his neck, making a point to skim my fingers along the red welt on his cheek. "But you're not. Never did I feel threatened or uncomfortable with you."

"You should have," he growls, digging his fingers into my butt cheeks. "Now I know your secret. I know what a bad, bad girl you are." He crushes his lips down on mine. He's rough and feral, forcing my lips open and shoving his tongue inside my mouth. His brutal outburst is confusing yet turns me on. I don't know where it's coming from. It's far from the flirt he's been the past two weeks. I want to ask what's changed in him, but my mind is starting to flip and that ache to be that bad, bad girl begs with need to come out and play.

PRIDE

"That's the risk I took. The high of knowing I was taking home a stranger to play my little game and hope he was the winning type. The dark type. The giving—*ahhh...*" I moan as both hands grip my ass hard, pulling my cheeks apart. He grinds into me, his cock hard against my stomach. The size of him sends a wave of sensations down every nerve ending, and I can't help but press into him. The friction has him growling in my mouth and deepening our kiss.

Too many scenarios swirl around in my mind. *Make him stop.* Have him fuck me against my table. *He's too young.* Take him to my bedroom and play. *He's your student. You have to stop this and make him leave.* Maybe just a little taste. I'll behave. *Dark.* Only foreplay. *Everything, everything, everything!* I beg to take him back to my bedroom and have him tie me up and whip me and fuck me in ways I can't stop fantasizing about.

I knew by the shocked expression on his face when I pulled out my toys, it was the first time he'd been so adventurous. But now, it all made sense. He was still so young. It also reminds me of all the things I have hidden in my bedroom. The stuff I swore I was going to throw away after I got the one night out of my system. But I never had the guts to get rid of it. *Do not go there, Megan. This is wrong.*

Mason rips his mouth off mine and goes for my neck. I bend to the side to allow him better access. "You're fucking with my head," he hums against my skin.

"Would you rather me be fucking something else? Fucking your cock?" Oh my god, my vulgar mouth! *Stop egging this on. Be the adult.* Or not. I embrace the layers of goosebumps over my skin at the fantasy of him doing just that. I should be ashamed at how much I've fantasized about being with him. Having him inside me. I squeeze my eyes shut at how shitty my willpower is, and how I let him do insane things to me—in my classroom, of all places. I should fire myself for being so reckless. He could cost me my job and reputation if we got caught. But there was something inside me that told me the wildness of it all was all worth it.

Snap out of this, Megan!

Dammit, this is so wrong. I squeeze my eyes tighter, willing myself to push him away. Ask him to go. And, most importantly, tame the dark beast inside myself before she ends up ruining everything I've worked so hard for. I take in a deep breath to clear my mind, but Mason's not making it easy for me. His hand finds its way to the back of my pajama pants and using his finger, he grazes my back hole. *Fuck.* My legs threaten to buckle, and I rock into him. "Mason…"

"Fucking dirty girl." He reaches forward, until his fingers are saturated with my arousal. Pushing one finger inside me, he pulls out, swirling the wetness between my butt cheeks. "How many guys have you let do this to you?"

I struggle in his arms, but he holds me tighter in place, going back and inserting two fingers inside me. "Why, want someone else to join us? Didn't picture you as the multi-player—"

He bites at my neck, and I whimper, my final words falling short off my tongue. "I'll fucking gut anyone who gets between this." He starts pumping me harder. His spite of jealousy ignites my already pulsating arousal.

"Just a two-player game then? Just your cock? Or

PRIDE

should we—ahhh, shit, *yes*..." I moan as he uses his thumb to breach my puckered hole. He works me faster, and I lose my will to hang on. My orgasm erupts through me, and I explode around his fingers. He doesn't let up, pumping in and out. My sensitivity kicks in, and my legs quiver around him. He pulls his soaked hand free and drops my legs to the ground while I attempt to catch my bearings.

He's yet to take his eyes off me, pinning me with his stare. "Who the fuck was that guy tonight?"

"Huh?" I reply, still chasing my orgasmic high.

"I saw you. Is he another conquest? Am *I* just a fucking conquest?"

At first, he confuses me, but then my awful forced dinner date comes to mind. "Wait, you saw me?"

A growl deep in his chest rumbles up his throat, shaking the floor beneath our feet. "Answer me," he demands.

I should be mad at the way he's talking to me—asking questions that are none of his business—but his intensity does something to me. "No, he wasn't a conquest. Far from it. It was a horrible date Aunt Lillian basically forced me on. She lied to me. It was supposed to be for a new fund-raising prospect for the Faith and Leadership program. As soon as we sat down, I found out it was far from it, and I kindly told him I wasn't interested and left. And if you want to know, no, you're not a conquest either. You're something more."

The angel on my one shoulder just conked me over the head with her sparkly wand. My confession was a bad, bad idea. But the devil in the other corner pricks me with his sharp fork and cheers me on. He praises my handy work and promises all things Mason are a great idea.

When Mason slams his mouth against mine, I

mentally flick off my angel while high-fiving my devil, grab the lapels of his jacket, and tug him toward my bedroom. When we step over the threshold of my room, my huge bed, filled with white pillows and layers of soft blankets, comes into view. Nothing close to the sex dungeon I bet he expected. But the truth is, Mason is the first and only person I've ever shared my secret desires with.

Even with the urge building inside me for years, I didn't muster up the courage until that night. The way I felt with Mason that night was nothing I'd ever experienced before. Alive. Empowered I'd orgasmed with such fierceness more times than I've ever had with any man or toy. When I left that morning, I wanted to wake him for more, ride his hard cock until stars exploded behind my eyelids, then do our night all over again. I was willing to never leave that motel. But as tempted as I was, I left, told myself I more than scratched my itch and it was time to go back to my normal, vanilla life and move on. I didn't bust my ass to lose it all. Get caught up with a guy from the wrong side of the tracks just to fulfill my overflowing sexual desires to be bad.

What I didn't expect was for him to turn up as a student in my classroom. The moment our eyes reunited, memories of that night hit me like a freight train taking the air from my lungs. My legs became weak and black spots twinkled in my vison. He was my dirty little secret. He was *not* supposed to show up in my pure, innocent world.

But the more I see him, the hungrier my urges become. I told myself one night. I taste the lies that spew from my thoughts even as I think them. The toys I never got rid of, the clothes that still smell like him. I don't know what I'm doing. This was insane. He's drunk, and I should turn him away, as well as my desires.

Student. Student. Student, I chant to myself, in hopes I snap out of the haze I'm in, but the closer I bring Mason to my bed, the more excited I become. My breathing is labored at the excitement of his hands touching every single inappropriate part of me. I tug at his arm and twist his waist so his back is to my bed. My anticipation sparks, and I push him and watch as he falls backwards, sprawling out on my mattress.

"It's your turn to play nice and my turn for control. No talking, understand?"

VII
UINCENDUM NATUS

THIRTEEN

Mason

My mouth is dry. My muscles sore. Strangely, I feel a cold breeze on my ass. I squint open an eye when the bright light sends a zap of electricity through my retina, sending pain straight to my skull. *"Fuck."* I lift my head and inspect my surroundings. *"Double fuck."* I came to Megan's last night after the bar. I catch sight of my backside, and realize the cold breeze is due to my naked ass hanging out, her soft white sheet resting just above my thighs. Flipping to my side, I notice she's not in bed with me. My mind spins for pieces of last night. Showing up at her door. The accusations. Her bringing me into her room. And fuck. Her wild, amazing imagination. My dick begins to poke against her mattress. I groan into her plush pillow, throw my legs off the bed, and sit up. The room

PRIDE

spins, but I manage to get up and find her attached bathroom to take a piss. Everything in the bathroom is neatly placed. Her color choice, a calming shade of white and lavender. I wash my hands and search for my clothes, finding my briefs halfway under the bed and my jeans tossed over a chair in the corner.

Partially dressed, I go in pursuit of Megan, which isn't hard because I follow the yelling. I find her sitting cross-legged in front of the television, a bowl of cereal in her hands as she yells at the screen.

"Oh, come on, Judy, that's a bad move, girl!" She waves her spoon at the TV, then takes a bite.

"Judge Judy, huh?"

Her head whips in my direction, and a small blush creeps along her face. "Uh, how could you not?" She waits for my agreeance while shoving another full bite of cereal into her mouth. Long gone is the wild sex kitten from last night, and back is my innocent professor, wearing ridiculously bright pajama pants, eating a bowl of Lucky Charms, and watching a tacky reality justice tv show. "Don't tell me you're not a fan." Her eyes widen at the mere thought that someone could possibly not enjoy Judge Judy.

"No, I used to watch her a bit back in the day at…" I catch myself. "She's okay," I finish. Her curious eyes wait for me to elaborate, but I don't. She lets it go by shoving another full bite into her mouth.

"She gives some of the best advice," she mumbles through her chewing. I stand there with my hands shoved in my jean pockets, admiring how cute she looks, a drop of milk falling from her spoon and dripping down her chin. It doesn't go unnoticed that her eyes fail to stay on mine and drop every few seconds to my bare chest.

"Sorry. I couldn't find my shirt."

She chokes, knowing she's been busted, and wipes at her chin. "Oh, yeah…uh, it was dirty, so I threw it in the washer. It's almost done." She continues to stare, and I'm uncertain where to go from here. I'm not sure if this is where I walk out, shirt or not, and pretend this never happened. I can't imagine what she thinks of me now after the shit I pulled showing up at her door.

Shockingly, she pats the open spot on the floor next to her. "I made you a bowl. Wasn't sure what kind of cereal eater you were, so I kinda put three different kinds in there." I check out the large mixing bowl beside her, noticing Lucky Charms, Captain Crunch, and I believe Cocoa Pebbles. "And I also didn't know how hungry you were going to be. So, I just put it in this." With a guilty smile, she says, "This is my third bowl."

Fuck, she's cute.

"Uh oh, what? Do you not like cereal?" She gawks, more devastated that I could possibly not like cereal than Judge Judy. I want to keep her in suspense longer just to stare at that cute little pout, but my stomach rumbles, and I actually do love fucking cereal.

"Love cereal," I say, and her relieved smile fucks with me as I sit my big ass down next to her. She hands me the milk sitting on the other side, and I waste no time digging into the best breakfast I've had in years.

"So, I gotta ask—"

"You're the first," she blurts out before I have a chance to say anything more. She doesn't turn to me, but continues eating her cereal, pretending she's immersed in the show.

PRIDE

"You're gonna need to explain that one further," I say, pushing her.

"The night at the bar. I'd never done that before. You were my first…and, well, I guess my only victim." She takes another bite. "And last night…I guess I kinda victimized you last night too." She keeps her eyes glued ahead of her. She can't hide the flush of her cheeks, and I'm not sure if she can see from the corner of her eye the smile spreading across mine.

"You think you took advantage of me last night?" I laugh.

Her head whips to me. "Oh my god, do *you* think that? Oh shit. You were drunk. I shouldn't have. Fuck, I should have sent you home. Shit!" She begins to panic, milk sloshing out of her bowl onto her cute little girly pants. I grab her bowl so she stops spilling it all over herself and place it on the ground.

"You didn't take advantage of me. I was messing with you. Anything that happened, I sure as fuck wanted it to. And I loved every goddamn second of it."

I love watching her eyes come to life. I'm learning she's a very passionate person in her work and play. And last night was no different. She has wants. Cravings I'm desperate to feed. I pour myself more milk and guide my eyes to the screen. "So, what's the case today?"

Sensing her relax instantly at my topic change, she jumps right in "This girl! So, she cheats on her boyfriend, right? Then tries to kick him out so her new man can move in—but! She and her *old* man share the lease. She's dragged his ass to Judge Judy 'cause she thinks since he's on the lease, he should still pay half the rent!"

Like I said, she has passion. I smirk while shoving a

huge spoonful of mixed cereal into my mouth and fight the wussy moan at how good it tastes. It's been a lifetime since I got a taste of hyped up sugar cereal. Before I realize it, I finish off the entire bowl, catching her curious eyes as I drain the leftover milk into my mouth.

"Wow."

"Wow what?" I ask.

"I think I met the one person who may love cereal more than I do." She grins, and I take note of her bowl, which is also empty. We stare back at one another, sharing a silent moment of recognition, then both burst out laughing. I could stare at her for hours. She's beautiful in a way I don't know how to describe. Her eyes shine with curiosity, adventure. Her graciousness makes me want to be someone better, just so she looks at me like I'm someone to be proud of.

I watch her stick her tongue out to wet her lips. Her throat bobs, swallowing, and I know—*I know* she's feeling the same whirlwind building inside me. Yelling on the TV breaks the moment, and we both face the screen to see the verdict being called. Judge Judy slams her gavel onto the sound block and the show breaks into commercial. I know this is where I get up and leave, but the thought of walking out that door seems impossible.

"So..." she starts, and I know it's time. I shouldn't have shown up here to begin with. It's time to go.

"Time to get—"

"If you don't have plans today, there's this Haitian voodoo tour..." she starts, cutting me off. "The voodoo queen of New Orleans is said to be buried there, and...I don't know, probably not your thing, but it's—"

"I'll go," I say.

PRIDE

"You will?" She ogles, shocked. "But you didn't even hear what it was."

"I'll go," I repeat.

"Are you sure? It's probably really—"

"I said yes." I couldn't give a fuck if it's to visit and test out torture equipment. I'd do anything in this moment to spend more time with her. Surround myself in her scent of cherries and sweet vanilla. My hands ache to hold her, and my cock even more so to violate her, but most importantly, I want to just be next to her. Hear her voice as she tells me stories about her life. A life I was less than fortunate to have. I want to hang on to every word she speaks as I imagine I'm in her world, living her life, peaceful and beautiful.

"Okay then." She nods with her glowing smile that threatens to ruin me every time, then gets up, grabbing both our bowls. "It's a date." Her cheeks instantly flare a deep shade of crimson. "I mean…not a date. Just…we can't…"

I get up also and grab the bowls she is threatening to drop during her outburst. "No date. Just two people who enjoy syncretic religion playing around a cemetery full of dead people."

Her eyebrows raise in surprise. "You read the book," she says, pleased.

"Of course. When your favorite teacher recommends a book, you read it." Silence falls between us. I should have kept the teacher comment to myself. Fuck, now I just ruined whatever plan she had for us.

"Just two people…" she repeats.

"It's a free country, Miss Benedict. There's no harm in two people being in the same place at the same time." My words win her over, easing any worry of what people may think if they see us together.

"Okay then. You're right. Just two friends. Taking a tour." She smirks.

We're silent, grinning at one another, until she finally breaks the moment.

"So…" she starts.

"Yeah, we should probably…"

"Get ready. We should get ready." She fidgets with her hands and I chuckle at how damn cute she is in those ridiculous pajama pants. I can't help but mess with her, just to see more of that glimmer in her eyes.

"Probably should change you out of those super sexy pajama pants. Don't want anyone trying to steal you on my watch." I grin and watch her mouth drop as her eyes fall to her pants. When they return to mine, her amused smirk has me grinning wider.

"Yeah? Well you should probably put a shirt on while we're at it. Can't have you wakin' the dead with those guns. Wait… technically you'd be killing someone with guns… I mean your pecs… Not that—"

I erupt into loud laughter. I can't help it. I start flexing my pecs and her hands shoot up covering her eyes.

"Oh my god, what are we doing?!"

"Having a pleasant Saturday. Now, if you're done with the gun show, let's get ready and go see some dead people."

"Sounds *dead on* with what I was thinking."

God, she's so fucking cute.

PRIDE

Megan

We're walking up the stairs to my front door after a long but fantastic day. Everything was perfect. Not that it was a date, but in my little fairytale head, it *was* the perfect date. I can't remember the last time I enjoyed myself as much as I did with Mason today. But now that the sun's set and night is luring in, I know it's time to say good night.

I insert my key in the lock, and the latch releases, opening just a smidge to my house. I turn to say goodnight, not realizing he's so close, I'm forced to raise my chin to meet his eyes. My heart does that girly little flippy thing at the way his stare penetrates down at me. He's not just looking at me, he's staring through me, to the deepest parts of my soul.

I want to invite him in. Beg him to do exactly what his eyes are silently telling me he wants to do. But I shouldn't. I can't. I've played on the wild side long enough. I need to stop whatever's happening between us before it goes too far. *It hasn't already?* Dammit. I need my heart to stop beating so rapidly.

Don't do it.

His aura surrounds me, and my skin begins to heat.

What you're doing is wrong.

His rugged attitude, those searing eyes. Anyone would mistake him for older. Maybe for just one night, I can forget he's my student.

Say goodnight, Megan.

Goodnight. Yep. I can do this. Two simple words, then turn around, go inside, and fill your gigantic need with ice cream, reality TV, and your vibrating collection of toys.

Good.

Night.

Meg—

"So, would you like to come in for—"

His head dips as he swallows the rest of my invitation in a kiss. His full lips still taste like the funnel cake we shared. I can't stop myself from leaning into him as he slowly yet hungrily devours me. This kiss, it's unlike the others. It's not wild or ravenous. It's slower. Gentler. He kisses me as if he's memorizing every part of me. This is where I should pull away. Send him home and ground myself. Rid myself of all the thoughts, urges, wrong feelings I'm starting to build for him. Why is my heart racing so fast? *'Cause you want this.* Goddammit! I do want this. I've wanted him since the moment I spotted him in the bar. And that forbidden need to be with him hasn't gone away.

I grab at his shirt and yank him into the house. I deepen our kiss as I walk us backwards toward my bedroom, both of us ripping at each other's clothes. "What are you up for tonight, Mr. Blackwell?" I pull away, peering into his heated gaze. I bite on my lower lip to stop me from jumping him right then and there, and reach for my nightstand, but he stops me.

"No. Not tonight." My mood plummets at his rejection. I've gone too far with him. I should have listened to my damn angel and sent him on his way. He probably thinks I'm some sort of fetish weirdo. Shame shatters my mood, and I retreat a step away from him.

"What just happened there?" he asks.

I'm too embarrassed to even make eye contact. "Nothing. Just…I shouldn't have been so…you probably think I'm—"

"Beautiful?" he lowers his lips to mine. He kisses

me, and it's so damn gentle and sweet, I want to weep. Without breaking contact, he lifts me up and lays me on my bed, his large body covering mine. "Tonight, I just want you. I want to savor you. Every inch of your body. Gonna be the fight of my life to go slow with you, but I need to. I need to show you just how beautiful you are." He lowers his mouth to my neck, leaving his print on my flesh, kiss by kiss, until his lips are wrapped around my breast. "You're like a gift, and I need you to know just how much I want to treasure you." His teeth graze my nipple. He doesn't bite down as he normally would; instead, he lazily works his tongue in circular motions over my bud, working me into a slow frenzy.

"Mason..." His words, his skin against mine. This sudden security he offers me. I buckle under his touch when his teeth finally close around my nipple.

"So, it's Mason now?" The vibrations of his deep chuckle bring my back off the mattress, whimpering from the overwhelming desire he's building inside me.

My trembling hands work their way into his thick hair. "Mason, please..." I don't know what I'm pleading for. He makes me want so many things, it scares me. He has me plunging deep into the thirsty sea of lust, drowning in everything he's offering me. But the deeper I plummet into the abyss of our forbidden attraction, the heavier my emotions become, and I know it's no longer just physical between us.

"Absolutely beautiful. You know that, right?" he whispers against my skin, dropping down to my ribcage, his tongue caressing my navel. "Your skin, so soft. The taste of you, Heaven on my tongue." The warmth of his breath and his praise completely unravels me. My eyes flutter shut as his teeth graze down along my pelvis. "God, your body is buzzing as I touch you." Spreading my legs apart, he presses his nose to my center. He opens me wide and licks between my folds. "I want to fuck you hard 'til you beg for me, but I need to fuck you slow. I need to cherish you. Will you let me?" He lifts his head to capture my eyes. His intense stare sets fire to my core. He's rendered me speechless, and I can only respond with a swift nod. His smile isn't predatorial. It's thankful. He's thanking me for giving myself to him. He lowers his head, pressing sweet kisses to my inner thigh. Taking his time to work back up to my center, he licks my sex.

I'm not sure I can handle this new side of him. His intensity is almost too much. "Mason," I whimper his name just as his tongue fills me. His strokes are measured, yet deep, sucking me until my legs begin to quiver. He knows he has me, yet he continues to relish in the slow build-up of my pending orgasm. He hasn't attempted anything beyond his simple tongue lashing, and I'm just as worked up as I am when he's taking me in the darkest of ways. "Mason, I'm gonna..." I warn him, because his slow assault is more intense than anything we've shared yet. My fingers curl into his hair, and my lips part on a silent moan as my orgasm brings me to an euphoric place unfamiliar to me.

He continues to stroke me, until my fingers release my death grip. He raises his head, and I start to sit up. "Where do you think you're going?" he asks, crawling up my body, using his lips to heat every inch of skin he presses down on.

"Your turn," I reply, but when I try sitting up farther, he pushes me down.

PRIDE

"I told you. Tonight, it's about you."

"Yeah, but—"

"This may never be anything more than what it is right now. You may wake up in the morning and regret what we're doing, and that battle in your head may finally win out, convincing you we ain't right together. So, tonight, I need to show you—prove to you, if just for tonight, how fucking important you're becoming to me." His head dips, and his lips are over mine, kissing me with the same slow intensity. He doesn't force my lips open but waits for the invitation. He wants me to show him, admit that this, us, together…we're a force. He wants me to surrender my doubts and allow him inside, not just the physical parts, but possibly the emotional parts too.

Fuck, fuck, fuck, what am I doing? So much of this is wrong, but I've never felt so right. He makes me feel so… wanted. I could be risking everything by going forward with this. Everything I've worked so hard for. And what if this is just a phase? For him *or* me? But what if I take a chance on someone who has never made me feel so cherished, needed, happy, fulfilled? What if?

What if I let him go? Could I live with the realization that something mediocre as age and status got in the way of being with someone who finally makes me feel so… perfect?

No. I can't.

I can't imagine pushing Mason away and giving up this happiness he envelopes me in. Maybe risking it all is, in the end, giving me even more? It all hits me like a ton of bricks and my lips part. I'm giving him my answer by wrapping my arms around his neck and bringing his head closer. This time, he kisses me back with the ferocity of him I crave.

"Fuck, I want you. Not just your sexy body, but your mind. I wanna own your fucking soul." He kisses me harder, his tongue dominating my mouth. I press my pulsating sex into him, in desperate need of a connection.

"Mason, fuck me. Please. I need you," I beg.

His mouth rips from mine, his stare, a fire of passion. "I wanna fuck you bare. I'm clean. I haven't been with anyone...not in a while."

There's a lot of carelessness in his request, and I should say no, but the thought of nothing standing between us sets a burn to my belly. "Okay. Yes."

His eyes darken, and for a moment, I fear he's changed his mind. His hand lifts, and he cups my face. "Fucking perfect. I don't even know how to say it otherwise. You're more than that. In every way." He aligns himself between my legs, and I feel the tip of him at my entrance. I'm way past wet, and my arousal allows him to easily push inside me. No words describe how good he feels bare, filling every part of me. "Fuck, you feel so good." He pulls out, the vein in his forehead protruding, and with a low moan, he drives back into me. He takes my mouth savagely and swallows my own cry of pleasure, his thick cock thrusting in and out.

"Oh, Mason." I want to weep from the overwhelming need. My legs wrap around his hips, and I beg him to take me harder, faster. This slow torment is killing me. He brings his hand under my butt and flips us.

"I want you to ride me. Wanna see your face as you take me."

My belly tightens at his request. He's all man, his muscles like stone on full display and bulging. He grabs my

PRIDE

hips and bounces me up and down his shaft. My hands press against his pecs, my fingers caressing the flower tattoo over his heart. Something dark flashes in his eyes, and he's pushing my hand away, sitting forward. His mouth is at my shoulder and his fingers digging into my ass cheeks as he continues to pump in to me.

Reverberations of sex and moans fill the room, our bodies heated, crashing into one another. Sweat builds between us, and I'm not sure I'll make it out of this one alive. My hands go back into his hair, and my fingers curl at how deep inside me he is in this position. I want to ride him harder and wilder, but his hand grips tighter into my skin, forcing me to slow down.

"Need to fuck you slow. Forever."

"Mason, I can't, it's too much," I plead.

"Let me be yours. I'll take care of you."

I shake my head violently. "We can't."

His grip only hardens, and he drives up into me. "We can. There's nothing stopping us."

"There is. My job. Your age, we can't—*ahhh*," I moan as his teeth bite at my shoulder.

"Fuck that. You're mine. You want this. I can't let you go now. Let me in. We'll figure it out."

"Mason," I pant his name, my hips grinding over his cock, my mind spinning.

"That's right. Say my name. The name of the man who's gonna own you. Fuckin' ride me." His hands are ruthless, slamming my ass into him, fucking me so deep, I can no longer think straight. I grind into him, my hand reaching for his face and cupping his cheeks while my mouth covers his. I kiss him hard and wild. "What's it gonna be baby?"

"Yes," I breathe, and he loses it. He flips us, and my back hits the mattress. He starts pounding into me, a hand at my pussy, rubbing hard at my clit. My vision begins to blacken as vibrations shoot down to my toes and I bite down on my tongue as my orgasm detonates and sends me over the edge of euphoria. With one last low growl from Mason, I feel the warmth of him explode inside me.

"Jesus Christ," he grunts, falling to his back and tucking me close to his chest. "I get you to agree we're good only for you to nearly kill me."

I laugh and slap him on his bare chest. "Blackmailing me into the orgasm of the century isn't technically agreeing."

He kisses the top of my head. "Can't take it back now. Plus, there's a lot more where that came from."

I lay my head on his chest, and his fingers thread their way into my hair. I'm listening to the beating of his heart and he suddenly becomes rigid underneath me when my fingers trail over the flower tattoo. "What's the story behind this one?" I ask. The flower is stunning. But wrapped around it are sharp, nasty thorns. It's beautiful, yet so angry. His hand, for the second time, stops my fingers from touching it. I raise my head. "I'm sorry. I didn't mean—"

"Don't apologize. It's just nothing I want to talk about."

I nod and rest my head back on his chest. "All right. Maybe, tell me something about you? Where'd you grow up? What kinda things were you into? I feel like you know what a geek I was, and I barely know anything about you."

He presses his lips to the top of my head again. "You know my cock has a fondness for ya." I slap him hard this time. "Ouch, okay. Fine, you win," he laughs. "I don't

PRIDE

have a very pretty story like yours, unfortunately. Jumped around a lot. Landed here."

"Way to keep it to the basics, Casanova," I joke. "You've gotta give me more than that. Why'd you pick St. Augustine? Are you from New Orleans? When's your birthday?"

His body tenses. "What's this, an interrogation or some shit?" he asks, missing a bit of the lightheartedness in his tone.

I raise my head to face him. "Of course not. I just wanted to get to know you. If we're gonna...you know, it's fine—"

"Shit, I'm sorry. I just have a past I don't like talking about, that's all."

His statement drips with sadness and makes me frown like a huge jerk. He doesn't have to tell me details for me to figure out he had a hard childhood. He doesn't dress like the rest of the bleeding rich college kids, not that I mind. His roguish bad boy attire is totally hot. Now I feel like an even bigger jerk for bragging about my fancy upbringing, loving parents, and adventures, when he probably had none of those things. "No, I'm the one who's sorry. I shouldn't have pushed."

He cradles me in his arms, adjusting us so we're laying on our sides. "I've lived in New Orleans my whole life. Moved around a lot so can't call any certain town our home. My parents died when I was eleven, my sister nine. She's here, so I followed her here to be close to her." He dips down, pressing his lips to mine for a short, sweet kiss. "And I got the tattoo to impress a girl who didn't wait around long enough to be impressed."

We stare at one another, until I lift myself up, push

him onto his back, and straddle him. "I'm sorry to hear about your parents," I start, leaning low to press my lips to his. I kiss him and pull back. "I'm sorry you had to move around a lot and didn't have a place to call home." I repeat my actions. He lets me. "And I'm sorry a girl broke your heart." This time, he locks his hand behind my head, keeping me in place as his lips fuse to mine. He then takes all control, kissing me, his tongue working its way into my mouth.

A hoarse squeal falls from my mouth as his hand reaches back and swipes along my bare butt cheek. My body jolts, thrusting forward. He bites my bottom lip and grabs at both sides of my ass. "Don't ever apologize for that shit." He grinds his hardening dick into me. "My misjudgments ain't any reason for you to say sorry." Another thrust, and his dick becomes slick from my building arousal.

"I just thought—"

"Don't need your sympathy. Need you for you. Need you to just understand." He thrusts up, and I adjust him so he's able to easily slide inside me. I rock back and forth, losing myself in the sensation of how great he feels filling me.

"I understand," I moan, back and forth, back and forth. I release his mouth and sit forward so I can watch his eyes darken as I ride him.

"Fuck, you're beautiful like this. Riding my cock."

And he has no idea how breathtaking he is. Watching him as our bodies connect, me taking all of him, riding him. There are no words to explain just how insanely, crazy, perfect this moment is. I moan loudly when he pinches my nipple and follow it up with a low purr when

PRIDE

he starts working my clit in a circular motion.

How fucked up is this?

How fucking *awesome* is this?

"This is crazy. We're crazy," I breathe, riding him faster.

"Fuckin' crazy for you." He throws his hips up, thrusting deeper inside me. I wince, almost pained at how big, and deep he is, but his hand squeezing my butt to the point he'll leave marks detours the pain into ultimate pleasure.

"This can't end well. We're gonna get caught."

"Then we deal with it. Ain't losin' you 'cause of some stupid rules bullshit." His grip slides forward, squeezing my hips and starts working me up and down on his cock. "You agreed. We're in this now." Up and down, hard and fast. "You're mine. Your beautiful fucking cunt and mind are mine." That does it for me. My inner walls threaten to choke his dick to death as my orgasm reaches a whole new level of ecstasy. My fingernails dig into his pecks, holding on for dear life as I threaten to pass out and float away. He takes no pity on me and flips me and continues to ram into me until I feel him grow in girth and explode inside me.

Once we manage to catch our breath, he lifts himself and presses a kiss to the middle of my breastbone, and I sigh in complete contentment. I'm sated, and my eyes are half closed. "I'm never gonna be able to convince myself you're a bad idea if we keep doing stuff like that."

He falls to my side, his head snuggling into the crook of my neck. "Then stop fighting it. Stop creating this rulebook for us to follow. Just be us."

"I know. I'm just scared."

His lips press to my neck. "There're bad people out

there. People who thrive to destroy. But I won't let that happen. I've got you. Hulk smash anyone who gets between us."

I can't help but chuckle. That darn silly name from the bar. But I believe him. I roll onto my side, catching his beautiful, sated eyes. "Yeah…well, maybe once you catch your breath you can Hulk smash that pretty cock of yours into me again."

His eyes light with a fire that instantly warms my belly. "You just call my cock pretty?" he asks, his brows up, that mischievous smile growing.

"Yep. Hoping that pretty cock finds its way into my mouth first too." I squeal in excitement when he jumps up and throws his body over mine and straddles my chest, stroking himself as he taps the tip of his semi hard dick against my lower lip.

"Well, open up, baby. Hulk's gonna feed ya."

Winner.

VII

UINCENDUM NATUS

FOURTEEN

Mason

The sound of Megan's alarm has me groaning and tucking her warm little body into me. "Call in sick," I mumble into her hair. Her warm breath against my chest awakens my dick, and I snuggle her closer.

"Mmmm...can't."

"Yeah, you can. Teachers play hooky all the time. Tell 'em you're sick. I'll take care of you. Tend to every single part," I murmur, pulling away and placing my mouth around her nipple. Her hands find their way into my hair, pulling me closer. I suck on her plumpness, earning a sweet moan. "That's it, baby," I praise, knowing she'll give in.

"Mason," she warns, but her voice is weak. I bet it won't take much to get my girl to play sick.

"It's *Doctor* Mason. Need to tend to my sick patient," I tease, dropping my hand down her stomach, dipping into her silky folds. I'm rewarded by her wet pussy, and she wastes no time rubbing against my hand. "That's right. Just the medicine my girl needs…" I insert a finger inside her when my phone goes off. The ring is the one I set for Evelyn.

"Fuck." I continue to pump into her slowly. The soft purrs falling from her lips fog my need to stop and answer the call. The ringing stops, then starts again. "Fuck, I gotta get that." I thrust into her faster, trying to get her off, but then her snooze alarm buzzes again, killing the moment.

Megan giggles in my chest. "Raincheck?" she says, and with a hard sigh, I pull my finger out of her warmth. Throwing my legs off the bed, I grab for my phone.

"What's up, Evelyn?" I start.

"Mason."

Just the way she says my name has me on immediate alert. "What happened?" I snap, searching for my shirt. "You hurt?"

"No. But I need to talk to you. Not over the phone."

I'm already throwing my shirt over my head and searching for my jeans. "Be there in twenty. Sit tight." I hang up and turn to a sleepy Megan. "Everything okay?" she asks, climbing out of bed and throwing a robe over her naked body.

"Yeah. My sister. I gotta go." I dip down and give her a rough kiss on her kiss-bruised lips. "See you in class?" I say, and I feel her smile against my lips.

"Don't be late, or I'm gonna need to keep you after."

Fuck, her little dirty side has me debating on delaying my sister and taking care of the growing bulge

PRIDE

in my damn pants. I throw my arm around her, pulling her into me, a squeal sounding like heaven leaving those plump lips I crave. "You better depend on me staying after. Gonna wipe that board clean with those beautiful tits of yours while I fuck you from behind, teach." I release her just in time to enjoy those pretty, turned-on eyes before I head out.

My thoughts are all over the damn place as I make my way to my sister's dorm. For one, I know I need to come clean with Megan. She needs to know. Every time she confesses her worries about my age, I fight myself from coming out with the truth. If she just knew my age, it wouldn't be an issue. But to come clean with that, I need to come clean with it all. My past. How I got here. The Elite. Her fucking psychotic aunt. But how would she take it? Would she believe me? I just know I can't risk what I have with her.

I'm hustling through the dorms, when I throw Evie's door open. She whips around from the window and I take in her frazzled appearance. Her hair's a mess and if I was a gambling man, I'd bet she hasn't slept at all. "What's wrong?" I spit out, examining her from top to bottom for injuries, bruising, anything.

"Nothing. Well…not nothing, but I'm fine."

"Yeah, doesn't ease my worry. You called me frantic. There's a reason behind it," I say, slamming the door and scoping her room to make sure no one else is in the room.

"I found something."

"What do you mean you *found* something?"

"Well...not found but heard. Early this morning, when I was walking back to my dorm." That comment strikes a nerve with me.

"What do you mean you were walking? Why the fuck were you out early walking home?"

Guilt washes over her as she struggles to think of a lie. I know her. "Evie?"

"I was coming home from a guy's house, but please! Mason, let it go. That's not important right now."

"Damn right it is. Now isn't the time to be escapading around campus with dudes you don't fucking know—"

"I know him!" she cuts me off.

"Who the fuck is he?"

She stalls.

"Evie—"

"None of your business. I haven't drilled you on why you're running around with your theology professor." That one catches me off guard.

"How the fuck—?"

"Listen, it doesn't matter. Just please listen. When I was walking home, I had to cut through the quad, passing the admissions building. It was still dark, but when I turned the corner, I saw two shadows. Then I heard their voices. One was Lillian." I'm immediately on alert. "She was arguing with some man. I couldn't get a good look at who it was. He was heavier set, that's for sure, but it wasn't anyone I've seen before."

"Did they see you?"

"No. I stood back and tried to listen. Whatever it was they were arguing about had something to do with The Elite. I'm sure of it. They were arguing about a book. The

PRIDE

wind was heavy and not blowing in my favor, so their voices trailed away from me, but it was definitely heated. I heard the word 'members,' and something about making sure no one gets ahold of some book."

"What fucking book are they talking about?"

"I have no idea, but it's obviously important to whatever it is they're up to. It also proves Lillian isn't the one heading The Elite. Mason, I think she's just another player. This club. It's bigger than just the Griffins. I know it, and I guarantee if we find that book, it'll prove it."

She's right. We need that book. I knew Lillian wasn't working alone. And this just proves it. But who the fuck is it? And what is this book?

"A few more heated words were said, then Lillian escaped into the building. I don't know if she had the book with her, but if she does, I bet—"

"It's in her office."

Evelyn nods. "We need to get that book. This could be our escape. If we expose them, we can finally be free— all of us."

I diverge my attention back to her. "What do you mean, *all* of us?"

There she goes, shutting down again. There's something she's not telling me. "Evelyn." I say her name in warning. Now is not the time to keep secrets. Especially from one another. If anything, the only people we should trust is each other.

"I just mean us, everyone else involved in The Elite. Micah, Megan Benedict." Fuck, she's right. If we blew this whole underground society out of the water, it would save Megan from the destruction heading her way. I'm not going to expose her. That's a fucking fact. I'm falling hard and fast for her, there's no way I'm going to put her in any danger. I'll take down the whole fucking organization before I bring harm to her front door.

"Mason, I know that look in your eyes."

I bring my thoughts back to Evelyn. "What is that supposed to mean?"

"You're falling for her. I can tell. I've seen that look in your eyes before. Once. With—"

"Don't even say her name." I stop her. Megan is nothing like Dahlia. She isn't a fucking liar. She's smart, and kind, and selfless. My knuckles clench at my sides as the anger builds from memories. Evelyn wraps her small palm around my hand and gently squeezes.

"She's not her. But if you love her. I think you should be honest. Does she know how old you really are?"

"No." And it's killed me every time she puts our age difference as a barrier between us. But how am I supposed to tell her why our lives have intertwined? That her aunt is a cunt, who wants to ruin her life and I've been placed into hers to do just that? "It's not that easy."

"Why isn't it? She would understand. If she shares the same feelings, she'll hear you out. We'll get the book and you'll have proof. Maybe she knows something that could help us."

"She doesn't know shit. She practically idolizes Lillian. Has no idea her loving aunt wants to fucking take away everything she worked for because of her hatred. Her jealousy."

"But why does she hate her so much?"

"I have no idea, but I'm gonna find out—"

I get cut off by the buzzing in my back pocket. I reach for my phone. A text from an unknown number. When

PRIDE

I open the attachment my stomach drops. "No," I whisper painfully under my breath. "What the fuck did he do?" Why? I thought...

"What? What is it?" Evie asks trying to steal a glimpse at my phone. I'm confused and pissed. A video of Rhett going at Chastity behind some carnival ride plays over and over on my screen.

He wasn't going to do it. He wanted out. Someone had to have gotten to him.

"Fuck!" I bite out, knowing just who it was. There's no way he would have gone through with this.

"Mason, you're worrying me. What's going on?" I can't tell Evelyn the truth. Not yet.

"Listen, I've got some shit to handle. I want you to lay low. Can you stay at your boyfriend's tonight?" Her face falls. "What, he ain't your boyfriend? What the fuck are you doing sleeping with him if he ain't claiming you?"

"It's not like that. And sure. I'll figure it out."

I don't accept her answer, but time is running out. I need to shut this shit down now and tonight. I give my sister a hug and head out, needing to hit up the library to do some research.

On my way, I shoot a quick text to Micah.

Me: Yo, need a favor. Need you to keep an eye on my sister. She's got some boyfriend. You'd be doing me a solid if you figured out who the fucker is. Also need you to keep an eye out for her tonight. I'm cashing in my IOU.

I'm leaning against Micah's car, waiting for Rhett. He pulls into the open parking spot next to me and I jump into the passenger seat.

"Hey," he says warily.

"I know it must have been hard for you to do it, but it's enough. You're in," I say, hurt and disappointed. I thought better of him. I never imagined he would put The Elite before his feelings for Chastity. I take the coin out of my pocket and toss it at him. "I've informed the others of your status." He's glaring at me, pissed off, but mostly confused. *Fuck*. It wasn't him who sent it. "The video?" I say, needing him to confirm it was him.

He continues staring at me, until I pull out my phone, but it seems the devil is one step ahead of us all. Because in the same moment, Rhett's phone goes off, and the same obscene sounds of sex chime through his speakers.

"You didn't send me that?" I ask, already knowing the truth.

"What? Fuck no. Where did it come from?"

"No number. I thought you must have sent it from the phone it was caught on. So, you didn't know you were being filmed?"

"No," he snaps, showing the same fury I am. "Have you shown that to anyone?"

I should just come clean now. Tell him the truth about The Elite and Lillian. But what kind of monster would I be admitting my part in it all? So I fucking lie, like a horrible friend, an imposter brother. "I handed it over to The Elite, Rhett. I'm sorry, brother. I thought you had a change of heart."

"Fuck. Fuck. Fuck," he roars, slamming his hands against the steering wheel.

PRIDE

"Maybe there's a way we can track the sender?" I offer, even though I know exactly where it came from.

"It doesn't fucking matter now. It's out there." he says, closing his eyes.

"I'm sorry, Rhett." I truly am.

With nothing more to say I jump out and walk away. I pull out my phone and shoot off a text to God. Rhett's gonna need a brother by his side for this. Racing across campus, I hustle through the old doors of the library. I walk passed the hag receptionist and slice my finger across my neck, not missing an opportunity to fuck with her. When the blood rushes from her face, I laugh and head down the aisles that pop me out to the community computers.

Throwing my backpack on the chair beside me, I get straight to work. All this time and I've been searching for the wrong stuff. The Elite, St. Augustine, secret societies. Of course, that shit wouldn't lead me anywhere. It would be too easy. After what Evie discovered, it hit me. Read between the lines. I shouldn't be searching for what's out in the open, I should be searching for what's hidden. There was no specific timeframe for when The Elite began, but I remember Lillian telling me it's been thriving since 1942. I start with unexplained deaths around that time. Unsolved crimes, or strange shifts in political heads and law enforcement officials. I even Google the location of the abandoned nunnery.

By the time I'm done, my brain is swirling. Nothing in the news articles links them to The Elite, but there's no doubt in my mind they're related. The nunnery itself was a landmine for deaths, unsolved mysteries, and cult sightings. Not to mention all the unsolved crime or travesties that had killers walking free without a lick of legal action. The most recent article on Rhett's little brother.

How the fuck have they been getting away with this? I'm sick to my stomach after reading the articles on the Masters' family tragedy, so I grab my backpack and leave. They—whoever *they* are—need to be stopped. Which means I need to get into Lillian's office—tonight. My next move is to figure out when Lillian leaves at night and how to break into her office.

It's past midnight when I arise from the shadows. I watch as the last security officer makes his rounds. Just like Envy said he would, the officer gets into his car, abandoning his post for a coffee run. It works out perfectly. It's just enough time for me to get in and out. I use the spare janitor key I snagged from the old guy earlier after telling him there was a gas leak and everyone had to evacuate the building. I took the time to locate all the motion detectors—not that they're active. I called in a favor with Envy, who's a hacking genius, and got him to mess with the system so it plays the same reel over and over, never picking up my body movement inside the building. One had to wonder why they go through such lengths to guard the admissions office, but I'm starting to realize why—there's something important they don't want anyone to get their hands on.

Even though Envy swore I was golden, I keep my back to the wall as I hustle down the hallway to Lillian's office. I use the first key to enter the reception office, and quickly

PRIDE

make my way through the waiting area to her door. With the second key, I slip it through the lock. "Bingo." The bolt clicks and the door slides open. He warned me I have exactly seventeen minutes until the security guard returns from his coffee run, so I waste no time and dart straight toward her desk. I drop to my knees and try the bottom drawer, but of course it's locked. Pulling out the small set of tools, I work on the lock until it pops open.

"That'a girl," I praise, clicking the flashlight app on my phone and digging through the drawer. Mounds and mounds of manila folders are stacked, names on each corner. "Shit, how many people does she have under her claws?" I open a few files and snap a few photos from my phone. I continue to push through the pile but find nothing that resembles a book. "Fuck, where is it?" I dig deeper, all the way to the bottom. Nothing. "Dammit!" I curse, looking at my stop watch and seeing I only have nine more minutes until I need to get the fuck outta here. I give up on the bottom drawer and begin digging through the top one. It not being locked tells me nothing important would be kept there, so I try the other ones. All unlocked. My frustration quickly builds, and I'm feeling the failure begin to hit me. I pull her middle drawer open. Fucking nothing. "Fuck!" I hiss, and pound on the desk. That's when a stack of papers, taped and hidden underneath the drawer, feather to the floor. I quickly bring my light to the documents and start taking snapshots of as many as I can. I stop on the final page, reading a few of the bold headings.

Conclusive of sexual—

That's all I get through before something metal smacks against the back of my head. The unexpected blow causes me to drop my phone, my head going down and smashing against the floor. I snap into fight mode, attempting to roll to my side, but another strike comes to my back, knocking me back down. I kick my legs out in hopes to trip my assailant, but they take a hard swing to my kneecap. I howl out in pain, grabbing for my wounded knee when two strong hands lift me from the ground. I try to swing, but I'm too dizzy from the crack to my head. A fist meets my eye, and begins pummeling my face in.

I'm fighting not to pass out when I'm dropped to the ground. The air in my lungs seizes, and I hear a gun being cocked. The feel of cold metal presses to my temple, and just as a low chuckle breaks the silence, they pull the trigger.

VII
UINCENDUM NATUS

FIFTEEN

Mason

Bang. Bang. Bang.

A thudding sound rings out in the distance. More like a muffled echo, because it sounds like millions of miles away.

Bang. Bang. Bang.

There is it again. I think it's banging, but I'm not sure. I sit up, and pain explodes in the back of my head. What the fuck? Throwing myself back down, I try prying my eyes open, but one seems to be swollen shut. From what I can see, I'm in my apartment, in the middle of the living room. I inspect myself, and there's blood on my clothes. I take note of my surroundings. How the fuck did I get back here? I remember being in Lillian's office. The files. The hidden document. I feel around for my phone, but it's not in my pockets. Fuck.

More banging sounds, but it seems so far away. I lift my hand to my ear and draw back with blood on my fingertips. The gunshot. Whoever that motherfucker was shot out my eardrum. Trying to stand, I groan at the pain radiating from my knee. When I make it to my feet, my door splinters and flies open. Cops explode around me, screaming and pointing their weapons. Their voices are too muffled, but I can understand enough to know they're telling me to freeze.

"I didn't do shit," I say, my own voice seeming distant. My words fall on deaf ears as my arms are ripped behind me and placed into cuffs. "What the fuck!" I fight the officer, groaning at the pain in my head and knee.

"Mason Blackwell, you're under arrest for the assault of Lillian Griffin. You have the right to remain silent..." the officer starts reading me my rights, and I go buck wild under the restraints.

"You're kidding me. I didn't touch that bitch! She's fucking lying!" A baton hits my back, and memories of two years ago come flooding back. I'm seventeen all over again. Fighting to get to my sister. Away from Lillian.

I'm being dragged out of my apartment when Sloth appears. "Don't worry. I'll have you out in an hour. Tight-lipped and quiet. One hour," he says as I'm hauled out and thrown into the cop car.

"Mr. Blackwell. What were you doing in Mrs. Griffin's office?"

PRIDE

Silence.

"Did you know she was going to be working late?"

More silence.

"Mr. Blackwell. The security system has you on tape entering the building and assaulting Mrs. Griffin. We don't need you to confess, we would just like some reasoning behind your attack."

"Bitch is lying. I didn't fuckin' touch her," I snap, pulling the restraints and leaning over the table. My hard stare doesn't faze the officer, and I don't give a fuck.

"Well, the bruises say something else. Can you tell me why you were there? Why you attacked her? She's told us you've been stalking her since the beginning of school. Making unprofessional passes at her. She said she's only tried to help you. Are you infatuated with your counselor, Mr. Blackwell?"

I try to jump over the table in a fit of rage, but the cuffs locked to my chair stop me. "The only infatuation I have with Lillian Griffin is the lust inside me that craves her blood splattered all over fucking campus."

The door throws open and Sloth fills the entryway. "I thought I said tight-lipped and quiet?" He rolls his eyes, as if he's just out for a stroll picking me up for study hour and not in an interrogation room being accused of the bullshit Lillian set me up for.

"Officer Campbell, Mason at this time, is free to go," says the officer who entered the room with Sloth. Officer Campbell's lips purse as I stare at the throbbing vein in his forehead. He slams his fist on the table.

"We're not done here, Mr. Blackwell. Better not go far. With a threat like that, we'll be watching you."

I want to spit in his face. The other officer unlocks

my cuffs, and I shoot up and follow Sloth out of the police station.

"What the fuck! I didn't touch Lillian."

"Didn't say you did, brother." Sloth walks down the police department stairs to his car. "Get in. We've got some shit to take care of."

Fuck that. "No, I gotta find that cunt and fuckin' do what I should've done in the beginning."

"Finding Lillian is not the key to unlocking this shitstorm, my brother. Plus, she's smart. She'll know you're coming for her." Good. 'Cause when I find her, she's done for. "She'll be one step ahead of you, man," he says, strangely calm, then lights up a smoke as he pulls away from the station.

I'm so blinded by hate and revenge, I don't give a fuck. "Text Rhett. His girl will know where she's hiding out." I massage my fingers around my bruised wrists. I lean over to get a look at myself in the side mirror and wince. My right eye is swollen, and dried blood covers my face and my shirt.

"Got Lust's location," Sloth says.

"Let's go."

I plow through the front door like a man on a mission. More like a beast ready to rip out the throats of his prey. I stop in the foyer when I'm met by Rhett.

"Whoa! What happened to you? Why are you covered in blood?"

"Where the fuck is she!" I yell through the house.

PRIDE

"Who, man?"

"Lillian!" I grab for the first thing near me and smash it against the wall, blind with rage. When Chastity suddenly appears, I jump toward her. "Where the fuck is Lillian?" I demand. Rhett steps forward, bringing a scared Chastity to his side.

"Where the fuck is Lillian!" I roar, not caring how fucking manic I look right now. Rhett becomes territorial over his girl, placing her behind him like I may attack her or some shit, but she pushes him away.

"Babe, it's fine. He wouldn't hurt me. She's at my uncle's, why?"

"Tell me what the fuck is going on," Rhett demands. "Whose blood is that?"

I don't wait around to explain. I storm out, leaving Sloth behind. Before he has a chance to get back in the car, I jump in the driver's seat and burn out. I need to do this alone. I can't, and won't, have another brother go down for me.

I race through the streets, breaking speed limits left and right, until I pull up to the gates of the Benedict mansion. The gate is closed, so I slam on the intercom, waiting for someone to open it—to no avail. Getting back in the car, I put it in reverse, then hit the gas and slam into the gate. The steel rods bend, but don't allow me access. I reverse again, then punch back down on the gas. Two more hits, and the gate opens.

I speed up the long driveway, and once I pull up to the house, I jump out and race toward the door. That's when it flies open. I'm about to haul myself at them when Megan fills the doorway.

I halt before crashing into her. Her eyes are swollen

and red. She's been crying. Fuck.

"Megan—"

"How could you?"

"Megan, listen to me—"

She smacks me hard across my already bruised and broken face. "You're sick, you know that? My aunt told me everything. I saw the bruises. How could I have been so blind?" She starts crying. I attempt to reach for her, but she swats my hand away as if my touch disgusts her. "Don't you *dare* touch me. Don't *ever* touch me again! I know your whole plan! I know everything!" she yells on a hoarse sob.

"Megan, no you don't. Lillian's fucking lying to you."

"How dare you. You think I'm gonna believe you over my own aunt? A felon with a record a mile long. Drugs, theft, *abuse*? You're not even eighteen. All this time…"

"Those charges were years ago when I was a fucking kid. That abuse allegation came from Lillian herself. I didn't do shit! It was her way of keeping her claws in me—"

"Stop lying! I know everything, you sick bastard. Your obsession with her. How you were stalking her. She told me you weren't even a student at St. Augustine. I looked into you. And there are no records of a Mason Blackwell registered."

The fuck? "Listen, that was all her."

"Get out of here, or I'm going to call the police."

"Babe—"

"GET OUT! I want you gone. I thought we…I thought…" She begins to sob harder. I take a step toward her, but she throws her hand out to stop me. "I've been so foolish with you. Little did I know I was just part of your plan to blackmail my aunt."

"What are you talking about? No! What we have is—"

"I saw the photos. The night at the motel. The ones you gave to Aunt Lillian, saying you'd expose me if she didn't give you what you wanted."

That fucking bitch.

Thud.

Thud.

Thud.

My heart is pounding viciously.

My lungs squeeze, and I start to panic. I'm losing her. I may already have. "Megan, no. Please, you have to listen to me."

"I said get out."

"No, she's fucking lying. LILLIAN!" I yell her name. "LILLIAN!" Megan blocks me.

"That's it, I'm calling the police!"

Two hands reach behind me, and I'm about to go apeshit when I hear Sloth's voice. "We gotta go. NOW."

"No, wait. Megan, please! You gotta fucking believe me!" But the door is already slamming in my face and Sloth is dragging me to his car.

VII

UINCENDUM NATUS

SIXTEEN

Mason
Two Days later...

"Mason?" I hear my sister's voice from the dark room of Micah's apartment. I've been holed up here the last two days trying to heal, mentally and physically. Sadly, only the physical stuff is mending. Lillian officially won. She fucked me. I tried to cross her, and she did exactly what she promised she would do: ruin me.

Envy hacked into the school records, and low and behold, there's no record of me ever attending St. Augustine. She set me up. At the least, deleted me before she went off on her bullshit assault story. He swore the security cameras were down, and they're lying about having me in the building. But there's no doubt she somehow knew

PRIDE

I was there. And framed me. She came out with bruises around her neck and cheek, but they sure as fuck weren't from me. Self-inflicted, if I had a say in it, but no matter what, it still showed up in the local university news that an imposter student attacked a well-known counselor on campus. The one thing she hasn't done is give my name to the press, which makes me super fucking wary. That just tells me she's not done with me yet. But I'm done with her. Megan won't talk to me. She thinks so low of me, and knowing what I could have done to her, I deserve her hate.

"Mason, can I come in?"

"Not a good time, Evie," I say, and roll on my side, offering her my back. Besides getting up to grab a new bottle of any sort of booze Micah has at his place, I haven't left the extra spare bedroom or even bothered to turn on a fucking light.

I feel the bed dip behind me. "Remember when we were kids? Before the Griffins?"

"Evie, just don't—"

"No, listen. Remember when I would get scared all the time and want you to sleep with me, but they felt it was inappropriate since you were older, so instead of sleeping in the bed with me, you built a fort in my room and slept on the floor for almost a month until I wasn't so scared of the dark anymore?"

"Yeah, I remember. You finally kicked me out 'cause my snoring was overpowering your fear of the dark." We both chuckle at the memory.

"Remember when we were living with the Kellers and they would force me to eat carrots? I swore I was allergic to them, but they made me eat double 'cause they said I was lying."

Even in the dark, I sense the sadness. "Yeah." What fucking foster parents force a ten-year-old to eat a food that was causing rashes all over her skin and her throat to swell?

"And remember eating them off my plate every time she would take a drink of her beer?"

I laugh. "I thought I was going to turn into a carrot myself, I'd eaten so many."

Her hand settles on my shoulder. "My point is you've always taken care of me. And I just wanted to thank you for that."

At that, I roll over. I find her face in the darkness and brush the back of my still scabbed knuckles down her cheek. "Evelyn, I failed at keeping you safe. I should've done more to keep you away from whatever the hell you lived through while I was away." My heart bleeds at the possibilities of what she endured.

"He didn't touch me, you know. Mr. Griffin. He never touched me. He would come into my room at night drunk and sit on my bed and just talk. As if I wasn't even there. As if he was confessing all the bad things he had done." I sit up and grab for her hand, offering her the strength to continue. "He was a sick man. He confessed he wasn't going to touch me because I didn't look like her and that's who he loved the most. He said every bad deed he'd done was their fault because they looked like her."

"Like who?" I ask.

"I assumed Chastity. It was the night he confessed that, Lillian walked in. She started yelling, accusing him of everything under the sun. But then there was this odd calmness that struck her. And then she turned on me. Before I knew it, the police were there, Mr. Griffin was

PRIDE

nowhere to be seen, and you and I were being separated."

"Evelyn, I'm so sorry. I should've been there."

"Mason, there was nothing you could've done. I'm not telling you this to make you feel shitty or take blame. I'm telling you this to make a point."

"And that is?"

"It's my turn to take care of you."

"Evie—"

"Mason, no. You've been taking care of me your whole life. It's my turn. And right now, you need me. I'm not going to let you sit back and let her win. By doing nothing, she is."

"And what the fuck should I be doing, Evie? She's taken everything away from me. I have nothing." I wound her with my words. "Shit, I'm sorry. I have you. I only need you."

"You *have* me. But you also have your brothers."

"And I have faith if Megan hears the truth, you'll have her again too."

The mention of Megan opens the deepest wound of all. I bleed the most from the hurt and pain of losing her. "It's over, Evelyn. Let it be."

"Is it, though? Since when have *you* been the guy to just roll over and allow someone like Lillian Griffin to call the shots?"

"Since I ran out of options."

"Stop. Don't give up. That night, think. Did you get a chance to look around? Anything that struck you as odd while being in her office? Was there *anything* that could help—"

"Wait…" I hadn't put much thought to that night except for the painful beatdown I received, then being framed. But having Evelyn talk about it, I remember… "My phone." But then I remember the crunching sound of the screen being shattered. "Never mind. I took some photos and fuck, now that I think about it, I'd found some strange documents, but my phone was smashed, along with my face when some asshole jumped me." My mood sinks again. I watch my sister, preparing for the disappointment in her eyes. She's stone still. "Evelyn. I know I failed you—"

She jumps off the bed, and a few seconds pass before the lights flicker on and I shield my eyes. "What? What's wrong now?"

"Oh brother, nothing yet." She smiles which confuses me. "Your phone, it's the one Lillian gave you, right?"

I nod. "Yeah, why?"

"And you told me before she was tracking you, right?"

"What are you getting at?"

"Your phone. If she was tracking you, she'd have to have had you connected to some sort of cloud. If that's the case, there's a good chance whatever was on your phone saved to that cloud. We don't need your phone. We just need someone who's tech savvy."

I watch her eyes light up, still reeling in what she's saying. "If we can find someone who can hack into the Apple system and pull the data from the cloud, we're in. We'd have what we need!" She beams, but her smile instantly falls. "But I don't know how to find that person without tipping off Lillian."

I sit up and throw my legs off the bed. "I've got a guy."

PRIDE

"Anything yet?" I tap my fingers on the frame of Envy's bedroom door.

"Almost, man," he says, not pulling his attention away from his computer screen. Whatever he's doing, he's been at it for a while.

"How does he know how to do this?" I spin around at my sister's presence, her focus on Envy's screen.

When I turn back, I see line after line of numbers, letters, numeric symbols all cluttered together. "No idea. Not askin' questions."

"Do you think he can get in? What if he can't—?"

"He will."

"But what if—?"

"In."

Envy's voice grabs our attention, and we both twist to see him facing us and wearing a shit eatin' grin. I push through the doorway with Evie right behind me. Envy swivels back around to face his computer and starts jamming on his keys.

"What the fuck is this? All I see is mumbo jumbo."

"It's the backdoor of her account."

"Yeah, and I can't read any of this shit," I reply, annoyed. This better not have been a waste of our time.

"And it's your lucky day, 'cause I can."

This time, Evie chimes in. "Why do you have all this stuff? How do you know how to do all this?"

Envy swivels back to face my sister, a lazy smile on his face. "Why are you asking to hack into the Master

Counselor's private cloud account? *Hmmm*?" He smiles wider once my sister fails to come up with a quick response. "Exactly. Let's keep our curiosity to ourselves." He turns back to the screen. Evie takes a step back, offering me an uncomfortable look. I nod for her to brush it off and bring my attention back to the screen. He continues to punch in numbers as I watch, confused.

"Seems you're in luck. Naughty Headmaster Counselor Griffin was definitely tracking you. This code right here?" He points. "That's you. These coordinates? All your locations. Anytime you took a shit, she knew about it."

I move closer to the screen, trying to decipher what he's looking at. "Any chance you can access the phone's pictures?"

"Yep." He's back at it, until a bunch of thumbnails appear. I peer closer, and sure enough, the photos I took of the documents are there.

"Hey, can we get a minute?" I ask.

Envy is already popping up from his chair. "Have at it. No peeking at any other tabs, though. Would hate for you to get more than you bargained for by snoopin'." He looks at my sister and winks. Then he's gone.

"Why—?"

"Forget him. Look." I take his seat and use the cursor to click on the first thumbnail. The photo enlarges, and I'm reading the screenshot document. My eyes widen at the bold titles. *Misconduct. Sexual abuse to a minor. Test result: positive.*

"Oh my god, do you think this is all true?"

I open another document and read. Police reports followed by large donations to the police department.

PRIDE

Another document, and another document, all showing a pretty sick discovery and a cover up. "Is this why? Why—?"

"It all makes sense now. Listen…" I start clicking on the file tab and sending each photo to his printer. "I need you to lay low. I'm gonna end this once and for all."

"Mason, no! You promised me."

"I promised I'd fix this. And that's what I'm gonna do." I press print on the last photo, then stand, Evie in a state of panic beside me. "I need you to hold on to something." I reach in my back pocket and hand her the gold trimmed card.

She unwillingly accepts it. "What is this?" She flips it from front to back. "No, Mason, no."

"If something happens to me, give it to Micah, he'll know what to do with it."

"No! You promised!" She starts to cry. "We'll find another way. We can go to the police with the information! They'll help us!" I begin to walk passed her, but she jumps in my path, her arms shoving at my chest. "You fucking promised me. This isn't you sticking to your promise. It's you *leaving* me—*again*." Her tears cascade down her face in rapid waves. My chest tightens at the pain I'm causing her. But this has to be done. I have to put a stop to her once and for all.

"Evelyn, calm down."

"No! I'm coming with you. You're not doing this alone."

"Yes, I am. I have to."

"No! You don't. Stop trying to be brave for everyone. You saw what happened the last time you went off alone. They almost killed you!"

And they should have. I'm done letting Lillian pull my

strings in this game. This is where I flip the tables, take those strings, and choke her near death. I grab Evelyn and pull her into my embrace, hugging her tightly to my chest. I kiss the top of her head. "I need to do this, okay? Nothing will happen to me, I promise. I won't stop until you're safe."

"I'm safe with you. Please."

"And with Lillian still around, I'll always be a target, which means I'll always be putting you in danger. Please. Don't make me have to worry about you right now. Stay low. Go to your boyfriend's. I'll seek you out once I'm done."

Her head raises off my chest, and I catch sight of her tear-stained cheeks. Her eyes are swollen, and it fucking kills me to see her this way. "You gotta trust me."

"I do trust you, it's them I don't trust. Mason, this Elite, if they can cover something as horrible as that up, what will they do if you cross them again?"

I'm about to find out.

I give Evelyn another squeeze and peel her away from me. "Do as I say. I'll be back as soon as I can. Keep your phone by you." She doesn't say another word. I walk out of Envy's room, and after discussing my plan, I'm gone.

VII

UINCENDUM NATUS

SEVENTEEN

Megan

The smoke alarm sounds for the second time in a row, and I rip the oven door open only to receive a gust of smoke to the face. "Shit!" I use my oven mitt to grab for the cookie sheet housing another batch of burnt cookies. "Seriously, this is just not my day!" I shout, fighting the quivering of my lower lip. How hard is it to cut, place, and bake? *Not hard at all if you weren't such a mess.* I take deep breaths, fighting back tears. I can do this. *No, you can't. You're on round two of failure.*

I take in my messy kitchen. I'm now going on round three of failure. But I refuse to give up. I'm too desperate to divert my thoughts so they don't go back to him.

I lay out a new tray, slide it back into the oven and sit on the couch to catch the end of a Judge Judy episode.

She's about to let some scumbag get spousal support from a girl he married while drunk off his ass for only two weeks, but my mind goes rogue, and I start replaying Lillian's frantic plea when she showed up at my door bruised and hysterical.

"Aunt—"

Aunt Lillian falls through my open doorway, forcing me to reach out and catch her. "I had to come straight here. You're in danger, darling." I gape at her, bruises forming around her neck and a welt growing over her cheek. "You need to know, Mason Blackwell, he's dangerous," she says, breathing heavily.

"Aunt Lillian, what are you talking about? Who did this to you?" I panic. She looks to have been assaulted.

"Megan, you must listen to me." She begins to shake me. "I know what's going on between you and Mason."

"What?"

"He's dangerous. He attacked me. Threatened me. If I didn't allow him to do...things to me, he would do horrible things to you."

My eyes go wide with shock, but even more confusion. "Aunt Lillian, you're not making any sense." How does she know about Mason? And why would he? He would never hurt me—

"Megan, he's not who you think he is..."

The blaring of the smoke alarm in the kitchen drags me out of the flashback, throwing me three feet off my seat. I run into the kitchen, fighting the dark cloud of smoke to realize I burnt my cookies. Again. Tears pool and fall, disintegrating on the hot tray. I scrape the charred cookies into the garbage. "Pull it together," I cry to myself. "If there is one thing you can control right now, it's making simple sugar cookies."

PRIDE

With a deep breath, I lay *another* batch on the sheet and shove them into the oven. I open my window to help get rid of the cloud of smoke. This time, I set a timer and go off to take a shower. It's supposed to help calm me and wash away the last two days of grime and pain over the lies and betrayal, but it only heightens the memories of him.

"Hold on to the wall," he orders, and I do what he says. My pussy is sore, but still pulsating for more. I throw my hands to the wet tile of the motel shower and hold on. He bends down, tossing a bare leg over his shoulder. My skin is pale compared to his colorful flesh. His tongue licks at me, pumping in and out of me, while he sucks my folds into his mouth. My head falls back against the shower wall, and my hands threaten to slip.

"Hold tight, or I might end up biting you."

My belly tightens, and one hand twitches, sliding an inch down the wall. He catches me, his strong fingers digging into my thigh. "Jesus Christ," I moan.

"Fuck, you taste like heaven." He pulls his tongue away to nip at my inner thigh. "Not sure I'm gonna ever be satisfied with you."

I know this is just a fantasy, but his words fill me just as much as his tongue and the pleasure he's giving me. "Hulk have big appetite?" I joke, and swallow my own whimper when he's up, flipping me, pushing my hard nipples to the cold tile, pressing his thick cock into my ass.

"Never knew it until you."

I'm struggling to catch my breath, my tears mixing with the water as I soak my body under the steaming hot spray. I'm using any effort I have to wash the suds out of my hair when the smoke alarm sounds again, causing me to slip and take out my shower curtain to avoid killing myself and falling in my tub. I stick my head out to check my phone where I set the timer, and low and behold, my battery's dead. With shampoo suds still thick in my hair and seeping into my eyes, I run in my birthday suit back to the crime scene of another batch gone bad.

"What the fuck, you stupid cookies!" I scream, whipping the oven mitt across the kitchen and knocking my plant off the counter. The pot shatters and soil explodes all over the floor. It was the perfect metaphor for how my world has felt since the moment Mason Blackwell came into my life.

Blackmail. Felon. Con artist.

One after another, I fight the sickness in my stomach, sitting in my parents' home as Aunt Lillian gives them her statement. Mason wasn't eighteen. He wasn't even a student at the university. He was obsessed with my aunt and using me to get to her. He threatened to expose my dark secret to the school and my family if she didn't give in to his sick obsession. He doesn't even want me. He wants her.

"He kept going on and on about how he's been stalking me since they were taken from our home. I tried to help him. We've wanted nothing but good things for those kids."

I cover my mouth in fear of expelling the small amount of food I have in my stomach. This can't be happening. I couldn't have been that stupid—that blind.

"Megan," my dad calls my name, not hiding the anger in his dominant tone. I look up, no doubt lacking any sort of color to my face. "Do you hear this? You're done with him. You're lucky I have the resources to hide this shameful scandal. How could you? Our name? Our legacy? Have you no sense of respect for yourself and your career? No less your family's?"

Trying to catch my breath, I wipe at my soaked

PRIDE

cheeks. Everything about us was a ruse. He lied to me. He fooled me. Or maybe I was just too wrapped up in the fantasy of us to see the signs. But everything felt so real. Genuine. My heart opened wide for him with every single promise he imbedded deep inside. But it was just to trick me. Get close to me as a ploy.

"Damn you." I grab for another set of oven mitts, removing the ruined batch of cookies. "So much for pulling a Martha Stewart move, making my house smell magical like warm sugar cookies." I sadly laugh at myself and dump the cookies in the trash.

The truth about Mason isn't the only shame I feel. The disappointment in my mother's eyes. My dad's anger. He wouldn't even look at me. I've spent my entire life trying to make my parents proud, and in an instant, I ruined everything. All because I had a desire and finally found a guy who made me feel normal.

"Yeah, well that guy doesn't truly exist." I throw the mitts and pull open my freezer to grab a frozen pizza instead. I'm washing my hands when my doorbell rings. My head whips toward the front of my house, curious who would be stopping be. My eyes search out the grandfather clock in the hallway. My family would still be in church. I dry my hands, grab a robe from the laundry room and cautiously make my way to the front door. Peeking through the curtain, I see a girl. It doesn't take a genius to see the resemblance. Her hair is lighter, and she may be shorter, but there's no hiding those steel eyes.

Unlocking the three bolts, I pull the door open.
"Hi, Megan. I'm—"
"Mason's sister."
"Oh...uh, yeah. Well, I was wondering if we can—"

"I have nothing to say to you or your brother. Now, if you'll excuse me." I start pushing the door shut when her hand slams on the door, stopping it. "Excuse me!"

"I think you'll want to hear what I have to say. This isn't just about Mason. It's about you too."

We stare at one another for a moment, her eyes haunting me, the same steel eyes as his, until I release the door. "Make this quick." I give her my back and walk into my living room. The sound of the door shutting, and her boots hitting the tile echo until she's sitting next to me.

"I'm sorry I didn't mean to be rude back there," she starts.

"This better be good. I have things to do."

She peers over my shoulder, her nostrils twitching. "Like what? Trying to burn your house down?"

"I was *trying* to bake cookies," I snap.

Her nostrils flare again, her eyebrows creasing as she takes another whiff of my living room. It does really stink in here. "Okay, well…"

"Yeah. Sure, get to it." She reaches to her side and shuffles into her purse until she retrieves a worn photograph. She hands it to me, and after some hesitation, I grab it. My eyes scan the photo. My aunt and uncle and cousin sitting proudly next to a younger Mason and his sister. It wasn't new information that the Griffin's fostered kids. I always thought it so admirable of them. But as kids, we were never exposed to them and my cousin, Chastity never spoke about them much.

"This isn't new to me. Aunt Lillian told me the story." I toss the photo back at her. The tears my aunt shed, rehashing the memory of Evelyn Blackwell and how she found my uncle in her room. The stealing.

PRIDE

"You don't know the real story."

"Oh, and what's that? You didn't lure my uncle to have sex with you? You didn't steal from them when all they wanted to do was help you? Mason's violent attacks on my aunt—"

"Those are lies," she spits at me.

"And you expect me to believe you? What, do you want me to feel *sorry* for you? I know how you got here, just like your brother. Blackmail." I jump up from my couch. "Actually, I want you to leave."

She follows suit and stands. "And I'm not leaving until you hear the truth. Afterward, if you still think your family is innocent, that's your burden to bear. I'm pretty sure my brother's in love with you and he's hurting bad, and it kills me to see him this way. I'd rather come over here and wipe your ass across the floor for the way you dismissed him, but I know you need to hear what I have to say. After that, it's on you. Now, sit the fuck back down."

Her fierceness sends my eyebrows up in shock. The fight in her to protect her brother. The acknowledgement that he loves me. My mouth goes dry. My tongue attempting and failing to wet my lips. I struggle to speak. I surrender to her demands and nod slowly, taking my seat. She does the same.

"The photo was taken about three years ago when we were first placed into the Griffins' home. To a passing eye, it looks like we're all happy. But there are lies behind those fake smiles." She hands me back the photo, and this time, I truly take it in. Mason is so much leaner. His arms are bare of any tattoos. His expression is still troubled, but not nearly as much as it is now. The permanent scars he wears behind those beautiful grey eyes.

"Nothing was as it seemed. Lillian was not the sweet, nurturing caretaker who made it her life's mission to help the helpless. She was the devil in disguise who had so much hate in her, she was suffocating herself with it."

The way she describes Lillian is unfamiliar to me. Far from the loving aunt I've grown up with. The one who would braid my hair at family parties or help me with my homework when she came by to visit with my dad. I want to demand she stop spilling such hate on someone who has been nothing but loving to me. But I also have this pinging feeling inside me that says I need to hear her out.

"We were with the Griffin's for a year. Our previous family, we thought we would stay with them until we chose to enter the world on our own. But she got pregnant, and well…when you finally get your own children, the temporary ones you have kinda just become that. Any who, Mr. Griffin, in that time, had been coming into my room late at night, drunk beyond comprehension." I clench my fingers at the fear of what may spill from her lips. "He never touched me. But the other girls they fostered weren't so lucky."

My lungs seize, feeling as if I just got kicked in the stomach. "No…"

"Yes. He'd come into my room late at night, booze making his tongue loose, and confess things. Stuff he'd done."

This can't be true. Uncle George would…could never. "I don't believe you. Why would he do such horrible things, but never to you?"

"Because I didn't look like his daughter."

The choked intake of breath causes me to sway in my seat. "Oh God, Chastity? Did he—?"

PRIDE

"No. He admitted he never touched her. He would cry sometimes because his desires were so intense, he was afraid one day he wouldn't be strong enough to restrain them. But from the time we were with them, he hadn't."

Oh, my poor cousin. The thought... I shake my head.

"The night we were removed from the Griffin house, Lillian caught George in my room. He'd come home from a business function. He was drunk and angry about something that happened. I would have never known what he meant then, but now it makes sense." I lift my hand to rest on hers. A tear escapes her sorrowed lids, and I give her the moment she needs before she continues. "The whole time, he was confessing secrets about The Elite. If I would've known to tell someone then...maybe...maybe I could have done something..."

"Honey, what are you talking about?" She's lost me. My uncle was part of many clubs. He was a high ranked member in our society. "He could've been talking about anything. His Golf Club maybe? The church had a—

"The Elite. Secret society run through the university. He's a part of it. Your aunt is a part of it. There's more. So many more."

I can't stop shaking my head. I think she's confused. This...a secret society? That's just nonsense. "Evelyn, listen. I know you've been through a lot, but—"

She stops me, reaching back into her bag, and hands me a gold piece of paper. It's thick like some sort of cardstock, the corner singed. "What is this?"

"This is proof." And the next twenty minutes burn into my mind, trying to diagnose everything she tells me. The years her and her brother were torn apart. The horrid things she went through. Mason. My poor Mason.

Lillian's true hold over them both. The Elite. I threaten to expel my breakfast, the color washed clear from my face. If all she says to me is true, then Mason and I haven't been a ruse. And Lillian…Lillian is exactly what she says she is: the devil in disguise.

VII

UINCENDUM NATUS

EIGHTEEN

Mason

My plan was in full swing.

Catching Lillian off guard was the only way to get her alone, and I needed her unarmed. If I was right on my theory, The Elite was bigger than just her. She may be the mastermind pulling my strings, but there's a higher power out there pulling hers. Envy, no questions asked, hacked into Lillian's phone sending a virus, creating an untraceable text. The message summoned her to the abandoned nunnery to discuss *Invidia*. The Latin name for envy. If she was a member, I was banking on everything, that was her sin. If I bet wrong, this will all blow up in my face and more lives will be ruined.

I pull up to the nunnery and my heart quickens when I see her car parked on the side of the abandoned structure.

I jump out of Micah's car and fight through the whistling wind to the front entrance. My hand dips to the back of my jeans, grazing over the outline of the gun shoved in my waistline. There's no guarantee how tonight will go, but I'm prepared for anything. If Lillian knows this is a setup, she won't be alone. And this may be the end of the road for me.

Before I headed out, I left clear instructions for Micah. If anything happens to me, I'm asking him to step in and watch out for my sister. If anyone will, it'll be him.

As always, the nunnery is dark, except for the sparing illumination of candles Lillian must have lit. When I step through the threshold, I see her standing at the fireplace, her back to me. When she turns, her smug expression vanishes. "What are *you* doing here?" she snaps, searching over my shoulder for the real person to show up.

"Don't bother. No one else is coming."

There's no hiding the sudden nervousness in her eyes. "What? What did you do?" She grabs for her cloak and tries to step passed me. My arm shoots out, and I grab her bicep and push her back. Her heel catches on a loose board, and she stumbles into the mantel. "How dare you," she hisses.

"No bitch, how dare *you*." I step forward and watch the authority drain from her face. "You know, it's funny. Fucked up people like you who abuse their power. Feed off the innocence of helpless kids."

She snarls at my words, trying again to get passed me. "This is absurd. I'm not gonna stand here listening—"

I shove her again, and this time, she does lose her footing, falling backwards right onto her ass. "You clearly didn't need the money, so why'd you do it? Why take us

PRIDE

in? Was it to get off on your own pleasure of torturing—"

"Please. It was him. *He* wanted you bratty kids." She straightens her posture from the ground, nurturing her scraped up hands. "You think *I* wanted you hoodlum children in my home? Your filth? It was him. Always him. And his sick obsession with *them*," she hisses, hatred radiating from her eyes.

"Is that why you hated my sister so bad? Why you'd cut her hair while she slept? Sent her to school with spoiled food? Fucking made her wear dirty clothes when you refused to allow her to wash hers!" The stories Evelyn confessed. The way she was treated, and I never knew. I thought I was protecting her, but I was too wrapped up in my own life, I'd missed all the signs of abuse.

"She was a little snob who needed to be taught a lesson. You think she was any different than the rest? Flaunting herself at my husband?"

"Your husband's a sick fuck who sexually abuses girls. And you let it happen."

She blanches at my accusation. "I did not. Those were his choices."

"And you never stopped him!" I yell, leaning over her. "You let a monster into the beds of these helpless girls. Girls who trusted you as their guardian to keep them safe!" Spit flies from my lips, the vein in my forehead popped. "I should fuckin' end your life right now. Make all your victims feel safer at night. Then put a bullet through your fucking husband's head next."

The color washes clear from her cheeks. "Mas—Mason, this is just a misunderstanding. Listen, I didn't know what he was doing."

"Liar! You fucking knew! And you let it happen. Why?

Was it your way of getting back at someone?"

"What? What's that supposed to mean?"

"Making others feel the same horrible fate you endured?" I stand straight, and watch the confusion set in her face. "Maybe it was you trying to deface all little girls the way you were."

"I don't know what you're talking about." That's when I rip out the documents stashed inside my jacket. She flinches and covers her face as I toss them at her.

"Oh, don't worry. I'm not going to kill you yet. I'm not done having fun. Look," I demand. With a scowl on her face, she picks up the pieces of paper and starts glancing them over. Seconds tick by until the acknowledgement of what she's reading settles in.

"How did you get these?" she whispers, whipping through each document, any color left quickly fading from her face as if she was just confronted by a ghost of her past.

"It all makes sense now. The hate you have for your brother's daughter. Is it revenge for what he did to you? How long was he abusing you before Mommy and Daddy caught wind? How long did it take for them to cover it up?"

"Shut up," she hisses.

"Pretty fucked up for your own brother to molest his little sister."

"Stop."

"Medical records show some pretty damaging stuff. Makes sense why Mommy and Daddy didn't want that shit to get out—"

"SHUT UP! Just shut up!" she screams and tries to scramble to her feet, but I kick her, pushing her back

PRIDE

down. "I ain't fuckin' done. Pregnant. Your own brother got you pregnant. That's how it came out, huh? Simple doctor's appointment for their little princess only to find out their son was a sick fuck. And you just let it all disappear."

"That's not true! I tried to tell them. Come forward with what he'd been doing. I told my mother. But you know what she did? She accused me of playing the slut. An eleven-year-old slut who was in love with her seventeen-year-old brother. She told my father, and you know what *he* did? He didn't hold me and tell me everything was going to be okay. Nooo," she hisses, tossing hair away from her face. "He made it all go away. Him and his secret society of brothers. The medical documents, the police report I tried to file. Even me. He made it all go away."

"Ahhh, explains the fancy boarding school. Man, what'd your poor brother do while you were away. Probably pretty upset lusting over his absent sister—"

"Fuck you!" She jumps and attacks me, her long nails slicing down my face. I allow her the one outburst, then raise my hand and wrap it around her throat. I press hard against her wind pipe, knowing I have the strength and anger flowing inside me to pop her neck.

"No, bitch, fuck *you*. Fuck you for the years I spent locked up and beaten to within an inch of my life. Nights where I starved. My skin scaled because I was so fucking dehydrated. You did that to me. Two years gone, because you wanted to play with my life. With my sister's life. And for what? So, I can be your little toy in your game of revenge?"

"And look how that turned out. A disgrace. A weak boy who—"

I press harder, causing her to struggle. Her wide eyes protrude as her skin transforms in a dark shade of purple. I have less than a minute until she dies under my hold. With the strength of a thousand men, I toss her across the room, her body smacking against the mantel and dropping to the ground. Her whimpered groans echo against the hollow walls as she scurries upright, backing herself into the corner.

"You're a fucking monster. Willing to ruin your own step-daughter, and for what? Vengeance? And why Megan?" I need to know.

"Why Megan, what?" She holds her limp wrist.

"Why her? What did someone as perfect and selfless as your own niece ever do to you that made you hate her so much? To ruin everything she's ever worked so hard for? Why do you hate her so—"

"Because she's *his*. He *had* a child. He took *that* away from me. You know what happens to a body when it's abused and impregnated at such a young age? Do you! I almost bled out when they scraped that growing monster out of me. The one *he* put there. When I woke up, I was told I would never bare anymore children. That's how my parents dealt with the situation. Not with their son or his disgusting sickness! They made sure he wouldn't get me pregnant again! He ruined my life, my future of having children. So, I decided to ruin his."

"Because of him, not—"

"Because he thinks he has everything! Perfect life. Perfect family. He needed to know how it felt to watch someone he loves suffer, just like I have."

"She didn't hurt you, Lillian. All she ever did was love you."

PRIDE

"She's a spoiled brat who, just like her father, deserves what's coming to her."

I take the minimal steps separating us, the sound of my booted shoes pounding with a ferocity on the old wooden floor as I make my way into her space. My hand reaches in the back of my jeans. My fingers squeeze around the cool titanium as I pull it forward and point it to the center of her forehead. "I will splatter your brains all over this place if you speak one more thing about her, you fucking hear me? You just signed your death warrant." My finger starts squeezing down on the trigger—

"Mason, don't."

My head whips behind me to the sweet sound of Evelyn's voice. "What the fuck are you doing here? You need to leave."

"Mason, no. Please."

I turn back to Lillian, my hand beginning to shake. "She needs to go. She's a virus for us all. You need to be free of her. We all do."

"This isn't the way, Mason."

"It is!" I snap, pointing the gun at her forehead. "You're fucking dead."

"Mason, she's right."

I sway on my feet as Megan steps out of the shadows. "Megan," I say her name on a strained whisper. God, I missed her. The peace she brought into my life. Her beauty that brought color into my dull world. "You shouldn't be here."

"Neither should you." She approaches me, raising her hand with caution, and stroking the back of her hand against my cheek. "This isn't the way." My eyes close at the intimacy of her touch. "Give me the gun, Mason." My eyes squeeze shut. It is the way. This is how everyone gets to move on and out from under her spell and the claws of The Elite.

"Yes, thank you, Megan. Listen to my niece, Mason."

Megan moves so fast, I don't even see it coming. With an impressive quickness, she seizes the gun from my grip and moves in front of me, the bottom of the barrel back between Lillian's eyes.

"You listen here, you sick, disgusting, waste of a life. For starters, I am *not* your niece. You are nothing to me. I'm sorry for what my father did to you, but that doesn't excuse all the hate and travesty you brought among so many other people. You are no judge, jury, and definitely no executioner. You don't have the right to play God with anyone's life."

"Oooh, look who's passing judgement, the little whore—"

I jump forward to snap her neck and end this, but Megan puts her hand out, stopping me in my tracks. "I got this," she says, then veers her attention back to Lillian. "Oh, Auntie. Your foul mouth doesn't suit you. And what doesn't suit me is murder, but you see, I can't allow you to just walk away either. You're done. This secret society? Your revenge on innocent people? It ends now."

Lillian's sadist laugh sends fury down my spine. "Oh, little girl, this is way bigger than just me. You can threaten me, get rid of me, but I'm the least of your worries."

"Then we'll figure out who's in charge and destroy them too."

Another burst of laughter. This time, Megan steps forward and punches her square in the nose.

"You little bitch!" Lillian howls, gripping her nose as

blood spews between her fingers, while Megan grips her sore hand. "You know nothing. You're just as foolish as I thought if you think you can take them down. There's no destroying The Elite. They will just grow back and flourish even larger and more powerful than before."

"That might be. But as they say, you have to start by weeding out the bad seeds." This time, it's Evelyn and I who laugh. God, she's so fuckin cute. "So, this is what's gonna happen. For starters, you're done here. At the university, in this secret *club*. I want you to step down effective immediately. If you don't, these papers will surface."

"They do, and your name gets dragged into the mud just as much as mine and your daddy's."

"Then so be it. But at least I'll go down for the better cause. Until then, consider this the last thing I'll ever do for you. I won't leak anything about this or The Elite. My focus is to shield my mother from any of this. Next, before you do so, I want Mason reinstated as a student. His classes, full housing, and his scholarship. I want it in writing and in the record books. Also, I want in writing about Evelyn's as well. Can't trust a snake like you won't go back on her word, ya know?"

My girl is so ferocious. I want to hug her and kiss those fierce lips of hers. Praise her for the strength even after learning the horrible things about her father.

"You won't get away with this."

"I already have. We've been here long enough, and thanks to modern technology, I have your confession. Talking about The Elite. Your abuse. Your husband's sick tendencies. The dean of the university. I do believe that will take a bigger hit than my job or smeared last name. I'll be able to move on. But will you?"

Lillian takes those words and allows them to simmer thick in her mind. Her expression gives us the answer. She won't. "I can't just disappear. People will ask questions."

"Let them. Take a spontaneous vacation, and when you come back, have a change of heart. Call it a midlife crisis. But you're done here. Understand me?" Megan cocks the gun. Fuck, I think I'm a little scared of her right now. She leans forward. "I'm sorry, I didn't hear you?" she taunts.

Lillian, looking so far from her normal, put-together self, finally nods. "Fine. I'll do whatever you want."

Megan nods. "That's more like it. Now, get the hell out of here before I decide killing is my new hobby and I shoot you right between your horribly Botoxed eyebrows."

Lillian scrambles to her feet, and races passed us. She doesn't look back as the old door slams shut and we hear her car roar to life and tires squealing down the long driveway.

We all stand there for another beat, until Evelyn finally moves and runs into my arms. "Oh, Mason. It's over. It's really over." I hold her close to me, feeling a lifelong weight being lifted off me. "I love you, brother."

I kiss the top of her head. "You too, Evie." I steal a glimpse of Megan, who's standing silent watching our embrace. I mouth, "Thank you," and she mouths, "Welcome," with a smile. Finally, Evelyn pulls away, looking between Megan and myself.

"Well, I'm gonna let you two talk. Um, Mason, I'm gonna just wait in Micah's car." She reaches up on her tippy toes and places a kiss on my cheek, then she's gone, leaving Megan and I alone.

PRIDE

"Listen, I—"

"Your sister told me you thought you were in love with me."

Her comment catches me off guard. Damn my sister. I slide my hands in my pockets. "I'm afraid to give you the wrong answer, with you still holding that gun and all."

Not realizing she still had it, she suddenly drops it. "Shit, not sure what came over me there." I laugh and take a step to eliminate some space between us.

"You were pretty bad ass."

"Yeah?"

"Real Judge Judy bad ass."

Her beautiful smile radiates, lighting up the entire room. "You think so?" She puffs her chest out. I throw my head back and let loose a loud chuckle.

"I appreciate the compliment, but you didn't answer my question." I bring my eyes back to hers. "Is it true? Are you in love with me?"

I stare into her beautiful hazel eyes, asking myself how to answer that question.

This wasn't in my plans. With the thirst for revenge and hate flowing inside me, there was no room for anything else. I could barely see passed the retribution I set to viciously achieve.

But then she came along.

My heart was dead inside—only beating for the love and survival of my sister—And then this beautiful spark of life revived me. My heart beat like crashing thunder inside my chest at the sounds of her musical voice the first time she spoke. The exact moment I touched her bare skin. Fuck, her laughter and every moment of solace I found in her beauty, her mind. Her innocence.

I walked into a bar one night searching for something to silence my demons, and instead I was gifted this dark angel, waiting to numb my pain. My fears. But she didn't just silence the bad shit in my head, she changed the course of it.

My plan was to hurt, deceive, kill. Nothing would stand in my way. My pride would destroy anyone beneath me to reclaim what I'd lost. Until her. Her humbleness broke me in every way. Cracked the hard shell that wouldn't allow me to see past my abhorrence. My destruction. But she showed me worthiness. It wasn't about my *pride*, but my *temperance*. It gave me the courage to restrain the hate and reform it into something worthy. She gave me the strength to forgive myself.

And now I stare at her needing to know how exactly I express all that shit without bringing myself to my knees. How do I tell her that her beauty gives me light in my dark world? That my heart aches at the mere thought of her not giving me another chance?

Her patience is quickly wearing thin, and the way she starts chewing on her bottom lip makes me want to throw her over my shoulder and take her home and fuck her until she knows just how much I do. So, I put her out of her misery. "I love you," I reply, three simple words that don't even sum up the whirlwind of emotions inside me.

I watch her chest deflate with the breath she's been holding. "Phew! Well…good. That was the answer I was hoping for. Now that I know I'm also not a cradle robber, there're some things we need to get clear. One, you're no longer my student. We're not to break any student/teacher rules, because I technically do love my job and want to keep it. But I think replacing the title, student

PRIDE

with boyfriend has a better ring to it anyway." She stops, waiting for my response.

"You want me to be your boyfriend?" I ask, a playful smile building.

"Yes. Along with my doctor, and a few more role-playing ideas I've been fantasizing about."

I step toward her, lifting her chin. "I think I can handle that." Dipping down, I cover her mouth with mine. I kiss her slow, but with intensity, as the weight of the world lifts from my shoulders. When I know it's time to stop, I pull away. I catch her glazed-over eyes and give her some time to fully come to.

"I was never going to go through with that task. I would never—"

"I believe you."

Relief washes over me at her words. "Thank you," I say, because I needed that. I needed her to know, even if we parted ways, I would have never done that to her. I cared too much. "I didn't want you to hear that shit about your dad." The reminder of the information she learned tonight hurts all over again, and I kiss her lips to help with the pain I know it's causing her.

"I don't know how to handle all the things I've learned today. I would've never thought my dad to do something so sick and horrible. Even my grandparents for covering it up." She pauses to take a breath. She's fighting back tears and it kills me. "But those things aren't your fault."

"But it still has to hurt. And I'm sorry."

This time, she offers me her lips. "And I can't imagine all the things you've had to endure. I wish I could take back all the horrible things my aunt did to you and Evelyn. I wish I would have seen the signs she was so evil sooner and put a stop to her."

I raise my arms and engulf her into my warm chest. She rests her head over my still wild beating heart. "Do you think she'll leave? Take my threat seriously?" she asks.

"I don't know. I think her reputation means a lot to her, and at least, for now, I think she'll back off. As for The Elite, I have no idea. What she said…it was bigger than her. That makes me wonder just how big it is. Who's all really involved? How safe are any of us really?"

She sighs into my chest. A part of me feels relief. Not to feel captive under the claws of Lillian is like seeing life in a whole new aspect. No longer having to look over my shoulder. The constant fear for my sister's wellbeing. If Lillian does what's she's been told, we're free. But if she's lying, we may have just started a whole new war, one I'm not sure we can win.

For now, I plan on still playing their game. Even though Lillian is out of the picture, there's no doubt some other Elite member will step up into her place. So, until I can take them down, I'm gonna continue to play their compliant little puppet.

"All we can do is hope." She untangles herself from my hold. "For now, maybe we should just focus on the present and make up for the time we missed out on." Her eyes light up, and anything and everything Lillian and The Elite fall to the back of my mind. "And what do you have in mind, *teach*?"

She giggles, but her eyes sparkle with that playful darkness. "Not sure. I was thinking you could play my underage student and offer dirty things to me to buy you beer or something."

A loud laugh echoes off the crumbling walls. "Does

being *almost* of age take all the fun away for you?" I joke and love the way her smile widens.

"I mean, I love a good taboo story. But I'll take one where the humble girl takes the proud man to his knees and shows him just how worthy he is. Then once I've filled him with all the greatness that he is, I'm going to allow him to thank me with his hands, his tongue and his mighty cock."

Fuck. My girl's cute.

"Well…we better get you home. I'm not one to deny a beautiful girl."

VII
UINCENDUM NATUS

EPILOGUE

Two weeks later...
Megan

"**O**h my god, stop!" I can't stop giggling. He knows I don't want him to stop, and the more I beg him to, the more he's gonna bite me. I wiggle under his hold, playing the damsel wanting to be free of her big bad wolf. "Someone save me!" I scream, but my voice doesn't sound convincing as a stifled moan pushes past my lips.

"I think my little girl wants me to bite every single part of her. I told you I was hungry, and you offered your sweet cunt for breakfast. You don't mess with a starved man," he hums into my thigh, then takes another nip. I thrash under him, his tongue does magic to my skin, teasing me so bad. He hasn't even made it to the promised land and I'm already on the verge of orgasming.

"I think you should get to it and eat away before we're both late." He doesn't waste another second and shoves his tongue into my wet center and goes to town. My fingers grip my sheets and hold tight as my back arches off the bed. "Jesus Christ all mighty," I cry when a finger enters me.

"I thought I was your big bad wolf, but I'll take being the higher power instead." His chuckle vibrates between my legs, heightening my pending orgasm. His tongue is rough and quick, and a few more seconds pass before I'm squeezing his head between my thighs as my orgasm explodes, shooting down to the tips of my toes.

Mason lazily lifts his head, his chin moist from my juices. His tongue traces along his lips, his smile sexy and feral. It sends tingles down to my toes, and I start conjuring up any reason to call in sick and stay in bed with my big fierce wolf. "I know that look. No skipping, teach."

"Wow, you getting bossy with me?" I tease.

"Damn right." He tugs at my legs, spanking the side of my butt cheek.

"Mmm…sounds super naughty. Maybe you should make me." Dammit, that smile. That hungry fire in his eyes that shows me he's not only going to make me, he's going to comatose me. I reach for the back of his neck and decide today is definitely going to be a sick day.

The morning quickly morphs into afternoon when I reopen my eyes and roll over to the beautiful sight of

Mason. A girly grin spreads across my cheeks as I stare at him. Even when he sleeps, he radiates dominance. His masculine forearms tucked under his head, his chest on complete display for me. I lick my lips wanting to wake him up, but I know even as delicious as he looks, my body needs a break. Especially after our morning. I also want to let him sleep. He looks so peaceful. I feel at ease, knowing I bring him that. Something he said never came easily for him before me.

I snuggle into my pillow, sighing at how perfect everything has been when the doorbell sounds. Mason stirs, opening his eyes.

"You expecting someone?" he asks, grabbing me and pulling me into him. His lips press against the top of my head when more banging echoes from the front.

"No, unless it's the hooky police," I joke, as we both peel ourselves from one another and climb out of bed. I throw on my robe as Mason pulls back the drapes of my bedroom window.

"The fuck...?" He releases the curtain and searches out his clothes.

"What? Who is it?" I ask, trying to keep up with his large steps as he makes his way to the front door. He unlocks the three bolts quickly, and when the door opens, his brother from The Elite, Rush, or his Elite name, Sloth, stands in my doorway. After everything went down at the abandoned nunnery, Mason took me home and told me everything. The Elite. My family's involvement. My mind couldn't even wrap around all the deception and scandal. But at the end of it, I did one thing. I swore I'd stand by him and fight this underground world of evil until it was disbarred and banished.

PRIDE

"Fuck you doing here?" Mason asks, not sounding very happy to see him.

"Don't mean to interrupt, brother, got some bad news. And it ain't good."

Mason's shoulders stiffen. "Explain then," he snaps. Rush's mysterious eyes find mine, then he brings his focus back to Mason. "She can hear whatever the fuck it is you have to say bro." He nods, and my body starts to hum with uneasiness. Even before the words leave his lips, we both know.

"Lillian's back."

The words quickly sink in, but it's not until the rumble of the floor and the fist through my entryway wall, does it fully register. I observe Mason, who's pulling his fist out of the smashed drywall. I step forward and press my hands to his shoulder for support. As much as we've avoided the elephant in the room, we couldn't deny the question lingering thick around us all. It wasn't a question of *if* Lillian would return, it was when. We knew she wasn't gone for good. But we used the time she disappeared to heal. But now, it's time to get our armor back on.

"How?" Mason snaps, his chest heaving.

"Not sure, but whatever she has up her sleeve she has Wrath at the center of it all."

"Where's Wrath now?" Mason asks, turning and grabbing his shirt off the couch and throwing it over his head. He's already slipping into his boots when Rush replies.

"Campus. We don't have much time. Need to get there before shit goes down."

Mason comes at me, kissing me hard, but quick. "Don't fucking leave this place. I need to know you're safe. Call my sister. Make sure she sits tight."

Then he's gone.

Mason

I shoot off a 9-1-1 text to all the brothers and head to campus. When we hit the crowded parking lot, I jump out and push through the mob to get in front of the commotion, but a band of cops refuse to let me go any farther. I look around, and spot Rhett. Screeching of tires has me searching out God's Escalade as he jumps out, heading in my direction. I scope out the crowd more, looking for the rest in the sea of cops and bystanders.

"Where's Micah?" I ask God as he comes up and stops next to me examining the scene.

"No idea. Not his babysitter."

I pull my phone out to check for any missed texts.

Something doesn't feel right.

Out of nowhere, Envy appears next to me. I turn to him and my stomach drops at the sight of him. "Where the fuck have you been?" I growl and give him the once-over, but he doesn't reply. "Don't tell me that's what I think it is, man." He better fucking convince me I'm not seeing what I think I'm seeing.

He still doesn't answer. He seems lost, staring out into the distance of the crowd. I follow his eyes, and that's when I see her.

Lillian.

She's in the way back, hidden behind an old cypress

PRIDE

tree. Her gleaming eyes break away from the ambulance, landing on mine. My stomach recoils again, and a heavy sickness swirls inside me at the way her evil smirk breaks across her face.

It's then I fully understand.

The one thing we've all dreaded: the war has begun.

I turn back to Envy. "Sebastian, talk to me. What did she make you do?" He's so lost in himself, he doesn't bother to even look my way. But his four simple words hit my eardrums like acid, burning into my brain.

"Wrath's gonna kill me."

The End.

MORE FROM J.D. HOLLYFIELD

Love Not Included Series
Life in a Rut, Love not Included
Life Next Door
My So Called Life
Life as We Know It

Standalones
Faking It
Love Broken
Sundays are for Hangovers

Paranormal/Fantasy
Sinful Instincts
Unlocking Adeline

#HotCom Series
Passing Peter Parker
Creed's Expectations
Exquisite Taste

2 Lovers Series
Text 2 Lovers
Hate 2 Lovers
Thieves 2 Lovers

Four Father Series
Blackstone

Four Sons Series
Hayden

ACKNOWLEDGEMENTS

First, and most importantly, it wouldn't be a proper acknowledgement if I didn't thank myself. It's not easy having to drink all the wine in the world and sit in front of a computer writing your heart out, drinking your liver off and crying like a buffoon because part of the job is being one with your characters. You truly are amazing and probably the prettiest person in all the land. Keep doing what you're doing.

Thanks to my husband who supports me, but also thinks I should spend less time on the computer and more time doing my own laundry.

Thank you to Ker Dukey for bringing me onto this amazing project and to all the other authors who got together to make this a bomb ass series. It's been a real blast!

Thanks to all my eyes and ears. Having a squad who has your back is the utmost important when creating a masterpiece. From betas, to proofers, to PA's to my dog, Jackson, who just gets me when I don't get myself, thank you. This success is not a solo mission. It comes with an entourage of awesome people who got my back. So, shout out to Amy Wiater, Ashley Cestra, Jenny Hanson, Amber Higbie, Gina Behrends, Elizabeth Clinton, my boo thang Kristi Webster and anyone who I may have forgotten! I appreciate you all!

Thank you to Monica Black at Word Nerd Editing for helping bring this story to where it needed to be.

Thank you to All By Design for creating my amazing cover. A cover is the first representation of a story and she nailed it.

Thank you to my awesome reader group, Club JD. All your constant support for what I do warms my heart. I appreciate all the time you take in helping my stories come to life within this community.

Big thanks for Stacey at Champagne Formats for always making my stories look so amazing!

And most importantly every single reader and blogger! THANK YOU for all that you do. For supporting me, reading my stories, spreading the word. It's because of you that I get to continue in this business. And for that I am forever grateful.

Cheers. This big glass of wine is for you.

ABOUT THE AUTHOR

J.D. Hollyfield is a creative designer by day and superhero by night. When she's not cooking, event planning, or spending time with her family, she's relaxing with her nose stuck in a book. With her love for romance, and her head full of book boyfriends, she was inspired to test her creative abilities and bring her own stories to life. Living in the Midwest, she's currently at work on blowing the minds of readers, with the additions of her new books and series, along with her charm, humor and HEA's.

J.D. Hollyfield dabbles in all genres, from romantic comedy, contemporary romance, historical romance, paranormal romance, fantasy and erotica! Want to know more! Follow her on all platforms!

Keep up to date on all things J.D. Hollyfield

Twitter
twitter.com/jdhollyfield

Author Page
authorjdhollyfield.com

Fan Page
www.facebook.com/authorjdhollyfield

Instagram
www.intsagram.com/authorjdhollyfield

Goodreads
www.goodreads.com/author/show/8127239.J_D_Hollyfield

Amazon
www.amazon.com/J.D.-Hollyfield/e/B00JF6U2NA

BookBub
www.bookbub.com/profile/j-d-hollyfield

NEVER MISS UPDATES!
Sign up for J.D. Hollyfield's Newsletter!
SIGN UP!

Printed in Great Britain
by Amazon

Collins

INTERNATIONAL PRIMARY SCIENCE

Student's Book 4

William Collins' dream of knowledge for all began with the publication of his first book in 1819. A self-educated mill worker, he not only enriched millions of lives, but also founded a flourishing publishing house. Today, staying true to this spirit, Collins books are packed with inspiration, innovation and practical expertise. They place you at the centre of a world of possibility and give you exactly what you need to explore it.

Collins. Freedom to teach.

Published by Collins
An imprint of HarperCollins*Publishers* Ltd.
The News Building
1 London Bridge Street
London
SE1 9GF

Browse the complete Collins catalogue at
www.collins.co.uk

© HarperCollins*Publishers* Limited 2014

10 9 8

ISBN: 978-0-00-758620-2

The authors assert their moral rights to be identified as the authors of this work.

Contributing authors: Karen Morrison, Tracey Baxter, Sunetra Berry, Pat Dower, Helen Harden, Pauline Hannigan, Anita Loughrey, Emily Miller, Jonathan Miller, Anne Pilling, Pete Robinson.

All rights reserved. No part of this publication may be reproduced, stored in a retrieval system, or transmitted in any form or by any means, electronic, mechanical, photocopying, recording or otherwise, without the prior written permission of the Publisher or a licence permitting restricted copying in the United Kingdom issued by the Copyright Licensing Agency Ltd., 90 Tottenham Court Road, London W1T 4LP.

British Library Cataloguing in Publication Data
A Catalogue record for this publication is available from the British Library.

Commissioned by Elizabeth Catford
Project managed by Karen Williams
Design and production by Ken Vail Graphic Design
Photo research by Emily Hooton

Acknowledgements
The publishers wish to thank the following for permission to reproduce photographs.
Every effort has been made to trace copyright holders and to obtain their permission for the use of copyright materials. The publishers will gladly receive any information enabling them to rectify any error or omission at the first opportunity.
COVER: iurii / Shutterstock.com

p6 SCIENCE PHOTO LIBRARY, p53 Zak Waters / Alamy, p63 © Deyan Georgiev Authentic collection / Alamy, p69 iStock.com / RapidEye. All other photos Shutterstock.

Printed and bound by Grafica Veneta , Italy

Contents

Topic 1 Humans and animals — 1

- **1.1** Animal skeletons — 2
- **1.2** Your skeleton — 4
- **1.3** Growing bones — 6
- **1.4** Functions of the skeleton — 8
- **1.5** Protecting your organs — 10
- **1.6** Muscles — 12
- **1.7** Moving your bones — 14
- **1.8** Investigate moving bones — 16
- **1.9** Drugs and medicines — 18
- **1.10** Different medicines — 20
- **Looking back Topic 1** — 22

Topic 2 Living things in their environment — 23

- **2.1** The importance of the environment — 24
- **2.2** Adapting to different habitats — 26
- **2.3** Investigating different habitats — 28
- **2.4** Identifying and grouping animals — 30
- **2.5** Using identification keys — 32
- **2.6** Human activity and the environment — 34
- **2.7** Waste and recycling — 36
- **Looking back Topic 2** — 38

Topic 3 States of matter — 39

- **3.1** States of matter — 40
- **3.2** Water — 42
- **3.3** Heating matter — 44

3.4	Cooling matter	46
3.5	Liquid to gas	48
3.6	Gas to liquid	50
	Looking back Topic 3	52

Topic 4 Sound — 53

4.1	How sounds are made	54
4.2	Measuring sound	56
4.3	Sound travels through different materials	58
4.4	Reducing sound levels	60
4.5	Soundproofing materials	62
4.6	Musical instruments	64
4.7	Pitch	66
4.8	Changing the pitch of a musical instrument	68
	Looking back Topic 4	70

Topic 5 Electricity and magnetism — 71

5.1	Electrical circuits	72
5.2	Building circuits	74
5.3	Why won't it work?	76
5.4	Electrical current	78
5.5	Magnets	80
5.6	Investigate magnetic forces	82
5.7	Magnets and metals	84
5.8	Using magnets to sort metals	86
	Looking back Topic 5	88

Glossary — 89

Topic 1 Humans and animals

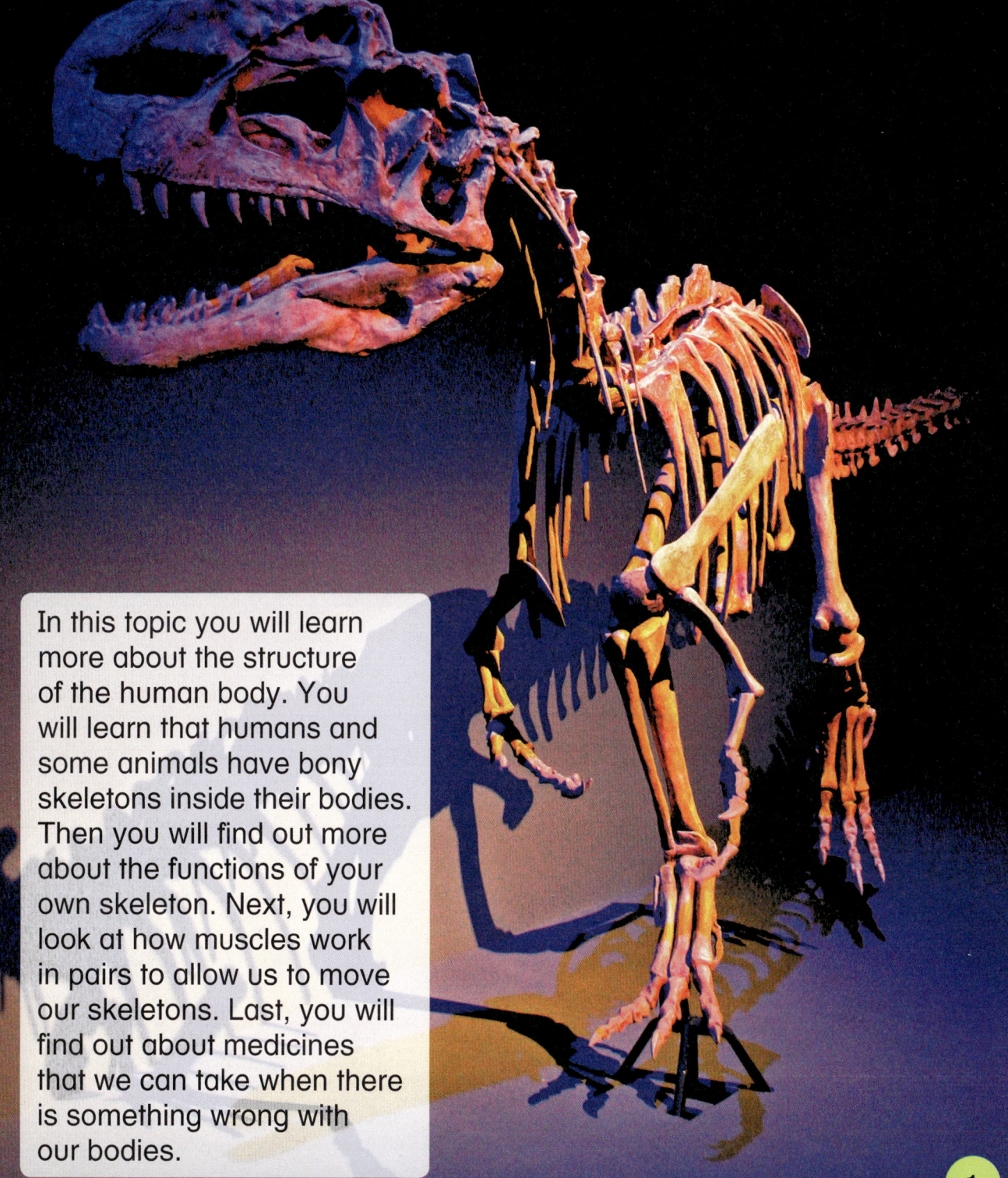

In this topic you will learn more about the structure of the human body. You will learn that humans and some animals have bony skeletons inside their bodies. Then you will find out more about the functions of your own skeleton. Next, you will look at how muscles work in pairs to allow us to move our skeletons. Last, you will find out about medicines that we can take when there is something wrong with our bodies.

1.1 Animal skeletons

Key words
- bones
- internal
- skeleton
- move
- support

Look at this photograph of a jellyfish. Jellyfish have soft floppy bodies with no **bones**.

1. Can you think of any other animals with soft bodies and no bones?

2. Some insects, such as locusts and beetles, have hard bodies. Do you think they have bones?

Some animals do have bones inside their bodies. These bones are joined together to form an **internal skeleton**. The skeleton helps the animal **move** and **supports** it, as well as protecting the soft parts inside its body.

Look at the skeletons of a frog, bird, fish and snake in the photographs.

jellyfish

bird

frog

2

Topic **1** Humans and animals

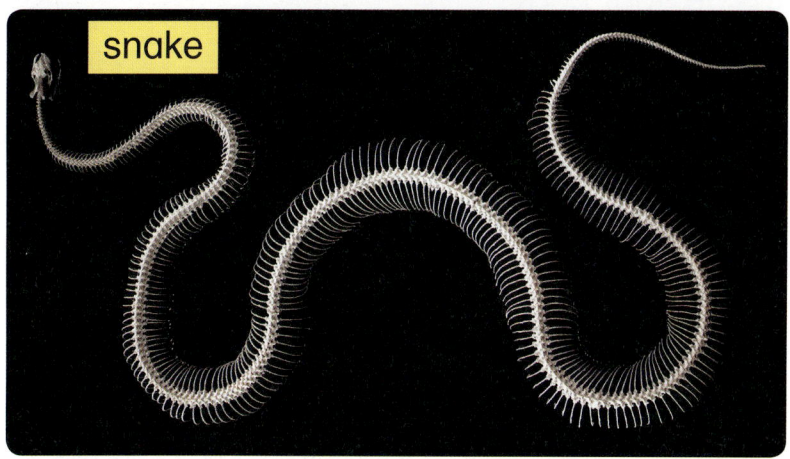

fish

snake

Hold one arm out in front of you. Feel your wrist with your other hand.

3 What do you feel?

4 Why isn't your arm soft and floppy?

5 What does this tell you about your own body structure?

Activities

1 Make a table of animals with no skeleton and animals with an internal skeleton. Try to find at least five examples of animals in each group.

2 Some animals have a hard covering on the outside of their body. This is called an external skeleton or exoskeleton. Make a list of at least five animals with an exoskeleton.

3 What is an X-ray photograph? What are these used for in modern medicine?

I have learned

- Some animals and human beings have bones inside their bodies.
- The bones are joined together to form an internal skeleton.

1.2 Your skeleton

Key words
- skeleton
- joints
- spine

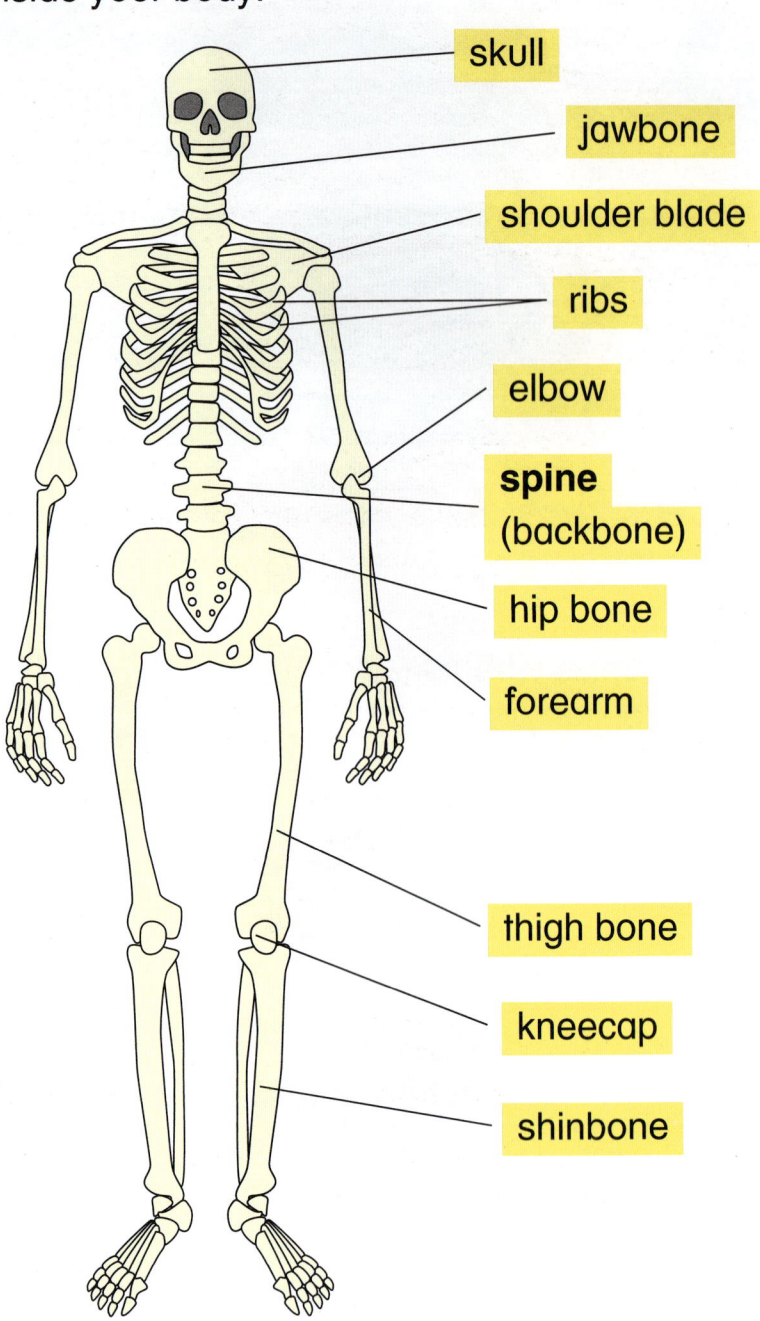

Like some animals, human beings also have a bony skeleton inside their bodies.

When you squeeze your arm you can feel the bones inside it. Bones are hard and strong and they form a rigid frame inside your body. This frame of bones is called a **skeleton**. Your skeleton helps you to move and supports your body, as well as protecting the soft parts inside your body.

1 Do you know the names of any of the bones in your body? Show them to your partner and say their names.

There are 206 bones in a human skeleton. On their own, bones are hard and stiff and they cannot bend. However, the bones in our skeletons are connected to each other at **joints**. Because joints are flexible, we are able to bend and move our bodies.

2 Find three joints on the skeleton. In what way does each joint allow you to move your body?

- skull
- jawbone
- shoulder blade
- ribs
- elbow
- **spine** (backbone)
- hip bone
- forearm
- thigh bone
- kneecap
- shinbone

Topic **1** Humans and animals

Bones in museums and the bones of dead animals in the environment are dry and they crumble easily. Living bones are not dry and are very strong.

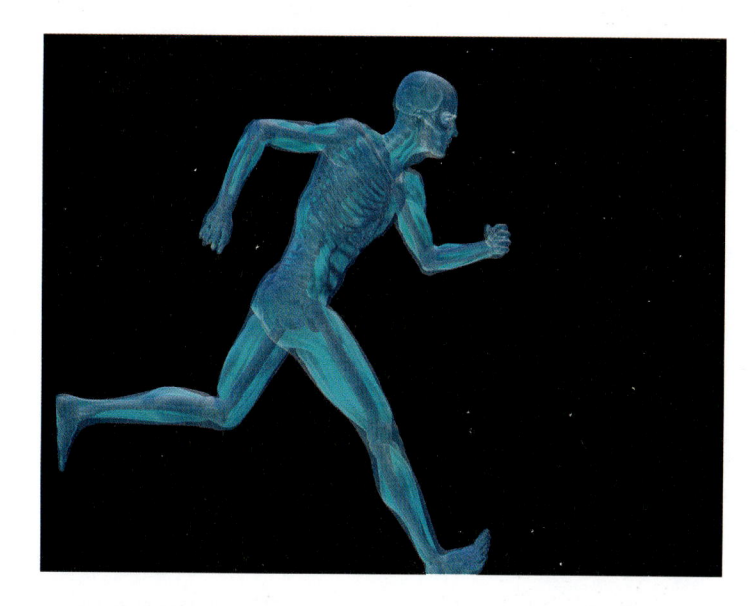

Activities

1 Describe some differences between the bones that make up the human skeleton.

2 Find out what happens when you break (fracture) a bone. What is the difference between a complete fracture, a greenstick fracture and an open fracture?

3 When you break a bone you may have to wear a splint or a cast. Make a poster to teach young children what they can expect if they have to wear a splint or a cast.

I have learned

- Humans have bony skeletons inside their bodies.
- Skeletons are made of different kinds of bones connected to each other at joints.

1.3 Growing bones

Key words
- X-ray
- bones
- cartilage
- calcium

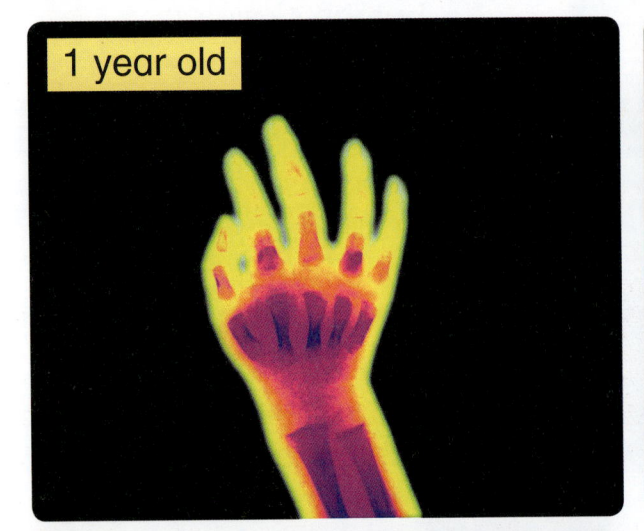

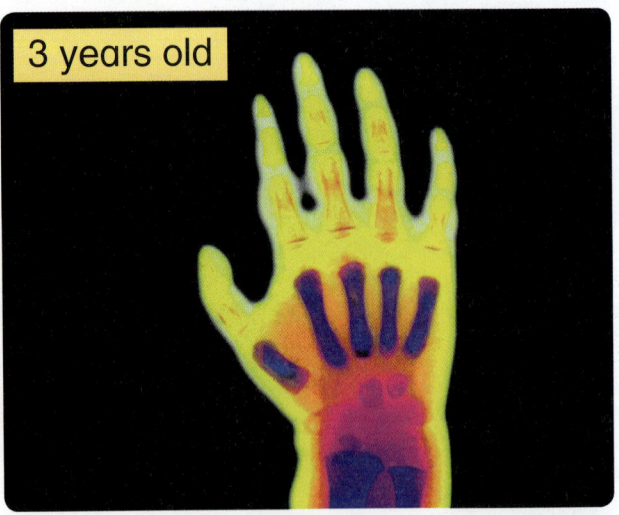

When you were a baby, you were much smaller than you are now. Your skeleton was also smaller. Our skeletons grow as we grow.

Compare these **X-ray** images of human hands.

1 year old

3 years old

13 years old

20 years old

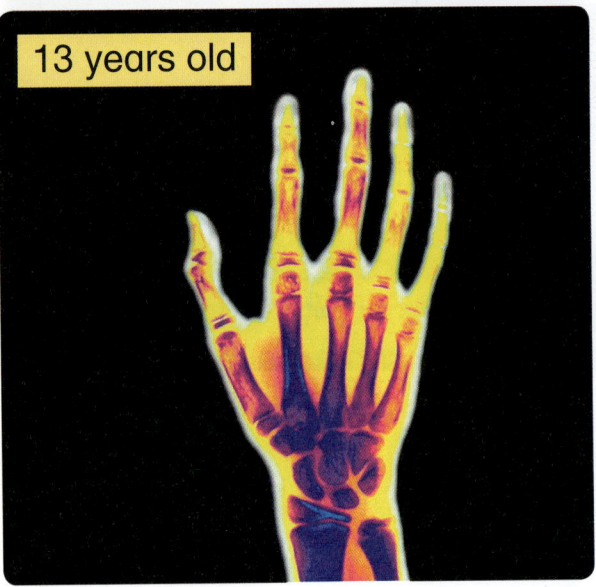

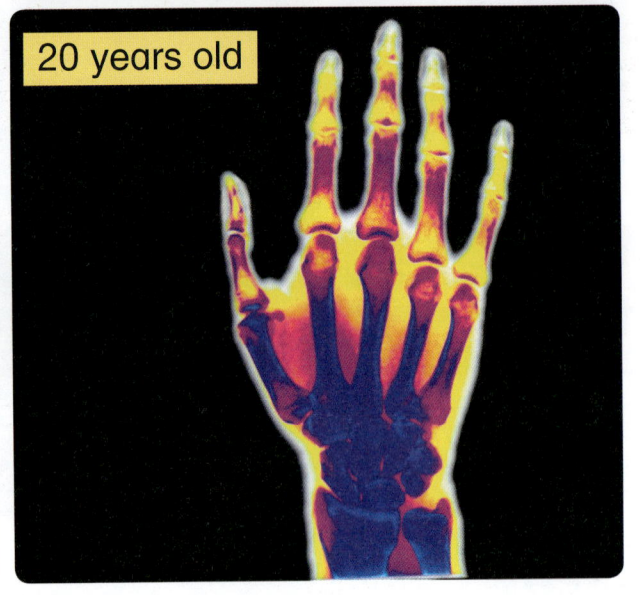

1. What differences can you see between the hands in the photographs?
2. Describe what you think your hand would look like on an X-ray.
3. What do you think happens to the bones and joints in the hand after 20 years of age?

6

Topic **1** Humans and animals

As we grow from babies to adults our bodies, including our **bones**, get bigger.

When a baby is born, it has more than 270 bones. Some of a baby's bones are made from a soft, flexible material called **cartilage**. As the baby grows, the cartilage grows too. Over time the cartilage is replaced by bone. This is why **calcium** is very important for young children – they need it to build healthy bones.

4   Your outer ear and nose are made of cartilage. Feel your ear and nose. Compare the cartilage in your ear with the bones in your hand.

As a baby grows, some bones grow together (fuse) to form the 206 bones in an adult skeleton. Between the ages of 20 and 25, your bones stop growing and your skeleton no longer increases in size as you get older.

Activities

1 Do taller people have bigger bones than shorter people? Work in groups of three or four. Use a tape measure to measure each person's height, arm length, leg length and head circumference. Record the measurements in the table on Workbook page 5.

2 Draw four separate graphs to compare the measurements. What do your results suggest?

3 If you took the same measurements using the same people in five years' time, would you get the same results? Explain your answer.

I have learned

- Bones are alive and they grow and change as we grow and change. Our skeleton grows with us.
- By the age of 20 to 25, our skeleton has grown to full size and it no longer grows.

1.4 Functions of the skeleton

Key words
- support
- protect
- organs
- backbone

Without your skeleton you would not be able to stand, walk or run. Your body would be soft and shapeless. Your skeleton allows you to stand upright and to move. It also **supports** your body and **protects** your soft **organs**.

1. Put your hand on the back of your neck. Can you feel the bones joining your head to your body? Now run your fingers downwards. Try to feel the bumps along your **backbone**.

Your backbone, or spine, is important for supporting your body. It also allows you to twist and bend.

2. What do you think the discs of cartilage do?

vertebrae

discs of rubbery cartilage

8

Topic **1** Humans and animals

Activities

1 Make a model of a thigh bone. Decide how you will make it light but strong, like a real bone. Use Workbook pages 7 and 8 to record your work.

2 What can you do to test the strength of the model bones? Work with another group to test the model bones. Whose bone was stronger?

3 The backbone is different from the thigh bone. Think about how you could build a model to show the backbone and the way it allows the body to move. Draw a labelled diagram of your proposed model.

Your backbone is a column of small, ring-shaped bones called vertebrae (vert-eh-bray). A single one of these bones is called a vertebra. The vertebrae are separated by small cushions of rubbery cartilage. The cartilage stops the vertebrae from rubbing together and acts like a shock absorber to cushion the vertebrae from jolts when you walk and run.

Your backbone also protects the nerves that send messages from your brain to the rest of your body.

Your legs are important for support too. The leg bones are large and strong. The bone in your thigh is the largest bone in your body.

I have learned

- The skeleton allows us to move.
- It also supports our body and protects our organs.

1.5 Protecting your organs

Key words
- skull
- ribs
- ribcage

Your skeleton protects the soft organs inside your body.

Your brain is the control centre of your body. Your **skull** acts like a helmet to protect your brain.

If you put your hands on the back of your head you can feel the hard curved bones of your skull. The back of your skull is formed of eight curved bones tightly fused together. You can see in the picture the lines where the bones are joined.

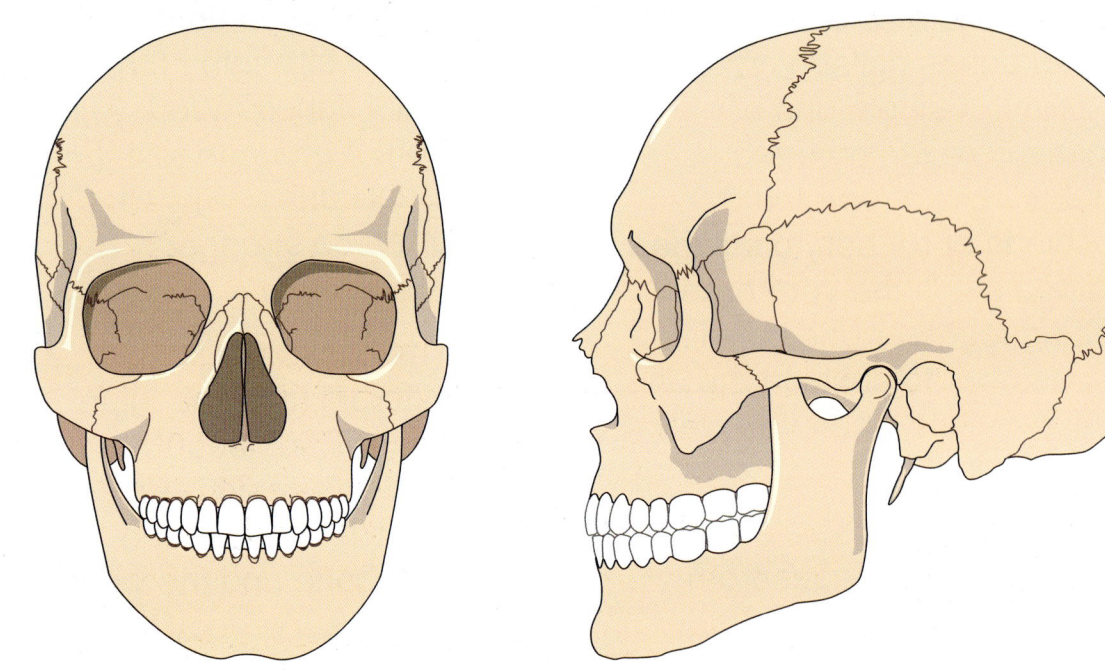

The front of your skull is made of 14 facial bones, which protect your eyes, nose and mouth. If you feel gently under your eye, you can feel the edge of the hole around your eye.

1. Why do you think the curved bones of the skull are fused together?

2. A baby's skull bones are not fused together. Explain why it is important to protect a baby's head at all times.

3. The only bone in your skull that can move is your lower jawbone. Why does this bone need to move?

Topic **1** Humans and animals

Your heart, lungs and liver are all inside your chest. These important organs are protected by your **ribs**. The ribs form a bony cage around your organs. This is called your **ribcage**.

4 Put your hands on your ribs. Take a deep breath in and then breathe out again. What happens to your ribcage? Why do you think this happens?

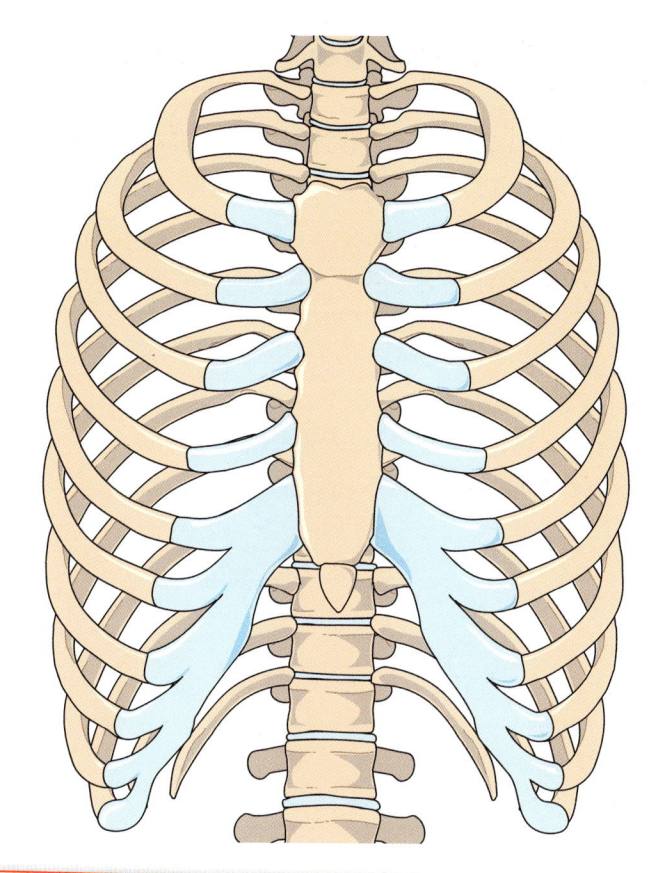

Activities

1 Using Workbook page 9, make a list of sports in which the players wear protective equipment.

2 Choose one piece of protective sports equipment. Photograph or draw it. Write a paragraph explaining the way it protects your body.

3 Make a poster or brochure to encourage young children to wear a helmet when they are cycling, skateboarding or riding a scooter.

I have learned

- The skeleton protects our body.
- The skull protects our brain.
- The ribs protect our heart, lungs and liver.

1.6 Muscles

Key words
- muscles
- tendons

You can feel your bones under your skin, but if you could take off your skin you would not see your skeleton because your bones are covered by **muscles**. All animals with bony internal skeletons have muscles attached to their bones.

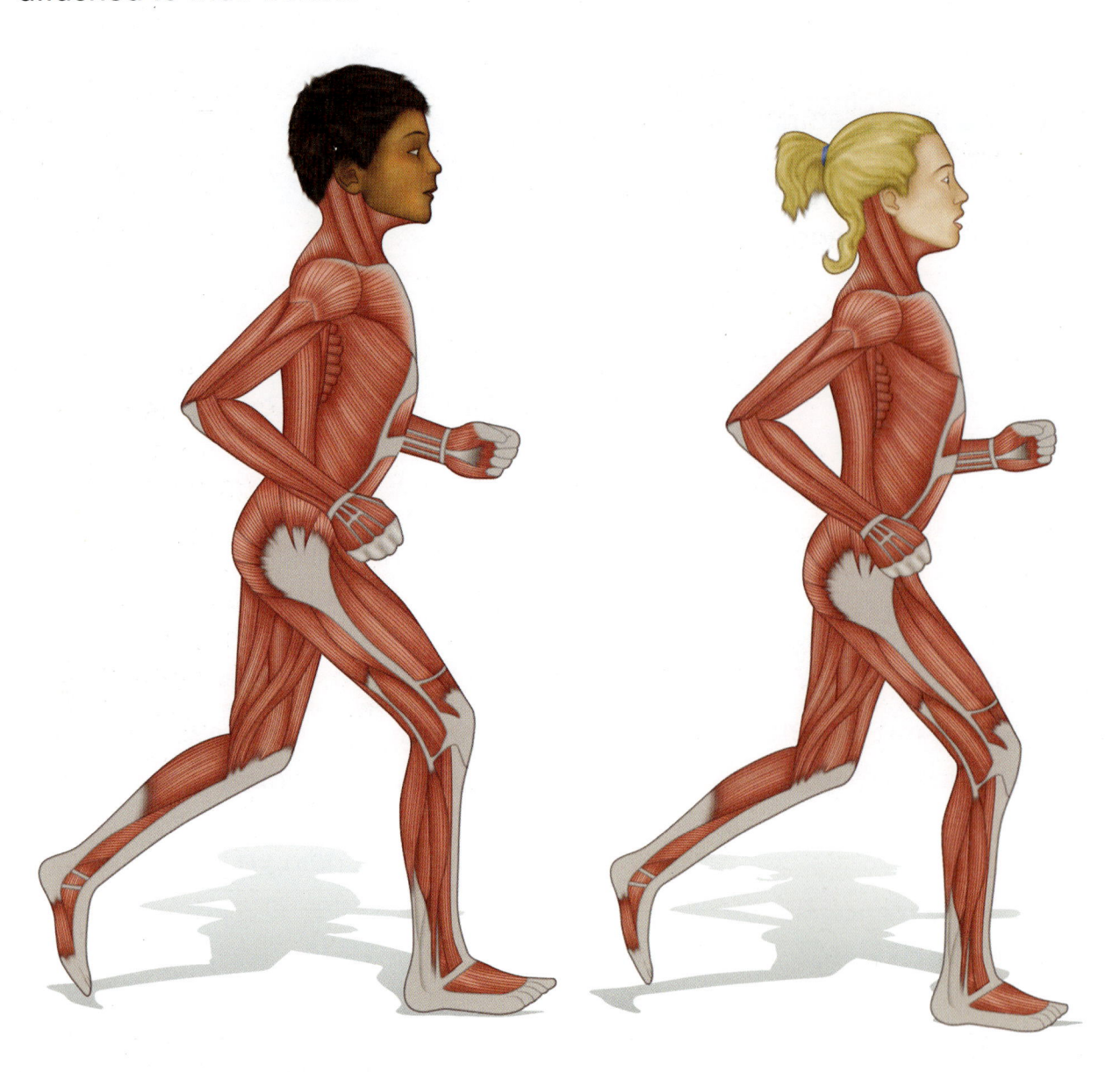

1. Describe what the muscles look like.
2. What do we need muscles for?

Topic **1** Humans and animals

Here are some muscle facts:
- Our muscles are attached to our bones by **tendons**.
- The strongest muscles are the muscles you use to bite things. They are found on either side of your mouth.
- The most active muscles are the six muscles that move the eye around in its socket.
- Your heart is a special kind of muscle that never gets tired.

Activities

1 Draw an outline of your body. Colour and label the following muscles:

the shoulder muscles

the jaw muscles

the thigh muscles

the stomach muscles.

2 Find out what the difference is between a tendon and a ligament.

3 What can we do to keep our muscles strong and healthy? Write a paragraph with at least three suggestions.

I have learned

- All animals with skeletons have muscles attached to their bones.

13

1.7 Moving your bones

Key words
- muscles
- contract
- relax

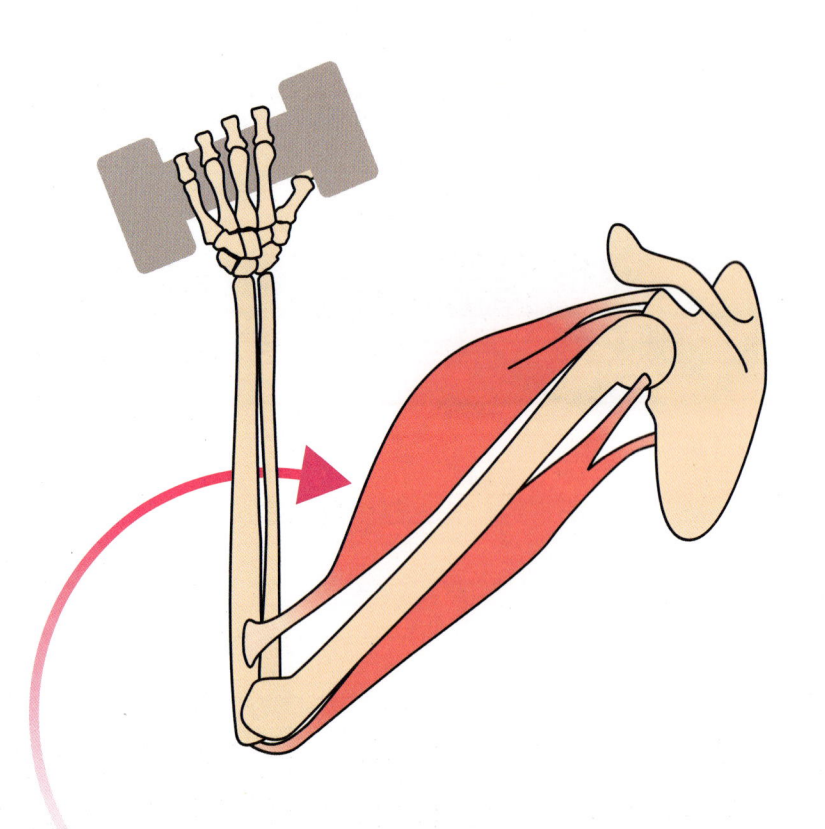

The skeleton and **muscles** work together so that you can move.

1 What are the muscles around our skeleton attached to?

Muscles move the bones they are attached to by **contracting**, or shortening. When a muscle contracts, it pulls against the bone and the bone moves. Muscles cannot push – they can only pull – so they need to work in pairs to allow each joint to move.

The elbow is an example of a joint. It is controlled by one set of muscles at the front of the upper arm and another set of muscles at the back of the arm.

Look at the pictures and read the information to see how one pair of muscles works together to allow you to bend and straighten your arm.

When you bend your arm:
- The muscles at the front of the upper arm get fatter, harder and shorter.
- The muscles at the back of the upper arm get thinner, softer and longer (they **relax**).
- The lower arm moves up.

Topic **1** Humans and animals

When you straighten your arm:
- The muscles at the front of the upper arm get thinner, softer and longer (relax).
- The muscles at the back of the upper arm get fatter, harder and shorter.
- The lower arm moves down.

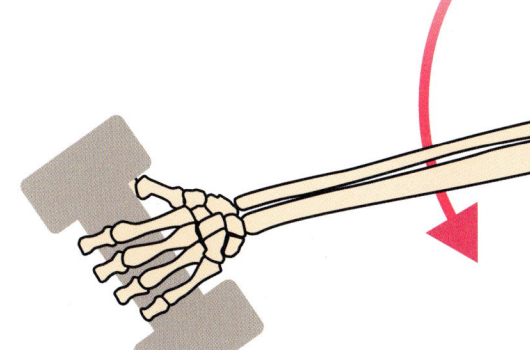

Activities

1 Draw a diagram to show what happens to a muscle when it contracts.

2 Test out the muscles in your legs. Explain to a partner which muscle is contracting and which one is relaxing when you:
- lift and lower your leg
- bend your leg at the knee.

3 Write a short paragraph in your notebook about why the skeleton and muscles need to work together as a system.

I have learned

- Muscles have to shorten to make a bone move.
- Muscles act in pairs around joints to allow us to move.

1.8 Investigate moving bones

Key words
- model
- muscles

You are going to make a **model** to show how the **muscles** in your arm work.

1. What is a model and why are models useful in science?

You will need:
- 2 elastic bands
- 5 paper fasteners
- stiff card

Follow these steps to build your model.

Use one paper fastener to join the two pieces of card together.

2. What do the strips of card represent in this model?
3. Why have you joined them with a fastener?

Push four more paper fasteners through the card as shown opposite.

Topic **1** Humans and animals

Fix the two elastic bands to the paper fasteners like this:

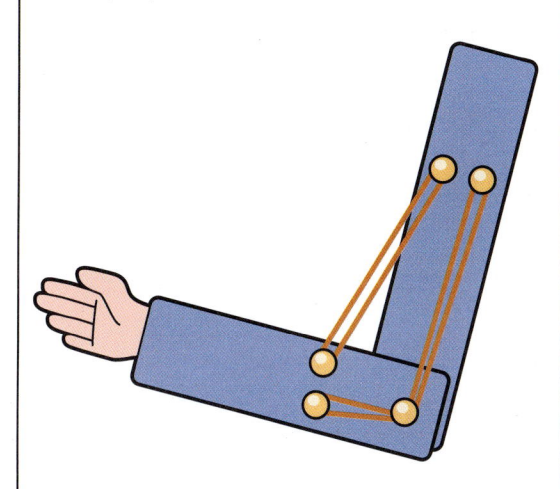

4 What do the two elastic bands represent?

5 What part of your model represents tendons?

Use your model to demonstrate how a human arm moves.

Try the same movements with your own arm.

Activities

1 Draw a diagram of the model arm changing from one position to the other. Draw another diagram to show the arm moving the opposite way. Label each diagram to show what the rubber bands are doing.

2 Could you use this model to show how your leg bends at the knee? Explain why or why not.

3 The muscles attached to your skeleton are voluntary muscles. This means that you can decide whether to move the muscles or not. Some of the muscles in your body are involuntary muscles. Find out what this means. Give some examples of involuntary muscles and say why it is important that they work without us thinking about it.

I have learned

- How to use simple equipment to model how muscles work.
- Muscles work in pairs. One muscles contracts while the other relaxes.

1.9 Drugs and medicines

Key words
- drugs
- medicines
- prescription
- pharmacy

A drug is any substance that affects how your body works. For example, some **drugs** kill germs, some stop you from feeling pain and some make you sleep.

Drugs that are used to treat illness are called **medicines**. Some medicines are taken by mouth (swallowed), some are injected into the body, some are inhaled and others may be absorbed through the skin.

Doctors sometimes give sick patients a **prescription** for these medicines to treat or prevent an illness. You have to take the prescription to a **pharmacy** or a clinic to get the medicines.

Some examples of prescription medicines are:

- an inhaler to treat and control asthma
- antibiotics to treat infections caused by bacteria (germs)
- anti-retrovirals to control symptoms of HIV/AIDS.

1 Have you ever taken any medicine? What was it for?

Medicines can help you to stay healthy or to recover when you are sick. But medicines are drugs and they can be dangerous if they are not used in the correct way.

2 Some pills or tablets that are given as medicine look like sweets. Explain why you should never eat things unless you know what they are.

Topic **1** Humans and animals

Activities

1 Read the information label from a box of Nopain medicine. What information does the label give you? Why is this information important?

2 Mrs Smith is a diabetic woman. She has a headache and wants to take some Nopain medicine. Read the information on the box and tell Mrs Smith what she should do. ▶

3 Prepare a list of instructions for storing medicines safely for a family with young children.

Nopain 200 mg tablets

Indications
Rapid relief from backache, muscle pain, aching bones and joints, headache and toothache.

Dosage and directions
Adults and children 12 years or older: 2 tablets up to three times per day.
Take after meals. Swallow tablets with water.
Do not take more than 6 tablets in any 24-hour period.
Do not give to children younger than 12 years of age.
Do not take for longer than 10 days.

STORE IN A COOL DRY PLACE OUT OF THE REACH AND SIGHT OF CHILDREN.

Speak to your pharmacist/doctor before taking this medicine if you:
- have asthma, diabetes, high blood pressure or kidney problems
- smoke
- are taking any other medicines.

I have learned

- Drugs are substances that can change our bodies.
- Drugs that treat illnesses are called medicines.
- You must never take medicines unless you know what they are.

1.10 Different medicines

Some plants give us medicines. The ancient Egyptians used the Aloe vera plant over 6000 years ago. We still use Aloe today in some medicines and **moisturisers** to soothe sunburn and other skin conditions.

Aloe

Aspirin is a common medicine used all over the world. It can reduce fever and relieve aches and pains. Aspirin is made from the bark of the willow tree.

Willow

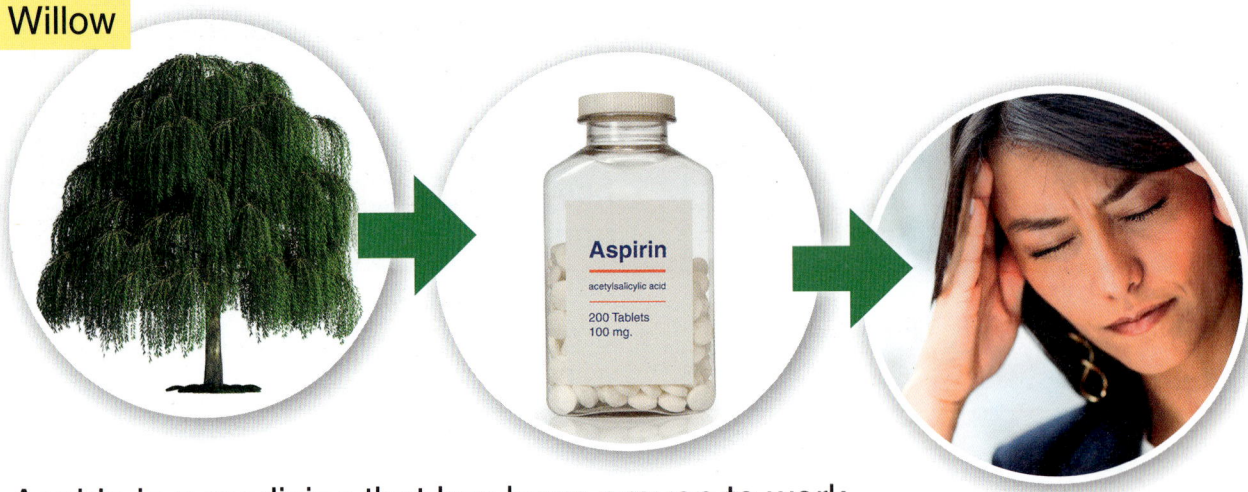

Aspirin is a medicine that has been proven to work by scientists, whereas scientists cannot provide any medical evidence that Aloe vera works, despite many people using it.

1 Name another plant used in medicine.

Key words
- moisturiser
- aspirin
- vaccine
- immune

Topic **1** Humans and animals

Some medicines, such as creams, are used on the outside of your body. Tablets and cough mixtures are used on the inside of your body.

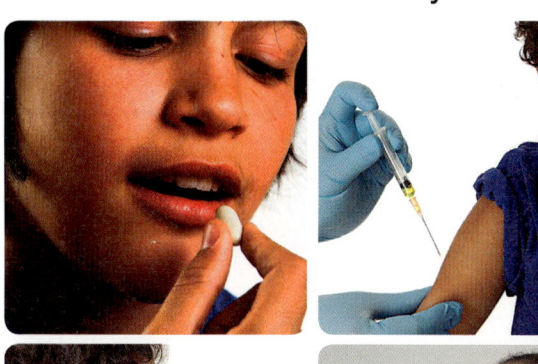

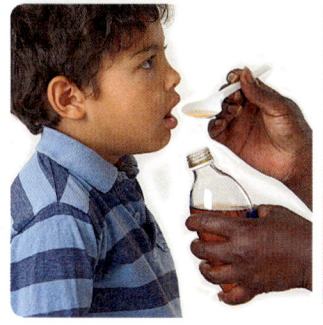

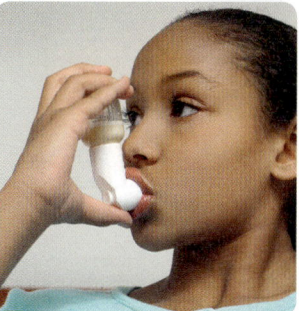

Some medicines are used to prevent us from becoming ill. **Vaccines**, such as those for measles and smallpox, are often given to children and young babies so that they become **immune** to the disease.

2 Explain how a vaccine works. What does 'immune' mean?

3 Why do you think it is against the law to sell or take certain drugs?

Activities

1 Sort some different medicines into two groups: those that are used on the outside of the body, and those that are used on the inside.

2 Prepare a fact sheet about how Aloe vera is used as a medicine. You can use PCM B2 to help you. Your fact sheet should include the arguments for and against how well it works as a medicine.

3 Do some research, using books or the internet to find out about two more plants used in medicine. Record your results on page 13 of your Workbook.

I have learned

- There are many different kinds of medicines.
- Not all medicines have been scientifically proven to work.
- A vaccine can make you immune to a disease.

21

Looking back Topic 1

In this topic you have learned

- Humans and some animals have bony skeletons inside their bodies.
- As we grow our skeleton grows with us. We stop growing when we are adults.
- Our skeleton allows us to move, supports our body and protects our organs.
- The bones of our skeleton have muscles attached to them.
- Muscles are attached to bones by tendons.
- Muscles allow us to move our bodies.
- Muscles work in pairs to allow movement. One muscle contracts while the other muscle relaxes.
- Drugs are substances that can change our bodies.
- Some drugs can be used as medicines to treat, control or prevent illness.

How well do you remember?

1. Look at the diagram of an elephant.
    a. What is the animal's skeleton made of?
    b. Name one animal that does not have a skeleton inside its body.
    c. Write down two similarities and two differences between an elephant's skeleton and a human skeleton.
2. What are two advantages to having a bony skeleton inside your body?
3. Why should you never take medicines that were prescribed for someone else?

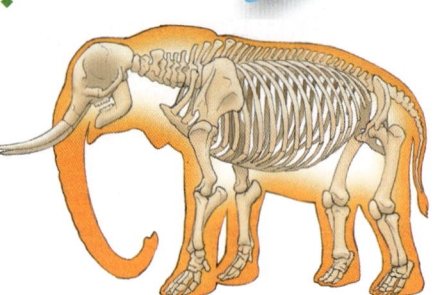

Topic 2 — Living things in their environment

You already know that different animals are found in different places in the environment. In this topic you are going to look more closely at the habitats in which animals are found, and you are going to investigate how animals are suited, or adapted, to different environments. There are many different types of animals and scientists use different methods to group or classify them. You are going to learn how to use a simple identification key to do this. Last, you will look at how human activities can affect the environment in both positive and negative ways.

2.1 The importance of the environment

Key words
- environment
- habitat
- adapted

The **environment** is the scientific name for our surroundings and the conditions found in them. The place in the environment where an animal (or plant) lives is called its **habitat**.

Look at these two pictures (below and opposite) carefully.

1 Describe the habitat in each picture.
2 Make a list of all the animals that live in each habitat.

There are many different habitats in the environment, each with a set of conditions that suit particular plants and animals. The habitat in which an animal lives must provide it with food, water and shelter. The rock-pool habitat is suitable for small sea animals such as crabs, starfish, limpets and anemones. It is also suitable for seabirds that feed on these small animals.

Topic **2** Living things in their environment

Activities

1 Choose one animal. Describe its habitat. Describe how it is adapted to suit the conditions found there.

2 Draw a picture of the habitat. Label it to show where the animal gets all the things it needs.

3 Which other animals are likely to be found in the same habitat? Why?

Many animals are **adapted** to suit their habitats. For example, the limpets are attached to the rocks by a strong muscular foot so they do not get washed off when the tide comes in or goes out. They also have a strong, pyramid-shaped shell that is difficult to break, so they seldom get eaten. Limpets feed at night on algae that grows on the rocks.

3 In what ways are the animals that you listed adapted to suit their habitats?

4 Why is the rock-pool habitat unsuitable for the rabbit and butterflies?

I have learned

- The place where an animal lives is called its habitat.
- Different animals are found in different habitats and they are adapted to suit the conditions found there.

25

2.2 Adapting to different habitats

Key words
- suited
- habitat
- adaptation

Most animals have some features that are **suited** to their natural **habitat**.

Giraffes are found in the grasslands of Africa. They feed on the leaves and branches of trees.

1. Why does having a long neck help the giraffe?
2. Giraffes have a spotty coat, a long, strong moveable tongue (up to 40 cm in length) and they can go for long periods without drinking water. In what ways do these features make them suited to their environment?

Some animals live in trees. Monkeys are found in most of the warm forests of the world. They eat fruit, nuts, leaves and seeds.

3. In what ways are monkeys suited to living in forests?

Topic **2** Living things in their environment

Some animals have features that help them live in freezing conditions.

4 Describe the polar bear's habitat.
5 In what ways are polar bears suited to living in such conditions?

Activities

1 What is the polar bear's fur like? Explain how this helps it to survive. What is likely to happen to a polar bear with no fur?

2 Design and carry out an investigation to see which coat would be best for a polar bear. Use Workbook pages 16, 17 and 18 to record your work.

3 Polar bears are endangered animals. Do some research to find out why these animals are endangered.

I have learned

- Animals have **adaptations** that make them suited to different conditions.

2.3 Investigating different habitats

Key words
- investigate
- habitat

You are going to find and **investigate** two different **habitats** in your local environment in order to observe and compare the animals found there and the ways in which they are suited to their habitat.

A good way to find different habitats for investigation is to draw a map of the local area.

Look at this map which Nadia drew of the environment around her school. She has circled four different habitats that interest her.

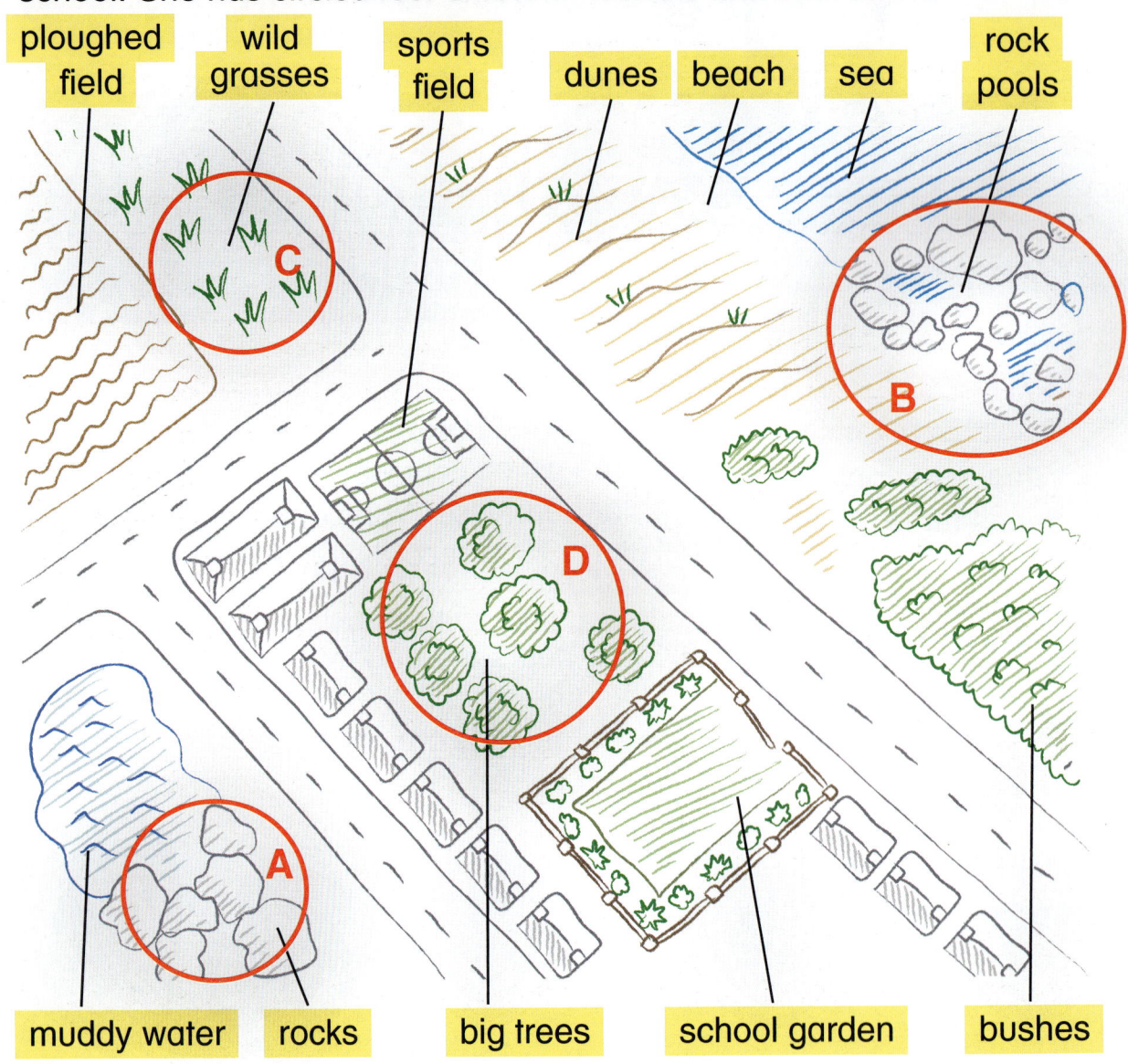

ploughed field · wild grasses · sports field · dunes · beach · sea · rock pools

muddy water · rocks · big trees · school garden · bushes

28

Topic **2** Living things in their environment

Activities

1. Work in groups to plan an investigation into two different habitats around your school. Use Workbook pages 20 and 21 to record your work.

2. Choose one of the animals you observed during your investigation. Complete a fact file to show what conditions it prefers and how it is suited to its habitat.

3. Choose one animal that would not be suited to the conditions in either of the habitats you investigated. Prepare a short presentation explaining why it is not suited to those conditions.

1. Choose one of the habitats that Nadia has circled and describe what you think it would be like. Consider all of the conditions found there. For example:
   - Is it hot and sunny or shady?
   - What plants are found there?
   - Are there rocks and other places for small animals to hide?
   - Is the ground wet or dry?
   - Is there a source of water?
   - Is the habitat likely to be disturbed during the school day?

2. What animals is Nadia likely to observe in the habitat you chose? Why?

I have learned

- Different animals are found in different habitats.
- Animals are adapted, or suited, to the conditions in their habitat.

29

2.4 Identifying and grouping animals

Key words
- classification
- key

You already know that we can group things into living and non-living. The group of living things includes all the plants and animals in the world, so it is a very large group.

Scientists divide living things into smaller groups using their characteristics. Living things that are similar in some ways are placed in the same group. Placing living things in groups based on their characteristics is called **classification**.

These animals all belong to the group called insects.

1. What do all these insects have in common?
2. What differences can you see between them?

All insects have some things that are similar, but each type of insect has some characteristics that make it different from other types. We can use the differences between insects to identify the type of insect.

On the next page is an identification **key** for the insects in the pictures. In keys such as this, there are usually two choices for each characteristic. Each choice divides the group into smaller groups until the key names each insect.

Topic **2** Living things in their environment

Follow this key to identify the insects in the group.

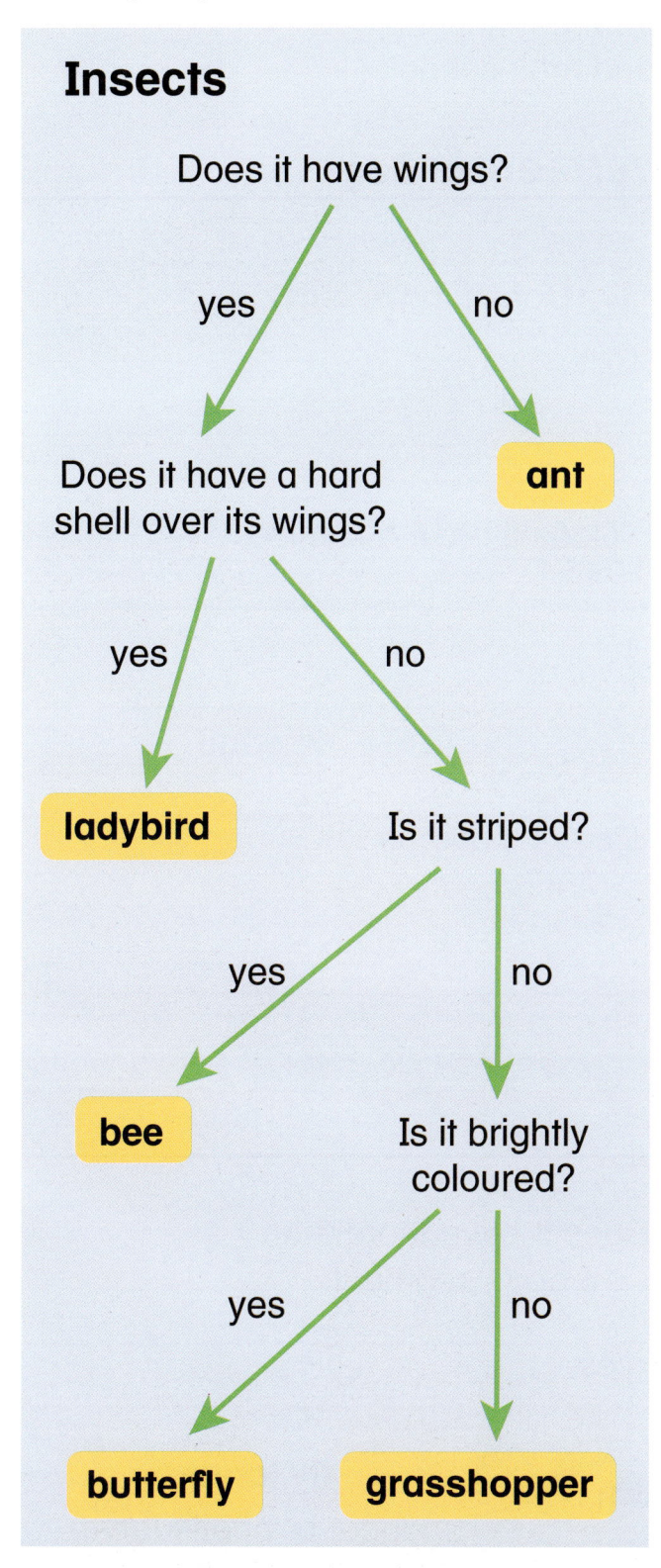

Insects

Does it have wings?
- yes → Does it have a hard shell over its wings?
  - yes → **ladybird**
  - no → Is it striped?
    - yes → **bee**
    - no → Is it brightly coloured?
      - yes → **butterfly**
      - no → **grasshopper**
- no → **ant**

Activities

1. Write a set of instructions for using a simple key.

2. Make a key to identify the following animals: brown bear, polar bear, panda, teddy bear.

3. Choose four of your classmates. Make a key to identify each person. Include yourself.

I have learned

- All living things can be classified into groups using their characteristics.
- The differences between animals in a group can be used to identify them.
- We can use a key with 'yes' or 'no' choices to identify members of a group.

31

2.5 Using identification keys

Vanessa and Joe found these nine different animals when they investigated habitats around their school.

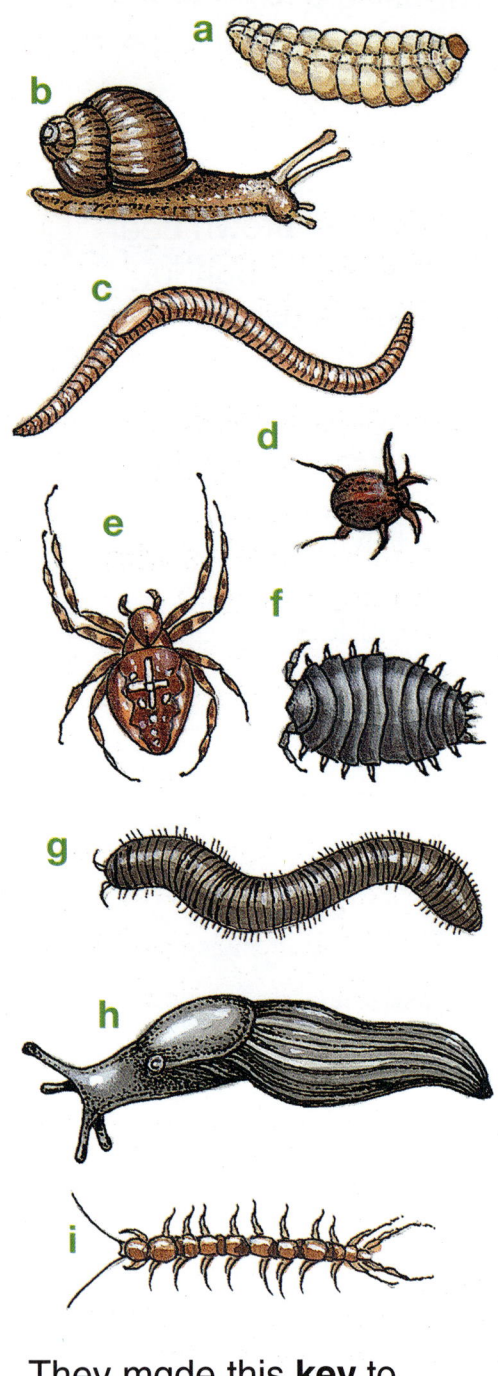

Key word
- key

They made this **key** to identify the animals.

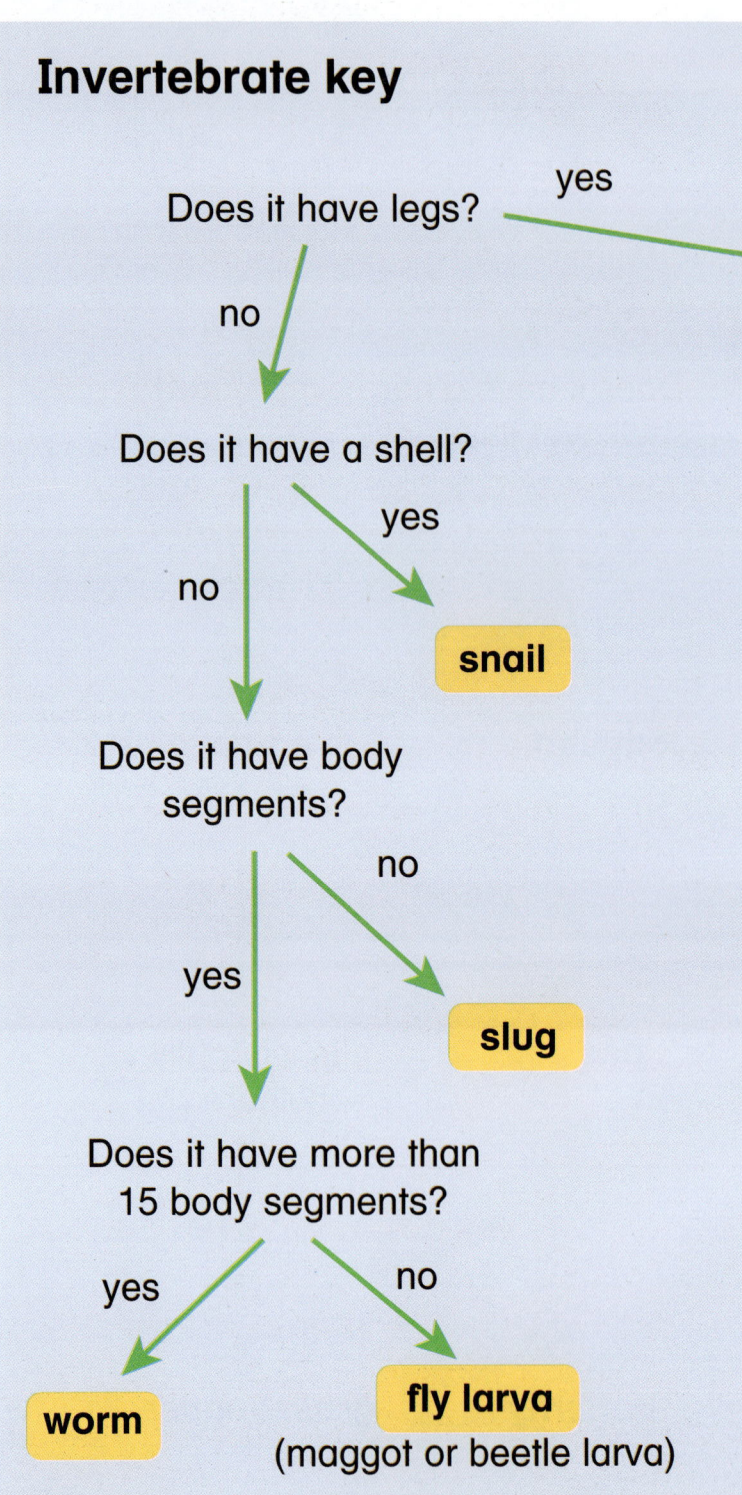

Invertebrate key

Does it have legs?
— yes →
— no ↓

Does it have a shell?
— yes → **snail**
— no ↓

Does it have body segments?
— no → **slug**
— yes ↓

Does it have more than 15 body segments?
— yes → **worm**
— no → **fly larva** (maggot or beetle larva)

32

Topic **2** Living things in their environment

1. Use the key to find the name of each animal in the pictures.
2. Name one difference between:
   - a spider and a woodlouse
   - a snail and a slug
   - a centipede and a millipede
   - a worm and a fly larva.

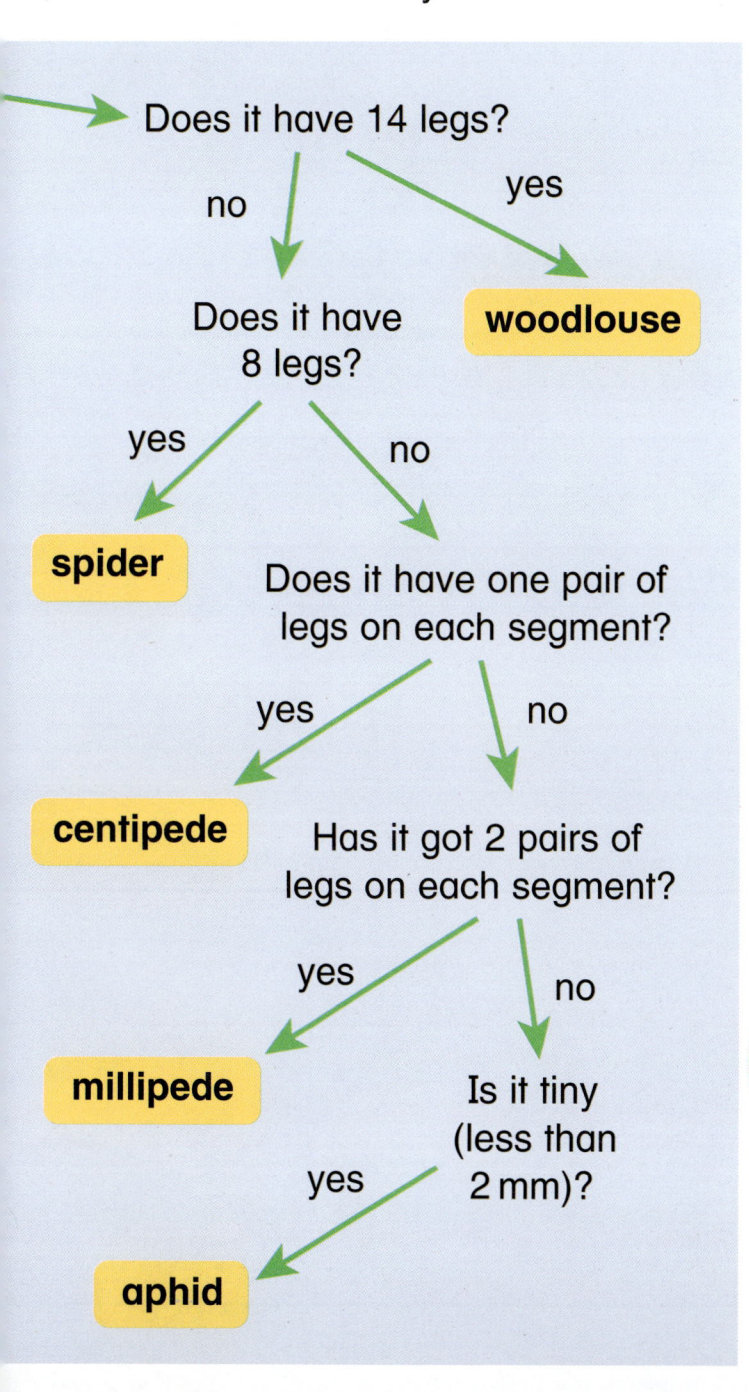

Does it have 14 legs?
- no → Does it have 8 legs?
  - yes → **spider**
  - no → Does it have one pair of legs on each segment?
    - yes → **centipede**
    - no → Has it got 2 pairs of legs on each segment?
      - yes → **millipede**
      - no → Is it tiny (less than 2 mm)?
        - yes → **aphid**
- yes → **woodlouse**

Activities

1 Nancy and Richard found these animals:

slug   butterfly
earthworm   snail
woodlouse   moth

Use the key on Workbook page 23 to classify the animals.

2 Design a different key to identify the same animals. Exchange keys with another student. Discuss whether the key was easy to use or not.

3 What would you have to do to change the key to include a palm tree and a hibiscus bush? Draw the new key.

I have learned

- You can use a simple key to identify different living things.

2.6 Human activity and the environment

Key words
- recycling
- pollution

Everything humans do as we live and work has an effect on the air, water and land in our environment.

Some of the things humans do can have a positive effect on the environment. For example, making compost from your kitchen waste and adding it to the soil can improve the soil quality. Fitting filters to factory chimneys can keep the air clean, and **recycling** waste can reduce the amount of resources we use as well as how much waste we produce.

Other actions have negative effects. For example, throwing litter on the ground makes the environment dirty, burning fuels to make electricity produces smoke that gets into the air, and dumping waste can pollute rivers and other water sources.

Pollution is anything that dirties or harms the environment. Many human activities cause pollution of some kind.

Topic **2** Living things in their environment

1. In what ways could the human activities shown here lead to water pollution?
2. What could be done to prevent the water from being polluted?
3. Explain how water pollution affects fish and other animals that live in the water.
4. Explain how water pollution affects people.

Activities

1 Look at the images. Describe how the environment is being affected in each case.

2 Read the sentences about industrial waste on Workbook page 24. Put them in order so that the paragraph makes sense.

3 Which is worse for the environment: pollution from industries or pollution from households? Organise a discussion about this and present your findings to the class.

I have learned

- Human activity affects the environment in positive and negative ways.

35

2.7 Waste and recycling

Key word
- waste disposal

Many human activities produce waste. Think about the things that you throw away at home or at school. All of this waste has to be disposed of in ways that are not harmful to the environment. **Waste disposal** is a big challenge for everyone.

1. What happens to the waste that you throw away?
2. Explain how the waste we produce affects the environment.
3. What could you do to reduce the amount of waste that your class throws away?

Topic **2** Living things in their environment

Look at the pollution in this river.

4 What is most of this waste made from?

5 Explain how this waste ends up in rivers.

Activities

1 Almost all plastics can be recycled. What other materials can be recycled? Make a list.

2 Carry out a survey to find out what materials are recycled in your community. Do you think enough is being done to reduce and recycle waste? Write a short report on your findings.

3 Produce a slideshow or leaflet that explains the positive effects of recycling and encourages people to recycle their waste.

I have learned

- Human activity affects the environment in positive and negative ways.
- Recycling can reduce waste and have positive effects on the environment.

37

Looking back Topic 2

In this topic you have learned

- The environment is the scientific name for our surroundings and the conditions found there.
- The area in which an animal lives is called its habitat. There are many different habitats in an environment.
- Animals are adapted to the habitats in which they live.
- Scientists group, or classify, living things based on the similarities and differences between them.
- A key is a diagram with questions that you follow to identify different animals in a group.
- Human activity affects the environment.
- Some effects of human activity can be positive, such as cleaning water, recycling waste or preventing pollution from reaching rivers.
- Other effects can be negative, such as polluting the air, land or water around us, damaging the environment or removing habitats.

How well do you remember?

1 Here are four different habitats.
   a Name two animals you would expect to find in each habitat.
   b State one way in which each animal you have named is suited to its habitat.

2 Look at PCM B7: Identifying wild cats. Petra has made a key to identify the five types of wild cat she saw at the zoo. The cats are: lion, black panther, tiger, leopard and cheetah.
   a Which animals should be written in spaces a to c?
   b Write a question for d that could be used to identify the leopard and cheetah.

3 Write down two causes and two effects of river pollution.

Topic 3 States of matter

In this topic you are going to learn more about matter and materials. You will examine solids, liquids and gases. You will work with materials to investigate heating and cooling further. You will focus on water to learn more about melting, freezing and what happens to steam when you cool it.

3.1 States of matter

Key words
- matter
- states
- solid
- liquid
- gas

Matter is the scientific word for what everything is made of. Matter is found in three different **states**: **solid**, **liquid** and **gas**.

Solid matter has a fixed shape. Some solids, such as sugar, can be poured but they do not always take the shape of the container you pour them into.

Liquid matter has no fixed shape. Liquids always take the shape of the container they are poured into.

Gases have no fixed shape and they spread out more easily and quickly than liquids do.

Your body contains matter in the three different states. Your bones and teeth are solid. Your blood and the tears in your eyes are liquid. Your lungs contain gas (air).

Topic **3** States of matter

The photographs below show some examples of different types of matter. Some are in a solid state, some are in a liquid state, and some are in a gas state.

Activities

1 Think about how you can tell whether matter is in a solid, liquid or gas state. Write down your ideas.

2 Test some solids, liquids and gases to find out about their properties. Use Workbook page 27 to record your findings.

3 Draw up a table to compare the properties of a gas with those of a liquid. Include similarities and differences.

1 Can you name five things around you that are solids?
2 Can you pick up liquids? Why?
3 Which gas is all around us right now?
4 Identify the solids, liquids and gases in the photographs.

I have learned

- Matter is the scientific word for what everything is made of.
- Matter is found in three different states: solid, liquid and gas.

41

3.2 Water

Key words
- water
- gaseous
- vapour
- change of state
- water cycle

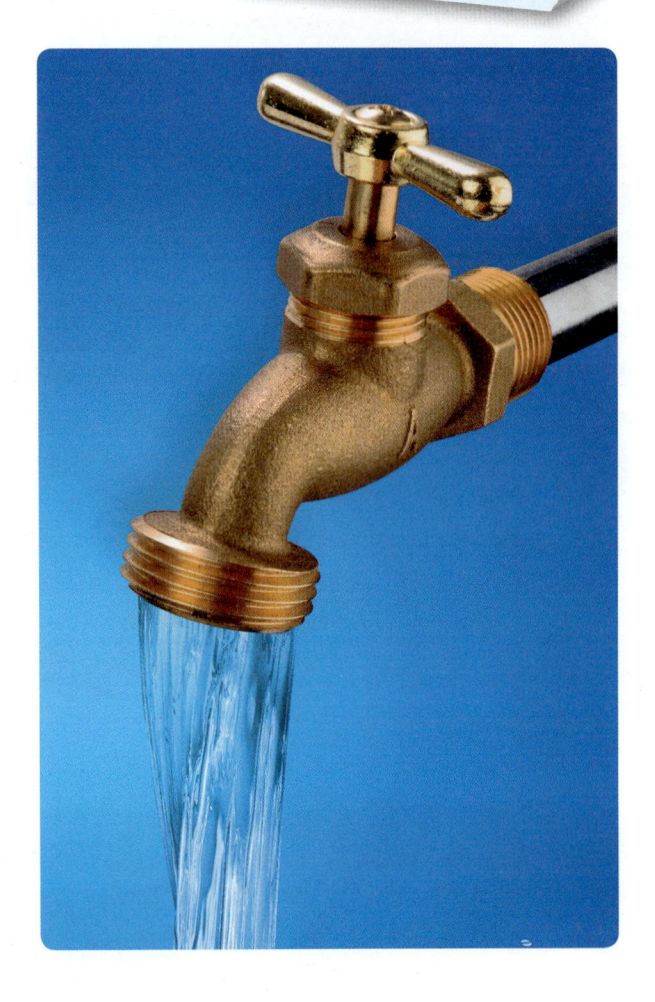

Water is a very common type of matter and it exists in all three states. Running or flowing water is in a liquid state. Ice is water in a solid state. You cannot see water or smell water in its **gaseous** state because water gas is invisible and odourless. However, there is water gas in the air around you all the time. We call water gas in the air water **vapour**.

1. Where have you seen water in a liquid state?
2. Where in the environment would you find water in a solid state?
3. Where does the water from wet washing go when the washing dries?

When matter changes from solid to liquid or from liquid to gas, we say it has undergone a **change of state**. Water is one of the few types of matter that we can observe changing from one state to another.

Topic **3** States of matter

This diagram shows how water changes state in nature. This process is called the **water cycle**.

Remember that clouds are not clouds of water vapour. They are actually made up of tiny drops of liquid water. The drops join up and, when they get too heavy, they fall to the ground in the form of rain. If it is really cold, then the drops freeze and fall to the ground as solid snow or hailstones.

4 Identify the three states of water in the water cycle.

5 Why do you think this process is called a cycle?

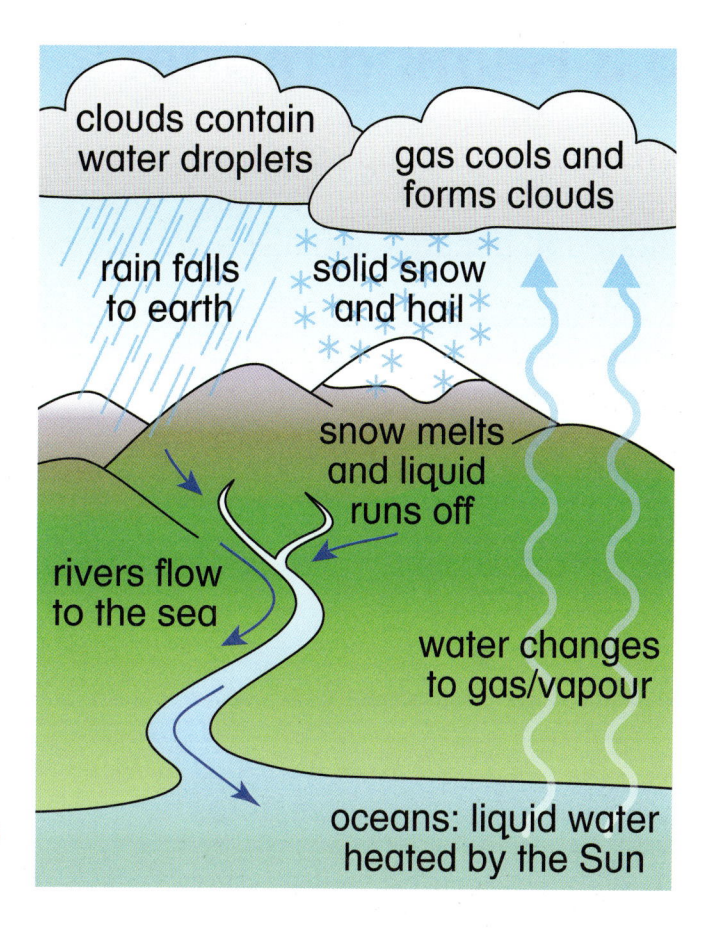

clouds contain water droplets
gas cools and forms clouds
rain falls to earth
solid snow and hail
snow melts and liquid runs off
rivers flow to the sea
water changes to gas/vapour
oceans: liquid water heated by the Sun

Activities

1 Imagine you are a water droplet in the ocean. Draw a cartoon story to show what happens to you as you move through the water cycle.

2 Set up a model of the water cycle in the classroom. Follow the instructions on Workbook page 29 to do this.

3 Compare your model with the real water cycle. What do the parts of your model represent and demonstrate?

I have learned

- Water exists in solid, liquid and gaseous states.
- Water can change from one state to another.

43

3.3 Heating matter

Key words
- melted
- heating

When you warm up solids, such as ice or butter, they get soft and then turn to liquid. When solids change state and become liquid, we say they have **melted**.

▲ This ice cube was left on a sunny window ledge for ten minutes.

▲ The solid ice cube melted in the heat and changed into liquid water.

1. What happens to ice when it gets warm?
2. Describe what ice looks like as it melts.
3. Do you think all ice will melt at the same rate?

Some solid matter needs more heat than other matter to make it melt. For example, if you heat butter in a metal pan, the butter will melt but the metal pan will not.

4. Name some solid matter that is easy to melt.
5. If you heated ice, butter and candlewax in the same pan, over the same heat, which one do you think would melt first? Why?

Topic **3** States of matter

Metals can be got from rocks by **heating** them at very high temperatures until the metal melts. Gold ore contains pure gold.

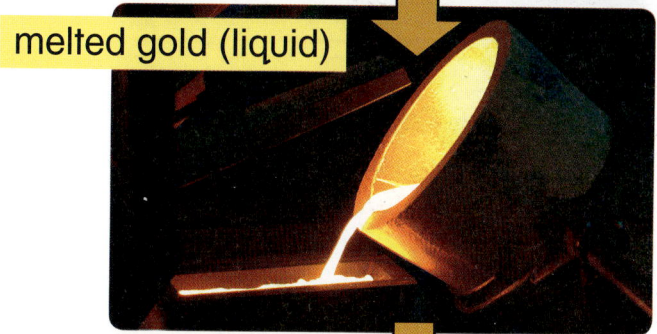

gold ore (solid)

melted gold (liquid)

pure gold (solid)

Activities

1. Have a class competition to see which group can make an ice cube melt the fastest. Use Workbook page 30 to record your work.

2. Investigate which solid matter melts the fastest by putting samples in foil dishes and floating them in hot water. Use Workbook page 31 to record your work.

3. Find out how heating is used to get precious metals, such as gold and silver, out of the rocks in which it is found. Draw a labelled diagram to show how this is done.

I have learned

- Some materials change state when they are heated or cooled.
- When a solid changes state to become a liquid, we say that it has melted.
- Some solid matter needs more heat than others to melt.
- Some solid matter melts faster than others.

3.4 Cooling matter

Key words
- freezing
- cooling

When a liquid is cooled enough, it turns to a solid. We say it solidifies, or freezes. **Freezing** is the reverse of melting.

1. Use the pictures to explain why we say freezing is the reverse of melting.
2. Give examples of liquids that solidify as they cool.
3. Do you think all liquids freeze at the same temperature?

Solid and liquid are states of matter. Melting and freezing are changes of state. Because melting and freezing are the reverse of each other, the change from one state to another is reversible. This means that if you melt a solid by heating it, you can reverse the change of state by **cooling** the liquid and causing it to freeze.

Topic **3** States of matter

Look at these two pictures.

4 Write a sentence about what is happening in each picture.

5 Can you think of some examples when the processes of melting and freezing are useful to us?

Activities

1 You use a thermometer to measure temperature. Draw a thermometer and write a clear set of instructions for using it to record temperature.

2 Record the temperature at which some substances freeze. Use Workbook page 32 to record your work.

3 Find out what the term 'freezing point' means. Compare the freezing point of water with that of candle wax. Explain why the melting point is actually the same as the freezing point in most matter.

I have learned

- Cooling liquid matter causes it to turn solid, or freeze.
- Freezing is the reverse of melting.

47

3.5 Liquid to gas

Key words
- evaporate
- steam

When water in liquid state is heated, it **evaporates** and turns to a gas. You cannot see this happening, but you can see the effects of evaporation by looking at how puddles get smaller and how levels of water drop in a lake. You can also observe **steam** forming when water is boiled in a pot or kettle.

You can see other examples of evaporation in daily life. For example, wet washing gets dry and puddles dry up after rain because the water evaporates. Paint dries on a picture or wall because the water in the paint evaporates.

1. What is making the water evaporate?
2. Which water do you think will evaporate faster, the water in the lake or the water in the kettle? Why?

Water is an important resource, particularly in hot, dry environments. When the rate of evaporation is high, we lose valuable liquid water. By understanding why water evaporates more quickly in some conditions than in others, scientists can find ways of reducing evaporation and saving water.

Topic 3 — States of matter

Jamie did this experiment to see what conditions affect evaporation from a lake.

3 Look at this experiment and discuss what is happening.

4 Why do you think putting the containers of water into a fridge would affect the rate of evaporation?

Container	Volume of water at start	Volume of water after two hours
A	100 ml	90 ml
B	100 ml	50 ml
C	100 ml	10 ml

Activities

1. Carry out your own evaporation experiment. Use Workbook page 34 to record your work.

2. Explain how you made sure your evaporation experiment was a fair test.

3. Based on what you have learned and observed, what advice would you give a community who wanted to reduce the rate of evaporation from a large, shallow lake?

I have learned

- Evaporation is the change of state from a liquid to a gas.
- Water in a kettle boils and turns to steam, evaporating very quickly.

49

3.6 Gas to liquid

Key words
- vapour
- cools
- condensation

Think about what happens if you take a cold can or bottle from the fridge and leave it on a table without opening it. Within a few seconds, drops of liquid will appear on the outside of the can or bottle. You can see this in the photograph.

1. What is the liquid on the can?
2. Where do you think it comes from?

This liquid is actually water. It forms because water **vapour** in the air touches the cold surface and **cools** down. The cooled water vapour changes state from a gas back to a liquid. The scientific term for this is **condensation**. Condensation is the reverse of evaporation.

A group of students did some experiments to show that when water vapour cools it condenses and turns back into a liquid state (water). Read the information and look at the diagrams carefully.

Experiment 1

We placed some ice cubes in the centre of some plastic film stretched over a container of warm water.

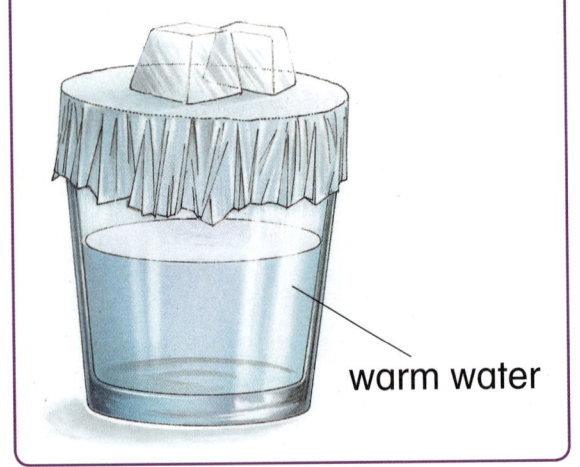

warm water

Experiment 2

We boiled a kettle on the stove until steam came out. Then we very carefully held a cold plate in front of the steam.

Topic **3** States of matter

3. What do you think will happen in each of these experiments?
4. Describe how the experiments are different from each other.
5. Water droplets form in all three experiments. Where do you think they form? Where do they come from?

Experiment 3

First, we rubbed the outside of a can with a duster until it was shiny. Next, we filled the can with ice cubes and then wiped the outside of the can to ensure it was dry. Then we put the can in a warm place. After a few minutes we observed the outside of the can.

1   2   3   4

Activities

1. Watch the demonstration of each experiment. Record your observations on Workbook page 35.

2. If water condenses on car windows, the driver cannot see. Find out what drivers can do to prevent the windows from 'misting up'.

3. Prepare a short presentation to show how evaporation and condensation occur in the water cycle.

I have learned

- Water vapour and steam will turn back into water when they are cooled.
- This process is called condensation.

Looking back Topic 3

In this topic you have learned

- Matter is the scientific name for what everything is made from.
- Matter is found in three states: solid, liquid and gas.
- When materials are heated they may melt or evaporate.
- When materials are cooled they may freeze or condense.
- When a solid changes to a liquid it melts. When a liquid changes to a solid it freezes.
- Melting and freezing are reverse processes.
- Water turns to steam when it boils. When the steam cools, it turns back to water.

How well do you remember?

Choose the correct scientific term in each statement.

Choose from this list.

condense   evaporate   air   reverse
freeze   gas   liquid   steam   melt   solid

1 This is a material with a fixed shape. It does not flow. _____
2 This is the word used to describe a liquid turning into a gas. _____
3 This gas is all around us. We cannot see it. _____
4 This is what happens when you breathe on a mirror. The water vapour from your breath will cool and _____.
5 When a gas cools, it will change state and become a _____.
6 When a solid such as chocolate is heated, it will _____.
7 To change a liquid into a solid, you need to _____ it.
8 When a liquid is heated it turns into a _____.
9 Melting is the _____ of freezing.
10 When water is boiled, it turns into _____.

Topic 4 Sound

In this topic you will learn about sounds, how they are made, how we hear them and how you can use a sound level meter to measure the volume of different sounds. You will do some practical investigations to find out how sound travels through different materials and how some materials can be used to stop sound travelling. Next, you will learn about the pitch of sound. You will explore how the pitch of a sound can be changed in different ways in musical instruments.

4.1 How sounds are made

Key words
- sounds
- vibration
- vibrate

Sounds are made when something moves forwards and backwards very quickly. We call this movement a **vibration**. When an object or material **vibrates**, we say it is a source of sound.

1. Describe what you would hear in each of these examples.
2. What is vibrating to make the sound in each case?

Human beings can be a source of sound. When you speak, shout or sing you are making sounds.

3. Put your fingers on the front of your throat and talk to your partner. Can you feel your throat vibrating?

You need movement to get sound. When you allow air to pass over your vocal cords in your voice box, the air makes them vibrate. You change the shape of your mouth to change the sounds.

We hear sounds because something causes our eardrums to vibrate. Vibrations move through air (or another material) in waves (we call these sound waves) until they enter our ears. When they do, the thin eardrum starts to vibrate and we hear the sound.

Topic **4** Sound

Robert Boyle was an Irish scientist. In 1658 he did experiments to investigate how we hear sounds. He placed a clock in a glass jar and slowly pumped out all the air. When he had removed the air, he could not hear the clock ticking any more. He concluded that sound is carried through the air to our ears.

Activities

1. Carry out a sound survey in your school grounds. Sit quietly outside for a few minutes and list all the sounds that you hear. Use Workbook pages 37–38 to organise and graph your results.

2. Carry out the experiment on Workbook page 39 to see how sound can make air vibrate.

3. Investigate how sound travels through air. Follow the instructions on Workbook page 40 to do this.

I have learned

- Sounds are made when objects, materials or air vibrate.
- You cannot see sound but you can observe the effect of the vibrations.

4.2 Measuring sound

Key words
- volume
- decibel
- sound level meter

Some sounds are soft and others are loud. The loudness of a sound is called the **volume** of the sound. Sound levels, or volume, are measured in special units called **decibels** (dB). This scale shows you the decibel levels for some common sounds.

1. What is the sound level of a jet on take-off?
2. What is the level at which sound damages your ears?
3. Most health authorities suggest ear protection for sounds above 85 decibels. Do you think you should wear ear protection when using a lawnmower? Why?

Whispering
Talking normally
Busy city traffic
Loud thunder
fireworks
Aeroplane taking off
Silence

decibels (dB)

Rain falling
Lawn mower
Train
MP4 player at high volume
Level at which the sound damages your ears

56

Topic 4 Sound

▼ We use a **sound level meter** to measure the volume of sounds in decibels.

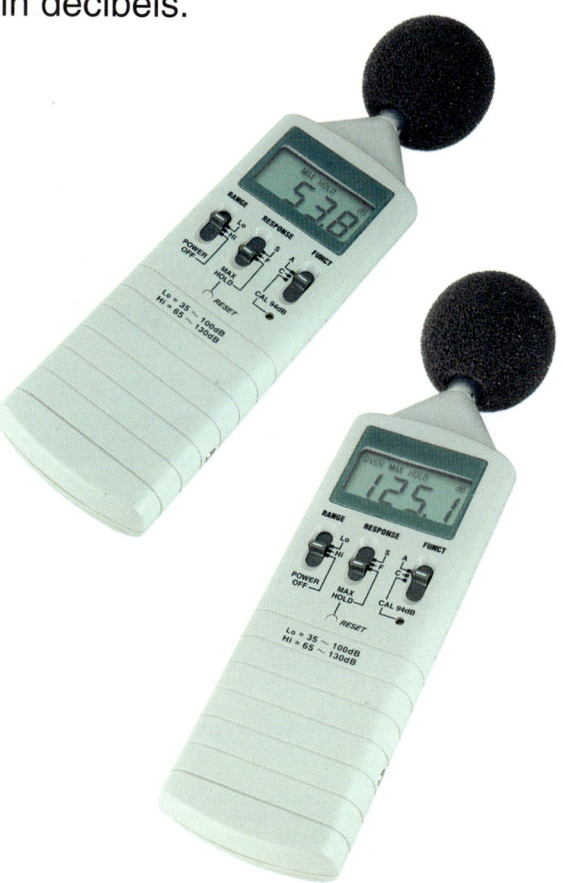

Activities

1. You are going to use a sound level meter to measure the volume of different sounds. Use Workbook pages 41–42 to record your measurements.

2. Choose one object that makes a sound. Investigate what happens to the readings on the sound level meter when you move the object further away from the meter. Use Workbook page 43 to plan and record your investigation.

3. Read the information about sound meters on Workbook page 45. For each use, say why it might be useful and/or important to record the sound levels accurately.

4. Explain how you think a sound level meter works.

5. What sounds might have given the readings on these two meters?

I have learned

- Sound levels can be measured in decibels using a sound level meter.
- The decibel scale is used to give the sound levels of different sounds or noises.

4.3 Sound travels through different materials

Key words
- source
- medium
- metres per second

We hear sounds when they reach our ears. To reach our ears, sounds have to travel from the **source** of the vibration, usually through the air.

Airplanes such as this one fly at heights of up to 10 km in the sky, but we can still hear them because the sound of the engine travels through the air to reach our ears.

1. Do you think we hear the sound at the same volume as the passengers on the plane? Why?

Sound can also travel through solids and liquids.

2. Put your ear on the table and ask your partner to tap gently on the table with a ruler. Describe what you hear.

Whales and dolphins make sounds underwater. The sounds travel through the water and they can be heard many kilometres away. Scientists have placed recording equipment underwater to record whale songs.

58

Topic **4** Sound

Next time you have a bath or go swimming, try making some sounds under the water. You will find that you can hear them quite well.

Sound travels better though solids and liquids than it does through the air. The sound travels at different speeds depending on the **medium** through which it is travelling. We measure the speed at which sound travels in **metres per second** (m/s).

Here are some of the speeds at which sound travels through different media (this is the plural of medium):

- air – 330 m/s
- water – 1430 m/s
- steel – 3600 m/s.

3 Does sound travel faster through solids, liquids or gases?

Activities

1. Work in pairs to design and make a string telephone. Use Workbook pages 46 and 47 to record your investigation.

2. Work with a partner to investigate how sound travels through liquid. Use Workbook page 48 to record your investigation.

3. Find out how ships use sound (SONAR) to navigate. Prepare a short presentation for the class explaining how this technology works.

I have learned

- Sound can travel through the air to reach our ears.
- Sound can also travel through solids and liquids.

4.4 Reducing sound levels

Key word
- soundproof

The photograph shows a recording studio where music is recorded. The microphones in the studio are sensitive and they will record sounds that are quite soft.

1. Think about the room you are in. Can you hear sounds from outside?

2. If you were recording a music CD, you would not want any sounds from outside to be recorded as part of your song. What do you think stops the sounds from outside the recording studio from spoiling the songs?

It is also important that people living or working near the recording studio do not get disturbed by the sounds made in the studios. Unwanted sounds are a nuisance. They can also be dangerous if they are very loud, as they can damage your ears.

Some materials are very good at stopping sound from travelling through them. These materials can be used to **soundproof** rooms or to make ear protectors that protect your ears and stop loud noises from reaching your eardrums.

Topic **4** Sound

Activities

1 Many people wear ear protectors like the ones in the photographs. Explain how you think they work. What sort of materials are they made from?

2 Make and test a set of ear protectors that can block the sound from a TV or radio. Use Workbook page 49 to record your work.

3 Find out which workers use ear protection devices such as earplugs and ear protectors (like the ones shown in the pictures). For each device, say what noise it is trying to reduce.

3 What is making the sound in the picture above?

4 What is the machine operator doing to protect his ears?

5 Why are ear protectors necessary for workers who use machinery like this?

I have learned

- Some sounds are annoying or harmful and we need to stop them reaching our ears.
- To protect our ears we can use ear protectors made from materials that reduce sound levels.

4.5 Soundproofing materials

Key words
- transmission
- muffle

Some materials prevent sound from travelling through them better than others. Look at these two apartments. Apartment A has wooden floors. Apartment B has a thick carpet on the floor.

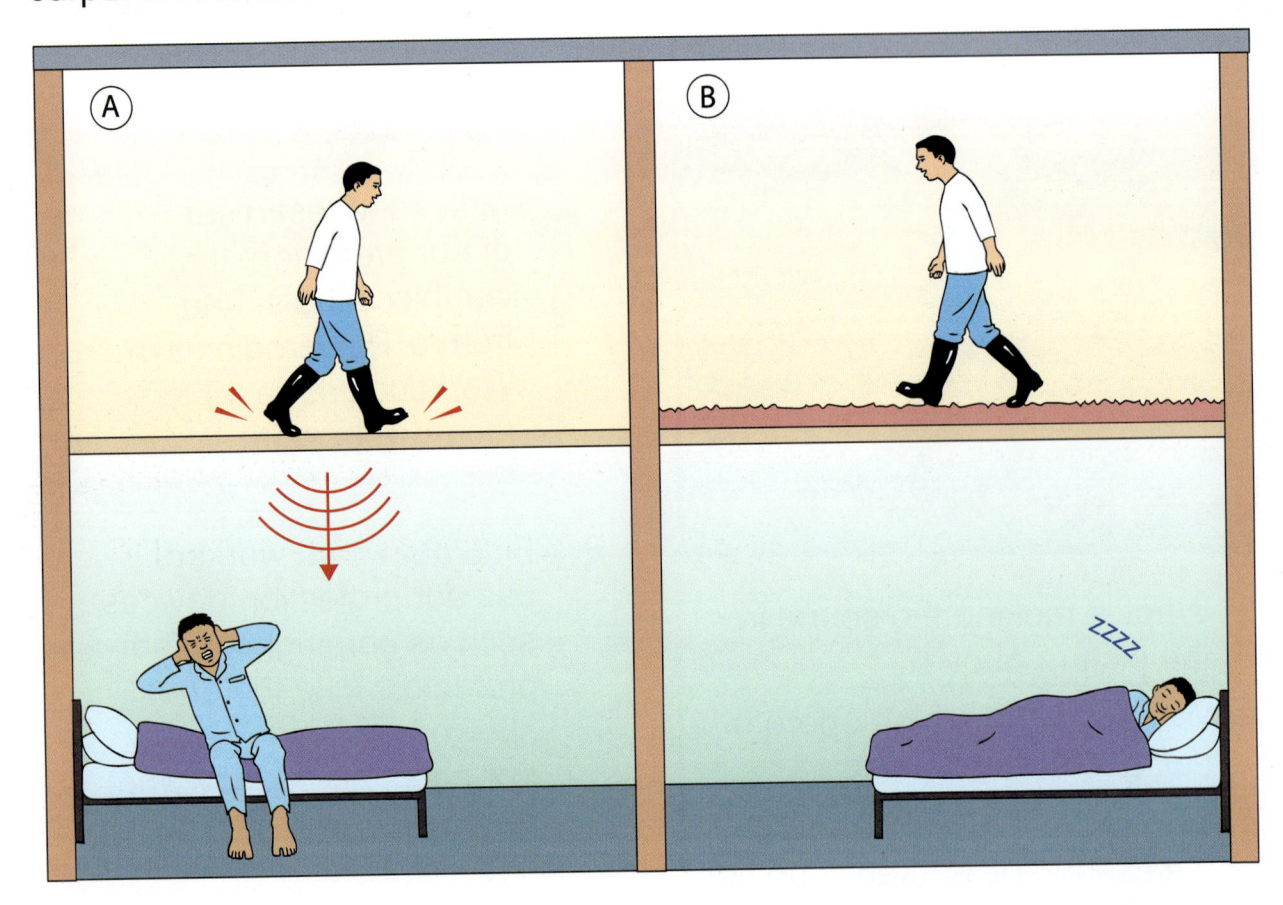

1. Whose downstairs neighbour hears a lot of noise? Why?
2. Think about your own home. What materials in your home stop sound from travelling between rooms and from outdoors to indoors?

Soundproofing materials work by absorbing sounds and preventing vibrations from travelling through them. They prevent the **transmission** of sound. Think of an alarm clock – if it is next to your bed you can hear it ringing loudly. If you put it under your pillow, the sound is **muffled** because the pillow absorbs the vibrations.

Topic **4** Sound

Look at these pictures carefully.

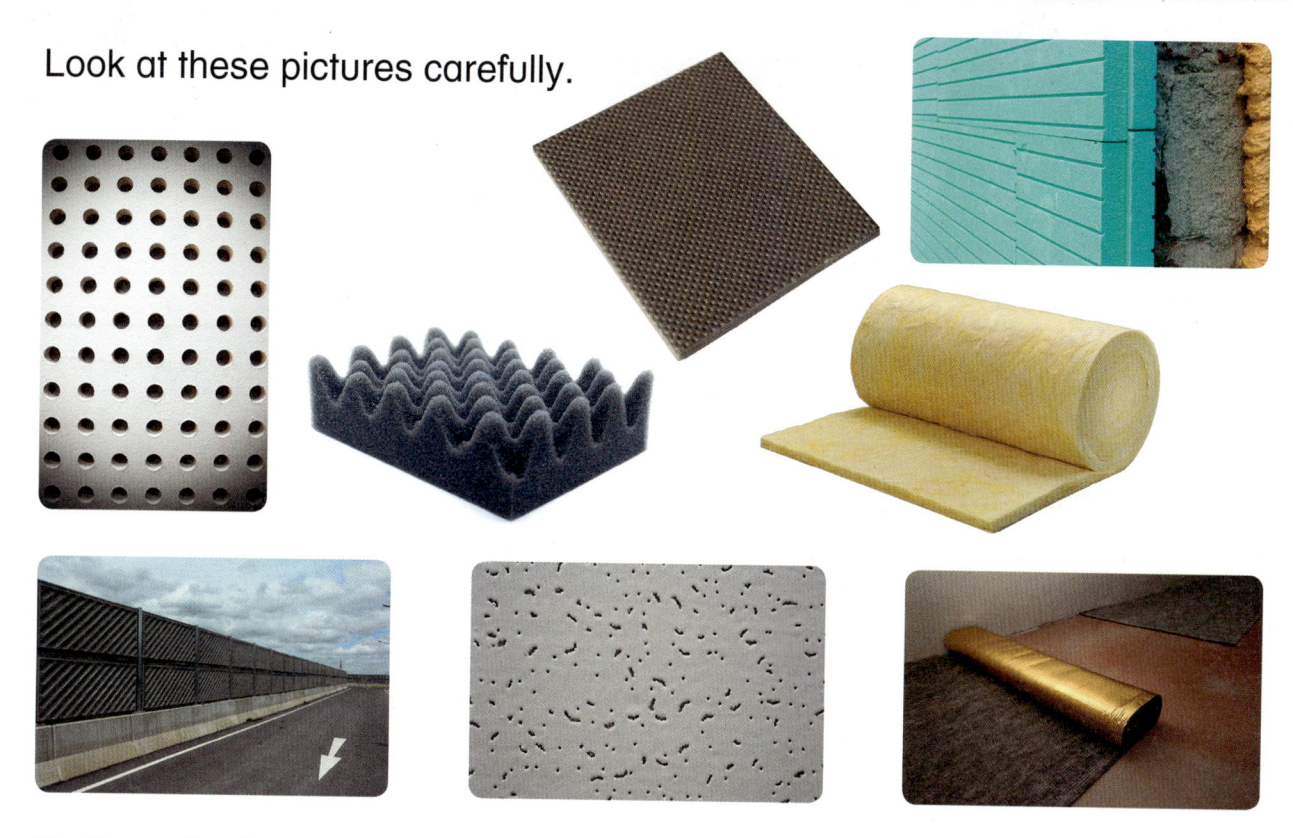

3 Describe how you think these soundproofing materials are used to reduce sound levels.

Activities

1 Which of these materials do you think works best? Use Workbook page 50 to rank the materials in order from most to least effective.

2 Carry out a test to see how effectively different materials reduce sound. Use Workbook pages 51 and 52 to record your findings.

3 Plan how to solve some noise problems in a busy workplace. Use the diagrams on Workbook page 53 to identify the problem areas and to show your solutions.

I have learned

- Some materials are very effective at reducing sound levels.

4.6 Musical instruments

Key words
- sound
- vibrate

A musical instrument makes a **sound**, or note, when part of the instrument **vibrates**.

1 Look back to the photograph on page 53.

   a Do you know the name of this instrument?

   b What are the children doing to make the instruments vibrate?

An orchestra or band is made up of several instruments that produce sounds in different ways.

Drums are percussion instruments. To make a sound you bang on them to make the skin **vibrate**. The sound you make depends on the size and shape of the drum. A larger drum will make a lower sound than a smaller drum.

2 Which of the other instruments shown here are percussion instruments? Explain how they make sounds.

Brass instruments, such as trumpets and saxophones, are wind instruments. You blow into them to make sounds. The sound depends on the shape of the instrument and the length of the pipe or tube.

3 Any instrument that you blow into is a wind instrument. Can you name some others?

64

Topic **4** Sound

Activities

1 You can use everyday items to model simple musical instruments and see how they make sounds. Use the ideas on Workbook page 54 to get started.

2 Complete the fact files and classify the different instruments on Workbook page 55.

3 Choose one unusual musical instrument and find out more about it. Prepare a short presentation about the instrument and how it is played.

Stringed instruments, such as guitars and violins, make sounds when you pluck the strings causing them to vibrate. The sound depends on the length, thickness and tightness of the string.

A piano has strings inside it. It is these strings that vibrate to make sounds. When you press a piano key it causes a hammer inside the piano to hit a wire. There are 88 keys on a piano and each one makes a different sound.

4 The strings of most instruments are not made of string. What do you think they are made of?

I have learned

- Musical instruments make sounds called notes.
- To make a sound, part of the instrument needs to vibrate.

4.7 Pitch

Key words
- pitch
- high-pitched
- low-pitched

You already know that sounds can differ in volume and that you can measure loudness in decibels. Sounds can also be high or low, depending on the speed of the vibration. The highness or lowness of sounds is called the **pitch** of the sound. For example, an emergency siren is a **high-pitched** sound and the roll of thunder is a **low-pitched** sound.

1. Can you think of two more high-pitched and two more low-pitched sounds?

When instruments are played together in tune, they produce music. Music is made up of notes with different pitches. A high pitch describes a high note and a low pitch describes a low note. If an object such as a guitar string vibrates quickly, it produces a note of a higher pitch than when the string vibrates slowly.

In general, the larger the object, the lower the pitch of the sound it produces.

Look at these three stringed instruments.

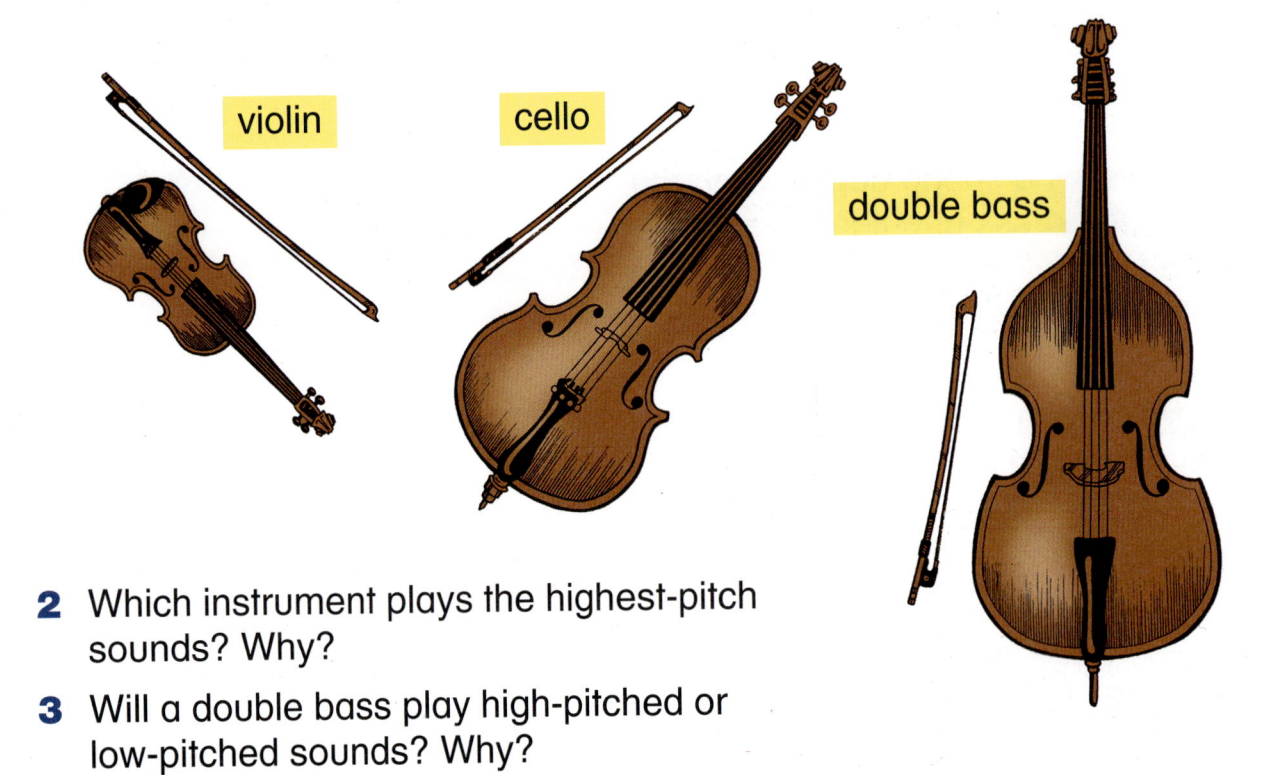

violin

cello

double bass

2. Which instrument plays the highest-pitch sounds? Why?
3. Will a double bass play high-pitched or low-pitched sounds? Why?

Topic 4 Sound

Sounds with the same pitch can be soft or loud. Loud notes are made by large vibrations. For example, if you hit a drum hard you will make a loud sound, and if you hit it gently you will make a soft sound. Both sounds will have the same pitch.

Activities

1. Use a plastic ruler to demonstrate how changes in vibrations can change the sounds produced. Follow the instructions on Workbook page 56.

2. Complete the sound wordsearch on Workbook page 57.

3. Do some research to find out what the tone of a sound is. Describe how tone is different from volume and pitch.

I have learned

- Pitch describes how high or low a sound is.
- High- and low-pitched sounds can be soft or loud.

67

4.8 Changing the pitch of a musical instrument

Key words
- pitch
- vibrate

The **pitch** of a sound can be changed in different ways. For example, in string instruments the musician can change the pitch by changing the length of the string. Musicians do not actually use longer and shorter strings; instead, they hold their fingers over the strings at different places to shorten the length of the string that **vibrates**. If you watch someone playing a stringed instrument, you will see how they do this.

You can demonstrate how this works using a simple model such as this one:

1. What do you think you will hear if you pluck the elastic?

2. Which length of elastic will make the highest-pitched sound? Why?

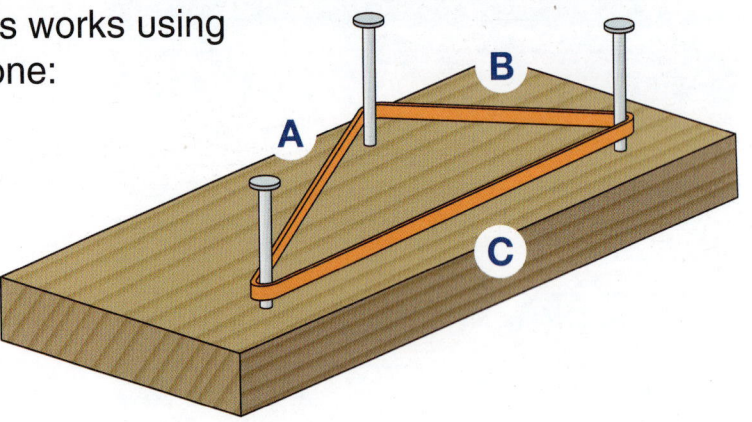

Wind instruments have keys that open or close valves or holes along their length. They can be closed by placing a finger over them. Opening and closing valves or holes changes the length of the tube in which air can vibrate, and this changes the pitch of the sound.

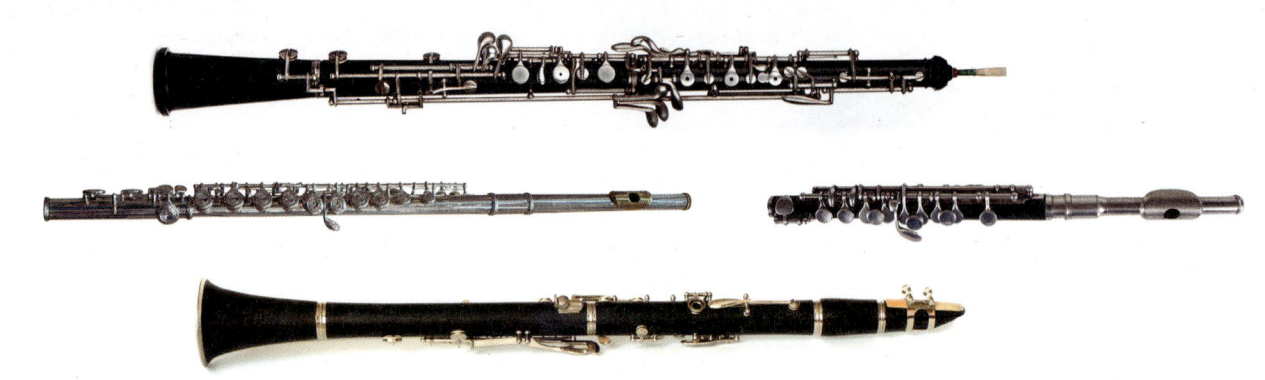

3. Which of these instruments will produce the most high-pitched sounds? Why?

4. Choose one of these instruments and explain how the musician would play notes of a different pitch.

Topic **4** Sound

Most drums can only play notes of one pitch because you cannot change the tightness of the skin. Other percussion instruments can play notes of different pitches.

5. Explain how you think the marimba player in the photograph produces notes of different pitches.

Activities

1. Make a family of straw whistles of different lengths. Explain how the length of the straw affects the sound of the whistle. Record your findings using Workbook page 58.

2. Use bottles and water to produce a wind instrument that can play different notes. Explain how to make sounds of different pitches using the bottles. Record your findings on Workbook page 58.

3. Design and make your own instrument made from only recycled materials. Your instrument must be able to produce notes of different pitch. Demonstrate how your instrument works to the class.

I have learned

- Pitch can be changed in musical instruments in different ways.

Looking back Topic 4

In this topic you have learned

- Sounds are made when air or an object vibrates. You cannot have sound without vibration.
- The volume, or loudness, of sound can be measured in decibels (dB) using a sound level meter.
- Sound can travel through air and other gases, as well as through solids and liquids, to reach our ears.
- Some materials absorb vibrations and this makes them effective at preventing sound from travelling through them.
- Pitch describes how high or low a sound is. The speed of vibration affects the pitch.
- Sounds of the same pitch can be loud or soft. The strength of the vibration affects the volume.
- The pitch of musical instruments can be changed by changing the length of the string or the amount of air that vibrates.

How well do you remember?

1. Write down two ways in which humans can produce sounds.
2. What vibrates to make a sound in each of the following?

    a drum   b guitar   c trumpet   d piano

3. Explain how you could stop sound reaching your ears.
4. Living and working in noisy places can be problematic for people.

    a List two problems that can be caused by unwanted loud noise.

    b List three things that make sounds loud enough to damage your hearing.

5. Mandy has three glass bottles. What can she do to make sounds with them? Write down and draw your ideas.

Topic 5 Electricity and magnetism

This topic deals with electrical circuits and how to construct them. Once you have built circuits you will find out what happens when there is a break in the circuit and begin to use models to understand how electricity flows around the circuit. Next, you will work with magnets to explore the forces between them and to see how they attract and repel each other. You will also learn that magnets attract some metals but not others.

5.1 Electrical circuits

Key words
- component
- circuit
- wire
- lamp
- battery (cell)
- switch
- break

In Stage 2 you learned about simple circuits and you built your own circuits using different **components**. Do you remember what the components are and how to join them in a **circuit**?

Look at this circuit.

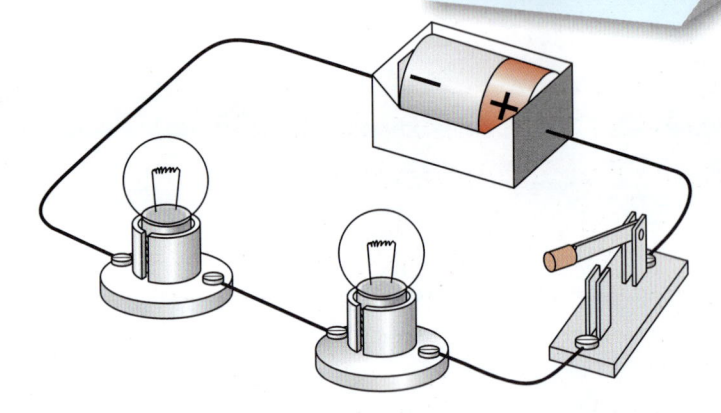

1 What are the components of this circuit?

2 Is this a complete circuit?

3 What would you need to do to this circuit to make the **lamps** light up?

A circuit is a path through which electricity can move. Circuits need to be complete in order for lamps to light up. A complete circuit means that the components are all joined in the correct way and that the circuit is closed.

Look at these diagrams:

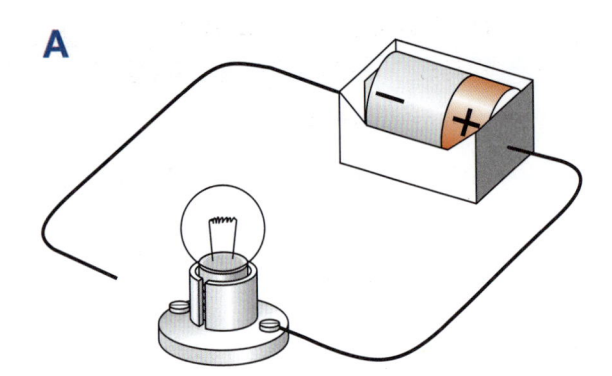

A

B

Diagram **A** shows an incomplete circuit. The **wires** are not joined to the lamp, so the circuit is not closed and the electricity cannot travel around the path.

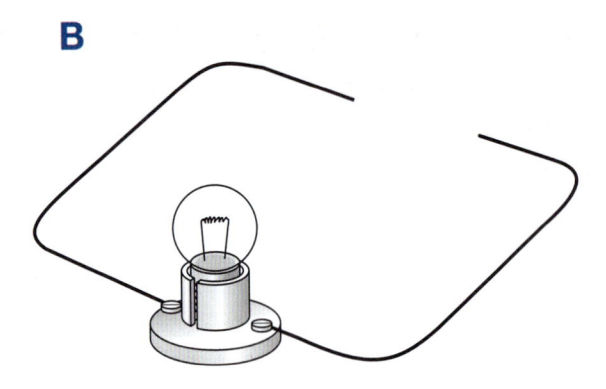

Diagram **B** has no source of electricity. It needs a **battery**, or cell, to make a circuit. Even if you joined up the wires, the lamp would not light up.

72

Topic 5 Electricity and magnetism

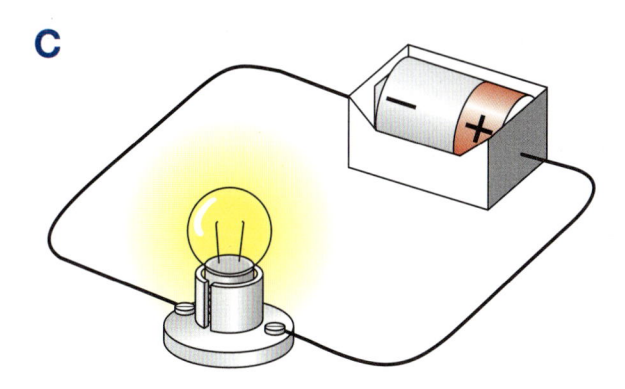

C

Diagram **C** is a complete closed circuit. The components are connected correctly, there is a source of electricity and the lamp is lit up.

If there is a **switch** in the circuit it needs to be in the 'on' position to close the circuit. Opening the switch, or putting it in the 'off' position, makes a **break** in the circuit and the electricity can no longer travel around a complete path, so the lamps don't light up.

4. Besides an open circuit, what else could prevent the lamps from lighting up?

Activities

1. Work in a group. Suggest all the things that you need to know before you can build an electrical circuit.

2. Make a poster to teach young children about circuit components, what they are for and how they need to be connected for a circuit to work.

3. Where do we use batteries in circuits in daily life? Make a list of devices that work with batteries. Show what type of battery is used in each one.

I have learned

- A circuit is a closed path for electricity.
- Circuits are built with components such as wires, batteries, lamps and switches.
- A circuit must be complete and closed for the electricity to be able to travel around it.

73

5.2 Building circuits

In this unit you are going to build some **circuits** so that you can learn more about them and understand how they work.

Key words
- circuit
- component
- bulb
- lamp
- switch
- wire
- connect

You are going to work with the following **components**.

battery

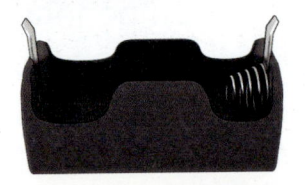

battery holder

bulb holder

lamp

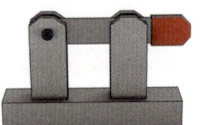

switch

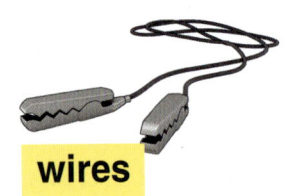

wires

1. Do you know what each component does in the circuit? Tell a partner.

Read through these instructions for building a simple circuit using these components.

Check that you have all your components.

⬇

Put the battery into the battery holder, paying attention to the positive and negative signs on both.

⬇

Screw the lamp into the lamp holder so that it fits firmly, but do not make it too tight.

⬇

Connect a wire to one end of the battery holder.

⬇

Connect a wire to each connection on the bulb holder.

Topic **5** Electricity and magnetism

- Put the switch in an off position (open).
- Join one end of the bulb holder to one side of the switch.
- Join the wire from the battery holder to the other side of the switch.
- Connect the other wire of the bulb holder to the free side of the battery holder.
- Close the switch to complete the circuit.

2 What would you check first if your lamp did not light up after you followed these steps? Why?

Activities

1 Use components to build different circuits. Follow the instructions on Workbook page 62.

2 Design a troubleshooting flow chart to show students what they should check if the lamp in a circuit does not light up. Use page 63 of your Workbook to record your work.

3 Does the length or path followed by the wires make a difference to a circuit? Read the statement and look at the diagram on Workbook page 64 and then do your own investigation.

I have learned

- Components must be connected correctly to form a circuit.
- In a complete circuit, the lamps will light up.

75

5.3 Why won't it work?

Key words
- circuit
- break

Electrical devices can only work if the electrical **circuit** to which they are attached is complete. If there is a **break** in the circuit, it is incomplete and the device will not work.

Consider the following problems.

Problem 1:
Harry's flashlight won't light up.

Problem 2:
Vanessa's reading lamp isn't working.

1 What could be causing each of these problems?

The devices in the pictures are not working because there is a break in the circuit. There are a number of things that can cause a break in a circuit.

▶ Switches are used to break circuits on purpose. When the switch is off, the circuit is broken and the device will not work.

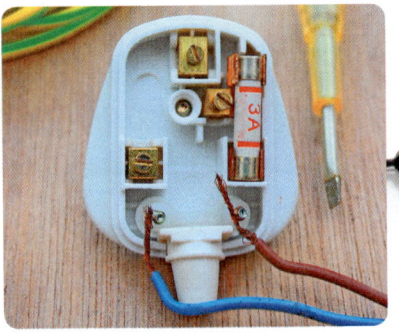

▲▶ Incomplete connections will also cause breaks in circuits. When a mains electrical device is unplugged, the connection to the electricity supply is broken and the device won't work. When wires or other components are loose or when there is something blocking the connection, the circuit is broken and the device won't work.

76

Topic **5** Electricity and magnetism

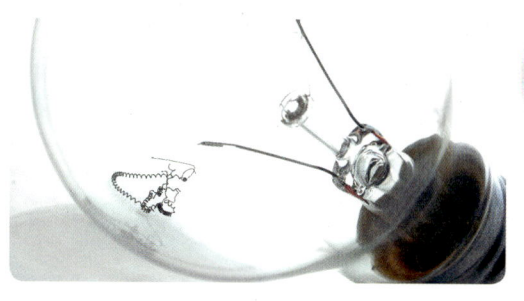

▲ Faulty components can cause breaks in circuits. Flat batteries, broken or spent bulbs, gaps between the connections in the switch and broken wires will all cause a break in the circuit and the device won't work.

▲ Special circuit breakers, such as fuses, are installed in homes and vehicles. If the electricity supply is too strong, or there is a problem with the supply, the fuse wire burns out and breaks the circuit by causing a gap that the electricity cannot flow through.

2 Many devices that you use at home rely on two switches to make a complete circuit. Explain how this works.

Activities

1 Write a set of instructions for Harry and Vanessa to explain what they should check to see why their electrical devices are not working. Refer back to your troubleshooting chart if you need to.

2 Look at the electrical devices on Workbook page 65 and read the information next to each one. Suggest where the break could be in each circuit.

3 Naadira has a length of electrical cord. She thinks that some of the copper wires inside the cord may be broken. Explain how she could test this before she attaches the cord to her new reading lamp. Use Workbook page 66 to record your ideas and show your solutions.

I have learned

- An electrical device will not work if there is a break anywhere in the circuit.
- Switches are used on purpose to safely break and complete circuits.

77

5.4 Electrical current

Key words
- flow
- current
- particles

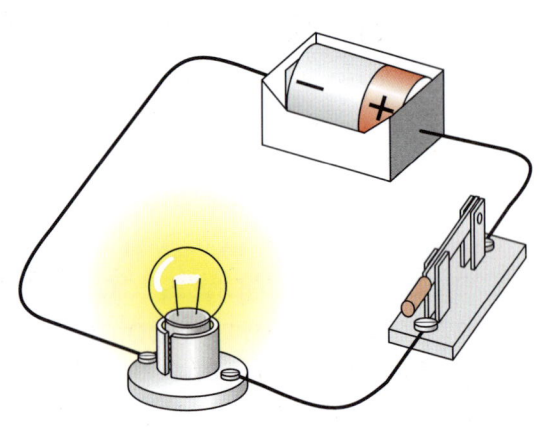

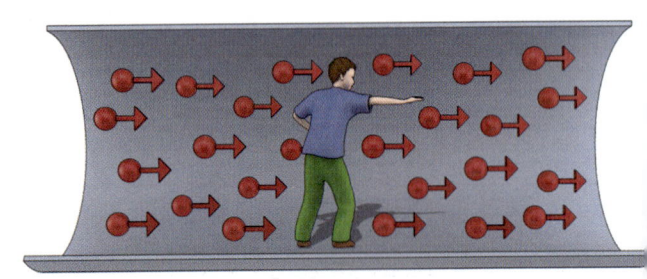

We cannot see electricity but we can observe its effects.

1. What happens to the fan when it is plugged in and switched on?
2. Where does the electricity come from to make the fan work?
3. Describe how the electricity gets from its source to the fan.

Think about the circuits you have built. When the circuit is closed the light bulb glows.

You already know that the battery is the source of electricity in the circuit. The fact that the lamp lights up shows us that the electricity has to travel from the battery along the wires and through the lamp in order to make it work.

The **flow** of electricity through the circuit is called an electric **current**. We cannot see the current, so we have to use models to describe how it flows.

You can think of an electric current as a flow of tiny **particles** (called electrons) though the wire. If you were small enough to stand inside the wire, you would experience the current as a movement of many tiny particles flying past you. You and the particles that make up the wire would be still while the current flowed past. Look at this diagram to see one model that describes the flow of electric current.

Topic **5** Electricity and magnetism

The circuit is a loop. The current travels around the circuit continuously until you break the circuit. This means that the current flows from the battery, around the circuit and back to the battery. The battery acts like a pump to push electrons around the circuit.

4 Use the diagram to explain how electric current flows around the circuit.

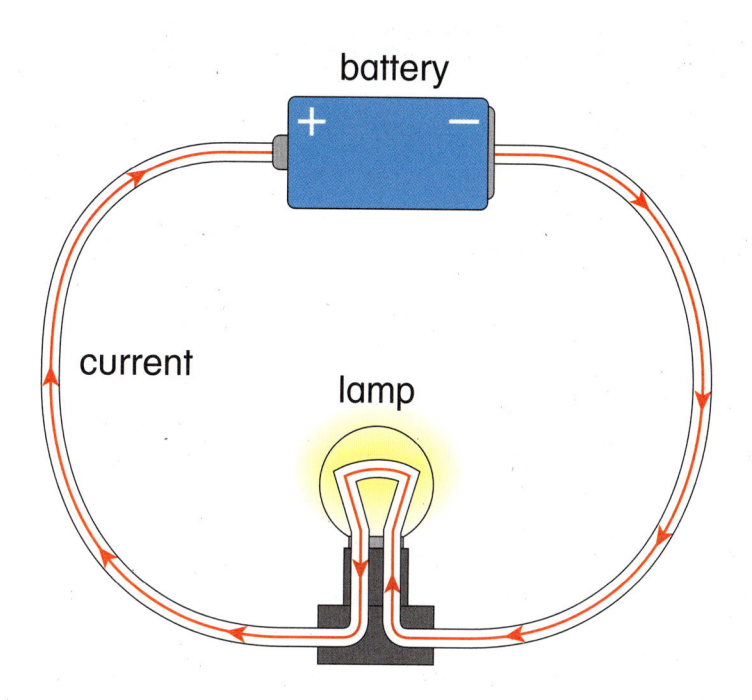

(Diagram labels: battery, current, lamp)

Activities

1 Label a diagram to describe the flow of electric current around a circuit in a flashlight. Use Workbook page 67 to record your work.

2 Work with a group to develop a role play to show how current flows around a simple circuit. You may not speak during your role play, so your actions have to show what happens.

3 The electrical current that flows through electrical cables is strong enough to kill a person. Find out how it is possible for birds to sit on electrical wires without being killed and what electricians have to do to work on these wires without getting killed.

I have learned

- Electrical current flows around a circuit in a continuous loop.
- We cannot see electrical current, but we can think of it as a flow of tiny particles.

5.5 Magnets

Key words
- magnet
- pole
- force

You have probably seen and used **magnets** before. The photographs show some of the magnets that you may have seen around you.

1 Which of these magnets have you seen?
2 Where else have you seen magnets? What were they doing?

There are also powerful magnets inside speakers and computer hard-drives.

3 What do you think makes one magnet more powerful than another?

Topic **5** Electricity and magnetism

Magnets come in different shapes. The most common shapes used in schools are bar magnets and U-shaped magnets, but you also get circular magnets, ring-shaped magnets and round magnets. The flat sheet-like fridge magnets are made from fine magnetic powder mixed with plastic.

4 Explain how you can tell the difference between a magnet and an ordinary piece of metal.

Look at this bar magnet. The two halves are painted different colours and labelled N and S. This is because magnets have two **poles**: a north pole (N) and a south pole (S). The magnetic **force** exerted by a magnet is strongest at its poles.

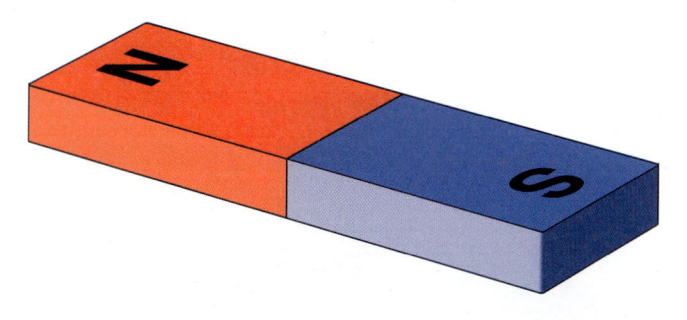

Activities

1 Make a poster to show some of the ways in which magnets are used in everyday life.

2 Do you think the north and south poles of a magnet are equally strong? What could you do to find out? Use Workbook page 69 to record your ideas.

3 Find out why the poles of a magnet are called the north and south poles. Write a paragraph summarising what you find out. Add diagrams if you feel they will help.

I have learned

- Magnets come in many different shapes but they all have a north and a south pole.
- The force exerted by a magnet is strongest at its poles.

5.6 Investigate magnetic forces

Key words
- force
- attract
- pull
- push
- repel

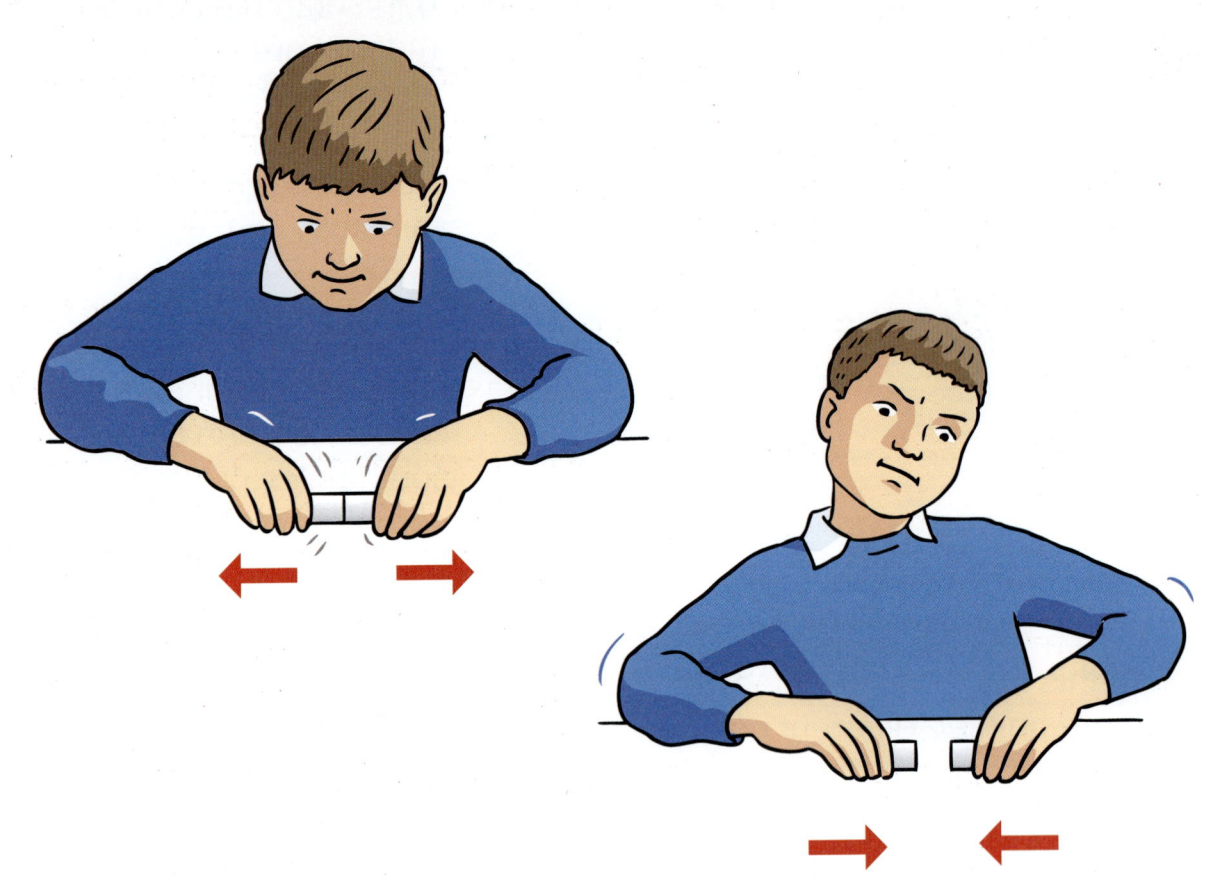

Last year you learned about forces. You discovered that pushes and pulls are both examples of forces. When a magnet sticks to a surface it is because the magnet is exerting a pulling **force** on the surface. The pulling force works to **attract** the surface to the magnet and they stick together.

1 What is happening in these pictures?

Magnets exert forces on other magnets. Sometimes this is a pulling force – the two magnets will be attracted to each other and will **pull** towards each other and stick together. At other times this is a pushing force – the magnets will be repelled by each other and will **push** apart from each other.

Topic **5** Electricity and magnetism

Look at this diagram.

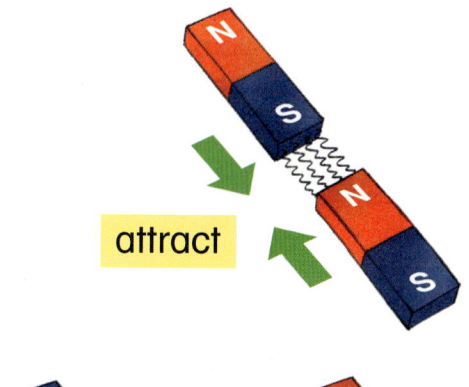

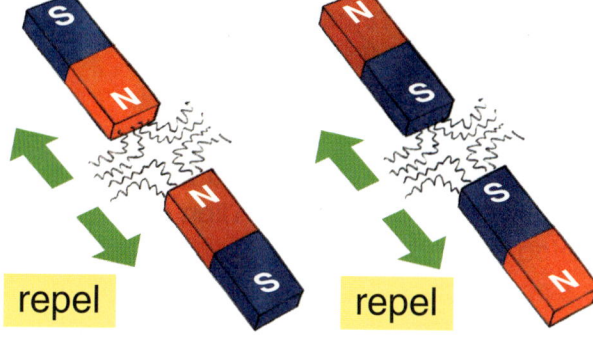

attract

repel   repel

2 What does this diagram suggest about the forces between magnets?

3 What is likely to happen if you turned the first two magnets around so that the north of the top one was facing the south of the bottom one? Why?

We say that the opposite, or unlike, poles of magnets attract each other and the like poles **repel** each other. In other words, if the two north poles or the two south poles are pointed towards each other, the force will be a pushing one and the magnets will repel each other.

Activities

1 Do an experiment with magnets to show how they attract and repel each other. Follow the instructions on Workbook page 70 to do the experiment and record your results.

2 Think about how you could design a toy that appears to float about the surface of a game board. Share your ideas with the class.

3 Explain how the forces between magnets can be used to work out where the north and south poles are on an unmarked magnet.

I have learned

- Magnets exert forces on other magnets and they can attract and repel each other.
- When like poles are facing each other, the magnets repel each other.
- When opposite poles are facing each other, the magnets attract each other.

83

5.7 Magnets and metals

Key words
- magnetic
- non-magnetic
- metal
- aluminium

Materials can be classified as **magnetic** or **non-magnetic**.

1 Predict which of these materials will not be attracted to a magnet.

Magnetic materials are those which are attracted to magnets. Magnets only attract other magnets and **metals** that are magnetic. Iron, steel, nickel and cobalt are all attracted to magnets, but remember they are not magnets themselves, so they are not attracted to other metals.

2 What happens to magnetic materials near magnets?

84

Topic 5 Electricity and magnetism

Non-magnetic materials are not attracted to magnets at all. Paper, wood, fabrics and other non-metal materials are non-magnetic. Some metals, such as gold, silver and **aluminium**, are not attracted to magnets.

3. If you placed a sheet of aluminium between the opposite poles of two magnets, what do you think would happen? Why? (You can test your prediction using aluminium foil.)

Magnetic forces can pass through non-magnetic materials including skin and bone.

4. Toys with powerful magnets are not suitable for small children as they may swallow them. Explain why this could be a problem.

Activities

1. Work in groups of four. Design a test to find out which metals are magnetic. Use everyday objects for testing, but make sure you know what metals they are made of. Use Workbook page 72 to record your work.

2. Are all coins magnetic? Test a range of coins to find out. Use Workbook page 73 to record your work.

3. Information is stored on debit and credit cards on a magnetic strip at the back of the card. Explain why it is important to keep these cards away from strong magnets.

I have learned

- Magnets attract some metals but not others.

5.8 Using magnets to sort metals

Key words
- magnetic
- non-magnetic
- aluminium
- recycle
- recycling

Magnets can be used to separate **magnetic** materials from **non-magnetic** materials. This is particularly useful in industries where metals are recycled.

1 Explain how you could use a magnet to find and remove steel pins from a pile of fabric cut-offs.

Aluminium is a non-magnetic metal that is light, easy to shape and rustproof. Many of the cans used for drinks are manufactured from aluminium. It is quite expensive and difficult to make aluminium from raw materials, so it makes sense to **recycle** cans and to use the aluminium gained from **recycling** to make other cans. Recycling cans also removes them from the environment and reduces pollution.

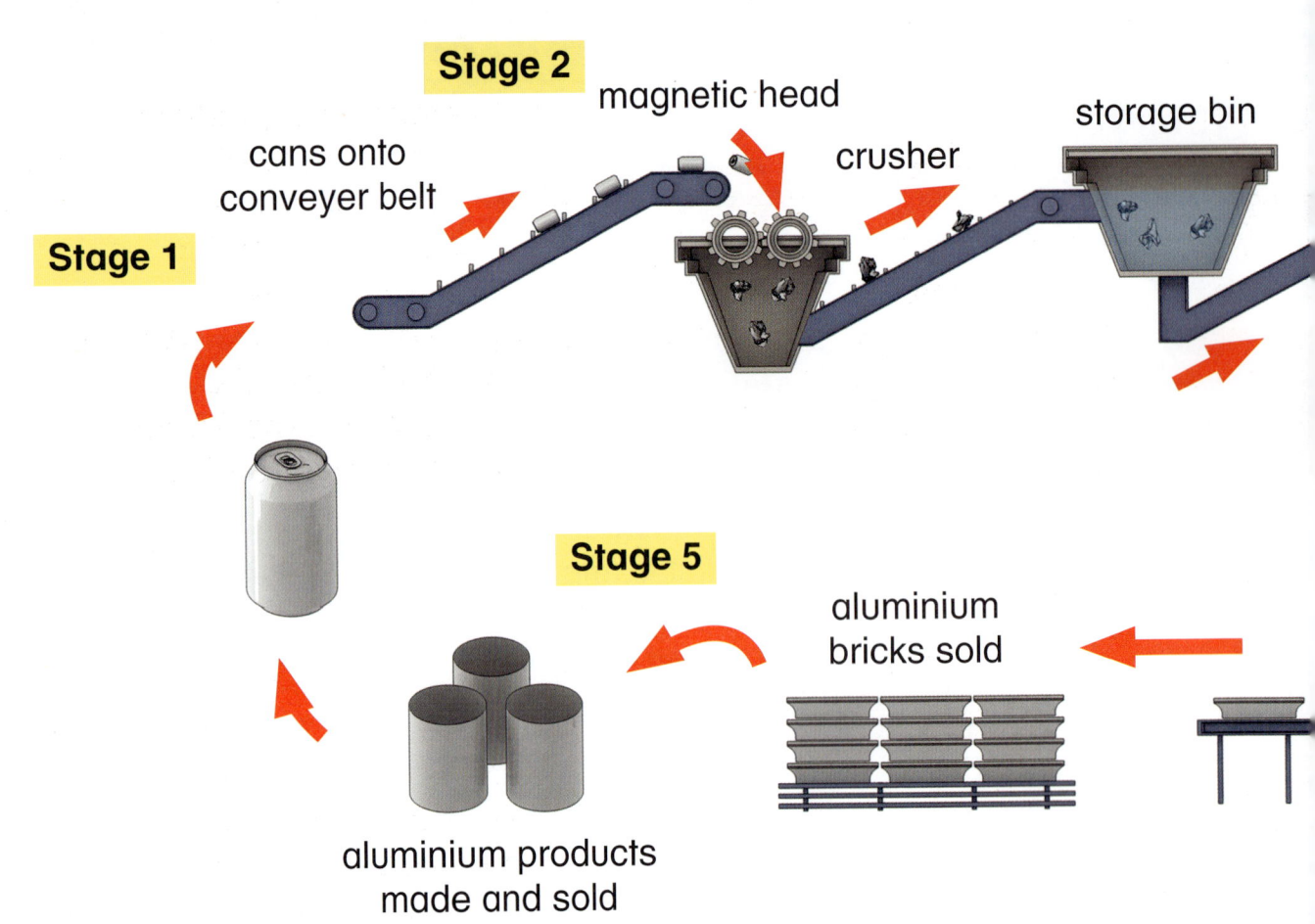

Stage 2 magnetic head

cans onto conveyer belt

crusher

storage bin

Stage 1

Stage 5

aluminium bricks sold

aluminium products made and sold

86

Topic **5** Electricity and magnetism

Other cans are made from steel or tin. These metals are magnetic, so magnets can be used to remove them from the recycled waste, leaving the aluminium behind for processing.

The diagram shows one method of separating steel cans from aluminium ones in a factory.

2 Where do the cans come from in this process?

3 Why do you think there are two magnetic heads?

magnetic head

Stage 3

metal crushed and made into blocks

blocks weighed and sold

Stage 4

blocks melted in furnace

aluminium bricks moulded

Activities

1 Describe how magnetic and non-magnetic materials can be separated. Use Workbook page 74.

2 Design a poster to tell people how their cans are separated and recycled at a recycling plant. Draw your poster on Workbook page 75.

3 Factories that produce prepared foods often place the foods on a belt and run them under a strong magnet. Why do you think they do this? Would this remove all metals from the food products?

I have learned

- Magnets attract some metals but not others, so they can be used to separate magnetic and non-magnetic metals.

Looking back Topic 5

In this topic you have learned

- A circuit is a closed path that allows electricity to flow around it.
- Circuits are built by connecting components to form a complete circuit.
- Electrical devices work when they are connected to a complete circuit. If there is a break in the circuit, the device will not work.
- Electrical current flows through the circuit.
- The flow of electrical current can be described as the movement of tiny particles from the battery, through the circuit and back to the battery.
- Magnets exert pushing and pulling forces and can attract or repel each other.
- Like poles repel each other, opposite poles attract each other.
- Metals such as iron and steel are magnetic. Aluminium, copper and gold are non-magnetic metals.

How well do you remember?

1 You have to build a circuit that has one bulb, a battery and a switch. Show two ways in which these could be connected to form a complete closed circuit.

2 Nadia's electric keyboard won't work when she switches it on. Suggest two things she should check.

3 Explain how you can tell whether an electrical current is flowing in a circuit.

4 What happens when the like poles of a magnet are brought together?

5 Does cardboard stop a magnet from exerting a force on a pin?

6 Name two non-magnetic metals.

7 Explain how you could use magnetism to sort a mixture of steel and aluminium clips.

Glossary

adaptation	If something has an adaptation it is changed or modified to suit new conditions or needs.
adapted	Something that has adapted has changed to suit conditions or needs.
aluminium	A light silvery-white metallic element that is used to make aircraft and other equipment, usually in the form of aluminium alloys.
aspirin	A drug used to reduce fever and relieve mild pain.
attract	If something attracts objects to it, it has a force that pulls them towards it.
backbone	A word used to describe the spine. All vertebrates have a backbone.
battery (cell)	A battery is a device for storing and producing electricity, for example in a flashlight or a car.
bones	Bones are rigid parts that make up the skeleton of a vertebrate animal.
break	A break in a circuit is an interruption in the flow of electricity; to break something is to shatter it into pieces.
bulb	A bulb is the glass part of an electric lamp.
calcium	A mineral found in the human body that is essential for healthy bones and teeth.
cartilage	A flexible connective tissue found in the human body, for example the ear.
change of state	When a substance undergoes a change of state it changes its state of matter, for example from a liquid to a gas.
circuit	An electrical circuit is a complete route around which an electric current can flow.
classification	The grouping of organisms according to their shared characteristics or features.
component	A part or element of something, for example a part of a machine or circuit.
condensation	Condensation is a coating of tiny drops of water formed on a surface by steam or vapour.
connect	To bring something together or in contact.
contract	To contract a muscle is to allow it to become firm and tight, and smaller. It is the opposite of relax.
cooling	The process of becoming cool.
cools	If something cools it becomes a lower temperature.
current	A flow of electricity.

decibel	A unit used to measure the intensity of a sound.
drugs	A drug is any substance that affects how your body works, for example aspirin.
environment	The surroundings and conditions in which something lives.
evaporate	When a liquid evaporates, it gradually becomes less and less because it is changing from a liquid into a gas.
flow	A flow of something is a steady continuous movement of it; also the rate at which it flows.
force	The force of something is its strength or power; pushes, pulls and twists are all examples of forces.
freezing	To turn a liquid into a solid; extremely cold.
gas	A gas is any air-like substance that is not liquid or solid, such as oxygen or the gas used as a fuel in heating.
gaseous	Having the characteristics of a gas.
habitat	The natural home of a plant or animal.
heating	The act of making something warmer.
high-pitched	Of a high sound.
immune	To be resistant to a particular disease or illness.
internal	Something that is inside.
investigate	To discover or examine the facts of something or a situation.
joints	The position in the body where two parts of the skeleton fit together, for example the knee or elbow joints.
key	A identification key is a list of the characteristics of an object or organism that is used to classify it.
lamp	A glass bulb that uses electricity to give out light.
liquid	Any substance that is not a solid or a gas, and which can be poured.
low-pitched	Of a low sound.
magnet	A piece of iron that attracts iron or steel towards it, and which points towards north if allowed to swing freely.
magnetic	A magnetic material is one exerting a powerful attraction.
matter	Matter is any substance.
medicines	Medicine is the treatment of illness and injuries by doctors and nurses. Medicines are drugs used to treat illness.
medium	A substance, such as water or air, through which a force acts or an effect is produced.
melted	Something that has changed from a solid to a liquid because it has been heated.
metal	A metal is a material such as iron, steel, copper or lead; metals are good conductors of heat and electricity.

metres per second	The number of metres something travels in one second, expressed as m/s.
model	To model is to imitate or to use something as an example.
moisturiser	A preparation, usually a cream or lotion, that is used to prevent dryness of the skin.
move	To change place or position; to go in a particular direction.
muffle	To wrap something up in order to reduce its loudness.
muscles	Bands of fibrous tissues in the body that contract to allow movement.
non-magnetic	Materials that are not magnetic.
organs	The parts of an organism that have specific and vital functions, for example the heart or liver.
particles	A particle is an extremely small piece of matter.
pharmacy	A shop where you can buy medicines.
pitch	The way something sounds depending on how fast or slow the vibrations are; the degree of highness or lowness of a tone.
pole	Either of the two ends of a magnet.
pollution	Pollution is dirty or dangerous substances in the air, water or soil.
prescription	Something a doctor gives to a patient who requires a controlled drug or medicine; a written instruction that authorises the purchase of the drug.
protect	To protect someone or something is to prevent them from being harmed or damaged.
pull	A force that makes an object move towards you.
push	A force that makes an object move away from you.
recycle	To recycle used products means to process them so that they can be used again.
recycling	Recycling is processing products so that they can be used again.
relax	To relax a muscle is to allow it to become loose and less tight. It is the opposite of contract.
repel	When a magnetic pole repels an opposite pole, it forces the opposite pole away.
ribcage	The bony frame found in the chest that is formed by all of the ribs. It protects the organs of the chest area.
ribs	The ribs are the bones that protect the organs inside the chest.
skeleton	Your skeleton is the framework of bones in your body.
skull	The skull is the set of bones that make up the head and protect the brain.

solid	A solid substance or object is hard or firm, and not in the form of a liquid or gas.
sound	Anything that can be heard. Sound is caused by vibrations travelling through air or water to your ear.
sound level meter	Device for measuring the sound pressure level of something.
soundproof	Something that prevents sound from entering or leaving, for example in a recording studio.
source	The place that something comes from.
spine	Your spine is your backbone.
states	The states of matter are solid, liquid and gas.
steam	Steam is the hot vapour formed when a liquid boils.
suited	If something is suited to its environment, it is right or appropriate.
support	A thing that bears the weight of something or keeps it upright.
switch	A switch is a small on–off control for an electrical device or machine.
tendon	A tendon is a band of tissue that connects a muscle to a bone.
transmission	The action or process of transmitting something, such as sound. To transmit is to cause something to pass on from one place to another.
vaccine	A medicine or drug used to provide immunity from particular diseases.
vapour	A substance in a gaseous state that is often visible in the air, for example water vapour or steam.
vibrate	If something vibrates, it moves a tiny amount backwards and forwards very quickly.
vibration	Vibration is the act or an instance of vibrating.
volume	A word that is used to describe the level of sound produced by something, for example musical instruments or radios.
waste disposal	The collection, transport and sorting of waste materials.
water	The clear, colourless, tasteless and odourless liquid that is necessary for all plant and animal life; when you water a plant or an animal, you give it water to drink.
water cycle	The water cycle is the continuous process in which water evaporates from the sea, forming clouds; the clouds break as rain, which makes its way back to the sea, where the process starts again.
wire	Wire is metal in the form of a long, thin, flexible thread that can be used to make or fasten things, or to conduct an electric current.
X-ray	An X-ray is made by exposing photographic film to electromagnetic radiation; it is a picture on film often used in medical diagnosis.